The Ringer

The Ringer

A NOVEL

JENNY SHANK

THE PERMANENT PRESS
Sag Harbor, NY 11963

For information, address:
  The Permanent Press
  4170 Noyac Road
  Sag Harbor, NY 11963
  www.thepermanentpress.com

Library of Congress Cataloging-in-Publication Data

Shank, Jenny–
  The ringer : a novel / Jenny Shank.
    p. cm.
  ISBN 978-1-57962-214-5 (alk. paper)
    1. Fathers—Fiction. 2. Police officers—Fiction.
  3. Drug dealers—Fiction. 4. Murder—Investigation—Fiction.
  5. Denver (Colo.)—Fiction. 6. Domestic fiction. I. Title.

PS3619.H35469R56 2011
813'.6—dc22   2010046149

Printed in the United States of America.

For Mom and Pop

CHAPTER 1

Ed O'Fallon
March 11

On the first day of tee-ball practice, Ed O'Fallon learned that his primary mission in coaching his daughter's team would be to convince the fielders to pay attention to the action at the plate. Instead, the girls preferred to concentrate on refilling aeration holes with the grass-topped earth plugs that littered the outfield like turds. While the girls arrived, Ed checked his watch. He had two hours to spend with them before he left for work. The SWAT team commander had summoned him to assist on a high-risk warrant that afternoon.

The dozen-odd girls assembled reasonably on time the Saturday morning of their first practice. The team's name—The Purple Unicorns—was a relic of the tee-ball league's first season, when the coaches allowed players to suggest and vote on names for each club. The schedule the league office had issued Ed listed such competitors as the Denver Dream Stars, The Butterfly Power, The Christinas—which Ed kind of liked—and the Colorado Princess Brigade, a coach-influenced name, Ed felt certain.

Ed stood on home plate, holding his clipboard, and surveyed his team: cleatless, capless, untutored six-year-olds, his girl Polly among them, their clothes the colors of an array of ice cream. Polly, at least, wore sweatpants, which she changed into after Ed insisted that she couldn't slide in shorts or jeans. Ed cleared his throat. "Hello, Unicorns," he heard himself say. He'd debated about what to call them. He'd always addressed his sons' teams as "Men," but "Women" didn't seem right, not for six-year-olds, "Ladies" sounded like a vaguely creepy term for a thirty-seven-year-old man to use with little girls, and "Girls" wouldn't have the appropriate, spirit-bolstering effect he was looking for. So he settled on calling them Unicorns. "We need to work hard today, Unicorns, because our first game is in two weeks." He looked down at his clipboard, and then added, "It's against the Southeast Denver Baby Kittens."

He should have been coaching his sons instead, as he had for years, in a league where the teams were named properly, after pizza joints, hardware stores, and rabid animals. "Okay team," Ed said, "Start with some laps."

The Unicorns looked up at him and blinked. "Laps," he repeated. "You know, where you run around the field a couple of times?"

As he waited for them to move, he could see a million questions burbling to their lips, which they opened slightly as if to speak, to ask him about the location of the bathroom, the availability of water and snacks, and what should be done with the unbroken-in gloves that they clutched to their chests like loaves of bread in famine times. But they wouldn't ask him their questions, because as Ed had learned from his wife Claire, many kids found him scary, ducking behind their parents or fleeing when he approached, especially when he was out of uniform and there was no way to tell whether he was a good guy or a bad one.

"Go on," Ed said to the still-motionless girls. "Follow Polly." He pointed his daughter toward the outfield and guided her off with a hand on her back. Some girls dropped their gloves, some girls clung to them, but they all began to trot away from Ed. He was proud to see that Polly ran the way he'd taught her, raising her knees high, her heels almost touching the seat of her pants.

At his sons' practice, the laps would be completed without a coach's request, and they would move smoothly through the warm up, two players gradually increasing the distance between them as they threw and caught, the team paired off and lined up in neat parallel lines.

Ed shielded his eyes from the sun and watched the girls jog. Polly chugged along in front, her brown curls bouncing, but others deviated, skipping, collecting fistfuls of dandelions that grew close to the outfield fence. Fine. That was fine. In this league, the standard kid sports motto about how it didn't matter if you won or lost was actually true. Which was why Claire insisted Ed give baseball coaching a rest this year and take on Polly's tee-ball team instead. "You just get too worked up when Jesse and E.J. play," she said. By that she meant he yelled too much and that parents had complained.

At work, raising his voice at a citizen would barely chart on a 1-to-10 use-of-force scale. Yelling was the most benign control technique Ed possessed, serving as the entryway to the arsenal of other options, like the warm-up scales of an opera singer. When Ed coached, yelling was the way he expressed his hopes for the team, being too superstitious to do it in any other way. He voiced ideas contrary to his wishes, trying to dejinx the team: *this pitcher's stuff's too fast—you can't touch him, the catcher's got a cannon—he'll throw you out if you try to steal.* He yelled when a boy swung at a bad pitch or took a good one. He yelled when hitters didn't run out stillborn hits. He yelled when fielders failed to back each other up on grounders or call fly balls. He yelled at loafers, lollygaggers, showboaters, and space cadets.

"You can't treat other people's children like potential noncompliants to be controlled," Claire often told him. "Only your own. And there's a time and a place. What can you do to help a kid, really, when he stands in the batter's box with a 0-2 count against him? You can say what you want before he goes to bat, but each person has to face the two strikes against him alone."

Claire had tried to save Ed's baseball coaching career before it was too late, steering him as she always did, like a rider guiding her horse, applying gentle, firm pressure toward the desired turn. Last season, she started bringing containers of cut apples to games and thrust them at him whenever a player committed an egregious error. The moment a grounder shot through legs, a runner took off on a fly without tagging up, or a pop-up tumbled out of a glove while the fielder's ungloved hand remained idle, Claire would produce the apples. Ed did as expected, took an

9

apple slice, bit into it and chewed, one after another, keeping his mouth full and silent until the urge to holler passed. Sometimes this method failed, and after he sprayed invective and partially chewed apple bits, Claire would banish him to another field while an assistant coach took over, so Ed could pace out his anger away from the team. After games Claire would remind him that the point of the Police Athletic League was to introduce neighborhood children to what decent and friendly guys police officers could be.

Ed couldn't account for how his steadiness at work gave way to madness at games, where he became the guy the mothers whispered about between sips of diet cola as they roosted in the stands. At work, Ed's temper held. One time he and his partner Mitch entered a house on a call for a domestic and found the husband and wife screaming at each other by the refrigerator, brandishing kitchen implements, she with a cast iron skillet, and he with an unplugged plastic toaster. Pitched on the edge of battle, they hardly registered Ed and Mitch's entrance. They told the couple to calm down, ordered them to drop the pan and toaster and back away from each other, but their eyes locked, and neither would move until the other did. Then Ed noticed a bottle of cleaner glinting on the windowsill. He grabbed it and began to scrub the grimy kitchen, while he watched the couple, then wiped down the counter and the stove with a stray dishrag, until they gleamed. The couple stopped yelling, put down their arms, and looked at him in wonder.

Because of stunts like this, the SWAT commander recently invited Ed to join the team. Ed declined to become a full-time member, preferring the unpredictable, alternately boring and energizing routine of the patrol officer. He enjoyed roaming the city, scouring the streets, answering calls, keeping his eyes open for young women on solitary jogs in parks full of miscreants, children at bus stops who were small enough to snatch, and the disheveled shamblers of Colfax Avenue, who could do anything to anyone at any moment. Instead of giving up patrolling entirely, Ed agreed to assist SWAT when they needed him, and he'd be part of the eight-man team that would enforce a drug warrant that afternoon.

The Unicorns returned from running after only one go around the field. Ed felt no urge to yell at them. Claire had been right about that.

"Laps," Ed said. "They're called laps. It's plural."

The kids just stared at him. He was Don Rickles, trying to work a room full of Japanese tourists.

"All right, Unicorns, now we get to decide where everyone will play. Why don't you all run out to the field and stand at the position you'd like to play."

No one moved. Then one girl, a blonde who was taller than the rest and wore glittery silver fingernail polish, sauntered out to the pitching mound—well, the pitching flat, really, Ed thought. What did you call it when there wasn't a mound there? Everyone followed her, and herded in the center of the field. Polly started to follow them and Ed reached out and stopped her with his hand on her shoulder.

"Hey, you don't want to go there, P. The pitcher doesn't even pitch in tee-ball." The manual Ed had read the night before was clear on this point. The pitcher merely stood on the rubber and made a gesture as if she were pitching, underhand or overhand, it didn't matter, which was the signal for the batter to swing the bat at the ball mounted on the tee in front of her. The part called for a little light fielding, but it was mainly mime. Ed kneeled next to Polly. "Why don't you go to short? You'd be good there."

"Okay," Polly said, and turned to go.

"Hey," he said. "What's all the rush on pitching today, anyway?"

"It's Anna," Polly whispered, indicating the blonde by jerking her thumb in that direction. "She's cool."

Ed walked over to break up the mob at the pitching flat. "Okay, we can't all be pitchers, Unicorns. There are lots of other fun places to play. Now, who are my lefties?"

They stared at him, silent, as though they were worried about what would be required of lefties, maybe another lap or something worse.

11

"Don't be shy," Ed said. "Raise your hand if you're left-handed." Two girls slowly lifted their hands, looking at each other.

"Great," Ed said. "Lefty, you get over to first base," he said, pointing to the taller girl of the two.

"My name's Bethany," she said.

"Well, now it's Lefty."

Ed detected a smile or two at last. He could do this. He began to divvy them up. "Okay, Shorty, you go to second. Speedy—yes, you, I saw you cooking during the run—you head out to centerfield. The one in the middle, that's right. Muscles," he said, resting his hands on the shoulders of a stockier girl, and getting a smile from her and a giggle from the team. "Muscles, you'll be our catcher. Catchers are special because they have their own outfit, just for them. Blondie, you pitch, that's good, you showed some initiative the way you hustled out here. Okay, Curly, Larry, and Moe," and now all the girls were laughing. See? He wasn't so scary. "Larry, you go to left field, and Moe, you go to right." The two girls took off toward the positions opposite the ones he had assigned them. "Well, whatever. Curly, you grab third, and the rest of you get to bat first." As long as you didn't think of it as baseball, it was fun, really. As long as you didn't expect it to resemble real baseball in any way.

"How did it go?" Claire asked when Ed and Polly arrived home from practice. Claire was standing on the front porch, waiting without her coat on though the March day was crisp. She'd hurried outside as Ed's car approached, as if she had expected him to report a catastrophe. She looked lovely to Ed as she stood there, the wind blowing back her auburn hair, her fair, freckled cheeks pink from the cold.

"Great," Ed said, "really great."

"Polly, I made macaroni for your lunch," Claire said.

Polly slipped inside, letting the screen door slam behind her.

"And?" Claire said, moving in front of Ed until he looked her in the eye.

12

Ed never looked in a suspect's eyes, because they would only mislead you. The hands were what you watched. Claire had to remind him to make eye contact with his family whenever he forgot. "And what?"

"You know."

"I didn't yell, Claire, not once. I couldn't yell at those little girls."

"Good," Claire said. "That's a start." She squeezed his hand. "Do you have time for lunch?"

"I'll have to grab something on my way to work. I've got to run. I've got that raid."

"All right. Be careful, would you? Be safe."

"Hey, always."

She turned her cheek to him and he kissed it.

At just past one in the afternoon, Ed and the other policemen approached a small brick house in west Denver, past Mile High Stadium, where the playing fields of the neighborhood schools were nothing but dust-covered ground fenced in chain link. They crossed the parched, pigweed-choked lawn. They mounted the cracked cement steps, rushing past a green plastic watering can and a battered lawn chair on the porch, a pile of dirty snow melting in the seat. The remnants of long dead plants in terracotta pots lined the edge of the porch. As discussed in the briefing, the men didn't ring the bell, they didn't knock on the door. They had obtained an immediate-entry search warrant for this raid, and they didn't even have to jimmy the lock. The door swung open when the breacher turned the handle and the officers passed through.

Inside the house, the sergeant yelled, "Police! It's the police!" No answer came. The eight men split into four predetermined teams and broke up to search. They prowled the ground floor first. Ed moved cautiously, scanning for signs of an occupant hiding or crouching in wait, but the first room he checked harbored only a ratty olive-green couch cloaked in a brown afghan somebody had crocheted long ago. The kitchen, piled with fast food boxes and dishes with geologic encrustations, revealed little. No sane, sober woman would abide living there, and that confirmed what Ed knew about the place. According to the briefing, it served as a flophouse for men who came from Mexico for part of the year to finance their families back home. They used a no-knock warrant for a better chance of securing case-building evidence against the dealers—so much drug evidence was flushable—but as the officers searched the ground floor for anything incriminating, they found nothing.

Ed followed Sergeant Springer up the stairs with his gun ready, and two other officers trailed. Springer was six-five and skinny, and he tried to fold himself smaller as he mounted the stairs. Ed scanned the dim hallway at the top of the steps, noted the two closed doors on either side. On the wall opposite the left-side door hung a dingy oval mirror, but with the house shuttered into midday dark, Ed could see nothing reflected in it. "Police!" Sergeant Springer shouted at the door to the left. No one answered. The breacher forced open the door with a handheld ram and stood clear as it swung forward, hit the wall, bounced halfway back. The breacher fell back, Ed took a position to the right of the doorframe behind the wall, and Springer assumed the left side.

That was the last time Ed noticed Springer. Because then Ed looked around the doorframe and saw a man, bleary from sleep, standing near the bed, keeping his left hand hidden behind his leg. He wore jeans and a crumpled white t-shirt with a hole in it just below his throat. Ed felt that he stared at that hole for minutes before he acted, pulling his head behind the cover of the wall.

Ed yelled, "Police! Policía! Let me see your hands!" He heard nothing but his lone voice as he shouted, and it sounded frail to him, barely audible, hoarse and off-pitch. "Policía! Policía!" he repeated. Ed ventured a glance at the man to check if he had complied.

The man seemed disoriented, as though just awakened, rubbing his eyes with his free hand. He drew his left hand forward, holding what looked to Ed to be a gun. "Drop the gun!" Ed yelled. The man lowered his hand, then suddenly raised it again. Ed saw the muscles of the man's forearm twitch, and thought *that's it*, the man had already pulled the trigger and Ed could tell from the angle the bullet would momentarily rip through him, somewhere between his throat and his heart. Ed heard a *pop* from the room, a noise too insignificant for a gun, and he heard the mirror shatter in the hallway. *Did he fire?* Ed pulled the trigger of his weapon.

Ed shot him once through the doorway and the man fell to his knees, and then tried to stand back up. Ed saw the muzzle flash and he fired again, but the sound was distant, muffled. He wasn't hearing right, he wasn't seeing right, just riding the wave of his training, his body having memorized what it was supposed to do. The man dropped to the floor as his blood pumped out onto the rust-colored carpet. The words the man cried out as he fell back sounded like names, but Ed could not make them out. The man writhed onto his side, spreading the blood with every motion. The front of the man's pants became wet as his bladder emptied. Was he dead already?

It was then that Ed realized that five other officers stood around him. The area that seemed so empty, spotlit only around Ed and the man, suddenly teemed with people. Ed's ears flooded with the sounds of their activity as if popped by a change in altitude. Ed remained in the position from which he'd fired the gun, his feet fused to the ground. His shaking hands could not holster his weapon. He stared at the man on the ground, unable to comprehend that he, Ed, had done this. Ed told himself that he had killed this person, his mind running over and over this idea, like the finger of a blind man trying to make sense of an inscrutable passage of Braille. Ed finally turned around and looked at the mirror in the hallway, which hung intact on the wall. He closed his eyes to clear them, still able to hear the sound of the glass shattering, louder in his memory than the blasts of the gun.

From his spot, he surveyed the room where the dead man lay, and saw the uniform for the man's job at the soda bottling plant hanging in the closet alongside little else. Embroidered on the pocket, the dead man's name: Salvador. *Not the name on the warrant*, Ed thought.

Scanning the room, Ed noticed a makeshift trophy case near the spot where the man had fallen, something he hadn't perceived before. On a plank of pine stretched across two cinderblocks sat an assortment of baseball trophies. An identical golden boy, his bat at the ready, topped each one, and every batter stood on a cylinder of varying size and color, glinting blues, greens, and reds, on a plastic base bearing a small engraved plaque. Ed finally reached for one of the trophies so he could inspect the inscription, but Sergeant Springer closed a hand around Ed's arm and gently pulled him away. Ed's fingers brushed against a trophy, toppling it. It landed next to the man's foot, and that was the last Ed saw of the claustrophobic room in the west side of the city. The sergeant led Ed away down the stairs.

CHAPTER 2

Patricia Maestas de Santillano
Monday, March 13

Patricia Maestas sat home too early on a work day, sunk in Salvador's chair, a seat no one had occupied since he'd left for Mexico again six months before. The chair was hard around the edges and concave in the middle, covered in scratchy brown material that resembled burlap, so it had always been Salvador's private throne in the corner of the room. She rubbed her hands over the armrests and settled into the dent left by his body. It had been an hour since Tío Tiger called her at work to say he'd seen the article about Salvador being killed by the cops in a drug raid. Salvador had been dead for over a day without her knowing and she couldn't understand how that was possible. The father of her children, the man of her life: shouldn't she have felt something when it happened? Bewildered, she'd made her way home.

When she first arrived she thought of taking the kids out of school but then thought, no, leave them a few more hours of not knowing. The afternoon sun began to fail, sending in a weak shaft that stopped just past the windows, but she could read the clock across the room as its red numbers flashed the day away: 3:45. The kids should have been home by now.

She walked out on the porch, shielding her eyes to scan the street. The litany of terrible possibilities unspooled in her head. Then she saw Mia approaching from the end of the block, alone, heart-shaped face angled toward the pavement, dragging her backpack by one strap.

When Mia ran up the porch steps Patricia sank to her knees and pulled her daughter close, burying her nose in Mia's long braids that smelled of strawberry shampoo. Mia's milky skin and delicate build came from Patricia, but her full lips came from Salvador, and Patricia kissed her on the mouth like she used to when she was a baby.

Mia wiped her lips with the back of her hand.

"Where's Ray?" Patricia asked. Mia was eight years old and responsible, but they lived near Federal, a busy street.

"He said he'd be home in a while. I'm not supposed to say."

"Supposed to say what?"

"That he let me walk home alone." She looked down at her shoes, as if consulting with them about how much to spill. "He was walking to Federal with those boys."

"What boys? Miguel?"

It had started after Patricia and Salvador separated. In sixth grade Ray stopped hanging out with the neighbor kids and picked up a new group that included Miguel, whose mother was barely thirteen years older than he was, her boyfriend tattooed with the insignia of the North Side Mafia. Patricia had agreed to drive Ray over to Miguel's once. Two blunt-bodied, short-necked dogs scrambled over the dirt lawn toward their car like a couple of slavering torpedoes. Three men with shaved heads slouched on a sun-faded floral couch on the porch. Patricia kept on driving, Ray saying, "What the fuck, Mom?" as the house with its gray peeling paint and sagging roof faded away.

Patricia screeched to a stop in the middle of the block, squeezing the clutch until her knuckles popped so she wouldn't smack him. The skill separating a good mother from a bad one was the same quality Ray often mentioned good pitchers possessed: superior muscle control. "We don't talk that way," she said. "You get that from Miguel?"

Ray fixed her with an ugly stare. "Maybe I got it from Dad."

"He doesn't talk like that."

"You act like he does," Ray huffed. "Don't say ain't," he added in a high-pitched tone meant to rile her in imitation of her grammar lessons.

She sped off. Miguel's people were the sort who shot their guns into the air at midnight on New Year's Eve, too drunk to care where their bullets fell, but Patricia cared, because sometimes the bullets landed in bystanders wheeled in to her at the hospital.

"You're too good for Miguel's neighborhood, too good for Dad's," Ray continued, testing his power.

She shot him a glance: *watch it.* She knew little about the house where Salvador had been renting a room, except that people moved in and out all the time. She couldn't keep track of the different men who answered the phone there, *Bueno?* The neighborhood was bad, too, one that often made the 10:00 news. Since they had separated, Salvador had been meeting the kids at places where Patricia dropped them off—Sloan's Lake, the Woodbury library, the museum on a free day so Mia could hunt for the elves hidden in the back of the animal dioramas.

Ray pulled up the hood of his sweatshirt and faced away.

"Fine," Patricia said. "Hate me if you want, but ask yourself: who takes care of you every time Dad takes off?"

After the day she'd driven past Miguel's, she'd kept Ray apart from him when she could, but she couldn't prevent the association at school, and a few weeks earlier they'd been suspended for flashing gang signs to each other on the playground. Salvador had told her not to worry about it so much, that Ray was a decent kid and he'd figure things out. Now Salvador was gone for good.

"You're not going to tell Ray I said he went with Miguel, right?" Mia asked, tugging on Patricia's sleeve. "Why are you still wearing your coat?"

Patricia looked down. She had forgotten to remove her coat when she arrived home two hours earlier, and when she let it drop now, she shivered.

"And you're still in your nurse scrubs," Mia said. "What about germs?"

"We've got to find your brother."

Patricia led Mia into the car and drove toward Federal Boulevard. She scanned the parking lots of businesses, churches, schools, and homes all jumbled together along one stretch of road. She was hoping he'd be outside, where she could see him. She'd revoke his allowance for a month. Two. The only way to keep them home was to keep them broke. Federal offered too many places to pass five bucks' worth of time.

"Why doesn't he hang out with Nino anymore?" Patricia asked Mia, who shrugged. Plump little Nino, who lived next door with his grandma, used to be Ray's sidekick. They had been friends since first grade, when they started playing baseball together on the same parish team, Ray pitching and Nino catching, because in some leagues, as in bad baseball movies, that's where the chunkiest player is put.

They passed the old Federal movie theater that had sat empty for years, its name in jaunty white cursive writing above the jutting marquee. She glanced at the little shop where her mother Lupe used to buy *chorizo* and *nopales* for their restaurant on 34th Avenue, a *panadería* with a BIMBO bread delivery truck in front, permanent fireworks stands busy on only a few occasions a year, stores with bilingual placards advertising the services of tax preparers, *curanderas*, bailbondsmen, money wirers. Places Salvador used to visit to send part of his paycheck home to Mexico, no matter how many times Patricia asked him to stop. Two men outside Rudy's Cash Express were dressed in jeans too tight and high-waisted for Americans, their shirts tucked in, just like Salvador when she met him. She took a deep breath so she wouldn't cry. How appropriate, really, was the term "alien" that her mother always used for such men, their experiences so different from hers that they may as well have originated from another planet. Patricia understood so little about how immigrants ran their lives, even after being married to one for thirteen years.

In the other direction, a chiropractor's sign read, *Dolor de cabeza—podemos ayudar!* A hairdresser's services were spray painted on the windows of a salon: *Tintes, Mechones, Rayos, Permanentes, Extenciones.* Outside the bars hung Broncos banners, offering 2-for-1 game day specials.

A group of boys of about the right age were hanging out in the parking lot of El Pollo Loco and Patricia pulled in. She rolled down the window as the boys backed away. "Hey guys," she said, "Do you know my son Ray?"

A skinny kid in a long-sleeved collared shirt buttoned all the way up to his incipient Adam's apple took a step forward. "Stingray?"

It was the nickname Nino had given Ray on their baseball team, for his blistering pitching. Patricia used it only to tease Ray when she was calling him to chores, but all the kids in the neighborhood seemed to call him nothing but Stingray. "That's the one."

"He's inside."

She found him crunching into a chicken *taquito*, sitting next to Miguel, who wore a pristine, all-white Colorado Rockies cap backwards and some matching snow-white Nikes that he must have scrubbed the street off every day. The bleached gear signified something and it scared Patricia that she didn't know what. Twelve years old and lanky, Ray wore his hair in a buzz cut, the shortest length Patricia would brook, covering it with a baseball cap the second school let out, where hats—with their potential gang affiliations—weren't allowed. She only let him buy caps in teams' regular colors. He had his father's sharp profile and pointed chin, but his eyes were Patricia's, brown and clear. He took a sip of his pop and choked a little when he looked up to see her.

"We need to go," she said.

"I'm not done eating."

"You are now." She grabbed his *taquito* basket and led him by the arm. Miguel bit into a *taquito* with a crunch so loud Patricia took the gesture for insolence. Ray shook off her grip. A girl sat near the boys, wearing the placid expression of an overfed lion, brown lip liner surrounding her sullen mouth. As Patricia stared at her, wondering if she was Ray's girl, she opened her purse—shaped like a woman's curvy torso in a black lace bustier—and drew out a compact to inspect her makeup.

"You going to yell at me for not bringing Mia home?" Ray asked, playing tough for his audience.

"Not today," Patricia said so only he could hear.

"Did you come home early just to spy on me?"

She put her hand on the nape of his neck, feeling the pulse beneath his warm skin, and gave it a squeeze. "Honey, you don't even know."

He turned his back to her and started to rejoin his friends. "I have to tell you something," she said softly, and he turned around. She didn't want to tell him here but Ray was too big to drag home and she didn't know how else to make him heed. She held Mia by the hand and backed away from Ray's friends, moving toward the exit. Something about her expression must have cracked his act. He approached, dropped his voice and asked, "What?"

She put her free hand on his shoulder. "Your father is dead."

Ray pushed away from her and searched her face for a sign he'd heard wrong. What he saw in her eyes made him turn his head.

"Papa died?" Mia screamed. The people in the restaurant looked up from their chicken nachos and quesadillas. The place grew silent except for someone slurping the last gasps of a drink through a straw.

Miguel stood and took a step toward them. "That's messed up," he put in.

Patricia shot him a glare and he faded back with a shuffle step like she'd jabbed him in the sternum. Then she put her arms around her children and led them to the car as everyone in the restaurant stared after them. The kids climbed in, Ray up front.

"Your father was killed by policemen," she said.

"You're lying," Ray said, "you are." He crossed his arms over his chest, his tough frown quavering at the corners.

"The cops were raiding the house he lived in," Patricia explained as she pulled out of the parking lot, "looking for drugs. And then, after that, I don't know exactly what happened."

"What do you mean you don't know what happened?"

"No one has given me an explanation yet. I'm trying to find out." When Patricia had spoken to the woman at police headquarters, all she'd say was that there would be an internal investigation and that Patricia could have a copy of the report when it was ready. Then she'd given her a number to call for victims assistance but she hadn't phoned yet. She glanced east toward Denver's modest set of skyscrapers, and wondered where the cops who had done this were, out living their lives, killing a man all in a day's work.

"I know what happened," Ray said in a distant voice, like he was a half-century old. "The cops shot him for no reason at all. They do it all the time, just like with Miguel's cousin."

"Miguel's cousin was a drug dealer and a gang banger," Patricia said. She slammed her fist on the steering wheel. How did he and Salvador end up in the same situation?

"Where is he?" Ray demanded. "I want to see him."

"I want to see him, too," Mia said.

"Take us to him," Ray said. "Take us to him now. I don't believe you."

Patricia shook her head. "I can't, baby," she said with no breath at all.

At a stop light three blocks from home, Ray looked up at Patricia. His wet eyelashes were clumped together in tiny triangles. "If you hadn't made him leave, he wouldn't have died," Ray said. "He would have been living with us like he was supposed to."

She felt a pain like an icicle popping inside her. Salvador had been living in the house where he died only because she had locked him out of their home. No—that wasn't right. It was Salvador's decision that put him there. He was the one who walked away when she'd told him not to. But before she could figure out how to explain this, Ray threw open the door and took off down the street.

"Ray, get back here!" she yelled. Patricia pulled out of traffic to follow him and stopped the car. "Mia, please stay," she said, locking the doors and glancing into the backseat at her daughter who was sobbing, huddled in the corner. Patricia regretted leaving her, but didn't know what else to do, performing the same quick calculation she'd been making since she'd had her second child, judging which one's need was rawer in that moment.

Patricia chased Ray down the residential street just off of Federal, pumping her arms to go faster, pains shooting through her lungs almost the moment she started sprinting. She cursed herself for not getting to the rec center more often as she lost him around a corner.

She was unsure which way to head. Then he began to scream. It wasn't a child's scream, centered in the throat, but a holler from the gut, the very place the pain settled at the bottom of his stomach. The neighbors who were already out on their porches drew forward and followed Ray's flight with their eyes. Others emerged from inside the little tile-roofed brick bungalows that lined either side of the street, walked out onto their lawns, planted their fists on their hips and stared. The Maestas family had lived in this neighborhood off of Federal Boulevard in north Denver for generations, since Patricia's great-grandparents' time.

Ray was still screaming and Patricia had to make him stop. She sprinted after her son down the uneven sidewalk, and finally tackled him as he slowed in the muddy part of Mrs. Salazar's yard, where the grass wouldn't grow in the shadow of a pine tree. But he didn't stop screaming. Even the heavy traffic from Federal Boulevard two streets over didn't drown out his sound.

Ray lost control of his breathing and the hyperventilating silenced him. Patricia kneeled in front of him, holding his hands in her own, telling him, "Take a deep breath," when she pulled his hands apart, "Blow it out," when she brought them together. Patricia counted twenty slow breaths like this, until her son's chest was rising and falling at a regular interval, then helped her boy—spent and shaking—to his feet. She covered his shoulders with her arm and walked him back to the car, her shirt damp with her children's tears, spring mud on the knees of her scrubs. The neighbors watched them pass in silence.

Back home, the children retreated to their rooms. Patricia walked to the living room and played the music of her favorite singer, Otis Redding. Just when she was building the courage to ask Salvador to come home, the cops killed him. Marched into his house and killed him. If he had to die, he should have died after Patricia had managed to tell him what she wanted to say: she still loved him. She wished she could be more like Otis, able to speak of his love so clearly, so constantly, the breaks and purls in his voice, the nonwords between lyrics conveying emotions that most people struggled to express. But Salvador died, as far as he knew, without Patricia's love.

She looked out the window at the little spruce that Salvador had planted on Ray's first birthday. Patricia asked him not to. She was born with a foreboding of disaster, and so she avoided moments that seemed too idyllic, so as not to create memories that would come back to wound her later. She could usually spot such scenes developing and measure how to avert them, like a farmer weighing the time remaining to load the newly mown hay into the barn before a storm hit. If something happened to Ray, the sight of the tree would serve as a slap. Because of her gloomy nature, her cousins from Pueblo had nicknamed Patricia *La Llorona*, after the weeping woman of Mexican folklore, and the nickname had proved prophetic.

"Don't, *mi vida*," she'd told Salvador, holding Ray on her hip, after he'd already dug the hole for the tree in the yard.

"My American wife," Salvador said, smiling as he settled the burlap ball at the base of the tree into the earth. "As superstitious as the *viejas* in my pueblo."

The doorbell rang and she opened the door to see Tío Tiger's sweet teddy bear face, round stomach and silver moustache. As soon as she took two steps toward him he held out his arms to her. He was her father's best friend and her Nino, but she'd

25

lost touch with him in recent years. She rested her head on his shoulder like he was her dad, and he rocked her gently. She buried her nose in the good tweed scent of his jacket, let the pine forest of his aftershave calm her. "I'm going to help you, Patricia," the old man whispered into her ear, and she believed him. "This isn't right. I'm going to help you fight the city."

Fighting the city. It reminded her of the stories Tío and her dad used to tell about the Chicano rights days in the '70s when they were always fighting for something. "What you could do for me," Patricia said, "is call Salvador's family in Mexico. My Spanish is so shaky." She knew just a handful of phrases that she'd learned from her grandmother, Salvador, and *Sábado Gigante*. Lupe had made her study French in high school. She copied the phone number onto a small piece of paper, and then pressed it into Tío's hands, which were brown and wrinkled as a walnut. "This is the number of the only family in his town that has a phone, the people who run the store," she said. "They'll tell his brothers."

Patricia sat with Tío at the kitchen table. "I need more information," she told him. "The cops are lying. Salvador had nothing to do with drugs. We had our hard times, but I know that about him, at least." She walked to the phone, picked up the receiver, then put it down. "I don't know who to call."

Tío shook his head. "*Hija*, the cops aren't going to tell you anything without a fight. You need legal help."

Patricia thought of the small amount that was left in her checkbook at the end of the month when the bills were paid and knew she couldn't afford a lawyer. Salvador had kept giving her money every month, but always much less than he earned, she knew. Now even that would stop. "It's too expensive." She sank back down on her chair.

"I know a guy who will help you out. Remember John Archuleta?"

"That chubby kid who used to come to my parents' parties?" Her mother had tried to set them up once, when Patricia was twenty and already in love with Salvador.

"He's still chubby. But he's a lawyer now."

CHAPTER 3

Ed

Saturday, March 11

Sergeant Springer led Ed and the other two cops who'd fired their weapons downstairs and told them to remain where they were until detectives came for them. Ed hadn't realized that anyone else had fired, and felt a slight sense of relief in sharing the burden of it. Maybe his shots wouldn't prove to be the fatal ones when all the reports came out. They stood in the man's living room, careful not to touch anything. Ed's bum right knee throbbed, but no way was he going to sit down on the couch with the afghan. He would not make himself at home. The air smelled stale to him, the stuffy, personal scent of a closed-up room in winter, and he hoped he'd be allowed to go outside soon. Ed kept his eyes down, studying his boots. He didn't want to see a photo or a child's toy or a sun-faded bouquet of fake flowers that would tell him any more about this man's life. He couldn't think about that right now.

"What happens next?" Cook asked, his pupils so dilated he looked like a fish. Cook, in his twenties, fairly green, no wife or kids yet, skinny, pale and freckled, shifted his weight from side to side like he had to piss.

"The detectives come," Gruber said. Gruber had been on the SWAT team for several years, and had been in a few shootings before this one. He calmly rested his hands on his gut like a pregnant woman, holding his weight back on his heels.

Ed sweated under his heavy gear. The dampness of his underarms bothered him and his nose itched but he didn't scratch it. Ed wanted to ask Gruber questions, but he knew better than to ask them now. He wondered if they were allowed to gear down yet.

"I mean," Cook said, "he had a gun, didn't he? I thought I saw something. You guys saw it too?"

"Shut up, Cook," Gruber said. "We're not supposed to talk. They should have isolated the three of us by now."

Squad cars rolled in outside and paramedics rushed up the stairs toward the man, Springer came back in through the front door, leading the D.A., a man with a face like an undertaker. Then a group of detectives entered the house and approached Ed, Cook, and Gruber. A gray-haired detective with watery blue eyes and lips so tight and dry his mouth looked like a coin slot in his face collected Ed's gun, then drew paper lunch sacks over Ed's hands and told him to leave them on until the forensic crew arrived and completed the shot residue testing. The detective, who said his name was Billings, put his hand on Ed's arm and led him out the door away from the other men.

The bright sun smacked Ed in the face, forcing his eyes closed until he lifted one of his paper bag hands to block it. Detectives and brass swarmed all over the lawn, and neighborhood busybodies drew as close as they could without arousing the cops' attention. The chief of police crossed the lawn and gave Ed a grim nod. Ed returned the gesture, feeling a slackness in his cheeks and mouth that told him there was no expression on his face. He looked across the yard and met the gaze of a chicken-legged little brown-skinned girl who must have been seven or eight, standing on the sidewalk, holding a lollipop in her mouth. She stared at him, impassive, sucking on her candy, as if he were a figure flickering across her TV screen. Billings held Ed by the arm and marched him forward. "Where are we going?" Ed asked.

"I'm putting you in a squad car until I get the go ahead to allow you to proceed to headquarters." The detective hustled Ed forward and opened the rear door of a vehicle.

Ed looked in the open car door but didn't make any move to climb inside. "The back?" Ed asked.

"Sorry, O'Fallon," Billings said. "You're a homicide suspect now." He held a medicinally scented lozenge in his mouth and

Ed could hear it click against his teeth as he spoke. "It's just the way we have to do things so that there isn't any confusion. You'll be cleared in no time."

Ed ducked his head and climbed inside the car. The detective reached to shut the door behind him and Ed said, "Can't I call my wife?"

"Let me get those other detectives over here and then I'll get you a phone." He reached again for the door.

"Just leave the door open," Ed said, still thirsting to suck fresh air into his lungs.

The detective shrugged and turned to walk back inside the house.

After the men freed Ed of the bags, Billings handed him a phone. Polly answered at home and Ed's stomach dropped. She was big on rushing to the phone as soon as it rang these days. He didn't want to hear her sweet voice while he sat in the back of someone else's patrol car after he'd just killed a man. He barely greeted her. "Put your mom on, will you P?" he said.

"K," she said. He heard her yell *Mom!*

"Ed?" Claire said. "What's the matter? I thought you'd call before now."

"I've been in a shooting."

"Oh my God," Claire said. "Are you all right?"

"I'm fine. I wasn't hit. I can't talk long, but I wanted you to know that I'm okay."

"Are you sure? Did someone shoot at you?"

"I think so—but it's hard to say. The whole thing went down so fast."

"Check yourself over for any wounds. Sometimes the shock hides the pain."

"I wasn't hit."

"Do it," Claire ordered. "If you're hurt, make them take you right to the hospital. Tell them to save their questions for later. Can I come see you?"

"They're taking me downtown. This could last all day. I'll call you when I know anything." Ed said goodbye and then handed the phone back to the detective. A couple of officers Ed didn't know approached and said that they would drive him to headquarters. They looked like kids to Ed, without a gray hair or a wrinkle between them, all jazzed because they'd been given an assignment during the aftermath of a shooting.

"I'm going to have to shut the back door," one of them said. "Is that all right?"

Ed reached over and drew it closed himself. Maybe they were carting him back to the station to lock him up. He projected his life forward five years, saw his kids grown without him, their hair cut to shock, cuss words painted in Wite-Out on their school folders, his wife removing the picture in the living room of a ship made out of nails that she had never liked, then pondering which perfume would please another man. But then they reached the station and Ed's patrol partner, Mitch Roybal, came to meet him as he exited the car, put his hand on Ed's shoulder and said, "We're with you on this."

Billings and another detective met Ed at the front door and began to lead him to a questioning room. A couple of guys from Ed's division handed him the business cards of their lawyers, as if he had just joined some club. He was thankful that the detectives were letting him follow at his own pace, and he was glad to see Mitch, who trotted down the chilly hall alongside Ed. Mitch was supposed to be off duty, but he'd come right down to headquarters the second he heard. He had gained a few pounds every year on the force so that now his belly strained against his uniform like a ball of rising dough. He maintained the thick moustache he'd worn since he concluded as a rookie that his face looked too boyish to convey authority, though he had retired the matching sideburns after losing a bet with Ed about the Broncos in '87.

"Did you call your lawyer yet?" Mitch asked as they approached the room.

"My lawyer?" Ed said. "I don't have a lawyer. I thought I'd just answer their questions."

"You don't want to do that," Mitch said, halting. "You're a homicide suspect now."

30

"So I've heard." Ed sighed.

"You can borrow mine," Mitch said. "I keep her on retainer."

Mitch rushed away to make a phone call and the detectives ushered Ed into a questioning room and began to close the door. "Wait!" Ed called out. "What happens now?"

"From what we can tell so far, you were the primary shooter," Billings said, "so we're going to interview you last. We have to interview all the witnesses and the other people involved first."

Ed whistled. "That means I'm here all day, huh?" he said.

"Afraid so." Billings clicked the lozenge once against his teeth and closed the door behind him.

Ed sat in the lone chair by the empty table in the room under the harsh fluorescent lights. The gray walls bore no windows, posters, or clock. They kept questioning rooms bare so suspects would have nothing to distract themselves with during the interview, nothing to fiddle with, leaving the room clear of objects that could prompt the suspect into the fabrication of a lie. There was nothing for him to do in here but think, and he didn't want to think. The wall was a blank screen on which Ed could replay the man's death over and over. Did he shoot too soon? Was the guy even intending to pull the trigger? Could he have convinced the man to drop his weapon without it all ending like this? Ed rose from the chair and began to pace.

The door flung open and Mitch entered.

"Are you supposed to be in here?" Ed asked. "They told me they were keeping me isolated until the interview."

"They said I could keep you company as long as we didn't talk about it."

"Good. I was beginning to go a little froggy in here." Ed eased back in the cold chair.

They looked at each other blankly for a beat. "So what do we talk about then?" Ed asked.

"When I got here," Mitch said, "the homicides were passing around some Polaroids—I think I forgot to give one back." Mitch reached into his pocket and produced a photo, keeping its black back to Ed. "So they answered a call to the scene of a suicide,

31

right? Turns out, the guy was a real big angler, and he hung himself in the garage next to all his fishing equipment. So they took turns posing for photos."

Mitch handed Ed the Polaroid and he looked at it. It was slightly out of focus, but its subject was clear. In it, one of the homicide cops, grinning, wearing mirrored sunglasses, held a rod and reel next to the hanged guy so that it looked like he was a prize fish that he'd landed. The dead man's head sagged to his chest, his feet dangled limp in the air. On any day before this one, Ed would have chuckled over the photo. Now it just made him feel nauseous. Ed turned the picture over on the table and slid it back to Mitch.

"Let's not talk about work," Ed said. "Let's talk about anything else—the kids, baseball, anything."

It wasn't long before Mitch's lawyer showed up and introduced herself. She was a heavyset, fortyish lady who said her name was Sylvia Bertagnoli, and waited for Ed to say something but he just nodded, tired of meeting so many people on a day he would have preferred to spend down at the bottom of a hole. Sylvia started telling Ed what to expect, explaining that she would sit with him during the questioning. "I usually don't stop cops who've been in officer-involved shootings from answering any of the detectives' questions," she said. "They usually don't cross the line." After the questioning, the detectives would turn over the information they gathered to the D.A., who would decide whether or not to file criminal charges against Ed. Later, the Firearms Discharge Review Board would decide if he'd violated any department policies.

"Tell him about the lawsuits," Mitch said. "The family of this guy could try to sue you."

People with a beef from years earlier could sue an officer, long after it was possible to locate any witnesses to back up the cop's story. They could make up anything, lie that a cop had beat them, harassed them for no reason, called them a name, and the city would usually pay off these people before it went to court, before the cop had a chance to clear his name. The complaint settlement ended up in a cop's package, and could affect his chance for promotion. Mitch had never forgiven the department for settling a lawsuit against him in which a man claimed Mitch had used excessive force on a DUI arrest. The department didn't back Mitch when he needed them, and he constantly threatened to quit.

"Lawsuits are always a possibility," Sylvia said, "but if this guy pulled a gun on an officer, they have no grounds. There are so many witnesses, and their statements are all being recorded."

There was a knock on the door and then it opened. Billings entered. "It's your turn now," he said. "Are you ready?"

"Sure."

Mitch slapped him on the shoulder and left the room. Billings drew the door closed. "Let's begin," he said, turning the tape recorder on. He read Ed his Miranda rights, and Ed looked to Sylvia to see if this was right. She nodded. Ed let out a nervous laugh. "I've never been Mirandized before," he said.

"Never?" the detective asked, glaring at him.

Ed swallowed.

"I'm just kidding," Billings said, his face brightening. "I'm simply going to ask you to lay out the whole timeline for me, to tell me everything you remember."

The detective asked him the usual questions first, what Ed's name was, how many years he'd been with the department, when he joined SWAT. Then he asked about the raid, about how they'd cased the house, entered and searched the ground floor.

"What happened when the door swung open?" the detective asked.

"I called out 'police,' I looked in, I saw a guy standing there with one of his hands kind of hidden so I told him to show me his hands," Ed said.

"Did the suspect comply?"

"I drew back to take cover behind the wall, so I had to duck in again to check on him, and I thought I saw that he was holding a gun in the hand that had been hidden before."

"You thought he had a gun? You didn't know for sure?"

"Well, it was kind of dark. But when he raised his hand, I thought I could make out the barrel pretty clear." Had all the stuff he'd seen—the gun, the muzzle flash—just been images drawn from his mind? "I mean, it was really weird. I got tunnel vision, like they say you will, and later when I looked at the room there were all these things I didn't notice, like this trophy case."

"Can we return to the gun?"

"Yeah, so the gun. I've got my weapon trained on him the whole time, and I tell him to drop the gun, but he doesn't, and then I hear this pop. It sounded like a BB gun going off or something, so I didn't know what it was, but I hear the mirror behind me shatter and I think shit, he's got his first round off before I did anything, and I have to protect the officers behind me, so I start to fire. I don't know how many rounds I shot."

Sylvia put her hand on Ed's arm. "Just answer his questions," she said, patting him. She smelled of soap and her round glasses reminded Ed of those of a babysitter he'd had as a child. "Short answers, yeses and nos."

The detective made Ed draw what happened on a whiteboard and explain everything again. Eventually the detective finished up, and the district commander came by to tell Ed he'd be placed on a two-week paid administrative leave.

"Two weeks?" Ed said. "So it was fatal then?"

"DOA," the commander said.

Ed had been hoping the guy would pull through. But that was it. Ed was a killer now. His heart started jackhammering and he remained in the chair for a while after they told him he could leave, taking slow breaths.

The shooting occurred at a little after one PM, and by the time they let Ed leave it was 10:00. Mitch drove Ed home, and he kept his eyes closed so that he wouldn't have to talk. Ed could tell Mitch wanted to ask him questions, but he made chitchat instead. When they approached the O'Fallons' driveway, Mitch asked, "Hey, don't your boys start that new team tomorrow?"

"Yeah," Ed said. "New team, new coach, new league, new everything. They'll be playing for the Zenith Homes Z's." For once, Ed was glad he wasn't coaching his boys' baseball team this year. He would have been too shaken to coach the next day. Ed's boys were moving up to a better league, the one that produced most of Colorado's Major League Baseball prospects. Jesse was twelve, E.J. eleven, the prime age when boys started to show if they had what it took to go farther, or if they lacked it. Ed hoped he could put off telling his sons about what happened, leaving their minds untroubled so that they could just look forward to baseball the next day. He didn't want to tell Polly, who knew little about what he did at work except that he "helped people." Not exactly how he or any of the other cops on the force would have described their work once they were past their rookie year.

"Take care, buddy," Mitch said as Ed climbed out of the car. "I'll call you tomorrow."

Ed waved at him as the car pulled away. He didn't want to go inside the house. He just stayed rooted in place. Ed thought of his father, dead for five years now, who wouldn't talk about his time in Korea until the end, when his lungs were riddled with tumors and he could hardly speak, and Ed had to lean close to hear his urgent whispers. Even then, his father only recounted the bare chronology, battles fought, wounds sustained, the party at the end. He talked mostly about a German shepherd who'd been his companion throughout the war. He'd wanted to bring the dog home, but his commanding officer forbade it. But when he entered the transport to go home, he saw that plenty of other people had brought their dogs. He never described what it felt like to kill someone, or whether it was possible to recover from such an act. It took weeks for Ed's father to come home after the fighting ended. Ed could now see that this time alone, which Ed's mother begrudged him, was useful to a man who killed and then had to resume his place at the dinner table.

Claire called out to him. "Ed, is that you?"

Ed walked from the driveway to the front porch, where Claire stood in the light of the porch lamp. She threw her arms around his neck, drew him close and buried her face in his chest. She wore her fuzzy bathrobe and Ed ran his hand absently over her back. He still felt as though he were weighed down with the heavy SWAT gear he had removed hours earlier, and Claire seemed smaller than normal in his arms.

"What did you tell the kids?" Ed whispered.

"Nothing yet," she said. "I just told them you were caught late at work, writing reports. Come on inside."

Ed followed her. The kids were tearing around the kitchen like it was midday. "I let them stay up with me," Claire explained, "for company." Ed began to head down to the basement as he always did, to lock his gun in the safe in the far corner before he saw his children. But when he checked his holster, he realized he must have left the replacement gun the commander gave him in the questioning room or in Mitch's car. He hoped he'd left it in Mitch's car—a knuckleheaded move like that in front of the brass could get him put on desk duty. Ed's face grew hot. Once when he was still on rookie probation, he had driven all the way to the station before he realized he'd left his gun back home in the safe. He had to turn around to retrieve it, and he'd been late for roll call. Guys had ribbed him for months about it. But that was long ago. He wasn't supposed to make mistakes like that anymore.

In spite of his empty holster, Ed went downstairs, opened the safe and pretended that he was putting something in it, because if he didn't, the kids would know something was wrong. What was he doing? The gesture was as ridiculous as that of a tee-ball pitcher who only pretended to pitch. He needed his gun back— he'd ask Mitch about it tomorrow. The kids knew they were not supposed to approach him until he'd locked his gun away, but Polly often waited for him at the top of the stairs to the basement, her toes a respectful inch back from the edge.

When Ed saw Polly waiting for him, her curly brown head backlit by the lamp in the hallway, the smile he gave her felt false and tight. The command expression he wore at work might one day completely overtake his face and refuse to budge. He'd develop that mask of stone like some of the older cops. He climbed up the stairs and picked up his daughter—she would still be the right size for that for a few more years. He hugged her, thinking that this was why people had kids—for those moments between tantrums and demands, for those good days during a sweet age, when they didn't care about whether you failed or triumphed at work.

The scene in the kitchen seemed choreographed, as if from a movie depicting an efficient household. His boys, Jesse and E.J., set the table, Jesse throwing down placemats and E.J. following him with plates, each of them rushing back and forth from the kitchen to the table on separate missions without ever bumping into each other.

"It's late—didn't you guys already eat?" Ed asked.

"Yeah," Jesse said, "But that was like five hours ago. We got hungry again while we were waiting for you." He set the table for three.

"You guys eat like you've got a couple of hollow legs," Ed said. They were astonishingly skinny given the amount of food they packed away. Jesse was more muscular than his brother, built like his father, but neither carried an ounce of flab. They grew so fast that Jesse passed his clothes to his brother, and E.J. gave them to the Salvation Army before they began to wear out. They played outdoors so much their skin was brown from last snow to first. People called them "Ed's boys" more often than they identified them each with a separate name—only their mother, sister, and teachers did that.

Claire charged through the last duties of dinner preparation, warming up the leftover spaghetti and meatballs, shaking bagged salad into a bowl and tossing in sliced carrots and tomatoes. Even after all he'd been through, she still was going to make him eat his vegetables. Polly stuck close to Ed's side, hiding so no one would detect her and demand that she help. Soon the boys positioned the last fork and cup, filled the glasses with ice and water. The flurry ceased when the family approached the table and assumed the same seats they occupied every night. Claire and Polly sat in their places, too, even though they weren't going to eat. Everyone acted like this was normal, like they usually ate a second dinner in the middle of the night, and the kids seemed excited, fiddling with the silverware.

"Thanks Claire," Ed said. "I haven't eaten since noon." Ed helped himself to everything, but the moment he held the first twirled forkful of spaghetti to his lips, he knew he couldn't eat. He didn't want to tip the kids off, so he tried to shovel food in and chew. The spaghetti was tasteless, despite Claire's meat sauce, which had achieved fame at a cop potluck Ed's rookie year, condemning Claire to prepare it for all subsequent gatherings. The sauce reminded Ed of the gore he'd seen earlier in the day, and he could eat no more.

"Aren't you hungry, Dad?" E.J. asked.

Ed looked down at his plate. It was plain that he had dished himself more than he could eat, which never happened. Ed was a man who knew the dimensions of his own stomach. He met Claire's eyes across the table before he delivered his lie. "I guess I'm not used to eating this late."

"I'll take it if you don't want it," Jesse said.

Ed handed him the plate.

The boys finished eating their second dinners, then shot out of the dining room, Polly zooming behind them, running downstairs to the TV.

"It's nearly midnight," Claire said, following them. "Time for bed."

None of them responded, keeping their eyes trained on the screen, as if Claire would disappear if they just ignored her.

"Hey you kids!" Ed barked. "Listen to your mother."

They leapt to their feet at the sound of Ed's voice and scampered upstairs to brush their teeth.

Claire and Ed made the rounds through the bedrooms, tucking the kids in and kissing them. When they finally entered their own bedroom, Ed felt so tired he wanted to sink to his knees. All of his old injuries now started to press their cases, screaming for attention like a nest of hungry baby birds. His joints pulsated. He'd hurt his rotator cuff and re-injured his knee back when he was a hard-charging rookie, tackling crooks without a moment's thought. He'd wrecked his back lugging the fifteen-pound gun belt for years. His gut occasionally acted up after a stressful day, producing worrisome burbling sounds and mysterious stabs of pain.

Claire stood inside the door of their bedroom, watching as Ed made his way toward her, the look on her face identical to the one she wore when Polly skinned her knee and she was waiting with her arms open.

"I know you want to talk," Ed said, "but I'm so tired right now."

"Of course," Claire said. "Why don't you just take a hot shower and then go to bed?"

Claire went into the bathroom and turned on the water in the shower to let it heat up. She took down a towel from the cabinet and put out his slippers and robe. Ed followed her, comforted by watching her putter about.

"I feel awful," Ed said, barely loud enough to be heard over the rushing water in the shower. He said it again, even though it sounded stupid. He sank down on the closed toilet lid to wait for the water to heat. "He died, Claire. I killed him."

"Sweetie," Claire said, kneeling in front of him, taking both of his hands in hers and kissing them. She kissed them slowly at first, and then more urgently, moving her lips over his skin. She looked up at him with clear eyes. "You had to shoot him. You know that don't you? Mitch said he pulled a gun on you, and you had to shoot him to protect yourself and the men you were with. If you hadn't shot him, I'd be here alone tonight."

"I've never killed anyone before."

39

"But you knew you might have to someday," she said. "We both knew." Her voice faltered, and she pinched her lips tightly together.

"Just cry," Ed said, squeezing her hand. "Just cry if you need to."

Claire let out her breath and lay her head on Ed's lap. He absently stroked her hair.

"This isn't yours alone," she said, "You know it?"

Ed nodded, but he didn't know it, not really.

Claire had fallen asleep by the time Ed climbed in bed, her breathing intense and deep. Ed was home safe, so she must have thought her worries were over. She radiated heat, warming them both. When Ed closed his eyes, the visions began, the faces and voices of all the officers who milled around the scene, the medicinal breath of the detective, the hot gaze of the little girl in the yard, the creak of the door swinging open, the rusty smell of blood, the after-burn of what he'd done to the man in that close, dim room. Ed opened his eyes and tried to keep them open until dawn.

CHAPTER 4

Patricia
March 14–17

Patricia studied the casseroles in the refrigerator that the neighbors had brought, the foil-wrapped items reminding her of all the unpleasant tasks ahead. She'd go to the morgue, then call the lawyer Tío hired and ask what he'd found out in that morning's meeting with the police. She planned to make up some lie for the kids, then slip out to identify the body when Mrs. Guerrero came over. She couldn't protect the kids from much, but she could spare them the sight of their dead father, at least. It was easy to recall all the bad images in her life, and difficult to bring up the beautiful ones. Sunsets melted into each other, but horror remained singular. And who knew what the cops had done to Salvador.

"What are you doing?" Mia asked, her tone accusing.

Patricia glanced up from the refrigerator at Mia. She'd left in her braids from the day before, and fuzzy hair haloed her. She held her El Johnway action figure close to her chest.

"I'm fixing something to eat," Patricia said. "Are you hungry?"

Mia shook her head, then sat down on one of the stools at the counter.

Patricia wasn't hungry, but hoped Mia would finally eat if she set an example. Patricia grabbed the dish closest to the front of the refrigerator and stuck it in the microwave. She thought about what to tell the kids when she went to the morgue. That she had to work, maybe. She hardly ever flat-out lied to them— mostly she was just evasive when there was something she didn't think they needed to know. Like when Mia was three and over-heard something on TV and then asked her what "sexy" meant.

41

Acting on a dormant reflex, Patricia shot out the answer her own mother always delivered when flummoxed with a question, usually about sex or death: "Never mind."

"You're really going to eat that, Mom?" Mia said over the hum of the oven.

"I'm going to try, baby. You should, too." Patricia opened the door when the timer sounded, plopped a spoonful of the casserole on a plate, and sat at the table. "You're sure you don't want any?"

Mia shook her head. "I told you already. I'm not eating any death food."

Ray wouldn't eat either. Patricia brought a full plate to his room for every meal, but she'd find it an hour later, pushed into the hallway, the cold food untouched. Patricia poked at the stuff on her plate with her fork. Tuna noodle casserole from the looks of it, beige chunks of fish stuck to dried-out noodles. She raised a forkful of it to her lips, stared it down, but couldn't do it.

Mia stood a foot away, watching.

"There's this old myth the Greeks have," Patricia said, returning her fork to her plate, "that as long as you didn't eat any of the food in the underworld—you know, the land of the dead people—you didn't have to stay there." Patricia had picked up this story from one of the countless books that she had read over the years. Mia took after her, and liked a story. "One girl, Persephone, ate some pomegranate seeds, so she had to stay in the underworld for a certain part of the year. That's why we have a change of seasons, or something like that."

"I don't want to stay," Mia said, trying not to cry. To hold back, she stuck out her bottom lip.

The bumper lip, which the kids had first showed as frightened infants, never failed to evoke a spasm of sympathy in Patricia. She pulled Mia close and kissed her head. "You don't have to be tough."

Mia's stomach rumbled.

"Okay," Patricia said, "you win. We'll toss this stuff." She scraped it into the trashcan. "I'll go to the grocery store on my way back."

"Where are you going?"

Patricia looked away to make it easier. "To work. I need to check on a patient," she said, "and then I'll be able to take some time off."

When Nino and his grandmother arrived from next door to stay with Ray and Mia, Patricia prepared herself to head to the morgue. What would it be like to see him dead, the husband she hadn't seen alive in weeks? Patricia was thankful Ray kept to his room so she didn't have to try lying to him.

"See if you can get them to eat something," Patricia whispered to Mrs. Guerrero. She had been fattening Nino on *churros* and *menudo* since he could eat solid food.

"I brought lunch," Mrs. Guerrero said, opening a Tupperware bowl to display some *chimichangas*, still steaming from her fryer.

As she drove, all Patricia could think about was how three days ago Salvador had been alive, five days ago, six. She wondered what he'd eaten that last day. Nothing as good as the meals she used to cook for him when they were first married, trying to impress him with pot roasts and hand-rolled pork tamales. Patricia's mother said the day she caught Patricia wrist-deep in a bowl of *masa* with a stack of wet cornhusks beside her was when she knew her daughter was in love.

Patricia could name every food Salvador liked and didn't, and she was probably the only person in the world who could. The first time she cooked for him, she'd baked a batch of cheese enchiladas. Spent half the day de-stemming and shaking the seeds out of a huge bag of desiccated red chile husks, boiling them in a great stew pot, then blending them into a fiery thick sauce. She'd watched Salvador as he sat at the table in her apartment, his hair wet from a hasty, after-work shower. He looked down at his plate and poked at the cheese glop that emerged from the end of the tortillas. He smiled, ate them all, lied to her that they were delicious, kissing his bunched fingertips with a flourish, then got sick an hour later, and spent the rest of the date on the toilet. She had married a man who couldn't stand the cheese-glutted Tex-Mex food that had earned her parents their living.

The office of the medical examiner was across the street from the hospital where she worked, but she had never really looked at it: a nondescript red brick building, an American flag visible through the front window, with a green handrail that she gripped as she mounted the small flight of concrete steps. She thought of all the other grieving people who had run their hands along the cold rail before her, pulling their protesting legs onward. How much time would she spend doing what at least part of her body didn't want to do?

Patricia walked to the front desk and spoke to the plump woman there, who held her large brown eyes in a look of what must have been perpetual concern as she asked, "Do you have a mortuary picked out?"

Patricia swallowed, trying to wet her dry mouth so she could speak as she searched in her purse for the piece of paper with the information Tío had written on it, then handed it over.

"I don't need that—just fill these out and we'll take care of it." She produced a clipboard with a stack of forms attached. "You probably know that the medical examiner ordered an autopsy on your husband. It includes a drug test."

"Why?"

"Because of the circumstances."

Patricia, smarting from the implied judgment, shot back, "You mean because the cops killed him."

The woman angled her head to her shoulder and gave a noncommittal half-shrug. "There's an investigation. You can request a copy of the report on one of these forms."

Patricia wondered if the words "drug dealer" were stamped in red on his file. "Do I get to see Salvador now?"

"We do the identifications from photos."

"I'd like to see him." If she couldn't see him anyway, she needn't have lied to the kids.

"I'm sorry, Mrs. Santillano. We can't take the chance that a visitor would contaminate trace evidence or be exposed to an infectious disease. The mortuary, I'm sure, will give you plenty of time to spend with him."

"But he's my husband," Patricia pleaded. She was aching to see him now, after all the weeks apart.

"I am so sorry for your loss." She shook her head, her liquid eyes looking so close to brimming that Patricia half-believed her. They must have hired her for those eyes. "If you're ready, you can take a look at the photos and then sign some forms and be on your way, back to your family."

The woman led Patricia to a private room with an empty table and handed her a manila folder. "Take your time," she said, closing the door behind her. Patricia put her hand on the folder, then drew it away. She'd fill out the forms first. She slowly wrote out his full name, probably for the last time in her life. When there were no papers left, she had to look. She took out the first photo. The color was off, the skin ashy, the features hanging slack, the eyes sunken, but it was him. She flipped to the next one—his hands, the dear hands that he'd been vain about, small and well-formed, the fingernails neat as he always kept them, the mole between the first two knuckles on his left hand that she used to kiss for luck.

"We have some of your husband's belongings for you," the woman said when Patricia returned the file. She pushed a small cardboard box forward on the table.

"This is everything from his room?"

"Probably some of it is still in the evidence locker."

Patricia added this to the mental list of all the questions she needed to ask the lawyer. Her brain hurt from it all. She took the box back to her car and placed it on the passenger seat. Maybe she should call Archuleta now, so she wouldn't have to speak with him in front of the kids. Instead, she opened the box and saw an Orange Crush Broncos t-shirt from the seventies that they'd found together at the Salvation Army on Broadway the first year they were married. Salvador had loved that team. He arranged his work schedule so he'd never miss a game.

She dug through the box, setting aside more clothes. There were dozens of photos, some framed, some unframed: the kids as babies, wallet-sized school portraits, their wedding pictures, and some of his family in Mexico. There was one photo Patricia had never seen before, of Salvador with his arms around a pretty woman and a girl in front of a whitewashed adobe house, the three of them squinting in the sun. This wasn't any relative she knew of, no one she'd been introduced to when she went to Mexico with him, and it was a recent photo, probably taken on Salvador's last trip—he wore a shirt Patricia had bought him for his birthday a few months before he left. The woman and the girl wore clothes that looked American, jeans and shirts that Salvador must have brought them. Patricia put the photo aside and sank back in her seat. Did Salvador have another family or at least a woman in Mexico? She'd suspected it on occasion. Her temples pulsed. She didn't have space in her head to worry about it now. She tossed everything back in the box, then carried it outside and shoved it in the back corner of the trunk under a blanket and some jumper cables, so the kids wouldn't see it.

"Where are the groceries?" Mia asked, jumping up from the couch when she returned. Mrs. Guererro watched a *telenovela* and Nino played with his handheld video game on the couch, thumbs flying.

"I forgot, baby," Patricia said, cursing herself for not carrying out the details of her lie. "Why don't we all go together—it'll give us something to do until grandma and grandpa get here."

"Ray didn't come out of his room," Mrs. Guerrero said. "But Mia had a snack." A pile of Twinkie wrappers from a stash she'd brought along lay on the floor between Mia and Nino.

"I'm sorry he didn't come out to see Nino," Patricia said, "he's been—"

"It's okay," Nino said in his surprisingly high-pitched voice. Ray's had begun to crack a few months earlier. Patricia would feel much safer if Ray hadn't ditched Nino for Miguel.

After they left, Patricia knocked on Ray's door. When there was no answer, she opened it and announced into the darkness of the room, "Ray, get up now. We're going to King Soopers."

Ray lay face down on his bed. He pulled a pillow over his head. "I'm not going."

On the floor lay orderly piles of baseball cards. Patricia picked up a stack and thumbed through it. As he had since he was a little boy, he'd been arranging his complete annual set in numerical order, consulting the checklist cards to make sure he had one card of each player in the major leagues, as promised on the box. He was still a kid, she reassured herself as she approached him and pulled on his shoulder. "Come on. Get up."

Ray threw the pillow off his head and flipped over. "Don't touch me."

Patricia took a step back. "Don't talk to me that way." She wanted to pull him into her arms and kiss his hair and neck like she used to when he was little. "Fine," she said, "Stay here if you want." She hoped he wouldn't—she didn't trust him alone. Maybe he'd skip out to Federal and see Miguel, who liked to hold court at the convenience store on the corner whenever he ditched school. She started to back out of the room, remembering how when he was little, all she had to do to get him to follow was pretend like she was leaving without him.

Mia came in from the hallway and touched the back of Ray's hand. "I'm going," she said. "Will you come with me?"

Ray looked at his sister for a moment, then raised himself and slipped off the bed. He stalked out of the room, brushing past Patricia without saying a word. He still wore the same clothes as the day before, one leg of his jeans hitched up high enough to show his white sock. Normally she would have had her hands all over her children, straightening their collars, fixing their hair, chasing them down to wipe jelly off their faces with a wet washcloth. Ray pulled the hood of his sweatshirt over his head and followed Mia, who held El Johnway in one hand.

When Ray was seven, he had saved his pennies to buy three-year-old Mia a John Elway action figure for Christmas. Elway

47

still reigned as Denver's lone celebrity, even after his retirement, and people talked about him so much that he was one of the first people outside of the family Patricia's children could recognize. When Mia had torn off the wrapping paper to reveal the toy on Christmas morning, she jumped up and exclaimed, "El Johnway!"

From then on, he was known only as El Johnway in their house. Mia loved the gift so much that at first she tried to keep the hard plastic figure in her bed at night, but El Johnway was no good for cuddling. He was a man of action, his arm permanently cocked to throw a football that was melded to his hand. She hadn't carried the doll around like this for years.

The cheery bustle of the bright grocery store made Patricia squint her eyes. She told the kids to grab whatever they wanted, something she'd never allowed before. Still Ray didn't touch anything, following Patricia at a distance with his hands jammed into the pocket of his sweatshirt, his shoulders hunched, his head ducked under his hood. They started in the refrigerated aisle because it looked the emptiest. Mia took frozen pizzas out of the case and studied the idealized pictures of the boxes' contents until she decided on one and placed it in the cart.

"Hey," Patricia said, "Why not get three?" She reached into the case and tossed two more pizzas into the cart.

"When do we get to see Dad?" Ray asked, his face shadowed in the depths of his hoodie.

"Tomorrow, I think," Patricia said, dropping her voice, "at the mortuary."

"I want to see him today," Mia said.

"They won't allow it."

"Who is *they*?" Mia asked.

"You went to see him without us, didn't you?" Ray said. "You never work five days in a row."

"I didn't get to see him, either," Patricia said, feeling caught. "It wasn't allowed."

"Quit lying."

"I'm not," Patricia said, defensive. "They only let me see photos."

"What was in them?" Ray demanded.

Never mind, Patricia thought, wishing they were young enough to still use that line on them. An old woman filling her cart with bags of frozen peas and carrots shot Patricia a look, as though she were personally responsible for all the mouthy kids these days.

Patricia pushed her cart ahead and blundered through the shopping trip, taking three times as long as usual because her mind was so numb that she couldn't locate the items she wanted, and kept doubling back after realizing she'd forgotten something in a previous aisle.

With her cart full of frozen pizza, cereal, snack foods and dessert, Patricia led her family to the checkout. They never ate this way. As usual, Patricia chose the wrong line. One lady tried to pass a pile of expired coupons that didn't match the items she had purchased. The next one asked for a replacement tomato upon noticing a bruised one, which prompted the cashier to summon one of the developmentally disabled bag-boys, who limped up in his grocery store smock, his ready smile marking him as the only apparently happy person in the store.

The others in line assessed the situation quicker than Patricia and fled to adjacent checkout aisles. The children simply stood behind Patricia, bearing the wait. Patricia wished Mia would ask for some of the candy or gum that lined the aisle so that she could say yes.

Tonight they'd eat frozen pizza because that's all she had energy for, tearing open a box and shoving its contents into the oven, retrieving it when a ding sounded. Patricia massaged her forehead with her fingertips as the checker rang up the items. Maybe she could call the lawyer tomorrow instead.

The kids were in their rooms and Patricia was dozing on the couch where she'd sat down to wait for her parents when the doorbell rang. She glanced at the clock, which read half-past ten. She padded to the door in her socks and flannel nightgown and peeked through the peephole: her parents, flanked by their matching red luggage.

Patricia opened the door to them. "Papa," she said, "Mama," as if she were a little girl. They left their bags and embraced her at once, together, holding Patricia between them for a long time. They smelled as they did when they used to collect her from the babysitter after a date—of night air and Lupe's perfume.

Her dad's hair was disheveled from the fourteen-hour drive, his glasses smudged with fingerprints. He leaned on Patricia and kissed the top of her head. The drive left Lupe untouched as ever, her white blouse and orchid pants still as pressed and fresh as when she put them on. Her hair was chopped short, with a touch of silver at the temples. In her early sixties, Lupe still rose at dawn most days for a brisk walk, and carried herself with impeccable posture, her back so straight you noticed it, her carriage always seeming to Patricia like an overcorrection, an affront to her daughter's tendency to slouch.

"Where are the children?" Lupe asked as she flipped on the lights.

"In their rooms," Patricia said. "They're not real happy with me right now."

"They're mad at you? What about? Their father?"

Patricia shrugged.

"You had nothing to do with all that," Lupe said flatly, and bustled off to Ray's room.

"Maybe I did," Patricia said to her mother's retreating back.

Patricia helped her dad carry their luggage inside. Then they stood in the entryway, Patricia staring at her toes, sheepish. Her parents were dignified people who'd never tangled with police. Patricia knew that Lupe was thinking that this was what came of her daughter marrying an immigrant, this was the sordid array that went with it—shootings and drugs and fatherless children.

"It's not fair, *Hija*," her father said. He and Salvador developed a camaraderie during the days they spent working side by side during visits, putting up a new fence in the yard, organizing the garage, and finishing the basement. It was Salvador's idea to name Ray after his grandfather, and Patricia knew her dad relished this, introducing him as Little Raymond wherever they went. "It's not your fault he lived with drug dealers," he said.

"He didn't," she insisted.

"Are you sure?"

"Of course."

"Were you going to work it out?"

"I'd hoped," she said. "It doesn't matter now."

"Sure it does." He looked off.

"You must be tired," Patricia said.

"That couch over there is singing to me."

"Go ahead, lie down."

He sat on the couch, took off his shoes, and stretched out. Patricia drew one of the afghans that Lupe had knitted over him. She sat down on the loveseat opposite the couch and watched her father sleep, his breathing becoming regular and deep.

Lupe charged around, opening cabinets and doors, flicking on lights, picking up clutter, rousting the house into life. The children finally wandered out of their rooms, looking dazed, and watched her rush about. "What have you arranged for the funeral?" Lupe asked Patricia during one of her passes through the living room.

"I haven't exactly gotten around to that yet."

Lupe looked down at her daughter with her arms filled with magazines, a pair of Ray's sneakers, and one of Mia's dolls. "I'll handle it," she said. "I'll start making calls—is Father Montero still at the cathedral?"

"No idea," Patricia said.

"You haven't been taking the children to Mass?"

"Not lately," she said, thinking *not ever.* It was Salvador who'd always insisted they go to Mass. When he left, Patricia let that slide.

"Tío said you were speaking to a lawyer today."

"I didn't find the time."

"Well, call now."

"It's late."

"I've known John Archuleta since he was in diapers. He can get out of bed."

Patricia handed Lupe the card with the lawyer's number on it. Lupe sat at the kitchen counter with a notepad and pens. They were still talking when Patricia went to bed, and she paused to listen to what Lupe was saying. "He was still an alien when they married . . . I *know* . . . He did get his citizenship later." An *alien*. The word was an accusation Lupe always used to highlight Patricia's poor judgment. "She says he wasn't selling drugs," Lupe continued, as Patricia slunk away.

She woke at two AM, covered in sweat from a nightmare she couldn't remember. Salvador used to come home at about this time from work, close the door quietly behind him, remove his shoes, and walk softly down the hall, then blast on the shower with a burst. He came to her with his hair wet, his face smooth from a quick shave, and kissed her throat. He spread a cool hand on her sleep-warmed belly, then nuzzled her until she admitted she was awake and returned his kisses. After they became parents, sex in the dead dark of night was the only kind, in a room with so little light they could have been anyone to each other. She couldn't recall their last time. She hadn't paid attention to it. Lasts could sneak past you in a way that firsts never did.

In the Cathedral of the Immaculate Conception, Patricia sat in the front pew beside her stunned children, choking on the incense that wafted from the priest's swinging censor. Salvador liked to go to the little neighborhood church's Spanish Mass. The cathedral was Lupe's idea. It was half-filled with neighbors and friends of her parents, people Patricia barely knew, and extended family up from Pueblo, people who had never before seemed interested in knowing her. Lupe had contacted the funeral director, selected a casket and haggled over a graveyard plot. Patricia had considered cremation, but then Salvador was

52

an old-fashioned Catholic. Salvador's family in Mexico was too poor to travel to Denver for the funeral, and Lupe insisted that she would pay for everything. "You've got two kids to raise," she said. "Save your salary for that." The draped casket rested on a black trolley in the center of the aisle, just in front of the altar. The priest slowly circled it, swinging the censor, sending out visible gusts of incense, rendering the air thick and spicy-sweet.

Snow fell outside, dimming the stained glass windows. The priest spoke the rites and Patricia's hand rose to cross herself at the proper junctures. Her body knelt unbidden, her mouth shaped the words. Whether she believed these phrases or not anymore, habit gripped her.

She watched the priest's lips move as he uttered the last words he'd ever have over Salvador. She thought she believed in heaven, but her concept of it was so vague—departed spirits dispersed like mist somewhere above—that it felt too insubstantial for comfort. She wished she could believe in the place her grandmother used to speak of, where Jesus, Guadalupe and all the saints, in the flesh, lived in a kingdom above the earth, holding their arms open, just waiting for you, just waiting for a spent soul to stagger into their embrace.

Her children didn't stir, Ray wearing the dirge of a suit Lupe had bought for him that he'd put on without protest, Mia draped in black velvet. Patricia wanted to hurt whoever had done this to her children, turned them into mourners so young. The luckless altar boys who had drawn funeral duty performed their silent tasks, careful never to turn their eyes on the crowd. She heard singing, from behind and above, an organ's garish, minor key blare, and then it was over.

When Patricia pushed through the door outside, someone snapped a picture. There were a few photographers and a couple of men who must have been reporters nearby. A reporter from the *Rocky Mountain News* had called the day after Patricia's parents arrived, seeking a comment about the shooting. Lupe spoke with him, and the article quoted her: "Salvador was not a drug dealer," she'd said, sounding more confident in this fact than

Patricia thought she would, "and we're pursuing all our legal options."

Patricia's father put his arm around her and led her and the children through the gap in the bushes around the courtyard to the parking lot while Lupe distracted the people, inviting them to the supper she'd arranged at the Knights of Columbus.

In the car, Patricia watched the wet snowflakes smack against the tinted windows and melt, the droplets skittering down the pane in a pattern she could never predict. She thought of Salvador, how young they'd been together, how old she felt now.

Her senior year in high school, she ended up falling in love with the man who delivered flowers to the shop where she worked, *Flora's Flores* on Federal Boulevard, sandwiched between a payday loan shop and a *taquería*. The little shop was busiest in spring and summer with orders for weddings and *quinceañeras*. She met Salvador in the autumn, the season of homecoming corsages for North High up the street.

Salvador had an old country name and wore tight jeans, a glinting belt buckle, and cowboy boots the way immigrants did when they wanted to look sharp. Even in his hick gear and dated haircut, Salvador was handsome, with terracotta skin, a sharp nose, and shining eyes. During his first delivery, she went out to meet the truck in the alley behind the store and he handed her a yellow daisy that had fallen loose from a bunch in the back of his van. "Thanks," she said. "Take the flowers over there," she instructed, jerking her thumb at the back door of the store. He didn't move or speak. "*Comprende?*" she asked. "Do you speak English, for Christ's sake?"

"For Christ's sake, I do," he said softly, as if to hide his gentle accent. "But also for your sake."

"Wonderful," she muttered, as a wrapper from a nearby fast food joint blew across the alley like a tumbleweed. "Johnny Smooth."

"Johnny? My name is Salvador. Sorry for not being quicker." He smiled, his grin endearingly crooked. "You are beautiful."

"Patricia Maestas," she said, extending her hand, as if she hadn't heard his last remark. He shook it. "The last delivery guy was an ex-con who smoked in the van and left the flowers reeking. Don't smoke in the van."

"I don't smoke."

"And don't let any of your buddies smoke around the flowers either."

"Why do you think I have buddies?" The grin again, the dark eyes that stared at her like they'd never look away.

Patricia's boss came out of the back door. "Where are my gladiolas? Mrs. Alfree just came in, and you know what that means."

"Here," Salvador said, handing her a bunch. "These I think are gladiolas."

"You know the names of the flowers?" she asked. "I don't think the last delivery guy even knew the names of all his children."

Patricia propped the door open and went back into the store. She watched Salvador walk back and forth, hauling the buckets of flowers all the way inside the store instead of leaving them out back. His t-shirt was tighter than the one an American would have worn.

As he walked away after his last trip, Patricia forced herself to keep her eyes down on her work, but Salvador approached her. "It is nice to meet you, Patricia," he said, making her name four syllables. *Pah-tree-cee-ah.* Her name was light when he said it, not heavy-hipped, the way her teachers made it sound. His tongue barely skimmed the roof of his mouth to make the word.

Patricia watched the snow fall outside the limo as she repeated the way Salvador had said her name in her head, practicing his voice to keep the sound of it from fading.

CHAPTER 5

Ed

March 12–13

The day after he killed the man, Ed kneeled next to his family at the 10:00 Mass at Risen Christ, a church that everyone called Ski Jesus because of the modernist, all-white building's odd shape, with one high end that swooped down dramatically like an alpine slope. Ed's bad knee smarted. He looked up toward the stained glass window that rose behind the altar and felt God's eye on him like a spotlight. He was a killer now, kneeling among children and old folks with their heads bent in prayer.

The kids jostled each other on the kneeler, and Jesse glanced at Ed to see if he was going to time the homily on his watch so that he could gripe about its length later, but Ed stared straight ahead and Claire hushed the children.

Ed's job meant that he often met people during the worst moments of their lives. Death didn't bother him nearly as much when it wasn't his or anyone else's fault, when it came as naturally as an old lady punching out her time card for the final time. A few incidents stuck out, times when he'd sped home to hold Polly's warm cheek in the palm of his hand and press his ear to Claire's freckled chest and hear her thrumming, alive. During his third year on the force, a teenage girl died in a car accident. When he arrived at the scene she was still conscious and screaming. Blood covered her face and the paramedics stood over her, shaking their heads. She must have been sixteen years old. But this was worse than that, because he had done the killing. He'd never killed anyone before. Most cops didn't—most never even had to fire their weapons throughout their careers. Still, in a city, casualties were more common. Ed should have expected it, he shouldn't have felt so unprepared.

The ritual of the Mass soothed Ed, the priest muttering the words he'd heard so many times, Ed mumbling back along with the others. It didn't matter what they said. The muttering of it, together, was what mattered. When the priest called for the congregation to offer their own intentions, Ed prayed silently, *God bless the man's family. Look after them.* He didn't even know the guy's name yet. He was Mexican, like the other men in the house, his family probably sweating through Mass in some pueblo, dust on their *huaraches.* Maybe the man's family would think that Ed had no right to pray for him, but Ed's mother had taught him that praying was what you did when you couldn't do anything else.

After church ended, Ed walked out into the sunny day with his family, his chest feeling somewhat lighter as he breathed the fresh air into his lungs. The boys trotted beside him as they walked to the car, one on either side, Ed resting a hand on each of their backs. Was now the time he should tell them about what had happened, to get it over with?

"Coach Boyd is handing out our Z's uniforms at practice today," Ed's younger son E.J. said. "He told us at the meeting this week."

"We get two uniforms," Jesse said. "A home one and a visitor one."

"Coach Boyd is going to show us how he wants us to wear our stirrups," E.J. added. "We don't know yet if he wants us to wear our pants down over them or up so they show like Mickey Mantle's."

"He wants us all looking the same," Jesse said. "The same colored sleeves under our jersey, and no long hair. No jewelry. And he wants our uniforms clean for every game."

"What about facial hair?" Ed said. "Is he going to shave the Franklin kid?"

"He talked a lot about how we shouldn't get any ideas from watching big leaguers," Jesse said. "He said that a lot of them don't swing the bat how we're supposed to."

"He's big on the fundamentals," Ed said. So was Ed, breaking down kids' batting stances and putting them back together, season after season. He'd have liked to coach such a talented team.

"I hope we win State, Dad," Jesse said. "The regionals are in New Mexico."

"New Mexico," Claire said. She walked behind them, holding Polly's hand. "Wouldn't that be nice? The land of enchantment."

The teams Ed had coached never traveled anywhere, and Claire complained sometimes that they were stuck at home all summer, going from one baseball game to the next. Ed gave a fleeting thought to heading to New Mexico right then, leaving everything behind, lighting out under the clear blue sky. But he was a dad, and plans like that weren't even remotely possible anymore. He wouldn't let on how badly he wanted the team to win State, too. Even after everything that had happened, it didn't matter any less to him. He was supposed to keep himself calmer this season, less involved. But Jesse was a big, strong kid, talented as any Ed had ever seen at that age, regularly smashing the ball, and it was hard for Ed not to project his son's path forward and hope for him to go on. To continue hitting towering homers right through high school, the stage at which Ed's knee had blown out, and past it to college ball or the minor leagues.

When they arrived home, Mitch was on the porch, waiting. Ed moved toward him sluggishly. The good feeling he'd clung to since Mass began to leech out of him, the energy he'd been holding in his chest now retreated to his places of worry, his head and his gut. The kids ran past them into the backyard. Claire joined Ed on the porch.

"You missing something, buddy?" Mitch said.

"Right," Ed said. "The gun. Please tell me you've got it. I don't want to go back downtown today."

"Maybe I've got it."

"Mitch."

58

"All right, all right. You left it in the car." Mitch took the gun from the holster he wore off-duty, hidden inside his pants.

Ed turned it over in his hand, feeling its weight.

"I came by to see if you wanted to go to the firing range. You're supposed to fire off some rounds pretty soon so that when you hear a gun go off again, it won't cause flashbacks."

"Where'd you hear that?"

"Learned it from that training seminar last summer that you conveniently ditched."

"I was coaching that weekend. I'm surprised you learned something."

"Hey, give me a little credit."

Claire stepped forward, her stance protective. "He needs to be home today," she said. "Tomorrow he'll go to the range."

"Okay, Boss," Mitch said, squeezing Claire's shoulder. She smiled at him.

The bright day beckoned, the crocuses and daffodils pushing up through the earth. They walked toward the fence that bordered the backyard. The kids ran in their church clothes, filling neon-colored water guns from the spigot on the side of the house. "I'm going to spend some time with the kids," Ed said. "I'm taking them to baseball practice."

"Tomorrow then," Mitch said, and headed toward his car.

Claire picked up the Sunday paper from the flowerbed and searched through the local news section.

"Is there anything about it?" Ed asked.

"Yes," Claire said, sighing, "but it's small. Buried in the back." She handed the paper to him.

He read the article, "Man killed after police storm house." It was only two paragraphs long, and it didn't name Ed or any of the other officers involved. But that didn't mean a future article wouldn't. The guy's name was Salvador Santillano. The name he remembered from the pocket of the uniform hanging in the room.

"See, it's just the facts," Claire said. "They didn't sensationalize it."

"You mean they didn't yet. Let's hope reporters don't start camping in front of our yard."

Claire folded the paper. "Let's take it one worry at a time." She looked tired, the skin under her eyes faintly violet.

Ed kissed her.

"Polly's soaked," Claire said, chuckling. The girl looked like a drowned cat, her hair and church clothes plastered to her. She held her arms out to the side, and water dripped off her fingertips.

The boys froze when they saw Ed approach, expecting him to give them hell for hosing down their sister. "Come on kids, get ready for practice."

"But we've still got an hour," E.J. complained.

"I thought we'd head over early, and you could treat your old man to a catch," Ed said. "How about that?" Maybe the exercise would take Ed's mind off the name that was running through his head: Salvador Santillano.

Greenwood Field stood empty when Ed and his children arrived, the sandy dirt naked of the white-chalked baselines that would be applied for spring games. In the outfield, a few green blades had begun to poke up among the drab mass of dead grass, but the sky above was mid-summer blue. Ed took a deep breath, as if inhaling all the possibilities of the season ahead, and though it was early, he could almost detect a whiff of clover, good dirt, and fresh-cut grass that baseball always smelled like to him. The wide-open scent of a well-kept ball field in summer was the opposite of the stench Ed routinely encountered at work—enclosed rooms reeking with the funk of cat urine, meth production, or musty neglect, the lived-in smell of the stuffy bedroom in which he'd killed Santillano.

Ed wished he could go back to his junior year in high school, just for a day, when he was playing centerfield, his body still lean and obedient, listening to the chatter of the infielders, regular as birdsong, *eybattaeybattaehhhy, eybattaeybattaehhhy*, standing there alert, his senses perked, his mitt ready, jumping with each pitch because he never knew when the batter would give one a ride and send him sprinting to the fence, gloved hand extended to meet the ball. Prepared as he was for each pitch, the chase always came as a glorious surprise. Just one more game, Ed pleaded silently with he knew not who. Just one more goddamn game. Hell, even practice had been fun, shagging flies in the sunshine, Coach yelling at him to move his lazy ass. Today of all days, it would feel great to put on a uniform and play ball for a few hours.

Ed dropped his equipment bag on the concrete walkway that separated the four fields of the complex, the aluminum bat inside producing a ringing ping as it struck the ground. He took off running through the field, holding his arms wide, the breeze rushing over the open palms of his hands. The kids, thinking it was a game, chased after him. The boys decided it was a race, Polly concluded it was tag. Ed didn't get very far when a pain shot through his knee, and he eased up, letting Polly tag him. "I got you!" she cried, exuberant, dancing around him. "You're it." The boys reached the chain link that bordered the outfield within moments of each other, sending a shiver through the fence. They turned to gloat. "We beat you, Dad," E.J. said. "You lose."

"I'm it and I lost," Ed said, breathing heavy. "What do you say we play catch instead?"

They grabbed their gloves, and instead of pairing off, they spread out across the field, each of them a point on a trapezoid. They began to toss the ball one to the other, allowing Polly a smaller distance to throw. "Don't throw from your ear, Polly," Ed said to his daughter after he caught her first toss. "Start your motion earlier." He demonstrated, holding the ball low to his side and bringing it back and over with a roll of his shoulder.

E.J. caught Ed's toss. "And don't throw from your elbow either," E.J. said. "Use your shoulders, use your hips." He threw the ball to Jesse, emphasizing his motion.

Jesse caught it. "And when you finish," Jesse said, "bring your arm down across your body, to the opposite side." Jesse threw it gently to Polly, aiming it so that all she had to do was hold out her glove to receive it.

"Can't I just throw?" Polly said.

"No way," Jesse said. "You're my sister. You're not allowed to throw like a girl."

Polly clowned, exaggerating everything they had showed her as she threw the ball wildly to Ed. It skittered off to his left, escaping his glove. He tried to disguise his limp as he fetched it from its resting place at the edge of the grass, and then returned to his spot. "Polly," he said, "if you're going to throw, throw like you mean it."

They hadn't been throwing long when Ed noticed the unmistakable silhouette of Coach Boyd approaching. Ralph Boyd, short and squat with a ruddy Irish face, maintained a perpetual squint above his bulbous tuber of a nose.

"Coach is here," E.J. declared.

"I guess we'd better knock off," Ed said, but kept throwing.

When the ball reached Jesse, he broke the chain, trotting over to Polly to hand her the ball before sprinting toward home plate to greet his coach. E.J. followed him.

"Looks like it's just you and me, P," Ed said. "We'd better clear off the field so we're not in their way." He looked expectantly toward Boyd, who gave him a businesslike nod. Maybe he should ask if Boyd needed a volunteer to throw at batting practice?

Ed and Polly sat in the bleachers and watched as the team assembled around Boyd, who wore his polyester coach shorts hip-slung, under his hard yet considerable belly. Cro-Magnon-thick hair furred his legs and he smelled of cigars even from five paces away. All the boys swarmed around him, turned their faces up to him, and peppered him with questions. One kid showed off by rolling a ball down his arm, across his back, and scooting it down the other arm into his glove.

The dreams of Ed's boys were no different from the dreams of other boys. Each heard his name announced in baritone over the loudspeakers, each came to the plate and hit the ball square, each trotted a glory lap under the lights. With so many boys dreaming the same dream, year after year, the same picture show, slightly altered, flickering, what did the dream become? Did the dream wear out, stretch thin, or did the strength of numbers make it grow? For Ed, like most, the dream faded over time. Now he'd passed it on to his sons, while he went about the gritty tasks of the job that earned his family a living.

When Ed looked at the faces of his boys as they listened to their coach, he saw the reels moving behind their bright eyes, and he wanted to make the world match, as best he could, the movies in their minds. Could he remember the way he thought when he was a boy, the way his opinions and hopes formed? Or was all this stored on some tape or reel or record that he no longer had the ability to play?

"Daddy," Polly said. "Can we go now?"

"I just want to see the first couple of drills, okay? It looks like Boyd starts the practice like I used to do, with laps and warm-up. But what does he do next? Pepper? Situations? BP?" Ed yammered as if Polly cared about any of this.

Polly leaned back over the bleacher behind them, rolling her eyes dramatically. "Booor-ring," she said.

"Okay, we're going kiddo. We're gone." Ed lifted his equipment bag, feeling ridiculous to have brought it now. What was he expecting, that Boyd would notice him and invite him to help coach?

As Ed and Polly walked to the parking lot, he kept glancing back, watching the boys rove and dive, until he could no longer make out the figures on the field.

The next morning, Ed drove to the shooting range downtown on Decatur Street. Claire had woken him up and made him get ready, even though he begged to put it off. "Mitch is right," she'd said, "you need to shoot." Ed pushed open the heavy metal door to the range and flinched as the regular reports of shotguns, rifles, and pistols assaulted his ears. He hurried over to the equipment counter to check out some ear protection. The indoor range had the feel of a bunker, cavernous and subterranean, full of empty space. Ed had spent days training there before he joined the force, the police technicians putting him through his paces on marksmanship, decision making, and team collaboration for sixty-four hours. He always emerged from the training sessions a little stunned, his eyes blinking in the bright light of day.

Though it still looked like a warehouse inside, the range's equipment had become fancier over the years, all the targets controlled by a computer so that they approached or fled the officer while he shot at them, the dummies turning this way and that so that you had to decide the best way to aim at center mass in a split second. The technicians adjusted the lighting, preparing you to shoot in a dark room or under the blazing sun. They tried to make the targets look as much like people as possible, some of them popping up armed with a gun or a knife, and then once you were all keyed up they'd throw a granny or a toddler out at you to see if you could hold your fire. Or an armed kid would pop out at you, and you were supposed to figure out what to do about that. Ed just wasted the sucker the first time he'd seen it—according to his training, he was well within his rights to fire at anyone who pointed a gun at him—but he wondered what he'd do if a real child tried to shoot him. Ed had convinced himself that his training was realistic, but now he saw that it had just been a game. No amount of training with dressed-up dummies could prepare you for what happened when you had to decide whether to shoot a real person.

Ed found Mitch in one of the stalls, firing off some rounds at the targets. Mitch unloaded into a dummy painted to look like it was wearing a Raiders jersey, the target that always seemed to take the worst abuse. Ed wanted to bolt, which was natural, he told himself. A technician with a clipboard came by and gave Mitch some papers to sign.

"I decided to come in early and finish my quarterly qualifiers," Mitch said, removing his headgear.

Ed took off his too, so that he could hear Mitch. "Maybe they'll just give me a pass this time," Ed said.

"But you've got to shoot. You've got to get back on the horse. I hear they usually give you your gun back in three to six days."

"Three to six days," Ed said. "That's classic. What does that actually work out to, two weeks?" He dropped his voice. "Do you think there's any chance that I might lose my job over this?"

"Oh, you won't lose your job," Mitch said. "The guy drew down on you. I don't care if he was John Elway, when he does that you're supposed to shoot him." Mitch waved over a technician and asked him to prepare the target for Ed.

"Just a stationary target for today," Ed told the technician. He waited until the man walked away, and then said, "There wasn't much in the paper about it, luckily."

"Yeah, but it's only Monday. Sometimes those journalists go back to digging up old news. The thing that could cause some trouble for you was that the guy you shot was a Mexican."

"So are you."

"My grandfather was. But look at me, I'm lighter than you. Put my photo in the paper and I look like any other white cop."

"I hardly had a chance to look at the guy." Before he shot him at least.

"You'll come out fine. I'm sure of it. As long as your head's on straight. Some guys are a little skittish for a while after a shooting, but I've never seen anyone crack. Except McGill. You know him?"

Ed shook his head.

"He was a good guy. Worked with the gang unit for eight years. Then one day he shot a thirteen-year-old Crip in the face. The kid had been in and out of juvie for years and pulled a gun on him. McGill was completely in the right, and the investigation cleared him. But he couldn't get over it. He cut loose, and now he's a river guide in Moab."

Ed saw that the target was prepared. He wasn't ready, but Mitch stood watching him and so Ed began to put his head-gear on.

Mitch stopped him with a touch on his shoulder. "But that's not going to happen to you—McGill's wife had just left him. He had nothing holding him here."

"Maybe he couldn't take killing the boy. Maybe it was too much for him."

"I don't know," Mitch said. "I took the family up to Utah for a camping trip once. I ran into McGill at a gas station in Moab. He'd grown his hair long and his skin looked like he hadn't had been under a roof in years. He kept looking up whenever a bird crossed above us in the sky. Then he would name it, in the middle of when I was talking. 'Red-tailed hawk. Turkey vulture.'"

"That's too bad," Ed said, thinking maybe he could look up McGill, talk to him to find out if he was doing any better. He imagined himself floating down the river, leading people in recreation for the remainder of his days.

Ed covered his ears with the protection and centered himself in the shooting stall. He picked up the Glock, feeling the cool, textured plastic of the handle. He squared his body to the target, a piece of paper with the outline of a body on it. Ed spread his legs slightly farther than shoulder-width apart with his gun-side leg back, bent his knees, and extended his arms, pointing the gun, a stance meant to minimize the impact of the recoil. When he put his finger on the trigger, his hands began to shake. He let the gun fall to his side and tried to master himself, filling his lungs slowly with air. He entered his stance again, and his shooting hand started to tremble, but he managed to steady it enough with his support hand. He put his finger on the trigger, aligned his sites, and squeezed the trigger, sending a bullet through the target's paper heart as he absorbed the kickback of the gun. He repeated the process, firing until he had emptied the magazine.

The technician brought the paper target forward for him, and Ed was inspecting the spray of shots when Mitch approached.

"I ran into Gruber at the equipment counter," Mitch said.

"He's good. Practicing like he's supposed to after a shooting."

"So are you."

"I wouldn't be here if Claire hadn't kicked my butt out the door this morning."

"Gruber said he's been talking to his lawyer."

"Why?"

"It turns out that the man you shot has a family in Denver. The guys he lived with said that his family was in Mexico, but apparently his wife called in today. That will make things worse for the department. You know, the weeping widow and half-orphaned kids. Stuff that goes over big on the 6:00."

"How many kids?" Ed asked. His hand rattled the paper target he was holding, so he dropped it to the floor. It caught a draft of air, and then settled to the ground. He fixated on the target, trying to hold the image in his mind so he wouldn't begin to picture the man's children. How old were they? He hoped they were grown. The image he had of the man's family south of the border somewhere disintegrated.

"I don't know how many," Mitch said. "But there's more." He looked off.

"What is it?"

"Maybe you should call your lawyer."

"Just tell me."

Mitch sighed. "There could be a problem with the warrant."

"What do you mean? Springer filled out the paperwork, took it to the judge and everything."

"Gruber's lawyer told him that during the beginning of their investigation, the homicides noticed a discrepancy with the address on the warrant. The original target had been the house next door."

Ed waited for Mitch's goofy smile to spread under his moustache, waited for him to confess that this was a sick joke he and Gruber had cooked up.

"I think you'd better call your lawyer, buddy," Mitch said.

In a haze, Ed packed his things, turned in his headgear, and started his car. He drove down the street and made a quick right turn on a red light, cutting off a pickup heading straight through the green. The car's honk set Ed's heart racing. He told himself he had to calm down, to pay attention to his driving. His hands sweated on the wheel and he tried to slow his breathing.

Polly was waiting for Ed on the front steps when he returned home. She wore a purple sweatsuit and sat with the baseball glove he had given her for her birthday that year in her lap. When he pulled into the driveway, she ran toward the car. She yanked on the handle and opened the door.

"Not until I've been to the safe, Polly," Ed snapped.

She ducked into the house, hanging her head. Ed cursed himself for the harsh tone as he carried the gun downstairs. He worked the combination on the safe, screwing it up twice before the door swung open, and placed the weapon inside, relieved to be rid of it.

Who was Salvador Santillano? What had his life been like? Was he a drug dealer or wasn't he? Ed had no idea what kind of trouble he was in now, or whether it would cost him his job. He didn't know what else he could do besides be a cop. The salary Claire earned for keeping an orthodontist's books couldn't support them all. He slammed the door of the safe shut and leaned on it, his head on his arms, and wept. The cold metal of the safe soothed his hot face.

"Daddy?"

Polly's voice came from the top of the stairs. "Practice is in five minutes," she said. "You're supposed to coach."

It had completely slipped his mind, tee-ball practice on Mondays, Wednesdays, and Saturdays. Saturday morning felt like a century ago. Ed rose, wiped his face on his forearm, climbed the steps on heavy legs, and gathered his daughter in his arms. He lifted her, held her close to his chest. He smelled her hair, breathing deeply the evocative scent of Johnson's Baby Shampoo. She rested her head on his shoulder.

"What's the matter?" she said, patting the bristles on his cheek with her hand. "Have you got the stress?"

Polly heard Ed and Claire discussing stress once and asked the meaning of the word. She had never mastered how to use it, though—she seemed to think it came on like the flu. Her brothers encouraged her mispronunciations and off-kilter phrasings.

"Yes Polly, I've got the stress. But it will be all right. Don't worry about me."

"A puppy might help." She was learning to read, and read everything aloud, street signs, cereal boxes, billboards. She would sound out the titles of articles if Ed left the newspaper lying around. "Pets Help Stress" was the only title she'd memorized, and she would blurt it out now and then.

"We'd better get to practice," Ed said. He thought of calling the lawyer. But whatever bad news the lawyer had would still be bad in a few hours. All the girls would be gathering at the field, waiting for him, their parents beginning to murmur about his absence. "Let's go play ball," he told Polly, trying to sound like he meant it.

CHAPTER 6

Patricia

March 27–28

Patricia sat at the kitchen table on a Monday afternoon. She looked out the window at Ray, who stood on the wooden bench that edged the back porch, winging a tennis ball against the side of the house. Patricia's father had returned to Arizona the week before, but Lupe remained, insisting she was needed. Patricia was glad she'd stayed, though she'd never tell Lupe that.

"The lawyer sent over these copies of the police reports for you," Lupe said, dropping a thick file next to Patricia.

"What am I supposed to look for?" She opened the folder.

"See if there's anything that strikes you, anything that can help us prove the cops made a mistake."

The ball struck the side of the house again with a dull thump, and Lupe crinkled the skin around her eyes, but didn't say anything. If Ray were Lupe's child, she would have barred him from the activity as soon as he began it, but Patricia was happy to see him out of his room and playing again. He flung the ball so it would careen at an unpredictable angle, then tracked the trajectory and leapt off the bench to catch the ball before it hit the ground. This often landed Ray on his butt in the grass, clinging to the ball as he fell the two feet down from the bench. After he made a spectacular catch, Ray threw up the hand that held the ball, as if to prove an out to some unseen umpire, then turned to display the ball this way and that, basking in the appreciation of an imaginary crowd.

"Look at him," Patricia said. "He's saying something to himself, doing commentary like he's a TV announcer. You know, 'And the crowd goes wild!'" Patricia breathed out, hard, through her open mouth, "Haaaaah!" producing the noise Ray often made to imitate the sound of a roaring crowd in a cavernous stadium. She turned some papers over in the folder until she came to one on Denver District Court stationary, labeled "Search Warrant."

"Wonder what the announcer will say when the MVP ends up with a broken leg." Lupe took up some of the papers Patricia had set aside.

When she and her mother spoke, they often held two separate conversations that barely intersected. "The kid's obsessed. Ray can name the winners of World Series from way before he was born."

"That memory should help him on tests," Lupe said. "When are you going to send the kids back to school?"

Patricia shrugged. If the kids returned to school, she would have no excuse to delay her return to work. "When they're ready," she said.

Lupe looked over to Mia, who lay on the couch with an enormous book held an inch from her nose, so close it looked like she wanted to crawl inside it. "That one is just like you," Lupe said. "She was ready to go back to school a week ago. Ray won't be ready until he's eighty. You have to send them back, whether they want to or not." Lupe stood, crossing her arms over her chest. "Children need a normal routine."

"Yeah, and I'm the living proof."

"Your father and I brought you up to the point where you were capable of making your own decisions. And you made them."

Patricia turned to the window. Lupe had pestered her as they planned Patricia's wedding, *It's not too late. You can change your mind. He's not as educated as you. You're so different from him, from such different cultures, from such different families, from such different countries.* But then once they were married Lupe didn't say anything about it again. Patricia took Lupe's eventual silence on the subject of their incompatibility to be her way of rooting for the marriage to work out.

71

The ball thumped against the side of the house and Lupe jumped. "That's enough," she said smacking her palm on the table. She stalked over to the back door.

"Where are you going?" Patricia asked, following her out.

Lupe rushed across the grass to where Ray stood on the bench, his left arm cocked and ready for another throw. She reached up and grabbed his right hand. "Raymond Salvador," she intoned, "come down from there now."

Ray dropped the ball and pried at her fingers with his free hand, but Lupe would not release him. "Ay," Ray said. "Let me go. I was just throwing." The tennis ball bounced away over the brick patio.

"You were making a racket, leaving dirty marks on the wall," Lupe said, gesturing toward the faint ball prints on the side of the house. "And leaping around like that, you could break your neck. You shouldn't even be here. You should be in school."

"Let him go," Patricia commanded. "You're not his mother, I am."

"You're not acting like it." Lupe tugged on Ray's hand, trying to induce him to step off the bench, but the tiny woman couldn't budge her twelve-year-old grandson, who stood firm.

"Mom," Ray pleaded, "get Grandma off me."

"Let go," Patricia said. "Let go," she repeated softly, directly in her mother's ear, saying it over and over until at last Lupe released Ray's hand. Ray massaged his squeezed wrist.

Lupe walked back inside the house, slamming the screen door behind her.

"Did she hurt you?" Patricia asked. Ray stood on the bench and towered above her. She opened her arms to him, hoping he would let her hug him.

He hopped down from the bench and entered her embrace. "Nah," he said, "She's just an old lady." Ray had grown almost as tall as Patricia over the past year, but he bent his knees and slouched so that his head rested on her shoulder.

"You play if you want to," Patricia said, holding her son close, stroking his hair, "you just play."

72

Ray backed away before Patricia was ready to let go of him. He gave a subdued wave to someone behind her. Nino approached through his yard.

"Hey Stingray," Nino said, "want to play catch?"

Ray shrugged. That gesture was as close as you'd get to a yes with Ray.

Nino clambered up the four-foot chain-link fence that separated their property from his grandmother's, his glove tucked under his arm, and launched himself into their yard.

Patricia edged away as the boys stood talking, Nino with his hands in his pockets and Ray with his arms crossed over his chest. She sometimes felt like a nature documentarian, trying to observe her kids in their typical environment without causing them to change their behavior because she was there. Before Ray had taken up with Miguel, Nino and Ray used to hop the fence to visit every afternoon even after they'd just spent the entire day together at school.

Ray picked up his glove and dug a baseball out from behind the juniper bush that always trapped balls in the corner of the yard. He instructed Nino to crouch, then paced off the regulation pitching distance.

"Hey!" Patricia barked. "What have I told you?"

Ray kicked the ground, then mumbled, his back to Patricia, "Not without the catcher's gear."

"I mean it. It's not safe."

Nino smiled at her, relieved for the reprieve. He would have stretched himself across train tracks if Ray told him to. Nino's grandmother approved of the friendship because Nino's affiliation with such a charmer prevented the other kids at school from teasing him. Patricia hoped Ray still stood up for Nino. It was useful for Ray to always have a catcher nearby. He liked to throw things, either a baseball or crabapples aimed at intrepid squirrels that approached within range. That was part of why Miguel was no good for Ray—Miguel didn't seem to play any sports. He just slouched around or hung out on corners.

"You can play catch," Patricia said, "but no pitching."

Ray began pitching his first year of organized baseball, and he threw so hard now that it wasn't safe for a kid to receive his pitches without a mask. For two years, no one but Salvador had been skilled enough to catch for Ray without equipment.

Pitching was the natural position for a kid who had been throwing everything he touched practically from the moment he took his first breath. When he was a baby, his meals always ended up on the floor, so Patricia began feeding him there, rolling out a clean plastic mat on the floor and letting him go at it. He threw cereal and toys, remote controls, magazines, pillows. His arm was a set mousetrap, waiting for the light touch of an object to spring.

When Ray was three, Salvador bought baseball gloves for the family, except for Mia, who was nine months old. A tiny blue one for Raymond, a tan one for Patricia, and a dark brown one for Salvador. Patricia teased him, saying he chose them just for color. But she knew that wasn't true—they all went to the huge Gart Brothers Sports Castle on Broadway and Salvador tried out half the gloves on display, pounding each mitt with his fist, while Ray stood two steps away, imitating the gesture.

They played catch with Ray, using a bean-filled ball, putting baby Mia in a playpen where she had a good view. Salvador stood across from Ray and tossed while Patricia stood behind her son, her hands on his, guiding them to try to make the ball land in his glove. Sometimes Salvador would take Ray outside and play catch with him until he had to go to one of his jobs or get some sleep before a night shift. But when Ray returned to the house, he'd still be throwing things until Patricia ran up to him and caught his little hands, holding them still, next to her face. "Stop, *mijito*, stop," she'd say, rocking him against her chest to calm him.

As Patricia watched Nino and Ray play catch, she started picturing Salvador there holding his brown glove open wide to give his son a broad target as he had on so many afternoons. She ducked into the house before the boys could see her cry.

The sun had shifted so the kitchen was dark when Patricia entered it, silent save for the ticking of the clock.

"You shouldn't let him get away with that disrespect," Lupe said, startling her. She waited in the shadows of the kitchen, her hands resting on the table with her fingers interlaced. Judging from her set jaw, Patricia guessed she had remained there, seething, since she'd come inside. Lupe pushed the copy of the warrant across the table to Patricia. "You barely looked at this. Check it over again."

"For what?"

"Just make sure it seems right. This is the piece of paper that sentenced Salvador to death."

Patricia took up the warrant. It didn't have Salvador's name, just an address of a house on Race Street where he'd rented a room. To be certain, Patricia walked to the bulletin board behind the telephone, took down the slip of paper where she'd kept Salvador's new phone number and address, and compared it to the warrant. "Something is wrong," Patricia said, a bitter taste rising in her throat. "The address isn't right."

Lupe took the paper from her. "It says 3885 Race Street."

"He lived at 3880 Race Street."

"Are you sure?"

Patricia handed Lupe the paper from the bulletin board.

"This could be it," Lupe said, standing. "This is how the police confused Salvador with a drug dealer. They went into the wrong house and figured any brown person would do."

"We caught their mistake," Patricia said, barely able to breathe. "But what can we do?" She was too tired and heartsick and didn't feel up to the task of battling the police bureaucracy. The only time that Patricia had anything to do with cops was when she had to go downtown to pick up a traffic accident report for her insurance company after another driver ran a stop sign and dented her car. The imposing police headquarters building was floored in dark, cold stone, and Patricia shrank as she made her way past the armed guards, waited her turn to speak her request into a phone in the vast hallway to an unfriendly woman, and then sat on a plastic chair next to the other civilians until her name was called. The setting made anyone who entered the building out of uniform appear shabby and guilty, and Patricia couldn't help but wonder what everyone else was in for, especially the many Mexican immigrants in flannel, paint-spattered work shirts who stared, bewildered, at a Latino cop who sat at an empty desk in the middle of the hall and translated the procedure for them.

"Don't act so helpless," Lupe said. "You have rights, you know? You're acting just like illegals do, letting people walk all over them."

"Nice, Ma."

"I can leave today," Lupe said.

Patricia sighed. "Wait." She held up a hand to signal a truce. "I appreciate all the help you've been giving me. But Salvador died only two weeks ago and I'm just trying to make it through the day."

"*Hija*," Lupe whispered, her tone softening as she drew toward Patricia. "Your husband didn't just die. He was killed by police who said he was a drug dealer. The newspapers say this, everyone we know has probably read it. And we know that's a lie. We can't let that stand. We need to call John and have him look into it."

"Fine." The lawyer's name never quite stuck with Patricia—she still thought of him as Gordo, what everybody called him as a kid.

"I am happy to help you all I can," Lupe said, touching Patricia gently on the cheek. "But you have to remember that you are a mother and you don't have the luxury of falling apart."

"I know," Patricia whispered. She shook her head. "I don't know how I'm doing as a mother lately. Yesterday Ray asked about his trophies, and I didn't know what to tell him."

"What about his trophies?" Lupe asked, her eyebrows shooting up as they always did before she was about to take action.

"Salvador mentioned how empty the room where he was staying was, and Ray gathered all his baseball trophies into a box and gave them to him. He wants them back."

"Surely his housemates or the police have them."

"I've been meaning to call," Patricia said. That day she had dialed the number three times and hung up, unable to continue. She was surprised an officer hadn't shown up at their door to check who had been pranking headquarters.

"I'll handle it," Lupe said.

The back door slammed and Ray and Nino clomped in. "Hey, Mom," Ray called. "It's time for practice. Are you gonna take us?"

"You're up for it this week?"

"Yeah, Nino said Coach Dufek has been sticking someone else in to pitch. I don't want to lose my spot in the rotation."

"Ray, you *are* the rotation." But Patricia didn't want to discourage his impulse to rejoin the world. "Okay," she said, "if you really want to go, get in the car. Nino, run and tell your grandma that I'm taking you."

"If he can go to practice," Lupe said as Patricia followed Ray out the door, "he can go to school."

Patricia drove Nino and Ray to the field and stayed to watch. She settled into a spot on the cold metal stands. Ray started playing tee-ball in the Catholic Youth Recreational League when he was five, working his way up to baseball. Salvador had signed him up after Patricia had read a notice about it in the parish bulletin. By the time Ray was ten, his pitches frightened the opposing teams and Nino, who closed his eyes and winced before receiving every throw. In between innings, Nino would sit in the dugout, blowing on his palm. The boys he played baseball with were normal kids, from better families than Miguel.

Ray started throwing to Nino, who was buried in catcher's gear, and smoked in a low pitch that caught Nino on his unprotected foot. He jumped up, yelping, and limped around the backstop in a circle, shaking his foot out.

The priest that coached the team walked up to Patricia. She steeled herself to receive a condolence speech from him about

77

her husband. Father Dufek was new to the parish, and this was his first year coaching Ray's team.

"Ray really should be playing elsewhere," Father Dufek said.

"But all his friends are on this team," Patricia said, afraid to lose this outlet for him. "Isn't he doing a good job?"

"He's doing a great job. But this is a recreational league, designed to foster unity among the parishes of the diocese. I hear Ray has been brushing back batters since he was in third grade."

It was true that all the other teams looked depressed when they were about to face Ray. The opposing teams hardly ever scored. Batters got on base—if at all—most frequently because of a dropped third strike. They had to invoke the ten run rule to end every game in the fifth inning that hadn't already ended with Ray's team fifteen runs ahead in the fourth. "But Ray loves baseball." She thought of Ray with nothing to do all summer, hanging out with Miguel.

Father Dufek explained that other, more competitive teams played throughout the spring and summer. There was a hierarchy of leagues, with rec teams, Y.M.C.A. and C.Y.R.L. on the bottom, then PAL and Little League in the middle. Then came the teams in which the coaches picked the players based on talent rather than where they lived, leagues without all-must-play rules.

Salvador had asked Patricia if there were any better teams for Ray to play on, but when she asked the other mothers about it, they acted insulted, like she was lording it over them that her son was better than theirs were, and she never found out anything. "What does it mean, that the teams are more competitive?" Patricia asked Father Dufek.

"The boys are more talented, and there is a greater time commitment—more practices, more games, and a longer season."

Patricia looked over at Ray, who was swinging two bats at once as he prepared to take batting practice. He had a distracted smile on his lips as he swung. She hadn't seen him that relaxed in weeks. Maybe more time on the baseball field would be the best thing for him. The safest thing.

"You should think about it," Dufek said. "Ray would be in the Pee Wee Reese division."

He made Patricia feel a little guilty for not knowing all this. But then, priests always made her feel a little guilty.

Father Dufek glanced around, as if to check if they were being watched, then handed her a folded piece of paper. "Don't tell any of the other mothers about this," he said. "The abilities of their sons are well met by our program."

The paper was an ad for Pete's Pizza on Pecos Street. According to the flier, they were running a two for one special. She looked up at the priest.

"Call that number and ask for Pete. Tell him Dufek sent you."

Patricia didn't know what to make of it, but later that evening when she saw Ray repeatedly throwing a crumpled paper ball against the refrigerator, scattering his sister's drawings with well-aimed strikes, she called the number. Salvador would have wanted her to.

"Pete? This is Patricia Maestas." She felt embarrassed, but she went ahead and said it. "Dufek sent me?"

"Good man, Dufek," Pete said. "He scouts promising twelve-year-olds in the northwest sector for me."

"Creepy."

"Not at all. Without Dufek, do you think I would have ever found Guillermo Sanchez or Joey Santiago?"

She supposed these were other twelve-year-olds, but Pete spoke of them as if they were famous. "My guess is no?"

"My team is almost filled up for the season, but if you bring your son around tonight, I might have room for him."

Ray had never asked her about joining a better team, but since Salvador left, Ray never talked much about anything. She wondered why Pete wanted Ray to meet him when it was already dark—he wouldn't be able to give him a proper tryout. But Ray had been interacting with her more that day than he had since Salvador's death, and here was another chance.

"Ray, get up. We're going to see a coach about getting you on a more competitive baseball team for this summer."

Ray jumped up and grabbed his glove and ball. She was surprised he didn't ask for any details before running out to the car. Patricia called out to Mia to be good for Lupe before she followed her son to the garage.

They arrived at Pete's Pizza around 8:00, after the dinner rush had subsided. Patricia opened the door and a waft of Parmesan and bread baking met her nose. Red-shaded lamps hung above the tables, red curtains shrouded the windows, darkening the restaurant except for dim circles of warm glow under the lights and the neon Bud and Miller beer logo signs that hung on one wood-paneled wall. A heavy metal band's ruminative ballad played softly from a radio on the front counter.

Behind the counter, a ruddy-faced man with a thick black beard and moustache labored, extending a long-handled wooden pizza board into the oven to retrieve a pepperoni pie. She guessed this was Pete. He winked at Patricia. "What can I get for you, honey?" She told him who she was and said she'd brought her son. Ray came up behind her with his glove on his hand, tossing the ball into it.

Pete came around the front of the counter. Under his red work apron he wore a Pete's Pirates polo shirt and skin-tight polyester coaching shorts, with striped athletic socks pulled to mid-calf. "I heard you can throw that thing," Pete said, nodding toward the ball in Ray's hand. "Is that true?"

Ray cocked his head to the side and shrugged.

"Well, come on, son."

Pete led them back through the kitchen, past the oven, the refrigerators and the prep counter, and unlatched a metal door that looked like the unpromising entryway to an alley full of trash bins. Instead, the door opened to reveal an astro-turfed expanse, lit from above like a baseball stadium at night, dominated by a green net batting cage in which a boy about Ray's age was taking some cuts. "Hey, Joey," Pete said. "That's enough for today. Knock it off."

80

"But, Coach!"

"I mean it, scram. And tell whoever is signed up for the next half-hour to watch the restaurant for a while instead."

The kid began to pack up his gear in a bag bearing a Pete's Pirates logo, a bearded pirate with an eye patch—who looked suspiciously like Pete—baring his teeth.

"You must be the legendary Joey Santiago," Patricia said.

The kid took off his hat and tipped it to her, bowing with a flourish, then shouldered his bag.

"Okay, Ray is it?" Pete said. "Let's get loose, then let's see some heat."

Ray warmed up quickly, before Pete was prepared for what he could do. After a few pitches Pete motioned for him to stop, grabbed a catcher's mask, and squatted.

"But can you control it?" Pete said. "Tight and in." Ray obliged. "High and out." Ray hit the target.

"What else you got?"

Ray gestured with a downward twist of his glove, the way he'd told Patricia that big leaguers signaled bullpen catchers to expect a breaking ball.

The ball moved so well that Pete couldn't catch it, stabbing at it with his glove like he was trying to trap a passing firefly. Pete took off his mask, rushed back toward the pizza parlor. Joey had stayed in a corner of the yard to watch. "Man, Coach," he said, "if you sign this kid, we'll smoke the Z's this year." Pete collared Joey with an arm and walked him inside the restaurant. Ray and Patricia stared at each other for a few seconds, until Pete returned with some paperwork that he handed to Patricia.

"Patty, can I call you Patty?"

"No."

"You had this kid playing in the Catholic Youth League?" Pete started to laugh, his face growing redder.

"Yes. That's where his friends played."

"I bet he didn't have too many friends among the boys that faced him." Pete continued to chortle. He turned to Ray. "You ever hit a guy?"

"Once," Ray said. After that incident, most batters who faced Ray stood so far away from the plate that they couldn't have reached the ball even if they could have swung fast enough.

"Okay, fill out these forms and bring Ray to Ruby Hill field at 4:00 tomorrow. I'll waive the fee."

"Who are the Z's?" Ray asked.

"Zenith Homes' team. Some rich kids from south Denver that think they're better than us. But they're not." He socked Ray on the right shoulder. "Would you like to play with a real team, son? Stop playing with these rec ball losers and get a proper uniform instead of a silk-screened t-shirt?"

Ray nodded.

"Well, welcome aboard." Pete handed him a black baseball cap with a red skull and crossbones insignia. "You're a Pete's Pirate now."

Ray's eyes looked brighter than they had in weeks. In the car, Patricia said, "Ray, I have one condition if you want to join the team. You need to go back to school tomorrow. I think it's time we started trying to continue our lives." She hoped she sounded more confident than she felt. She hated giving in to Lupe like that, but her mother was right, she couldn't keep the kids locked up in the house with her forever. Besides, she needed to return to the hospital and work hard enough to support the family by herself.

Ray stared out the window, then answered, "Okay."

"Good. You and Mia will go back to school and I'll go back to work, and you'll start this new team and we'll all try to pick up and do the best we can."

"Hey, Mom?"

"Yeah?"

"When you fill out that form, could you put your last name down for mine, instead of Dad's? I don't want everyone to know."

Patricia stopped at a red light and turned to look at her son. As was the custom in hers and many Mexican-American families, Patricia had kept her own last name instead of taking Salvador's. The newspapers and TV anchors were calling what happened to him "The Santillano Shooting." Ray's teachers and many of the kids surely had found out about what happened to Salvador. Neighbor told neighbor until everyone knew, and whenever Patricia left the house, she felt like she and her kids were wearing neon signs that flashed: "Please, stare at and whisper about us! We've had a tragedy!"

"Are you sure about that?" Patricia asked.

"Put down Ray Maestas," he said with a firm nod.

The next day Ray left for school without protest. Mia was up and dressed, ready to go before Patricia had even managed to flick on Mr. Coffee. When they returned in the afternoon, Ray darted into his room. Patricia thought he'd sulk in there for hours again, but he emerged a few minutes later, wearing sweatpants and a ball cap, and asked Patricia for the time. He kept asking every three minutes until she finally took him to the field a half-hour early.

Patricia stayed to watch. She didn't feel comfortable leaving Ray alone with strangers, even though he begged her to at least hide in the car. She sat down on the bleachers while Ray ran around the base path, tossing his ball in the air and racing to catch it. The puppyish enthusiasm vanished as soon as another kid arrived.

"Hey," Ray said. He stood on home plate, a few yards away from where Patricia sat on the bottom bleacher.

"My team has practice here now," the kid said. He was lean and lanky, wearing his cap low so that his eyes were almost hidden. "You're going to have to leave."

"What team?"

"Pirates."

Ray turned his new cap around to face the front.

"So what position do you play?" the kid asked, then blurted, "If it's second base you'll be on the bench most of the time. I've been playing second base for Pete since I was ten."

"I pitch."

"We've got a bunch of pitchers already."

"None as good as me."

Patricia shook her head. Where did he learn this arrogance? Salvador, of course—his gamecock swagger.

The field began to fill and Patricia was struck by the assured way the boys stretched and warmed up, so different from the chunky kids on the church team. There wasn't an ounce of spare flesh on them, their bodies nothing but muscle and go. They looked more like Ray than his old teammates had, diving head-long and hustling after everything, dispatching the ball with a graceful flick of the wrist. Salvador was right—there was a better league for Ray, and she'd found it.

The boys stood apart from Ray at first, not talking to him. Pete announced that Ray would pitch batting practice. He approached the mound and handed Ray the ball, telling him to go easy at first. Pete himself donned the mask to catch. The batters bounced in their stances and scuffed their cleats in the dust, like they wanted to nail Ray, to show him that they could. But Ray mowed them down. At first they managed to pop up a few off him, but once Ray was warm they couldn't touch him.

After practice the kids crowded around Ray, asking him what school he went to, where he learned to throw like that, where he played before.

"Nowhere," Ray said, his face shadowed by his ball cap. "I just started today."

"What's your name?" one of them asked finally.

Ray paused. "Maestas," he said. "Ray Maestas."

CHAPTER 7

Ed

March 29

"You didn't answer the last time I called," Ed told Claire when she finally picked up the phone. He sat alone in the house, the rain coming down outside as it had all morning, pattering against the rooftop, gloomy light filtering through the windows. He tried to fold some laundry, but couldn't figure out how to collapse a fitted sheet into the neat little packet Claire always produced.

"I'm working." She covered the phone with her hand and asked someone for his insurance card.

"I could come pick you up for lunch."

"I'm going out today."

"You didn't say that earlier."

"I just made plans."

"Who with? Dr. K?" Ed didn't entirely trust the orthodontist, who had become wealthy straightening the teeth of children in the burgeoning city. He didn't work Fridays and was too casual for his age, dropping teen lingo and keeping up on his patients' favorite bands. He made the women who worked in the office wear coordinated outfits instead of scrubs, usually sweaters paired with khaki slacks or plain skirts. They'd gone out to dinner with the orthodontist and his second wife once, and he kept complimenting Claire on her dress and her hair. Ed hadn't liked the way she'd blushed, looking down into her chardonnay.

"No. Just with the girls. Why don't you go to the grocery store? We're out of milk."

She'd been asking him to help out around the house more since he'd been on leave. But Ed had no knack for keeping the refrigerator stocked, the house clean. "Sure," he said.

When Claire hung up, Ed dialed his lawyer for the second time that day. This time Sylvia answered, which meant he'd be billed at least a quarter of an hour for it no matter how short the conversation.

"Look," Ed said, swearing that he could hear her clicking the mouse on her computer's billing program. "I'm sorry to keep bugging you. I just wanted to check if you've found out anything more about why they've extended my leave." The department had told him to stay home for another two weeks, and each morning Ed tore through the newspaper, searching for any news that they might have made public. In the week after the shooting, Ed spotted a smattering of articles, a few of which named him, Gruber, and Cook as the shooters, a matter of public record. But for the last week there had been nothing, which meant that the department wasn't talking to the press about it or that the press wasn't asking.

"I called around and came up with a few more details about that warrant discrepancy today," Sylvia said. "Apparently the problem began when the informant gave the wrong address for the house where he did a drug buy."

"And Springer just took him at his word?"

"According to the affidavit, Sergeant Springer said he personally saw a man purchasing drugs from the address that you raided. But the neighbors' complaints about a crackhouse all pertain to the address next door."

"Maybe Springer could tell me more," Ed said, trying to fold some of Polly's socks. What was the point? They were so small already.

"That isn't a good idea," Sylvia said. "What if he admitted he'd signed off on a falsified warrant? That's perjury, and you could be called in to testify against him. All this warrant business does nothing to harm your case—the man still pointed a gun at you, no matter what the warrant said. It could be that the department is worried about how this will look to the public, and they want to keep you off the street until it's settled."

"But I haven't seen anything about the mistake on the warrant in the papers," Ed said. "The public doesn't know."

"Not yet. But they will. It would have been better if the department had just held a press conference the second they noticed something wrong. Now when they come out with it, as they'll eventually have to, it'll look like they're trying to cover something up."

"And when that happens, people are going to demand a cop's head and I could lose my job, right?"

"I'm going to do everything I can to prevent that from happening," Sylvia said. "I'll call you when there are developments."

Ed wanted to keep her on the line, even if she billed him for another quarter hour. But he knew that the rest of the questions he wanted to ask weren't the sort a lawyer could answer. Maybe a priest.

Ed didn't care about Sylvia's warning. He couldn't stay home anymore. Mitch had mentioned that Springer frequently ate lunch at Pete's Kitchen on Colfax, a busy corner diner built in the '40s, its original neon sign with a cook flipping burgers glowing out front. Ed used to frequent the place before he was married, ordering pancakes at midnight.

He drove out in the rain to the diner and then sat in a beige vinyl booth, where he swilled coffee for a half an hour until Springer showed up, a golf magazine tucked under his arm. Ed waved to him, but Springer stared straight ahead as he walked through the diner. He sat at the far end of the laminated wood counter that overlooked the grills.

Ed waited until Springer had ordered his food, then approached and sat on the stool next to his. Springer kept his balding head ducked over his magazine. He looked vulnerable out of uniform, in a collared shirt and a crew-neck sweater. When Ed greeted him, Springer's shoulders twitched. They'd never been pals, but Ed tried to dredge up some personal details.

"How are the girls?" Ed asked. "How's Ferdinand?" That was his daughters' pet iguana that Springer always griped about.

"Fine," Springer said, glancing at the short order cooks who were frying up his lunch.

"Do you happen to know if they turned up any drugs at the scene of the shooting?"

"You know they didn't," Springer said into his magazine.

"No, I don't. Nobody tells me anything. No drugs. That's not good. So is there anything behind this warrant rumor I've been hearing?" Ed asked, trying to keep his tone casual. "Did we really hit the wrong house?"

"The investigation is supposed to remain secret," Springer whispered. "It's my business, not yours."

"I'm kind of involved," Ed said. "Don't you think I should know?"

"Involved how? It's my ass they're going after." Springer shoved his magazine aside to make room for his Greek omelet, and then dug into it with his knife and fork.

I killed a man because of your mistake, asshole, Ed wanted to say. "But you know if it was the right house or not, don't you? I mean, you signed the affidavit."

He tore at his eggs. "No comment. I wouldn't be in this mess if you hadn't wasted the guy."

"He drew down on me."

"Is that what you remember?"

"Of course that's what I remember. That's what happened."

"Different guys gave different stories."

"They found his gun."

"That rusty Burgo they say he had? They haven't been able to trace it, and I doubt it even worked."

"But he fired it at me."

"So you say."

Ed watched him chew. So people were doubting Ed's story now? He wanted to grab Springer around the neck and make him say what he knew. But he didn't want to alienate him because he didn't know how the whole thing would play out, and the guy outranked him after all. "Sorry to interrupt your lunch, Dale," Ed said as he pushed away from the counter. On his way out, Ed stopped at the register and paid for Springer's meal, just to piss him off.

Ed forgot to pick up milk on his way home, but felt too weary to head out again. He hadn't slept well in weeks, lying awake thinking about how when he was six years old, his father lost his job at the Gates plant. He'd hear his mother crying downstairs late at night as she and his father discussed the bills that were due. He would sit up in bed, straining to hear what their fate would be. They ate sandwiches of tinned meat and halfway-stale, discounted bread, and his mom saved watermelon rind and brined it to make cheap pickles. A light bulb in the hallway burned out and no one replaced it for months. His mom started taking him to weekday afternoon Mass, and after communion she would hand him a dime to put in the donation box so they could light one of the white votive candles for Ed's father and then kneel by it and pray. Ed walked to school in pants that hit him above the ankle and at Christmas the people from Our Lady of Mount Carmel sent over a box of food. He could still remember the pasty taste of those reconstituted potatoes that had rattled like rocks in the cardboard box when he shook it. Then Ed's mother went to work at the post office, saying they needed at least one government job in the family, a job no one could take away. Ed's father never felt like playing catch, just sat around smoking cigarettes and drinking Jim Beam cut with off-brand cola, even after he found work again at a gas station. It seemed as though the moment Ed's father realized he couldn't meet his obligations to his son, he ceased being able to even look at him.

Ed rubbed his gritty eyes and lay down on the couch in the living room. The rain pattering on the roof lulled him. When he woke, the clock read half-past-three. His muscles ached, and his face was imprinted with the nubbly weave of the couch's fabric.

The day was shot already, so he wandered down to the basement to fetch a beer.

When he stepped off the bottom stair, still rubbing his eyes, he heard a splash and felt the shock of frigid liquid. He looked up to see dirty rainwater rushing into the basement from the window well in the front. "Shit fire Mother Cabrini!" he hollered. His cry echoed, bouncing off the basement walls, and he could think of nothing to do to remedy the situation that would not involve a lot of backbreaking labor, so he yelled it again, and again, *Shit fire Mother Cabrini*, stomping through the water, sending up splashes that soaked his jeans to the knee, cursing the local saint in the manner his father had before him.

Ed hesitated over whether he should try to stanch the cascade from the window well first, or attempt to rescue some of the soaked boxes on the floor. Buckets. They had buckets, he knew, but where were they kept? Claire was the keeper of things, storing everything away in some closet, shelf, or cubby known only to her, growing miffed whenever Ed asked her where something was, producing the object and then lecturing Ed about how the cheese grater didn't change its whereabouts every time he asked for it and had been stored in the same drawer—third one down, on the right—since they'd first moved in over a decade earlier. Claire would gesture toward the drawer, saying, "See?" and Ed would nod, pretend to be storing the information for future use, but would really be thinking nothing but, "Oh good, here's the cheese grater." Ed tried to recall a similar conversation about buckets the previous spring, the last time the basement had flooded, but couldn't dredge up the crucial detail. A beer might help him think.

Was it possible that he hadn't seen what he'd thought he'd seen on the day he killed Santillano? What was Springer implying about the gun? He thought of the mirror he heard shatter only to turn around and see it intact on the wall. Mitch had loaned him a book a psychologist had written for cops who'd been in shootings, and it said that people imagined all kinds of things while the adrenaline was coursing through them.

When Claire came home from work and rushed downstairs to check on their flood-prone basement she found Ed there, standing by the offending window well, finishing his beer.

"Ed? What are you doing?" she screamed. "Why aren't you doing something about this?"

"I was just about to find the buckets," Ed said.

"And drinking a beer. Look at all the crap the kids have spread around on the floor down here. How many times do I have to tell them not to leave stuff out in the basement?" Claire kicked the water, sending up a spray.

"Yeah," Ed said, "those rotten kids." He heard them entering the front door just then, home from school.

"Well, go on," Claire said, "go fetch the buckets."

"Right," Ed said. "Why don't you just keep them down here, where we need them? It would make more sense."

"You don't even know where they are."

"'Course I do." Maybe Jesse would know. "Hey, you kids," Ed barked from the top of the steps, "Get down here!"

The children responded to the tone of his voice and scurried down. "What's the matter, Dad?" Jesse asked.

"We've got another flood," Ed said. He exaggerated the baritone in his voice, happy to have a mission to complete, troops to rally. "You know what that means. Man the positions."

"Aw man," E.J. said. "Floods suck."

"I have homework, Daddy," Polly said, having heard her brothers use this excuse before.

"Polly, you are six years old. You don't have homework. You have coloring, which can wait. Now go find those old towels in the garage. E.J., you grab the mops, Jesse—buckets."

The kids scattered. Claire sloshed around, trying to determine what she could salvage. They had never finished the basement because of these periodic floods, so the concrete floor's only covering was a layer of olive drab paint. The water had risen an inch high now, dispersed over most of the floor. They tried to keep everything elevated, but still things filtered down: ruined magazines, baby furniture, roller skates, Matchbox cars and action figures, cases of beer and pop, sacks of potatoes and onions, outgrown clothes that Claire was too sentimental about to donate, old paperbacks, souvenirs of past vacations, holiday decorations. In the corner stood a beat-up couch heaped with half-forgotten items, the lamps, drapes, and electronic gadgets of their youth, tapedecks and turntables, the sad detritus of their passing lives.

The only space free of heaped junk was the corner where the safe that held the gun stood. Ed stood in front of it, clapping his hands together when the children returned. "There are three squeegee mops—Mom, Jesse, and I will take those. E.J. and Polly, I want you to roll up those towels, and line them up to form a canal leading toward the drain."

"Aw, Dad," E.J. whined, "Why don't I get a mop?"

"Because there are only three. I need the strongest people on them."

"I am strong," E.J. said. "I hit a double in practice Tuesday."

"Ground rule double, you mean," Jesse said, turning to Ed. "The ball rolled into a bush, so they let him take an extra base."

Jesse was always trying to diminish his brother's achievements. Wasn't he successful enough already? "I didn't mean strong," Ed said, "I meant old, I need the oldest people on them. E.J., you can either build the towel canal or empty the buckets under the window. Let's get moving."

"Aye aye, Captain," Claire said, giving him a military salute with her middle finger.

She was pissed at him, that was for sure. How many times had he called her that day? That week? He couldn't remember. He never felt he had to keep track before. Ed needed to tell Claire about his conversation with Springer, but he couldn't in front of the kids.

Claire, Ed, and Jesse pushed the water forward from where it gathered under the window toward the drain in the opposite corner. Polly constructed a serviceable canal, and E.J. rushed back and forth carrying one bucket at a time from the window well to the drain.

E.J. was built from an entirely different blueprint than his older brother. Jesse was the tallest in his class, with a broad chest and strong arms, a body that wouldn't quit growing for a long time. E.J. stood a foot shorter than Jesse, with Claire's wiry build, the graceful neck of Ed's mother, features any girl would have traded him for in a second. But family attributes weren't distributed in the manner their recipients would prefer—Polly was a strong little bear of a girl, poised to take after Jesse.

The stream of water flooding in from the window well abated. Ed stopped for a moment to survey their progress, pleased that he'd broken a sweat and gotten his family working together.

"Is it your break time?" Claire said. Her pants were wet to the knees, her hair hung limp in her face, and mascara ran under her eyes. She didn't stop pushing the mop. "The kids aren't quitting," she said.

The kids simultaneously sneaked a glance at their parents, and then turned back to their work.

"I'm just catching my breath. I'll be here until the water is gone." He slammed the water forward with a mighty blow of his mop, creating a mini-wave that breached the banks of Polly's canal. Polly rushed forward with towels to repair her creation.

Ed kept pushing the water forward with his broom, but turned to look at Claire and held his gaze on her until she met his eyes. He smiled at her, trying to throw up a white flag. She gave no hint of accepting it.

"Kids," she said, "That's good enough for now. Dad and I will finish up. You can go do your homework."

"Great," E.J. muttered, but joined the others in scampering up the stairs before Claire changed her mind.

The standing water had receded, but the floor still glistened from the flood. Claire picked up Polly's towels and wrung them out over the drain. Ed joined her. She kept her eyes down, her knuckles turning white as she gripped the towel and twisted. Finally she looked up. "I can't believe you still haven't told the kids yet," she said.

"So that's why you're mad."

"I'm mad because I come home from work after you've been bothering me all day like you have nothing to do, and I find you down here, standing in a pool of water in front of a torrent, and you're tossing back a Coors like you're enjoying the show."

"I fell asleep, Claire. I took a goddamn nap, all right? That's why I didn't stop the flooding earlier. I was up all night worrying and then I spend the whole day trying to figure out what's going on with my leave, and I was just so frustrated and exhausted that I passed out on the couch," Ed said. "How was your day, honey? Did you have a nice lunch?"

"That doesn't explain why you haven't told the kids yet."

Ed took the towel from Claire's hands to make her look at him. "Every time I try to tell them, I just can't," he said. "I was going to talk to them yesterday after school, but they came home so excited about baseball and springtime, busting up about some kid at school snorting milk out of his nose, and I didn't want to drag them down. You know how I don't like to tell them all those gory work stories."

"But they know, Ed. Do you think they don't notice that something is wrong? E.J. asked me why there's never anything to eat anymore when they come home from school, not even cereal."

"Sorry," he said. "I guess I've been eating a lot." He patted his stomach, feeling how soft it had become. "Nervous habit."

Claire wrung out a towel with a violent twist, pulling her mouth tight. "Jesse asked me why you didn't work these last two weekends in a row. You've worked either Saturday or Sunday almost every weekend for as long as he can remember. I told him that he would have to ask you about it. Didn't he?"

"No," Ed said. "He never mentioned anything."

"Maybe he's afraid to ask."

"Why would he be afraid?"

"Maybe he thought you'd yell at him for asking about a gory work story."

"Why would I do that?" Ed said.

"I don't want to lie to my children anymore." She pushed the wet towels into a heap with the side of her foot.

"You're right," Ed said, "I'm sorry. I just don't know how to do it."

"Figure it out."

She picked up the pile of filthy towels and walked up the stairs, turning back to look at him at the top. "Can you bring up the wet junk to throw away? I've got to start dinner."

Ed looked around the basement at the soaked mementos. Claire had never called any of the stuff in the basement junk before. It was Ed that called it that.

By the time the kids went to sleep that night, he still hadn't found the right moment to tell them. Claire confined herself to the extreme right side of their bed, barely taking up a quarter of its width, and every time Ed tried to move closer to her she scooted away. Ed lay awake for a few hours, now and then glancing at Claire who slept with her back to him, the moonlight spilling in from the window making the pale, freckled skin on her arms glow.

He pulled on a sweatshirt and went downstairs. He turned on the TV, the volume low. PBS was showing *Star Hustler*, a program Ed enjoyed even though he didn't own a telescope. On it, a mustached man in a velour tracksuit delivered a peppy lecture about the current constellations in the sky. He'd get really worked up when there was something unusual to report, like a good view of Venus or an approaching comet. At the beginning, the man took a stroll through the cosmos, accompanied by synthesizer music that played softly throughout the show.

"I love this show," Jesse said, startling Ed. "The sets are so ghetto."

Jesse wore pajama pants dotted with little baseballs, but he had recently decided that he was too old for the top, and ditched it in favor of a white t-shirt.

"You up, too?" Ed said. He'd started his kids on *Star Hustler* when they were infants and he was walking them though fussy, sleepless nights. Jesse would drop off to sleep, his head resting on Ed's chest, before the Hustler closed with his tag line, "Keep looking up!" Ed made room for Jesse on the couch. "Did you have a nightmare?"

Jesse nodded and sat on the cushion that Ed had already warmed.

"You want to tell me about it?" Ed said.

Jesse shrugged, the tough man, but then he started spilling. "So I was catching in the state tournament with the Z's, right? But it wasn't Kitagawa pitching. Remember that kid Zeke, who used to be on our PAL team?"

"Sure," Ed said. "How could I forget him? Zeke pitched like the ball needed an invitation to enter the strike zone."

"Zeke sucked," E.J. said, walking in to join them on the couch like it wasn't the middle of the night, sitting on Ed's other side. "You guys woke me up. So what happened with Zeke?"

"I felt ready," Jesse said, "like I could stop anything he threw. So I squat down for the first one. But then I get a funny feeling that I should look behind me, and the backstop wasn't where it should be."

"It was a far one?" Ed asked. Catchers liked a good, close backstop, so if a pitch sailed past them there would be some hope of either retrieving it on the rebound or fetching it before the runners could steal an extra base.

"Yeah," Jesse said, "It was far. But it wasn't like, regular far. It was way back, like a mile away or something. And a tumbleweed blew by, and I heard a coyote howl."

"Geez, it was like the Old West back there," Ed said. "So what did you do?"

"I turn back around," Jesse said, miming the move, hamming it up to keep Ed going, "and the bases were suddenly loaded, with Reggie Jackson on third base, and he's wearing that tight uniform like he used to for the A's, his afro all big, puffing out of his hat. He wasn't wearing a batting helmet, and he starts dragging his heels back in the dirt and snorting, like a bull does before he charges you."

"This is getting interesting," Ed said. "What happened next?"

"I called for a fastball, straight down the middle. I didn't care if the batter hit it a ton, I just didn't want the ball to get past me so that Reggie Jackson could plow into me. But when I flashed one finger, Zeke got this goofy look on his face. I knew he wasn't going to throw me anything I could catch. And it woke me up."

"Why do dreams always end before the good parts?" Ed leaned back, putting his hands behind his head.

"Good parts? Like before your face hits the pavement?"

"But you could have collided with Reggie Jackson. That would be something, to have a tooth knocked out by Mr. October, even in a dream." Ed put his arm around Jesse and E.J.'s shoulders. "But it's all right now, see? You haven't lost the tournament. The whole season is before you."

The boys dropped their heads on Ed's chest. The weight comforted Ed. He liked the way his chest lifted them as his lungs filled with air and gently lowered them as he exhaled.

"So what woke you up, Dad?" E.J. asked. "Nightmare?"

"Oh, nah," Ed said. "Just couldn't sleep. I wanted to go down to check the basement to see if the flood had come back." Ed felt a pang from having fed his sons another lie. They accepted it so readily.

Ed worked his fingers through his sons' sandy hair. He felt so awkward, tongue-tied around his own sons, like one of those divorced cops who didn't spend any time with their kids and then treated every meeting with the over-eager nervousness of a first date. "Look, guys," Ed said, "maybe you've noticed I've been on a different schedule?"

"Um, yeah," Jesse said, scratching his nose. "I was wondering about that. Were you fired?"

"No! Nothing like that. I just didn't want you guys to worry."

"Worry about what?" E.J. asked.

Ed sighed. Here it came. "The other day—no, not the other day," Ed corrected himself, "like two-and-a-half weeks ago—I had to shoot a guy while I was on a raid."

"Did you kill him?" Jesse said, sitting up straight.

Ed nodded. "I did. I killed him. Me and the other guys got off some rounds."

"He pulled a gun on you?" Jesse asked, his body tensed. "Did he shoot?"

"How many times did you fire?" E.J. asked. "What did it look like?"

"He did pull a gun on me, I didn't get hurt, but I don't really want to get into the other stuff. I just wanted you to know that after an officer-involved shooting, standard procedure is that they put the cop that did it on paid leave. Which is what I've been on since it happened. It's just a formality," Ed blurted, as if to assure himself of this, "I'm not going to lose my job."

"But he shot at you?"

Ed nodded.

"Did the bullets hit your armor?" Jesse asked.

"Not that I noticed."

"You were wearing extra equipment because it was with SWAT, right?"

"Yeah, we wear all kinds of stuff to protect us on those raids. Shields, vests, helmets."

"But you could still get hurt, right, like in your face or arm?"

"Well, technically, yes. But I'm real careful, Jesse, you know that."

Jesse's shoulders relaxed. "The man was a drug dealer?"

"That's what the warrant said." Ed swallowed. Telling the boys was enough for tonight. He didn't have to get into the whole mess of it with them.

"Was he a gang member?" E.J. asked.

"He could have been, I guess," Ed allowed. "I really don't know much about him."

"Will his crew come seeking revenge?"

"I don't think he was a gang member," Ed backtracked.

"But you just said he might be. And gang members have those cop killer bullets."

E.J. had heard a story on one of the news programs about "cop killer bullets" that could pierce body armor, causing bad dreams for a week. Ed had to show him all his protective equipment and reassure him that he was safe. All parents lied to their kids in the night, telling them they'd always be there to take care of them. Ed wasn't the only one. "I'll protect you if anyone comes around," Ed said. "I promise."

"I'm not worried about me, Dad."

"Is this that shooting Tyrell told me about?" Jesse asked. Tyrell Pendergrass was his team's shortstop. "When he found out you were a cop, he asked me what I thought about those cops that busted into that Mexican dude's house and shot him dead."

"You heard about that?" Ed should have known. Why did everyone fixate on the fact that Santillano was a Mexican? "Yeah, that's why I'm on leave, so they can sort the whole thing out."

"I told Tyrell that there must have been a good reason for it, right?"

"Well, like I said, they're sorting it out." Ed stood. "Now come on, let's go back to bed. *Star Hustler* is over and you've got school tomorrow. And then the big scrimmage." The Z's first scrimmage was the next evening, which probably accounted for Jesse's nightmare.

"Maybe I can stay home with you?" E.J. wheedled.

"Maybe not," Ed said, standing by the light switch and waiting for the boys to head up the stairs. He'd always loved, as a kid, how he could tuck himself safely in bed with the hallway lights blazing and then call out to his mother to turn them off. Now he was usually the last to go to bed, flicking the switches as he moved forward, stumbling through the dark. When they were halfway up the stairs, Ed whispered to them. "Hey. Don't tell Polly—I'll talk to her. Don't talk about it at all, in fact."

They nodded and disappeared into their rooms. Ed grabbed an extra blanket from the couch before heading back upstairs. The bed was chilly without Claire near his side.

CHAPTER 8

Patricia
April 6

Patricia wandered around the living room, trying to find her keys, shoes and purse to prepare for a late shift at the hospital, and Lupe sat on the couch, watching the local news. "Listen to this," Lupe said, turning up the volume.

Channel 7 cut to a conference with the Denver chief of police. A "Breaking News" banner crawled across the bottom of the screen. The chief stood at a podium in front of a navy blue curtain, bright lights trained on him, bleaching his skin. "We have discovered a discrepancy with the warrant that was used in the immediate-entry raid on 3880 Race Street on March 12th," he said. "We are turning the matter over to our disciplinary unit for an investigation into possible wrongdoing, and the D.A.'s investigation is already underway."

The camera cut to a young reporter, who used the same stock inflection as all the others, artificially deepening her voice. "That's right, due to the investigative reporting of Denver Seven's own Ernesto Montoya, the chief of police has just admitted possible error in the Salvador Santillano shooting."

She turned toward Montoya, who was middle-aged with a thick moustache, wearing suspenders over his starched white shirt, and asked him how he discovered the cover-up. Montoya looked into the camera with a wounded expression. "Well, Kendra," he said gravely, "I was working on an upcoming story about Denver police's recent string of no-knock raids, when I noticed *something fishy* about the Santillano case."

"Please," Patricia said to the TV. "It was our lawyer who gave you the tip." When Patricia had pointed out the mistaken address, their lawyer had gone to the police. But when they stalled, Archuleta called Ernesto Montoya, an old school friend who used to go by the name of Ernie. "Look at this jerk."

"I'm trying to listen," Lupe said.

"Sergeant Dale Springer, who authorized the warrant," Montoya continued, "was last brought to our attention in September of 1999, when a young man he arrested claimed he'd used racial epithets and unnecessary force. And in 1997, Springer and two other officers shot and killed Miguel Abeyta as he charged them with a car."

"It's been a month," Patricia said. "They hid this for a month."

"What does this mean?" Ray asked, turning to Patricia.

"I don't know," she said. "It sure as hell doesn't bring your dad back." She felt like pulverizing something, but there wasn't a dish or a glass she could spare for dashing to the ground. Ray's baseball bat lay temptingly in his Pete's Pirates bag by the front door, but she couldn't think of an object she could afford to smash with it. Everything they owned, they needed to make last.

Patricia paced around the room, stumbling over a lunch sack that Ray had left out next to his school papers, sending an uneaten apple rolling under the couch. Patricia kneeled down to fish out the apple, telling herself the same thing she always did when faced with a household task she'd rather not do: she was the mother, if she didn't pick up the apple, no one would, and it would rot there. She drew the lint-covered apple out from under the couch. "Did that cop think that nobody would notice if they accidentally killed the wrong man as long as he was Mexican?" she asked.

"Would they kill me?" Mia asked. "Would they kill you?"

Patricia knew she should say something comforting, but couldn't. "I guess they could," Patricia said. "There's nothing to stop them."

Lupe shot her a horrified look, took up Mia's hand and kissed it. "That's not true," she said. "We're working to change that, to make us all safer."

Patricia held the apple up in Ray's face. He sat slumped on the couch, hands in the pocket of his hoodie sweatshirt, face hidden under hat and hood. "How many times do I have to tell you that you need to eat what I pack for you, Raymond?" She flicked up the bill of his hat so she could see his sullen face. "We can't afford to have you wasting food." Patricia twisted the apple with both hands in opposite directions. She ripped it apart, grunting as it gave, easing a tiny portion of her frustration.

The kids glanced at each other silently. Patricia didn't know what to do with the two halves of the apple. So she raised one to her mouth and took a bite. Lupe walked into the kitchen, and they heard her taking down a glass bowl from the cabinet, setting it on the counter, opening and closing the refrigerator, starting the microwave.

"Come here, Patricia," Lupe called from the kitchen.

Patricia walked into the kitchen. A mixture of yeast and sugar and warm water bubbled in a bowl on the counter and Lupe dumped a cup of flour into it. She stirred and added flour a cup at a time until it formed a ball. Lupe spread a white cotton cloth over the counter, floured it, and then turned the ball of dough out onto it. Lupe put an apron over Patricia's head, making her feel like a child being dressed by her mother.

"The lighter the leavened bread," Lupe said, standing next to the counter, "the angrier the woman behind it."

"You expect me to knead this dough?"

"Wash your hands."

Patricia obeyed, some part of her believing she deserved this penance, and rubbed her hands with soap under the water from the kitchen tap. She inhaled the smell of yeast and stared at the dough, lying on the counter, vulnerable. She clenched her hand into a fist and punched it. The dough flattened under her assault, leaving a fist print indented in its center. The smoothness of the surface and the density of the dough felt satisfyingly similar to human flesh. Patricia slapped, poked, jabbed, and banged the dough. She picked it up and flung it back on the counter, beating it with the sides of her fists. Maybe this

102

was why old TV shows depicted good mothers always baking so much—all the pies and cookies were really ugly feelings channeled into something that wouldn't frighten the children.

When Patricia was a kid and her parents had one of their momentary spats, the scent of bread rising and baking often followed. The aroma filled the whole house and the home felt safe, her family tight, even when the tension between Patricia's parents remained. After kneading the dough, Lupe would always leave the kitchen and then return, wearing a red dress. Later when the bread had emerged from the oven, golden brown, Lupe would say nothing, and place it on the table in front of Patricia's father. Patricia would watch her dad as he cut into the hot bread without meeting Lupe's eyes—the crust cracking, steam escaping—and buttered the first slice. The butter surrendered to the bread, and her father would raise the slice to his mouth, bite into it, and close his eyes.

Patricia's hands ached from kneading the dough, and she looked up to see Lupe leaning against the wall between the kitchen and the living room, watching her. "There," she said. "Do you feel calmer now?"

"A little," Patricia admitted.

She backed away from the counter and Lupe prepared the dough for the oven. "I've never understood why people buy bread machines," Lupe said. "They are missing the point entirely."

"Mom!" Mia shouted from the other room. "There are people!"

Patricia walked into the living room. Mia kneeled backwards on the couch by the front window, peering through the slats in the blinds. Strong beams of light poured in through the windows, illuminating Mia's face. Ray stood behind his sister, looking out over her head.

"There are three vans," Mia said, "and lights and people setting up equipment. There's the channel 7 news lady that was just talking."

Patricia pressed open the slats to look out, and found the normally quiet street in front of the house jammed with traffic

103

and activity. Porch lights across the block flicked on and neighbors stood outside, staring, conferring with each other. The reporter stood with her back to the house, occasionally turning toward them to gesture with her hand, glowing in the lights her camera crew trained on her. Patricia read the logos on the vans: "Denver's 7," "KCNC Channel 4," "Univision," were arriving.

"They can't do that!" Patricia said, turning to Lupe. "What right do they have to come over here and just start filming?"

"As long as they stay on the street," Lupe said, "I think they can do whatever they want. Remember during the salmonella scare at the Penagos' restaurant?"

Patricia had taped the news segment that showed the enraged Anita Penagos decking a reporter in front of her restaurant, and then giggled over it repeatedly with her friends. It didn't seem funny anymore.

"Mia, come away from there," Patricia said, pulling gently on her daughter's shoulder. "Don't let them see you."

"Why not?" Mia tightened her grip on the back of the couch.

"Because it isn't dignified," Lupe said. She took Mia's hand and led her away from the window.

"Why now?" Patricia said.

"It's a good story," Lupe said. "The police admitted a mistake. Yesterday you were nothing but a drug dealer's wife."

Patricia grabbed Mia by the shoulders and steered her in the other direction whenever she tried to dart toward the window. The heat from the oven made the house too warm. The phone began to ring.

"It's sure to be reporters," Lupe said. "You'd better think of a statement to give."

"Is there some rule that when your husband is killed by the cops, you have to talk to any stranger who shoves a camera or a tape recorder in your face?" Patricia pulled the phone cord out of the wall. She thought of the Columbine families, how some of them turned up in the paper frequently, rallying against guns or discussing their religious beliefs, and others you never heard from. There were enough of them that reporters had let them decide for themselves whether or not they wanted to appear in newsprint on the breakfast table every morning.

A helicopter beating overhead joined the general din. The scent of bread baking permeated the house. "What are they going to do with a helicopter?" Ray demanded of Patricia. "Land on our roof? Where were the helicopters when they shot Dad?"

"Hey," she said, holding up her hands. "I'm on your side."

"You couldn't be," Ray said, "because I'm on Dad's side." He turned and walked down the hall to his bedroom.

"But Ray," Mia called after him, "you could be on TV."

Patricia shook her head. Mia was probably thinking of all the times Ray pretended to be on TV, pitching in the World Series.

"I don't want to be on TV for this," Ray said before he slammed the bedroom door behind him.

"Oh, come on, Ray," Patricia said, following him. "Don't go hiding again." She rapped on the door. He didn't answer.

Lupe switched on the hall light. "You have to decide how you want to respond. If you want people to help you, you're going to have to become a public figure to some extent."

"What are you talking about?" Patricia said. "Help me with what?"

"Do you think the city is going to respond to one woman's demands?"

Patricia hated when her mother started speaking in rhetorical questions. She reached over and flipped the hall light back off.

Lupe continued, "Cops and politicians never budge for one person alone. Look how long it took for them to admit that there was a problem with the warrant." She looked as fierce as she did in the photograph Patricia's father kept in a frame on his desk, of Lupe on stage at a '60s Chicano rights rally, wearing bellbottom jeans, legs spread wide, long hair flowing, a bandolero empty of ammunition strapped across her chest. "Do you think they would have ever said anything if this reporter hadn't pressed them?"

"Obviously not."

"You are going to have to rely on the community if you ever want to get some restitution. Many of my old friends have been calling, offering to help. We should form some sort of committee."

"Come on. You used to do all that committee crap and what good did it do? There's nothing a committee can do to bring Salvador back."

Lupe put her hands on Patricia's arms. She was backlit by the glow from the living room and Patricia could barely make out her familiar features in the dark of the hall. "You are going to need the money," Lupe said, her eyes serious. "It sounds callous, but you have two kids that you're raising on just one income now, and you can't afford to turn your back on settlement money because of stubborn pride. Now I am going to talk to those reporters. You think about what I've said."

"You don't have to do that," Patricia said, but Lupe walked away. The image of proper, domesticated Lupe as a radical protester didn't seem as ridiculous anymore.

Lupe wrapped herself in a blue cloak. She took a deep breath, then stepped outside, pulling the door shut behind her so that Mia wouldn't follow.

Mia ran down the hall and shouted into Ray's closed door. "Ray, you're missing it! Grandma is going to talk to the news people."

Patricia turned on the TV again. The anchorwoman announced breaking news, cut to a reporter, and Patricia saw her mother standing on her porch, microphones held before her. She looked tough and tiny and beautiful.

"We are saddened that it took so long for the police department to admit their wrongdoing," Lupe said, "but we are not surprised. We demand a full investigation into the matter, and we hope that the truth will finally be uncovered. My son-in-law was an innocent man, gunned down by police." Reporters stuck their microphones forward and began to shout out questions.

106

Lupe raised her hand, shook her head, said, "That's all for now," and turned to come back into the house.

After Lupe closed the door behind her, she began to tremble. Mia ran up to Lupe and took her shaking hands. "You were just on TV," she said. "Maybe they'll show it again."

Patricia, feeling dazed, glanced at her watch. "How am I supposed to get to work?" She couldn't afford to miss any more shifts.

"You can't go to work now," Lupe said. "You need to stay with your kids."

"I need to feed my kids," Patricia said, picking up her purse.

Patricia took Mia's advice, walking out into the backyard and scaling the chain-link fence that separated their house from Nino's. She knocked on their back door until Nino's grandma shuffled up in her robe and slippers and let her inside. Nino's grandma, with her sweet, liver-spotted face, didn't even ask her what she was doing there—she'd probably seen everything on TV. Patricia asked if she could borrow her car and Mrs. Guerrero pressed the keys to her turquoise Datsun in Patricia's hands without hesitation.

She arrived at the hospital in time for the start of her shift, relieved to let her mind turn to her work. The ICU felt calm and quiet after the media siege at home, nothing but the steady beeps of EKGs, the whooshes of air pumps, and the sounds of doctors and nurses going about their duties, their purposeful strides down the hall, scrubs rustling as they moved.

That night an elderly woman named Mrs. Alba died of heart failure. Patricia clocked in just before she passed and went straight to see her, as Mrs. Alba was a favorite. Many of the members of her sizable family were assembled in the room, but they eventually filtered out and left the hospital to make arrangements. As the crowd broke up, Patricia thought of Salvador dying alone, in the company of nobody but the cops who had killed him.

Patricia talked to her patients when they were alive, she talked to them when they were comatose, and so she couldn't help but talk to them when they were dead, as she took out catheters and I.V.'s and prepared their bodies to be moved. The only difference was that while her patients lived, Patricia asked them questions about their lives, and when they were dead, Patricia spoke about her life to them instead.

"Let me get these out of you," Patricia told Mrs. Alba after they were alone together in the room. "You asked when I put them in if you'd ever take a breath without these tubes in you again. I pretended I didn't hear you, but I did. People couldn't tell what you were saying, toward the end, but I could. I asked about your grandkids. You ticked off their names and ages like beads on a rosary."

Patricia eased the I.V. out with the same care she would have taken if Mrs. Alba were alive. "It made me think, you know, there's a last everything. There's a last time you're free of tubes and needles, and a last time you'll smell lilacs, and a last kiss, and a last ice cream. Maybe that's the saddest one of all, thinking about how there's going to be a last ice cream some day. What flavor was Salvador's? Probably vanilla. He liked vanilla. And all of your lasts, did you enjoy them enough, Mrs. Alba? How are you supposed to make sure that you do? Throw yourself into ecstasies every time you eat a chocolate bar because it might be the final chocolate bar, the one you take inside you to the grave?" Patricia shook her head. "You can't live like that."

Patricia gathered Mrs. Alba's belongings into a box, a task she routinely performed for families too grief-stricken to attend to details. Once she had presented a woman with her deceased husband's false teeth in a plastic bag, and the woman stared at them in her hands and asked, "What should I do with these?"

Patricia studied the photo of Mrs. Alba and her husband for a long time before she placed it next to the cross folded from dried palm fronds, reading glasses, and get well cards from Mrs. Alba's grandchildren. In the photo, plump Mrs. Alba, her hair a brown bouffant, and her husband, a round-faced man with a comb-over, posed in front of a blue backdrop, gentle smiles on their faces. His hands covered hers at the bottom of the frame. "Fifty years as a wife, your daughter was saying." Patricia whistled. "Mrs. Alba, you won."

Patricia brushed Mrs. Alba's fine gray hair back from her face. "And me, I'm barely past thirty and already I've blown any chance at the serenity that you lived in."

Patricia felt she did her clearest thinking when she was with the dead, processing moments she had no time to reflect on when pressed with the needs of the living. But then she would remember she had other patients, way too many, and the rest of them were alive and deserving care.

Before she left the room, Patricia turned and looked at Mrs. Alba one last time. Her face was still and pale. Patricia sometimes wondered if conversations like this meant she was going crazy, and she occasionally thought about leaving nursing and switching to a job that offered less drama. Less dead people time. But then what would she do? She didn't understand work that wasn't physical, that didn't involve touching and lifting and being on her feet. Sitting on your ass wasn't work, no matter what you did while you were on it. Maybe she learned that from watching her parents run their restaurant, always on their feet, in motion, greeting and cooking and cleaning and taking orders, Lupe especially, just a blur in the frame. And so Patricia had become a nurse, a job that meant her feet swelled at night.

That evening's shift was quiet as Patricia went about her tasks, comforting her patients, checking their medication levels, consulting with their doctors. One of her patients was a young woman in a body cast, the result of a car accident that was her drunken sweetheart's fault. He sat there next to her every night until the end of visiting hours, touching her pink fingertips where they emerged from her cast, looking at her with his sorrowful eyes. It always took Patricia a lot of coaxing to convince him to depart for the night.

Patricia tried to remember how it was back when she and Salvador were first in love and couldn't bear to part. It became harder and harder to leave each other after dates. They'd start to move toward the door, still kissing, stand there at the door kissing, kissing with the door open, Salvador with one foot over the threshold, one hand on the small of her back.

On Sunday mornings after a Saturday night with Salvador, Patricia would sit in Mass, half-ashamed, even before she and Salvador began sleeping together. The priest's homily always seemed directed at her, a message sent by Lupe through God. Patricia would go to the earliest Mass because she was so agitated with infatuation that she couldn't sleep, and she'd be the only person there under seventy. Her parents had moved to Arizona by then, so Patricia went to church alone, still worried that Lupe would find out if she skipped. She was incapable of breaking all of Lupe's rules at once. The priest would sometimes deliver a brimstone message against abortion and the acts that led to it, and the old ladies would smile at Patricia warmly as they took her hand during the sign of peace, as if to acknowledge that Patricia was the only one in the church to whom the priest's message could possibly be relevant.

Salvador held off from pressing further for many months even as their kisses became more desperate. Patricia prayed to her favorite saints for strength—the ones with stigmata—then one by one let them go. She prayed to Otis Redding, but he was no help at all—he rooted for it, always begging in his songs: *Pleeeease*. People die too young every day, she had reasoned. Why shouldn't I live a little, now? What if I died or he died? Being in love made her think about death all the time.

The apartment building where Salvador lived when they were first dating was a two-floor, nondescript seventies box. The doors to all the apartments opened off either side of a long corridor. Tenants stuffed their rent checks into a slot in the wall downstairs, next to the laundry room where a pair of washers and dryers always tumbled loads of children's clothing. The rent was cheap, the location undesirable—too near the dog chow plant—and the building housed immigrants of many nations.

As she came and went, Patricia heard people speaking Spanish, Arabic, and a half-dozen languages she couldn't recognize. At dinner time the hallway hung heavy with cumin and curry, garlic and ginger. Veiled women, thick-bearded men, Mexican immigrants in tight cowboy jeans. The little children were all the same, running wild together in the parched grass surrounding the building, leaving their sun-faded toys out at night just as suburban kids would in a fence-enclosed lawn. Patricia felt uneasy entering this foreign world, but at the same time she felt freed of all the rules she'd lived under in her sheltered life with her parents. Patricia's family had lived in Colorado for generations, and she felt so different from these tenuous Americans. Wasn't Salvador more like her than them?

The morning after they made love for the first time, the arresting Muslim prayer music of Salvador's neighbors awakened her. The plaintive sound came in through the open window, the voices so strange and pained and wonderful that they were impossible to distinguish from instruments. The sky was pink and the song was achingly lovely. Without understanding a word, Patricia knew they were singing about God. She could tell by the way Salvador's breathing quieted that the mournful song had woken him too, but they didn't say anything or move, just listened, trying not to break the spell. This felt sacred to Patricia: lying close, her arm over his shoulder and her lips pressed to the recess of his back between his shoulder blades, while around them strangers prayed.

Patricia wished she could hear that music once more. She tried to recall its melody as she adjusted her patient's morphine drip. For the first time, she didn't care if Salvador had cheated on her. He was hers once, and he didn't deserve to die like that.

CHAPTER 9

Ed

April 7

Ed sat in front of the desk of his lawyer, who gave a long-haired calico the run of her Capitol Hill office. Mitch had called that morning with some bad news: he'd heard that the gunshot residue on Santillano's hands didn't match his gun. The cat turned figure eights between Ed's ankles, rubbing its head on his leg, begging for an ear scratch. No way was he going to pet it. Cats should know that just by looking at him. Eventually it stalked off and settled on a pan of kitty litter next to a carton of case files on the floor. Ed's nose wrinkled. What kind of rinky-dink lawyer had Mitch set him up with? Mitch said she worked on a lot of cases for cops—lawsuits, divorces, and disability settlements. Judging from the décor of the office—two pastel southwestern cactus prints that reminded Ed of some he'd seen in a Motel 6 in Albuquerque—it either didn't make her much money or she didn't want to spend any of it.

"Coffee?" Sylvia asked.

"I'm allergic to cats," Ed said, his tear ducts beginning to swell and itch.

Sylvia made no effort to banish the animal. "Didn't Mitch tell you I had cats?"

"There's more than one?" Ed searched the room and spotted a black cat perched on top of a filing cabinet, its tail twitching, green eyes burning down at him.

Sylvia plopped a legal file down on her desk and eased into her chair.

"It certainly makes things look bad that the department didn't come out with a statement until that reporter confronted them about the warrant, but it still shouldn't affect your case."

"My division commander called yesterday and said they're probably going to extend my leave until the D.A. decides whether or not to press charges against me."

"That's a good idea," Sylvia said. "People are going to be angry, especially the anti-cop kooks, and the department wants to evaluate the situation with great care—or at least look like it is. The media scrutiny is going to be pretty intense from this point until they find something else that interests them. Any reporters showing up at your house yet?"

Ed shook his head.

"If they do, don't talk to them, and don't let your family talk to them, at least not until the D.A. clears you. Is your phone number listed?"

"No."

"Do you subscribe to a newspaper?"

"Yeah, the *Rocky*."

"Did you sign up under your real name for it, with your real phone number?"

"I don't know, I'll have to ask Claire about it. Why?"

"I had another officer-involved shooting case where the guy had an unlisted phone number and was always very careful to register everything that might end up in the public domain under his wife's name. But then he subscribed to the *Post* with his real information. The first thing the reporters did was check the subscription rolls and then they started ringing his phone night and day until he changed the number."

"I'll check on that."

"Now, is your yard picked up?"

"My yard? The grass is starting to turn green and Claire put some pansies in last weekend, but it isn't going to make the Parade of Homes or anything. Why?"

"I had another case where a reporter figured out a cop's address, but he wouldn't talk to her. So she wrote an article describing his recent heart attack, his two divorces, and his weed-filled lawn. You could tell she was a frustrated poet or something, because she even threw in a vignette about dawn breaking behind a broken-down pickup with an expired registration parked by his sidewalk. If she'd checked the plates, she would have found out that it belonged to his neighbor. The thing is, they're going to try to dig up anything they can to make you look as though you've been walking around like De Niro in *Taxi Driver* for years, just waiting for the chance to cap some guy."

"I'll haul out the weed whacker, first thing." He sighed. At least tidying up the lawn would occupy his time alone at home. He looked at her, waiting for her to say more.

She interlaced her fingers and rested her hands on her desk. "I'm afraid that's all the advice I have for you today. Nobody's filed a lawsuit or criminal charges against you, so we're in a holding pattern until anything changes."

"Have you heard anything about Santillano's gun?"

"What about it?"

"Somebody said that the other guys' stories don't match mine, and that Santillano couldn't have fired the gun they found. Plus, they can't trace it, and Mitch said the gunshot residue on the guy's hands didn't match." It gave Ed vertigo trying to fit what he remembered around this fact. Could Springer have planted a gun? Or did something mess up the test?

"You said in your statement that Santillano had a gun. Don't ever say anything different." Her glasses slipped down her nose as she leaned forward and she jabbed them back in place with a forefinger. "Who have you been talking to about this?"

"You know, just the guys."

"You need to stop talking. Anything you say to anyone that's different from your recorded statements can be used against you. Just stick to your original story. He didn't need to even fire for you to be justified in shooting him."

"I saw a gun. But could I have mistook something else for a gun?"

"I don't care if you hallucinated a gun. As long as your hallucination stays consistent, and they've got a weapon matched to him, we're good."

"Then why do I feel so guilty?" Ed asked, absently stroking a cat at his feet. When he realized what he was doing, he scooted the animal away with the side of his foot and wiped his hand on his pants.

Sylvia rose from her seat, Ed's signal to do the same. "I think your extended paid leave might be a blessing," she said, holding the door open for him. Ed wondered what that meant—did she think he was nuts?

After pulling out of the parking lot, Ed found himself steering his car toward the McDonald's on Colfax. He ordered his food at the drive-through window and ate in his car, his Big Mac so freighted with cheese and sauce and ketchup that it spurted out with each bite and dripped all over his hands. He scarcely paused for breath until he had demolished two Big Macs and a large fries. He sat in his car with greasy lips, a pile of hamburger wrappings and mustard-drenched paper napkins littering his lap. He felt nothing but a vague desire for a chocolate shake. He had to stop eating like this or he'd end up looking like Mitch. He glanced at his watch. The boys' practice would begin in a couple of hours and then he wouldn't have to be alone anymore.

Ed nodded hello to all the fathers in the stands when he arrived at his boys' practice that afternoon. He had attended every practice of the Zenith Homes Z's. Among the regulars in the stands was the ex-Bronco lineman, Darnell Pendergrass, whose son Tyrell played shortstop.

Pendergrass scooted over on the bleacher to make room for him, and Ed felt honored to seat himself on a place still warm from an NFL alum. Recently retired, Pendergrass had begun to purchase Laundromats and electronics stores in the twilight years of his career, and now he rented a few billboards overlooking I-25 and Lincoln Avenue to advertise his businesses, a caricature of his face grinning down at the people of Denver. Pendergrass always brought a big bunch of grapes to the practices, and after he offered them around, he reclined on his elbows and popped them one by one into his mouth. Three-hundred-pound Pender-grass explained that he stuck to fruit for snacks because he was "slimming."

Ed watched Jesse, confident, broad-shouldered, at the helm of his team, as he stood by Coach Boyd at home plate, handing him baseballs and receiving throws from his teammates. Boyd led the infielders through a session of situations, calling out "Bases loaded, no outs," and hitting the ball to the third baseman, or "Runner on first and third, one out," and hitting it between the first and second basemen.

"I don't know," Hank Badgett said loudly, "I think Boyd has the wrong philosophy about building a team for high altitude." Badgett worked for Zenith Homes, the developer that sponsored the team, and his son played left field. He tried to disguise his scotch breath with wads of peppermint chewing gum, and always wanted to talk during practice.

"Why do you say that?" Pendergrass asked. The dads listened when he talked. Pendergrass was a personal friend of John Elway, and his thoughts counted for more than those of most men.

"Where are the mashers?" Hank said. "Besides Jesse and Roy, nobody else routinely takes it long. You've got to make use of the thin air, and round up boys who can send the ball sailing."

"That's not all that matters," Dr. Kitagawa said. His son Matt was the Z's ace, and during practice Dr. K always took notes on a steno pad. "The most important thing is putting the ball in play. Striking out is the worst outcome for a team at altitude, even more damaging than it is for a team at low altitude. Putting the ball in play here yields a better result than it does in any other state. Mashers tend to strike out more." Ed snuck a glance at his notepad. *Keep front leg flexible*, it said.

"What you want is someone with a good on-base percentage but with power," Pendergrass said. "You've got to balance the two."

"What matters more than the hitters," Ed said, "is building a solid rotation of pitchers who can keep the ball down. Fast-ballers, because a curve doesn't break like it should in Colorado.

If anybody gets a good piece of aluminum on it, it's going for a ride. There's nothing you can do about that."

"But what about after the Z's win the state tournament?" Hank said. "When they're playing teams from Texas and Oklahoma, at low altitude in high humidity?"

"That's different," Dr. Kitagawa said. "Texans require strategy. At least our boys will have a higher red blood cell count and greater lung capacity going for them."

"Shit," said Hank. "A higher red blood cell count is nothing compared to fourteen-inch biceps. Those Texans are monsters, even at twelve years old."

Badgett kept yammering to Dr. Kitagawa, who ceased to respond. Badgett's face grew ruddier and his mop of hair more disheveled as the practice progressed. "Say Ed," Badgett said, leaning forward. "What was it you said you did?"

"I didn't," Ed said, hoping Badgett would drop it. Ed purposely avoided telling people that he was a cop. When you told people you were a cop, they took it as an opportunity to vent their opinions, like you were the community's walking suggestion box. Or they'd tell you a story about a cop that had pepper-sprayed them for no reason back in '69 and wait for you to apologize for it or admit that, yeah, cops were pretty much scum.

"Well?" Badgett said.

He could say that he was a consultant, a nice ambiguous job that lots of people seemed to have. And it wasn't exactly a lie, because he consulted all day, with winos on Colfax, with freaked-out mothers, with meth lab technicians. But what if the reporters checked up on him and found out he'd been lying about his job like he was ashamed of it? Ed sighed. Badgett was just the sort of sucker who'd be happy to spill for a reporter. "I'm a cop," he said.

"DPD?" Badgett demanded, with a little too much interest.

"Yep." Ed didn't turn around to look at the guy.

Badgett climbed down a bleacher and sat next to Ed. He smelled like a cask of Balvenie. "And the name's O'Fallon, right?"

"Last I checked."

"So you were in that shooting last month? I read about it in the paper. Sounds pretty nuts. Did you guys really shoot the wrong man?"

Ed took a deep breath, reminding himself that if he collapsed the guy's larynx with an elbow to the throat, that would be a total DeNiro in *Taxi Driver* move: TRIGGER HAPPY COP ATTACKS DAD AT LITTLE LEAGUE PRACTICE. He turned and faced Badgett. "It's like this, Hank," Ed said. "Did you ever have a bad day at work? I don't know, did one of your deals fall through or something?"

"Sure. Everyone has bad days." He chuckled. "That's part of the business."

"When you had that bad day, did you have to read about it in the paper the next morning? Did you turn on the TV and see them going on and on about your bad day, describing it in detail so that everyone in the city knew about it, that you, Hank Badgett, had fucked up, and by the way, everyone should know?"

"Can't say that I have," Badgett allowed, flashing his teeth.

"The incident you're referring to was just about the worst day of my life, save the day I put my mother in the ground. I'd rather not talk about it."

"Amen," Pendergrass said. "When I had a bad day with the Broncos, they'd run a huge color picture of it in the sports page and replay it over and over on the news. Then a half-dozen sports television and radio shows would discuss it because this town has *nothing else to talk about*. And then there'd be assholes Sunday quarterbacking it in every bar and restaurant I went into for weeks. This city needs to get a life." He handed Ed a bunch of grapes. "So let's agree not to talk about work." He leaned back on his elbows. "It's baseball season and the weather is fine."

Ed popped a grape in his mouth and started chewing, working his jaw. Was there something about him that made people hand him fruit every time he got angry? Ed swallowed. "Why can't we all play baseball for a living?" he asked no one in particular, trying to lighten the atmosphere.

"I hear that," Pendergrass said. "If I'd played baseball instead, I might still have both my original hips."

Badgett rose and walked to the fence, clung to the chain link with his hands, and called out to his boy. "Hey Matt, let's see a little hustle out there."

Matt held up his glove and flipped his dad the bird behind it so that everyone at the field except his father could see. Ed was relieved that E.J. and Jesse would never disrespect him like that.

At the end of the drill, Boyd turned to his assistant coach, Chase, and said something inaudible that prompted him to whistle, two fingers in his mouth. The boys responded by sprinting in. Ed had always been hoarse after practices from shouting instructions and advice from home plate. Maybe controlled silence was the better way to go.

Boyd sent the pitchers and catchers to work on the sidelines and started the rest on batting practice. He didn't appear to have a life outside of youth baseball, though Ed learned from the other fathers that Boyd was an accountant. That day job made sense when Ed considered the sort of players Boyd assembled for the Z's.

He employed the services of multiple volunteer scorekeepers who kept track of everything from pitch count to opposite field hits. He gathered up their score sheets and entered them into a program on his computer, running a battery of calculations and issuing each boy a weekly stat sheet. Boyd coached methodically and he favored boys who played that way, picking pitchers with good control over those with messy velocity, and the consistent hitter of singles over an undisciplined batter who could occasionally pull it. Boyd's manner seemed to induce more terror and respect in the boys than Ed's had. Boyd hardly said anything during games, but the boys knew he was a careful witness, toting it all up. They played knowing he would reshuffle the batting order the next week according to how the numbers fell.

Tyrell Pendergrass let a ball go through the wickets, then chased it down and chucked it to second base. He snuck a

119

nervous glance at Boyd, who remained as outwardly impassive as ever. So this was how an expert coach did it, Ed thought. He exploited the kids' natural fear of numbers, their fear of data that could be processed to show them as less skilled than the others. At least Polly and the Purple Unicorns wouldn't understand the concept of batting averages for years yet, and considered the outcome of a game favorable only if the grape soda in the cooler afterward was abundant.

On the way home the boys chattered about how they wanted to save their allowances to buy batting gloves like the ones Tyrell wore. "Tyrell said he's going to retire a batting glove each time he steals a base this season and hang them on his wall, just like Ricky Henderson," Jesse said.

"That's a lot of gloves. I hope for his dad's sake that those Laundromats are doing well," Ed said.

"When are you going back to work?" E.J. asked.

"I still don't know," Ed said, a familiar wrench of inadequacy tightening the muscles in his jaw.

"Maybe you won't have to go back all summer and you can come to all the practices," E.J. said.

When Ed drove into the cul-de-sac where his family lived, Polly was circling around on her bicycle with a group of other kids. Ed tapped the horn and waved and the kids stopped their bikes, letting him drive through. The kids spent all summer turning endless loops around the cul-de-sac, usually with somebody's mother out watching on the porch, her arms crossed over her chest. Whenever a new kid grew old enough to take his maiden voyage on a bike and joined the parade, all the parents would come out of the houses and clap throughout the first lap. Polly had hammed up this moment the year before, waving like a beauty queen as she pedaled her purple bike around, the handle streamers flying back in the breeze.

Polly pedaled up the driveway behind Ed's car, and the boys climbed out. E.J. kicked at Polly's little white training wheels with his toe. "Dad didn't let us have training wheels," Jesse said. "You've got to work past those."

"She will when she's ready," Ed said. He had eased up on his rules with his third child. Sure, he didn't use training wheels when he was a kid, but what harm did they do? He'd been worried that the boys would become dependent on the crutch, and he wanted them tougher than that. He made them wait until they were old enough to learn to ride a bike properly from the start instead of having to learn it over twice. But when it came to Polly, he just gave in.

Polly downed her dinner in seconds and returned to her bicycle. While the rest of them ate, Ed left the door open so they could listen to the sounds of the kids cycling and come to the rescue if someone started howling over a scraped knee.

"Claire," Ed asked between forkfuls of macaroni and beef, "What name is the newspaper subscription registered under?"

"I don't know," she said. "I could check for you. Why?"

"My lawyer said reporters will probably be after us soon." He looked at his sons, who focused on their food, their heads ducked over their plates as they shoveled in their second helpings. "Did you hear that, guys? It's really important that you don't talk about the shooting with anyone now. And don't go around mentioning that I'm a cop. There are a lot of people out there who don't like cops."

"Okay, Dad," Jesse said, his mouth full of food. E.J. stopped eating and looked across the table at Ed, his eyes worried.

Ed finished chewing a bite, then put his fork down and listened. He hadn't heard the bikes going around for a few minutes, and no car had pulled into a driveway to explain their pause. His instincts commanded him to rise.

"What's the matter?" Claire asked, moving her hands to the edge of the table. The boys stopped chewing and looked up at him.

Ed said nothing and rushed down the hallway to look out the window. He didn't see the kids anywhere and his throat constricted. *Polly.* He opened the front door and stepped out onto the porch. He finally spotted the group of kids down at the far end of the cul-de-sac, gathered in front of the house with the weeping willow tree, Polly in the middle of them, talking to a grown man that Ed didn't recognize. Ed pounded down the porch steps and sprinted down the street, his hand moving to where his holstered gun would normally be before he could make a coherent analysis of the scene.

When he drew close he could see that the man was taking notes on a reporter's pad, and the mother of a couple of the kids stood off to the side smoking a cigarette and watching, as if she had given permission for the man to speak to them. Ed wanted to throttle her. He grabbed Polly off the seat of her bicycle and held her close to his chest. She put her arms around his neck.

"I'm Kyle Schmidt from the *Denver Post*," the man said. He was a little pudgy, his skin a vulnerable shade of pink, his mouth obscured by a droopy moustache a shade darker than his dishwater blond hair. "Are you Ed O'Fallon?" His demeanor was calm as a lizard's, which Ed found infuriating.

"I don't care who you are," Ed said, pointing his finger in the guy's face. "You stay away from my children. I don't care if they're not on my property."

Ed hauled Polly away in his arms before he gave the reporter anything else to print. She reached back and kicked her feet, trying to free herself, shouting, "My bike, Daddy! My bike!" Ed was too angry to respond. He'd get the bike later.

He didn't put Polly down until they were safely inside their house, the door shut and dead-bolted behind them. He kneeled down to look in Polly's eyes, and held her by her shoulders. Polly lowered her eyes but Ed raised her head back with a finger under her chin. "What did I tell you about talking to strangers, Polly Ann?" he demanded. "Did you listen to me? For Christ's sake, you're a cop's daughter and you're out there in the street, talking to a stranger."

Polly's green eyes filled and her mouth trembled. Claire rushed forward. "What happened, Ed?" she asked, her tone accusing. "You really upset her."

Ignore her, stay focused on the suspect, Ed thought, then shook his head. This was his daughter. "Stop crying, Polly. Crying won't help you. This is serious. When I tell you something's important, you obey. You don't talk to strangers, I don't care if they say they've got some fancy job. That's what strangers do—they lie to you."

Polly's sobs took over her breathing then, the whites of her eyes reddening until her irises shone, incandescent by contrast. Claire gathered Polly into her arms, rubbing her back, whispering, "deep breaths, kiddo, deep breaths." She shot Ed a fierce glare over Polly's shoulder.

Ed stood and turned away from his wife and his daughter, grabbing his head with his hands. Jesse and E.J. followed Ed as he paced. "What did she do, Dad?" Jesse asked.

"It's all right. She didn't know," Ed said. Maybe he'd been too harsh with her, he thought, struck by that sick feeling he got whenever he took discipline too far with the kids. But he couldn't ramp down. "Some reporter was out there talking to kids, trying to find out where I lived, probably to ask me questions about that shooting. I don't know how he figured it out but, well, now they know where we live. So you've all got to be extra careful. Don't talk to anyone about this. They might come to your school, to your baseball practice, anywhere."

The boys nodded. E.J. walked over to Claire and Polly and took his sister's hand, rubbing the back of it with his thumb.

The doorbell rang and Ed jumped. E.J. darted forward to answer it but Ed reached a hand out to stop him. "I'll get it," he said. "In fact, I don't want any of you kids answering the doorbell from now on. Claire, could you clear the kids out of the hallway? It might not be safe."

"Ed," she whispered, throwing him a cautionary look. "You need to calm down. You're scaring everyone." But still she hustled the kids away, into the kitchen. The kids huddled around her, clinging to their mother like a bunch of refugees.

Ed looked through the peephole and saw no one. Was it kids playing a trick or something worse? He unlocked the door and slowly drew it open, keeping himself covered behind it. He cautiously looked around it. The red-haired girl from next door poked her head out from behind the wall where she'd retreated after ringing the bell. He felt himself uncoil a little. "Yes?" Ed said, his voice sounding stern even to himself, his father's voice coming out of his mouth.

The kid stared at him with wide eyes. Her freckled skin was stained with the traces of a purple Popsicle around her mouth.

"I just brought Polly's bike," she said, taking a step back, her fingers playing with the streamers on the handles.

Ed breathed deeply, trying to calm himself. "Thanks," he said, and opened the screen door to take the bike in. The girl split without a word, running down the sidewalk toward her house, the sound of her flip-flops slapping against the pavement gradually fading away as she fled.

After the kids were asleep, Claire and Ed lay in their bed. "You frightened Polly," Claire said. "She was in no real danger, and you terrified her."

"No real danger? How was I supposed to know who that guy was? What am I supposed to do, wait until after someone abducts her before I ask questions, just so I don't unfairly judge the guy?"

"She was with a group of people. They wouldn't have let anything happen."

"Oh yeah? What about that seven-year-old last year in north Denver, out playing in the street with her little friends when some sicko scoops her up, drives off, rapes her, and dumps her back in the parking lot of a 7-Eleven? And that's a best-case scenario. It happens all the time."

"It doesn't happen all the time, Ed."

"It happens often enough that shit like this is all I hear about. All I think about. You have to guard your kids, Claire. The world is full of scumbags. If you want them to have any chance at a childhood, you have to fight for it."

"But you said that Mrs. Peterson was standing right there."

"Yeah, and she's a fine specimen, a chain-smoking, witless, worthless individual. I bet the reporter slipped her a twenty to let him have a crack at the kids."

"Not everyone is bad."

"Enough are to keep the department busy twenty-four hours a day. I don't regret what I did, Claire, not for a second. The only thing I regret is that I have to explain all this to Polly in greater detail than I would have liked—the shooting, the media."

"Polly knows plenty already."

"She's six years old. What could she know?"

"You know how Polly always insists on hugging you before you leave for work?"

"Yeah. It's mutual," Ed said, thinking about the day his daughter came tearing outside onto the driveway one time when he forgot to hug her goodbye. He'd been pulling out, but he parked his car and stepped out, embracing her, Polly's little hands moving over his back.

"What do you think that's about?"

"I don't know, she misses her dad when he's at work?"

"Do you know what she told me? She hugs you before you go to work so that she can make sure that you're wearing your bulletproof vest."

"She said that?" Ed said, raising himself up on his elbows.

"You'd better brace yourself. Things will probably get worse."

"Why?"

"Any day the reporters will learn that they didn't find any drugs in the house. And then they'll question his gun."

"But he shot at you."

"Yeah, but Springer said they can't trace it. And the gunshot residue on the guy's hands didn't match, for some reason."

Claire turned and her face was lost in shadow. "Did you plant the gun?"

"How could you ask that?" He looked at her, pleading.

"I'm just asking."

"Of course not. Honey, you know me."

125

"Sure," she said, but didn't seem assured. She turned over onto her side. Ed traced a pattern on the back of her bare arm, her skin as cool and inviting as a chilled peach. They hadn't had sex since before the shooting.

CHAPTER 10

Patricia
April 15

Patricia, Lupe, and Mia needed to head straight from Archuleta's office to Ruby Hill field to make it on time to Ray's first Pirates game. Mia stayed in the hallway reading *The Secret Garden*, while Lupe and Patricia sat in the lawyer's office, listening to his news. Archuleta showed them copies of police documents he'd requested, indicating that the tests didn't show gunshot residue on Salvador's hands. "They hit the wrong house," he said, "They found no drugs, and now we have evidence to suggest Salvador didn't fire the gun. In court, they'll say gunshot residue tests can be inconclusive, but this is a solid report we can use on our side." Patricia dug her nails into the meat of her palms. She knew so little about Salvador's life in the weeks before the shooting. She wished she at least knew if he'd owned a gun.

"We'll tell everyone at the committee meeting tonight," Lupe said, examining the documents. Patricia felt acid rise in the back of her throat at the thought of the meeting Lupe had scheduled, and said it was time to go.

At the field, Patricia absently sat down on the nearest bleacher filled with fans decked out in blue.

"We can't sit here," Lupe said. "It's the wrong side."

At Ray's old team's games, no one paid attention to where they sat, but the Pirates fans grouped together, wearing red, their caps and sweatshirts endorsing the team, a few mothers holding babies dressed in Pirates-themed onesies. As Patricia, Lupe, and Mia moved over to the red side, people murmured about the team's prospects. The grass on the field looked shaggy, brown interspersed with green blades, small mounds of black snow hanging out in the shadowed corners near the fence. The atmosphere of concentrated excitement and focused attention reminded Patricia of the energy she'd felt in the crowd at the Colorado/Nebraska football game she attended one year with her father, when he'd wanted her to go to Boulder for college, before she'd met Salvador and settled on staying in Denver.

Patricia looked down at her blue shirt. She could run back to the car and grab a coat to hide the opposing team's color, but the game was about to begin. The other parents brought blankets, stadium seats, warm thermoses, and bags full of food. Little finches hopped around the pavement near the bleachers, pecking at popcorn and sunflower seed shells, their heads and throats stained red like they were rooting for the team. The parents had settled into their territory well before the first pitch, and hardly an open space remained. Lupe squeezed them into a row, Patricia's blue sweatshirt sticking out in the sea of red. She shivered as she sat, the chill of the ridged metal stands reaching through her jeans.

A thin, middle-aged man perched on the lowest bleacher, preparing to keep score. He wore his visor low and leaned over a portable table, his scorebook, half a dozen pencils, erasers, and a pencil sharpener spread across the surface.

Pete walked by in tight polyester shorts and a jersey, and the scorekeeper looked up and asked, "You want me running pitch counts today, Coach?" Pete grunted vaguely but the man seemed to understand his reply, and set out a new tablet. At Ray's old games, they had been lucky if anyone could scrounge up a slip of paper from an old grocery list and a functioning pen to keep a rough tally of the score. When it was Patricia's turn to keep score, she'd add a few runs to the other team's tally now and then to extend the game.

"This is like the Rockies," Mia said, taking El Johnway out of the pocket of her red sweatshirt, "there's white lines on the field and everything. And a batboy!"

The batboy looked to be about five years old, and he wore the same uniform as the team members, though his pants bagged a little around his knees. He hustled in and out of the dugout, lugging the older boys' equipment around with a serious expression. "Somebody should tell that kid he isn't forty years old," Patricia whispered to Lupe.

Pete carried a radio out to the plate and blared loud rock songs from the era when he must have first begun to think of himself as a stallion: AC/DC, Scorpions, Guns N' Roses. Then the boys burst from the dugout, each dressed in an impeccable uniform, fanning out to their positions at a dead sprint. Pete hit a ball to the shortstop, who winged it to first, then the first baseman fired it back to second, the second baseman tossed it to third, and the third baseman sent it home to the catcher, who handed the ball to Pete so the process could begin again. The boys took an exuberant hop as they threw, beginning every movement with a bounce and ending it with a snap.

"Everything they're wearing is brand new," Lupe said. "Those are satin, appliquéd warm-up jackets!" She lowered her voice. "How much money did it cost for Ray to join this team?"

"Pete said he'd waive the fee," Patricia said. It hadn't seemed like a big deal, but maybe it was a lot of money. "He didn't say anything about paying."

"He didn't *yet*."

The man sitting behind Patricia whispered to his wife, "Who are those people in front of us?" Patricia almost turned around to introduce herself, but then the wife suggested that Patricia could be a spy from another team. A spy! Well, that was something more exciting than a nurse. She would let them think she was a spy for a while longer. The tips of Patricia's fingers and nose grew cold in the crisp air, and she put her arm around Mia, her assistant spy, for warmth.

A mother with puffy hair shellacked into place around a red Pete's Pizza visor bustled over to the scorekeeper's table and read the lineup over his shoulder. "Who is this Maestas? Leading off and pitching?"

The scorekeeper shrugged. "He's new," he said, guarded insolence in his tone.

The woman faced the parents and announced, "Coach Pete is having a new kid pitch. Someone named Maestas. Someone who wasn't on the official team roster I sent out last month. Someone who didn't attend the meet-and-greet potluck last month at Valverde Park. I thought you should all be aware." The woman pursed her lips, then turned back around.

Lupe elbowed Patricia. "Speak."

"Excuse me," Patricia said, "he wasn't on the roster because he just started."

The woman turned and stared at her, squinting in judgment. Patricia swallowed. "He's my son, Ray," she continued. Based on her look, Ray must have displaced her son as the starting pitcher. She was the sort to haggle with the scorekeeper over how he judged her son's hits and plays, arguing to keep his statistics elevated.

The ump yelled, "Play ball!" and everyone quieted and turned to face the field. Ray stood on the mound, sporting his new red uniform like plumage. He wore his ball cap low, the brim nearly to his eyes, shadowing his face from temples to chin. As he reached out a gangly arm to receive the ball the ump tossed, he revealed muscles primed from daily push-ups. He bent low to make out the signals from the catcher. Ray shook off the first one and there was an intake of breath in the stands. Patricia hoped he knew what he was doing.

Ray approved the next signal with a businesslike nod. He started his motion, rising to full height, bringing his glove up, his elbows out, his hand with the ball tucked inside the glove in a pose that mimicked prayer. Then he brought the glove down and raised his knee, cocked his arm, kicked his leg, and fired. What came out of his hand was the nastiest fastball a twelve-year-old ever saw, moving like a perfectly aimed bullet. It smoked by the batter, high and tight, tying him up. He'd always been good, but Pete's coaching had improved him.

The batter raised a hand, stepped out of the box, shoved the dirt around with his cleats like a confused steer, then resumed his position in the chalked box, standing farther away from Ray this time. Beyond the plate, the fielders' chatter was tentative, not the full locust chorus it would be in summer's heat. The batter lowered his hand slowly, and Ray took the signal, wound up and threw. The batter swung, behind it by eons, knocked off balance by the force of his whiff. The third pitch moved something crazy, the batter flailed, and one of the dads in the stands exclaimed, "He's got a *slider*?" The ump crooned, "Steeeeriiiike three," clocking the batter out with a pump of his arm.

The pushy woman turned around and extended her hand to Patricia. "I'm Gloria Sandoval," she said, "the team mother." As they shook hands, Gloria's skin felt soft against Patricia's hand, chapped from repeated washing at the hospital. "Patricia," she said, "Ray and Mia's mother." Then came hands from everywhere for Patricia to shake, Gary Arlen, Janet Sanchez, Jo Randolph. Lupe fielded some of the handshakes, smiling and greeting people with the easy grace of a politician's wife.

Gloria continued talking as if no one else were speaking, "I'll enter Ray into the official team roster tonight and send out a new copy. You want to bring the Cokes next game? We take turns based on the batting order, so you should have been up today. But I guess you couldn't have known about that. Is this your daughter? Such a pretty thing."

"Thank you," Patricia said, when Gloria paused.

Mia looked at Gloria hard, then opened the battered spiral notebook she always carried with her and wrote something in it.

What would Salvador have thought of this—Ray transformed into a star overnight now that he was playing before an audience that could appreciate him. Several of the fathers that began the game sitting in the bleachers started pacing along the first base line fence for a better view. "The Z's won't know what hit them this year," one of the men said as he walked away. Salvador would have been with them, whistling the piercing trill he reserved for joy whenever Ray struck someone out.

If Salvador hadn't taught Ray how to throw, they might never have discovered Ray's gift. There were no hints that this skill ran in either family, though the Santillanos never had the free time to test their talent for games. But that was the thing with kids. They were so much more than merely the qualities of one parent added to those of the other. Ray and Mia were relentlessly their own people, capable of surprising Patricia on any given day.

The Pirates won easily, with Ray throwing four shutout innings before Pete subbed in another pitcher. For the trip home, Lupe ceded the passenger seat and control of the radio to Ray, in honor of his performance. Patricia rolled her window down to let the mild evening air rush in to ruffle her hair, and the stereo, set to Ray's favorite station, blasted skittering hip-hop beats, bass thumps that confounded the rhythm of her heart and made her feel younger.

Stopped at a red light near the Pollo Loco, Patricia reached over and slapped Ray on the thigh. "You were pretty sweet tonight," she said.

Ray shrugged.

"You shut those parents up pretty quick. I don't think I realized what you could do before."

"It was just four innings of a game that doesn't even count," Ray said. "That team isn't in our league."

"Don't diminish it." Patricia held up her hand as if to stop his words. The light turned green and she stepped on the gas. "Whenever we have something to celebrate from now on, we're going to celebrate it. Let's get Chinese takeout tonight."

"You're going to jinx me, talking like that," Ray said, looking off, speaking toward his window.

It sounded like something Patricia would have said. "I don't know how I didn't notice before," Patricia said. "It took Dufek sending us to this new team and seeing how the parents reacted. I knew you were good for the team you were on, but I didn't know you were special. I bet you were holding back on the church team, right? I don't know if I can take those parents on the Pirates, though. Such locos."

"Patricia, you're driving too fast," Lupe said from the backseat.

"Oh," she said, glancing at the speedometer. Fifteen over. "I guess I was excited," she said softly. She glanced at Mia's puzzled face in the rearview mirror. Patricia was tired of being sad. But apparently a little happiness made her act crazy.

"We can get takeout if you want," Lupe said, "but the kids will have to carry it over to Nino's to eat. We have that meeting at our house tonight, remember?"

"Oh yeah," Patricia said. She felt like a balloon letting all its air out, the rude noise it made the perfect expression of its diminishing state.

After the kids took the food over to Nino's, Lupe asked Patricia to help her arrange the living room furniture for the meeting.

"Can't I eat first?" Patricia's appetite had returned when she smelled the Moo Shoo Pork, and she hated to let it grow cold. Having her mother order her around reminded her of how she'd felt when she turned eighteen, raring to escape.

"There isn't time," Lupe said. "The game went on longer than I'd expected. If they hadn't done all of that strutting and preening to that music beforehand, we would have had plenty of time."

"I think that's just part of this new league." The doorbell rang. "Here come the hordes," Patricia said.

Lupe stuck a finger in Patricia's face. "You'd better get your attitude right about this. These people are taking time out of their lives to help you. Don't be so ungrateful."

Patricia reached up to grab Lupe's finger, but her mother took it away before she could catch it and went to answer the door. She felt herself regressing, turning back into the teenager that her mother saw her as, the girl she'd been before she'd met Salvador.

133

"Tío Tiger!" Lupe said, the tone of her voice like arms thrown open in welcome. "Come in."

Tío hugged Patricia and she kissed him on his scratchy cheek. The doorbell rang again and Patricia left to drag in the stools from the kitchen, leaving Lupe and Tío to greet. She wasn't ready to accept all these people in her home, whether they were there to help her or not.

"Patricia, you shouldn't be doing that!" said a bearded man with blond hair that grew just past the collar of his lumberjack shirt. He took the stool she was carrying out of her hands. "I can manage fine," she told him. But nobody heard, and several other men quickly assumed the task. She didn't even know the guy's name. How did he know hers? He put down the stool and extended his hand. "I'm Greg Thompson from Denver Cop Aware."

She shook his hand, pressed her mouth into a smile. "What's Cop Aware?"

"We keep tabs on the police, try to raise public awareness whenever they do something disgraceful like this." He shook his head. "These pigs keep us pretty busy."

She wanted to ask how he made a living doing something like that, but then someone grabbed another chair out of her hands. She felt like she should be shrouded in a black lace mantilla, weeping like *La Llorona*, sitting in the corner and fanning herself so she wouldn't faint.

Patricia retreated to the kitchen and snuck a couple of bites of her Moo Shoo Pork from the carton, tasting the salt on her lips. Lupe's people swarmed over her house, moving her furniture, settling themselves in, accepting the coffee Lupe offered and drinking it out of the delicate teacups printed with roses that Salvador had given Patricia for their second anniversary. One woman of about Lupe's age took a careful sip from her cup and imprinted it with her magenta lipstick. Patricia leaned her head on the doorframe.

"It looks like we're ready to begin," Lupe said as she walked across the living room over to where Patricia stood. Lupe guided her to a chair, saying, "Here's your seat, dear." Lupe never called Patricia "dear." She sank in the chair, surprised to see over two dozen people gathered in her living room.

"Go ahead, Tío," Lupe said.

The old man stood in front of the assembled crowd, dignified in a tie and tweed jacket. "Thank you all for coming. As you know, I used to be known around here as Tío Tiger—I never wanted to pass up a fight back in the seventies."

Tío was big in Denver's Chicano rights movement back then. Patricia spent boring dinners as a kid sitting at the table and pushing around the leftover peas on her plate while her father and Tío drank too many cans of Bud and talked about the old days. Lupe would never excuse Patricia from the table, insisting it was good for her to learn a little history. But it seemed like all Tío had done was stage elaborate protests at school board meetings—he had nothing to do with any of the bombs the radicals were planting back then. What good had all their protests done, anyway? With busing in place in the late seventies, the Anglos fled the district. The mayor ended busing in 1995, and the public schools immediately became more segregated than ever before.

"But my age has caught up with me these past few years," Tío continued, "and I'm going to have to share the leadership of this committee with a volunteer who has all the energy we're going to need. Lupe, would you join me?" Lupe rose and stood next to him, poised, her eyes bright.

"Hello, everyone. I speak for Patricia and our entire family when I say that we are deeply grateful to you all and touched by how many people have turned out for the first meeting of the Justice for Santillano Committee."

So that's what they were calling it. Patricia could picture the banners with the committee title in red, her husband's name transformed into something public and distant, like the poor murdered children whose names became laws.

"Seeing all your familiar faces makes me wonder why I ever moved to Arizona," Lupe continued. "I've decided to stay on for a while, to be involved with the committee."

This was the first Patricia had heard of it. She should have been angry that Lupe had made this decision without her, but instead she felt the acquiescence of a tired child being buckled in a car by her mother. She wasn't ready to be alone yet. She liked sharing her bed with Mia so that Lupe could use Mia's room, no matter how many times her daughter's bony elbows jabbed her awake in the night. Lupe always claimed she had moved to Arizona to escape the constant obligations brought by having so many friends and family members near, but here she was, heaping them on again.

"Now I thought we'd just brainstorm," Tío said, settling into a chair at the front of the room and taking out a notepad. "So go ahead, give me your ideas. We want to think of every possible action we can take."

After Tío and Lupe coaxed a bit, people started speaking out, suggesting ideas for picket lines around police headquarters, various legal actions they could pursue, calling the ACLU. Patricia looked from one speaker to the next, unable to think of anything constructive to add. It sounded like a revolution was brewing in her living room.

"I have a question I'd like to ask Patricia," Cop Aware Greg said, standing.

"Go ahead," she said.

"I was wondering, if it's not too painful for you to answer, did you know before this that Salvador owned a gun?"

Patricia cast her eyes down and swallowed, alarmed at how intimate the question felt. Before this ended, the particulars of her marriage would become like the contents of a junk drawer spilled onto the floor for all to see. "No," she said. "I mean, I guess he could have bought one without my knowing." She didn't want to go into anything about the separation with these people, though they all must have known about it because Salvador was killed in a different house. "It doesn't seem like him, to have a gun."

"We just got some documents released that show the cops didn't find gunshot residue on Salvador's hands," Tío said.

"Is it possible," Greg continued, "that the police could have planted the gun after the shooting to make it look like they'd been attacked?"

The people behind Patricia murmured. In moments of anger, Patricia had thought the cops planted the gun, but she'd never suggested it to Lupe or the lawyer. "None of us know exactly what happened except the police who were there and Salvador," she said.

"I've been looking into this guy who messed up the warrant," Greg said, his voice growing louder. "He's killed another Hispanic man prior to this, and a few years ago he beat up a teenager and called him a wetback."

Tío pointed his pen at Greg. "That's good thinking," he said. "We'll form a subcommittee to look into the possibility that the cops planted the gun." He wrote on his notepad. "We'll have to get access to the ballistics test results, see if we can trace the weapon that they claim Salvador pointed at them."

If Salvador didn't have a gun, that would absolve him of any blame, but it would also leave Patricia's children growing up in a city where the cops executed unarmed people. She worried for Ray especially, as he grew older, one day going out on the town, lashing out at the slightest insult, no matter who dealt it to him, without considering the consequences. She was trying to keep him safe, out of the orbit of Miguel and his uncles and their pack of fighting dogs. But the cops could just as easily find Ray behind the locked door of his home. Maybe they would move. Was there any place where this wouldn't happen?

Patricia held a hand to her mouth. "Excuse me," she said, rising and leaving the living room, feeling her mother's eyes on her and hearing the sympathetic murmurs—*poor thing, look what they've done*—as she walked to her bedroom.

She closed the door behind her. She picked up an old crumpled t-shirt of Salvador's that lay on the closet floor. She'd seen it there before but left it alone. She pressed the shirt to her face. Soft with wear, its color faded to battered blue, she rubbed it over her cheek and inhaled it with desperation. She searched for a scent that had nothing to do with the shampoo he used or the cologne he wore, or the smells of his labor—motor oil and road-crew sage. Those were fleeting imprints. It was his pure scent she sought in that shirt, the smell that concentrated while he slept. But it was gone. She sat on the bed, holding the shirt against her cheek, listening to the voices of the strangers that filled her house, mobilizing to protest the murder of a man that none of them really knew. She buried her head under pillows until she couldn't hear them anymore.

CHAPTER 11

Ed
April 21–22

Ed sat with his feet propped on the coffee table and turned up the TV volume with the remote control. The 10:00 news reported that activists had posted hundreds of signs in downtown Denver protesting the Santillano shooting. Claire hustled back and forth across the room picking up stray clothes, toys, and school supplies. When she passed in front of the TV, she punched it off. "I don't want to hear this." She had a cold and the skin under her nose was tender and pink. She swiped at her nose with a crumpled tissue.

"What if I do?" Ed asked, jabbing the power button on the remote. But the anchorwoman had moved on to another subject.

Three hours later, Ed couldn't sleep as he lay next to Claire, listening to the slight squeak that her congested nose made every time she took a breath. She smelled like Vicks VapoRub. Maybe he'd sleep better after an excursion.

Ed took his gun from the safe in the basement and then lodged it in the holster around his waist. It was almost 2 AM on a Friday night, and Ed headed north on Colorado Boulevard toward downtown. When he stopped at a light on Colfax, a crowd of kids poured out from a concert at the Bluebird Theater onto the street, teenagers wearing thrift-store t-shirts that bore slogans and emblems they disdained—4-H and Girl Scouts, rainbow-colored messages about keeping teeth healthy or staying off drugs. A skinny kid in black horn-rims straggled across the street before the light changed. He was wearing a faded Kansas City Royals t-shirt that dated from the era before the Yankees had resumed their sullen domination, the time when the Royals had Brett and Bo and Saberhagen. The kid wore it as a joke, and Ed thought that's it, he was through rooting for teams that couldn't win.

He took a left on Broadway and headed toward the capitol, and the city and county building. Claire wouldn't understand his urge to see the signs. She wanted to ignore the protests, but Ed needed to face them. The signs stuck up from grassy dividers in the middle of streets, lining Colfax, Speer Boulevard, and Civic Center Park. Ed squinted at them, reading all that he could make out from his headlights and the streetlamps above. They bore simple messages, in English and Spanish. "Blame Springer, Not His Victim." "Justice for Santillano." "Accountability."

The mayor was taking heat, and he'd probably allow the signs to remain for a few days to avoid provoking the protesters. If this kept up, the mayor might have to host a community grievance airing, or fire someone in the department. Ed kept expecting to see his own face on one of the signs. It would be a blurry, black-and-white mug shot, he decided, him with a five o'clock shadow, sweat on his brow, dilated eyes. The people driving by would glance at his face and judge him without ever once having been in that situation themselves. He'd like to drop a hundred of the people he protected every day into the middle of his nightmare and see how many pulled the trigger.

Ed drove a couple of slow laps around the signs. Cars behind him honked. He hit the brakes to read a banner-sized sign at the corner of Civic Center Park. Some punks in a souped-up Civic cursed him as they passed on the right. A beer can clinked against the asphalt. "RACIST COPS MUST BE STOPPED!" the banner read in lurid red paint. Ed stopped altogether, his knuckles squeezing the wheel. He sped up until the signs rushed past him, forming a solid strip of white in his periphery.

That was the first thing they did: call you a racist without knowing anything about you, without knowing how Ed grew up; going to schools where kids muttered *stupid honky* or phrases of indecipherable Spanish under their breath at him until he

140

proved he could play pickup basketball better than everyone else, and they finally allowed his entrance into a room to pass without comment. Without knowing how he felt every year during elementary school on Cinco de Mayo, when the girls wore bright Mexican dresses that twirled when they spun, edged with satin ribbons and frilled with lace, their dark hair braided in glossy loops behind their ears, practicing dance steps, moves that made the bottom of their skirts flare like ripening peonies. He envied the boys who would get to kiss them, the boys who wore the tight black pants with fake gold coins sewn down the side that one day a year when no one would call them pussies. The boys were flashy and tough, fought with little provocation, and started romancing the girls in the fifth grade. They made Ed feel like a kid, stunted and slow to become a man. They were all on the inside of something and Ed was out. They were secure in that community, that culture, safe in their belonging, sharing something rich that they didn't even seem to appreciate, calling him a racist without knowing anything about him, he who had no culture to watch his back.

Driving south toward home on deserted streets, Ed woke from a fraction-of-a-second nap in time to straighten out his car in the lane. He was approaching a Catholic church on Colorado Boulevard, the cross-topped building of perhaps the only tribe he could claim, so he pulled into the parking lot and fell dead asleep in his car until the sun heating his face through the windshield at daybreak woke him. He looked at his watch—half past six. Claire wouldn't be awake for another two hours, not on a Saturday. An elderly woman took a large set of keys from her coat and unlocked the heavy front door of the church. Ed jumped out of the car and followed her inside before the door swung shut.

She turned around in the foyer, startled. "May I help you?" she asked, holding the keychain in front of her defensively, with frail, blue-veined hands.

Ed groped for a reason a bleary-eyed man would follow an old lady into a church at dawn. He was like one of those homeless men he'd seen staggering off Colfax into the cathedral to escape the freezing weather the moment it opened its doors in the winter. They had to start locking the doors after bums began pissing in the holy water fonts and desecrating the marble busts of past bishops. "Confession," he muttered.

"Reconciliation?" she corrected him. "Open reconciliation hours are on Sundays from nine to ten AM. Do you have an appointment?"

He shook his head.

She looked him over. He was unshaven, wearing old blue sweats, his eyes red: every inch a bum.

Ed started to turn around to walk out when she said, "Well, I'll just go over to the rectory and see if Father Bill has some time for you."

She told him to wait in the confessional. Ed ducked into the tiny booth. He kneeled inside, thinking about something he'd learned in a psych class in college, about how people were always coming up with stories to make sense of their own actions. He'd camped out at a church all night, he'd followed an old lady inside, and so here he was, pretending he'd come for confession all along so that his brain wouldn't get confused. A card on the wall outlined the procedure and Ed was glad to see it, as he couldn't remember how to do this. The confessional's other door opened and the shadow of the priest moved behind the screen. Ed opened his mouth but couldn't speak. "Go ahead," the priest said, sounding irritated.

"Bless me, Father, for I have sinned," Ed read from the card. The priest blessed him and Ed crossed himself as the card instructed. "I confess to Almighty God, to Blessed Mary ever virgin, to all the Saints, and to you, my spiritual Father, that I have sinned," Ed read. He glanced at the door handle and considered bolting. The spicy smell of incense permeated the wood, taking him back decades to when he was a boy with nothing more than mild disobedience to confess.

"Go on," the priest said. "Tell me when your last absolution was."

"It's been—I don't know—twenty-five years or something since my last confession. Look, Father, can I just tell you what I've done?"

"All right."

"Father, I killed a man."

The bench on the other side creaked as if the priest were rocking back, consulting his mental list of what he was supposed to do in this situation. "Have you notified the authorities?" the priest asked, hesitant.

"I am the authorities," Ed said, "I mean, I'm a cop."

"And you shot him in the line of duty?" the priest offered, eager.

"He pulled a gun on me, and I shot him."

"Well, then," the priest said. "That isn't a sin."

"It feels like one." Ed started to explain his doubts about what had happened during the raid, the mistake on the warrant, and the protests, but the priest cut him off.

"I know this is a difficult time for you, but perhaps the church's teachings on this subject can ease your mind," the priest said. "Legitimate defense is a grave duty for those responsible for the lives of others. It is not a sin. You protect people. Now I'm sorry to rush, but I need to prepare for Mass."

"Look, the last time I was in one of these things was 1977," Ed said, rapping the wooden ceiling of the confessional with a knuckle. "I was fourteen years old, and my mother forced me to go in before Mass. She all but shoved me in there, and I didn't know what to say to the priest. But I finally said that I'd had impure thoughts, which was probably true, but I was saying it just to say something, to get out of there. And the father hits me with three rosaries and an Act of Contrition, which my mother made sure I did, I can tell you that. I don't know what the inflation rate is for this kind of thing, but all I'm saying is, I got three rosaries and an Act of Contrition for impure thoughts, and I don't get anything for killing a guy?" Ed raised his voice, "Not even one lousy *Hail Mary*?"

The priest remained silent for a while, a technique others had used before to calm Ed when he was yelling. "Praying the rosary might ease your mind," the priest said, "but you should know that what you have done is not a sin in the eyes of the church. Maybe you need some counseling. I can hear your anguish. But first, would you like me to absolve you of your other sins?"

"Other sins," Ed repeated. The confessional suddenly felt as roomy as a coffin. "No, thank you," Ed said. "I can handle them myself."

It was a little after 7 AM when Ed pulled into the driveway. Claire waited out on the porch in her bathrobe, her hair unbrushed, her face drained of color, her eyes as puffy as they'd been after long nights when Polly was an infant. He rushed up to her.

"Where were you?" she said, sniffling, either from the cold or because she'd been crying.

"Honey," Ed said softly, touching her face with his fingertips. He hugged her to his chest, working his fingers through the fuzzy bathrobe.

"Where were you?" she said, resisting his embrace. "I woke up in the middle of the night and you weren't there. Your car was gone. There are so many people out there who are angry at you."

"I'm sorry I scared you. I was at church," Ed said, the half-lie jumping out of his mouth easily.

She pushed away from him. "Tell me the truth."

"That is the truth. I was at church."

"All night?"

"I didn't want to wake you."

"So you went to church and stayed there all night? Jesus, Ed, that sounds like the kind of crap that people feed you at work all day. Can't you come up with something better?"

"I didn't stay at the church all night. I went driving first."

"Driving where? Where did you have to go at that hour?"

Ed opened his mouth to speak.

Claire held up a hand. "No, don't tell me. If what you were doing was something you couldn't tell me about last night, then I don't want to know."

"Honey, I didn't think you'd wake up before I got back."

She laughed. "And that makes it okay?"

"It's not what you're thinking," he begged. "I mean—what are you thinking?"

She turned and walked inside the house, letting the screen door slam in his face.

Twenty minutes later, Claire fixed pancakes for the kids, who wandered downstairs in their pajamas. She cracked eggs, measured flour, and beat the batter like she bore it a grudge. The kids must have been hungry because instead of watching cartoons until they were called, they sat on stools by the island in the kitchen, their heads propped in their hands, following their mother with their eyes. "Are you going to put chocolate chips in those?" E.J. asked her.

"Since when do I put chocolate chips in pancakes?" she asked.

"I hear that people do it," he said. "It's not like I'm crazy."

"Blueberries," she said. "We'll throw in some blueberries."

Blueberries weren't in season, but Claire produced a bag of frozen ones from the depths of the freezer and threw it on the counter. She was like a magician that way, how she could anticipate every need and cause the desired supply to appear out of nowhere. He couldn't remember ever running out of toilet paper since they'd been married. Ed sank down on a stool next to the kids and watched her, his fingers interlaced before him on the counter like a child awaiting punishment, but she didn't look at him until the batter was ready. She flung a pat of butter onto the hot griddle and met his eyes as it sizzled violently, as if to give him something to think about.

145

The kids held out their plates to receive the golden brown, steaming pancakes, and Claire divvied them up, one for each in a row to prevent arguments. Polly loaded hers with enough syrup for three people, taking a furtive glance at her parents as she squeezed the bottle to see if they would stop her—the youngest at a crowded table always like a coyote over her kill, leery of larger predators. Ed felt too sheepish to hold out his plate, but Claire walked over with a pancake on her spatula and flung it down in front of him.

"You'd better eat breakfast," she said, "the Unicorns have a game at 10:00."

"He knows we're playing the Dream Stars today, Mom," Polly said. "He's the coach."

Polly gave him too much credit, Ed thought, as he checked his watch. He'd completely forgotten.

The Unicorns' uniforms—silk-screened purple t-shirts—had arrived the day before. They'd played three games without them because Ed had neglected to order them at the beginning of the season, a detail he'd never overlooked with the boys. Claire finally took care of the uniform order. The girls asked about them constantly. He planned to distribute the t-shirts after the girls warmed up, but while he was helping Moe fix a busted rawhide lace on her mitt, Blondie noticed the cardboard box in the dugout. She pawed through the uniforms, and then held one up and shrieked, "Here's mine! Here's mine!" The girls stopped warming up and sprinted over to the box of uniforms, moving faster than Ed had ever seen them. Blondie began tossing the shirts out, and the girls jumped up and down and shouted as they caught them.

"Hey!" Ed hollered. "What the hell is going on here? Get your butts out of there!"

The girls froze. Polly looked down at the shirt in her hands, then up at Ed, stricken. The rest of the girls studied their shoelaces.

He'd used his command yell, the one that had gotten him in trouble with the boys he'd coached. A couple of mothers in the stands stared at him over ducked newspapers, judging him. What did they expect from a coach? How were the girls ever going to learn a little discipline if he mollycoddled them all the time? He took the uniform from Polly's hands. The other girls silently passed theirs.

Ed took a breath and told himself to speak in a moderate tone. "Blondie, did anyone tell you to get into that box?" It came out too loud. A couple of mothers stood.

Blondie shook her head and bit her lip.

"Ed," Claire whispered fiercely from behind the chain-link fence. "Watch yourself."

Ed sighed. Blondie wasn't used to hearing *No*, and would be a pain in the ass by the time she was fourteen, he could see. Skimpy skirts and red lipstick and secret fumblings in the dark, nothing to say to her mother that wasn't the piss and vinegar of backtalk and sass.

Or maybe she wouldn't. That was what was great about kids—they stored all their potential tightly within them like bulbs waiting for spring. All the decisions that would send them down one path or another were before them, and anything was still possible. Blondie moved the toe of her sneaker back and forth in the dust. "Well," Ed said to her, "honest mistake, right?"

She nodded so hard her pigtails swung back and forth.

"I guess we might as well pass these out now, then," Ed said. At this the girls raised their heads, turning their faces up to him, their spirits brightening. Moe and Curly exchanged smiles and Speedy clapped her hands.

"Okay," Ed said, "First up, Amelia," thinking, *Who the hell's Amelia?* Luckily, Larry reached forward to claim it. "Wait a minute," Ed said. Larry-Amelia withdrew her hand. "That's not right. These should have your last names on them. Who's ever heard of uniforms with first names on them?" He looked to Polly.

She shrugged. "When Mom ordered them, she called the league lady and that's what she said to do."

"First names on a *uniform?* Well, okay, if that's the way it's got to be." He tossed Larry her shirt. "I guess for tee-ball it's all right, but Unicorns, when you move up to softball, don't let them disrespect you like that." At least during the game, he could check the girls' shirts to see what their real names were so if he had to talk to any parents afterward they wouldn't figure out that he knew their daughter solely as one of the Stooges.

"All right," Ed said as he handed the last shirt to Lefty.

Blondie had already pulled hers over her head and the rest of the team wriggled into them as well.

"Now," he said, drawing his hands together, savoring the moment, "Laps!"

The game began, and like the Unicorns' other games it wasn't so much a competition as it was a display of two teams of six-year-old girls making a supreme effort to catch the ball without letting it pop out of their mitts, to swing the bat at the stationary ball on the tee without falling over, to run in the correct, counter-clockwise fashion around the bases. In the third inning, Ed walked in front of the other team's stands and heard the parents talking. "That coach is a cop," a woman announced. "He was in that shooting last month." Ed kept his head down, feeling like an inmate of an ant farm, under constant observation. He hoped Claire hadn't heard.

After that it felt good to see the Unicorns crush the other team. Tee-ball had lots of rules to help the game along if neither side could string together three outs—inning time limits, scoring limits, limits against batting around more than once, and the Unicorns used them all. The Unicorns extended their undefeated record on sheer speed from all those laps, they kept rounding the bases no matter where the ball was, and the fielders for the Dream Stars usually bobbled the play at the sight of a Unicorn galloping toward them. The whole production ended after an hour and a half with a round of grape soda and girls sitting willy-nilly in pairs in the outfield grass, braiding dandelions into each other's hair and tracing shapes on each other's backs for the other one to guess.

As the girls lined up to slap hands with the other team, Ed looked off past the stands. The reporter from the other day stood in the shadow of an oak, his hands in his pockets. He wore a baseball cap that didn't look broken-in, as if purchased for disguise, the flat brim shading his pink skin from the sun.

Ed dismissed the girls, swung open the door in the chain-link fence and marched up to the reporter. Claire called after him to stop but he kept walking. "You need to leave," he told the reporter.

"The park is public property," the reporter said, smirking as though pleased with the smell of his own fart.

Ed had to be careful, or he'd be quoted. "There's nothing for you to write about here," Ed said. "It's a tee-ball game."

The reporter took a notebook and pen from his pocket. "Did Santillano actually have a gun?" he asked, throwing it out there like a cherry bomb.

"This is not an interview." Ed yanked the notebook from the reporter's hands and tossed it on the ground.

Claire rushed over and picked up the notebook, dusted it off and handed it back to the reporter. "We were just leaving," she said, grabbing Ed around the wrist and tugging him away.

He walked off with her, but she wouldn't let go of him, like he was a child. He twisted his hand to isolate her thumb from her fingers and popped out of her grip.

"That hurt," she complained, looking like he'd slapped her.

"Just let go of me." Ed felt accused, when he hadn't done a single thing wrong.

That evening Ed and Claire bumped into each other as they cleaned the kitchen, silent, too aware of each other. "I need to get out of here," Ed said, grabbing his keys from the counter.

Claire trapped his hand on the counter with hers. "Where are you going this time?"

"To see Mitch." The keys dug into Ed's palm under Claire's pressure.

She stared at him for a while as if to see whether he'd change his story. Finally, she let go. "Ask if he's heard anything about when your leave will end."

Mitch had just returned from working overtime at a Rockies game and he was still in his uniform when he opened the door. Ed hadn't worn his in weeks. "You wear your uniform around the house now?" Ed asked.

"I'm still on duty," Mitch said. "It's Saturday night, Mavis is working dispatch, and I've got two teenage daughters. How are you doing?"

"Not too good."

"A double, then." Mitch poured a glass of whiskey on the rocks from the small bar in the corner of the living room and handed it to Ed. A car honked outside and Mitch froze. Mitch's youngest daughter, Mimi, a petite, fine-featured sixteen-year-old, pounded down the stairs. Mitch cut her off at the bottom of the steps, his legs in a sturdy cop stance, fists on his hips.

"You're not going to go out with him unless he comes up here and rings the doorbell like a gentleman," Mitch said.

Mimi tried to get around her father, faking him out with a feint to the left and darting right, but Mitch simply shifted his weight and stopped her.

"Let's see how long it takes the latest Einstein to figure it out."

Ed sipped his whiskey and watched through the window as the kid outside turned off his ignition and walked up the path toward the house, his head ducked between hunched shoulders.

When the doorbell rang, Mitch opened the door. "Yes?" he said.

"Uh," the kid said. "Is Mimi here?" He was skinny, all Adam's apple and elbow, with the sort of big-eyed, soft-jawed baby face that all the movie stars seemed to have these days.

"Yeah, she's here all right," Mitch said. He began to close the door. "Is that all you wanted to know?"

"Um, Mr. Roybal, I'm here to pick her up to go to a movie."

"I gathered that when you honked at her like she was some Colfax floozy." Mitch opened the door wide and the kid hesitantly stepped over the threshold.

"Sorry," he said, staring at Mitch's holster.

Mimi snuck a glance at the boy and gave him a shy little wave, fluttering her fingers at waist level.

Mitch drew a clipboard from the table by the front door and put on the reading glasses that he kept in his shirt pocket. "Name?" Mitch barked.

"Rick," the kid said.

Mitch looked at him over the top of his glasses. "Full legal name, son."

"Richard A. Miller," the kid said.

Mitch started filling out the chart on his clipboard. "Destination?"

"We're going to see a movie." When Mitch remained silent, Rick added, "at the Continental."

"Start time?" Mitch asked.

"8:00."

"That means it'll be out at 10:00, and you can have her back by 10:30."

"But Dad," Mimi said, "We were going to meet up with some friends after."

Rick shot her a terrified glance. "10:30 is fine, Sir."

"Make, model, year and license number of your vehicle?"

"It's a '93 Chevy Impala." Rick scratched his chin. "I think the plate begins with an 8?"

"I'll record it myself, Richard. At 10:31 if you aren't back with my daughter, I'll enter this information into the police database and find you. The city has eyes, son."

Mitch held the door open and followed the kids out to the car, saying, "Let me take a look at your driver's license, too," before the door swung shut behind them. The production seemed a bit

151

extreme, but then Ed wouldn't have wanted Rick taking out his daughter either. "Enjoy Polly while you can," Mitch said when he returned, "but down the line a few years, I've got a date night spreadsheet all formatted that I can email you."

Ed swirled the ice in his glass watching Mitch's household dramas, glad to forget his own problems for a moment. Mitch's older daughter Shelley glided down the stairs, dressed like Stevie Nicks, her gauzy black clothes billowing. "I don't know why she even bothers," Shelley announced. "I'm not going on any dates until I'm away at college. Far away. And then I'll go on many dates, Father, with totally inappropriate people."

Shelley's hair was two shades darker than Ed remembered and she wore it cut in a precise bob that sliced forward when she looked down. Her burgundy lipstick set off her pale skin. "May I have the keys to the Toyota, Father?" Something about the way she deliberately pronounced the word "Toyota" seemed to mock it.

"Where are you going?"

"Downtown. I have my poetry group meeting. We've been through this before."

Ed sipped his whiskey, enjoying the scene while knowing that his own combative time with Polly would be coming. Mitch had bitched when Shelley insisted on adding the second "e" to her name so that it would be spelled like the poet. "Remember that sickly guy who wrote poems about birds and crap that we had to read in high school?" Mitch had said. "That's who she wants to be named after. Not her grandmother. No, she's too good for that."

Mitch dug into his pocket for the keys. "Why can't you meet somewhere around home? Meet here—we built that rec room for you girls."

"Atmosphere is everything, Father."

"Shelley, how many times do I have to tell you to just call me Dad? Any boys in this group?"

She laughed. "I'm not interested in boys."

Mitch handed her the car keys, his ears crimson. Shelley made straight A's and never got into trouble, so Mitch couldn't do much to control her. Ed had seen Shelley hanging out at Paris on the Platte down by the river, a little bohemian coffee shop that poetical Denver kids had frequented for as long as Ed could remember, seeking a taste of nightlife in the city.

After he locked the door behind Shelley, Mitch leaned against it and said, "So that's my life."

"I'd trade you, these days," Ed said. "Do you ever think that what we do is over the top?"

"How do you mean?"

"I mean you giving poor Rick the third degree, me going ballistic on that reporter the other day." Ed threw the rest of his drink down his throat, savoring the burn. "He came to the Unicorns game today. After I'd told him to stay away from my kids."

"Maybe he's got a crush on you." Mitch collected Ed's glass and refilled it. "We know what's out there. What if something happened to one of your kids and you hadn't done everything you could think of to prevent it? It'd be as bad as those yahoo mothers in Boulder who don't get their kids vaccinated."

"I think I might end up like that guy you told me about, McGill, drifting down a Utah river for the rest of my life."

"Why do you say that?"

"I've been having nightmares. I'm fighting with Claire, I can't seem to do a thing right around her."

"That's women. Join the club."

"No, it's not just women." Ed reached for his refilled glass and Mitch handed it to him. "It's never been like this between us. I mean, today she grabbed my wrist and dragged me away from the reporter like I was five years old, then said I hurt her when I broke out of her grip. For a moment, I wished I actually did hurt her."

"But you didn't."

"No."

"Thoughts don't count. I'd be in trouble if they did."

153

"What if I won't be able to come back to work? I'm so jittery."

Mitch sat next to him on the couch. "Don't go thinking like that. When you start back up, I'll make sure we take it easy for a while. No answering hot calls or anything, just helping old ladies locked out of their cars. You can do that, can't you?"

Ed shrugged. "Old ladies are some of the worst."

"It's sitting around home that's eating you. When I was at court yesterday, I talked to one of the lawyers from the D.A.'s office, and he told me that they're going to issue their decision about your case this week."

"This week?"

"Yeah, you'll be back on the street in no time."

"Great," Ed said, trying to hide his worry by throwing back the rest of his drink, holding his nose in the glass until the fumes made his eyes water.

Chapter 12

Patricia
April 24

Patricia came home from work and found Lupe in the kitchen, her sleeves rolled to her elbows, scrubbing something in a sink full of soapy water. Just once Patricia would like to catch her mother with her feet propped up, eating potato chips and watching soap operas. The countertops in the kitchen shone, free of clutter except in the corner by the phone where Lupe had set up a station for her work on the committee, stacked high with papers, file folders, and notepads covered with Lupe's clear, even cursive.

"You can just use the dishwasher," Patricia said, throwing her car keys on the counter. "It works fine."

"These aren't dishes." Lupe reached into the water and held up one of Ray's trophies. "They were sitting in an evidence locker all this time."

"They were dusty?"

Lupe looked at Patricia. "You don't want to know what was on them." She turned back toward the sink.

Patricia fished out one of the soapy trophies. According to the plaque, Ray received it when he was in first grade, before his pitching became so good that the team started to win official league trophies. Still, the coach had always badgered the parents into chipping in enough money for participation prizes every year. This habit of rewarding kids whenever they did anything more ambitious than staring at the television seemed peculiarly American to Patricia. Salvador had never won a thing.

Patricia blew the soap bubbles off the batter's head, revealing a golden face with a vacant expression, the boy's gaze on a nonexistent ball. "How did you find them?"

"I called around," Lupe said, handing Patricia a dishtowel. "John had to submit his request for their release on legal letterhead before the police let us have them."

"Did they give you anything else?"

"Just some of Salvador's work uniforms."

Patricia toweled off a trophy, picturing the box of Salvador's final belongings sitting in a cold basement warehouse. "No photographs or letters?" She couldn't look at Lupe as she asked the question.

"No. Why?"

Patricia said nothing as she rinsed another trophy in warm water. The figure was the same skinny one in tight pants, year after year, with thin lips and a patrician nose. Under his batting helmet, he must have been blond, modeled on some idealized boy derived from Lassie or Hardy Boys books. Ray had once brought home a basketball trophy with a black player on it, but they still had the poor kid in an afro, striped socks pulled to his knees like it was 1972.

"The police are acting like they have something to hide," Lupe said.

"More than they've already hidden?"

"I wouldn't trust those bumbling thugs to direct traffic," Lupe said, wringing out a dishrag with a sharp twist.

"You adored Officer Smithson," Patricia said, reminding her of a charming policeman who used to eat at their restaurant, using a napkin to wipe salsa away daintily from his Clark Gable moustache. Patricia's parents served cops platters of complimentary enchiladas, enticing them to patrol the block more frequently.

"They're not like him anymore," Lupe said, an edge to her voice.

"I've never seen you take Salvador's side like this before," Patricia said.

After Lupe found out Patricia and Salvador were engaged, she used to call from Arizona and ask what she saw in him. What Patricia saw in him made no sense when she tried to articulate it. When they got engaged, Patricia was twenty, had never had a boyfriend before, and it was as if Salvador had stepped out of some dream of what a gentleman should be, dressed in clothes that fit instead of baggy *pachuco* gear, walking like an unhurried cat, so unlike the boys her age who led with their chests, swinging clenched fists around. Salvador never failed to open her car door first before letting himself in. He always gave her his elbow to hold when they walked down the street, and he brought her a glass of water when she said she was thirsty. But all that sounded stupid when she was trying to explain it to Lupe. "Child," Lupe had told her, registering none of it, "you don't marry the first man who brings you a glass of water."

Patricia pulled another trophy out of the sink. She knew she shouldn't pick at an old fight with Lupe, but she couldn't help it. "Why didn't you figure out that bad-mouthing Salvador would drive me toward him?"

"You were my only child," Lupe said, "What did I know?" Lupe scrunched the corners of her eyes the way she did when a headache was coming on.

Patricia felt like thunderheads were building inside her chest as she thought of the different life she might have had if she'd listened to Lupe and dropped Salvador. The first thing Patricia planned to do if Ray ever started dating a girl she didn't like was invite her over for pie. Every afternoon, until the girl grew too fat for Ray to like her anymore.

"Salvador wasn't my first choice," Lupe continued, washing another trophy. "He was uneducated and I wanted you to finish school first."

"I wouldn't want Mia to marry too young," Patricia allowed. Once Patricia had kids and that desperate instinct to protect them gripped her, she was able to perceive an extra layer to every memory, the inscrutable logic behind what her parents and grandparents had done suddenly revealed.

"Salvador is my blood now," Lupe said, "the father of my grandchildren. I'll do whatever I can to clear his name."

"He might have cheated on me," Patricia said quietly.

"What?"

Patricia walked over to the box of his belongings, hidden behind the trashcan under a pile of newspapers, and took out the photo of Salvador with the woman and the girl who might well be Salvador's daughter. "They gave this to me at the morgue."

Lupe inspected it. "You don't know this woman?"

Patricia shook her head, her eyes stinging.

"He talked to your dad a lot. Maybe we should ask him about it, see if there's another explanation." Lupe looked lost then. "Or we could just let it be."

Patricia took the photo back. Salvador had his arm around the woman and the girl stood in front of them, each of them wrapping an arm around her. She put the picture back in the box and piled the newspapers on top. "Marrying Salvador was probably the least rational thing I ever did," Patricia said. She hadn't inflicted little rebellions on her mother like most girls: applying eyeliner too thickly, ditching class, or sneaking out through the window at night to do the forbidden thing. She'd rebelled only once, with a decisive gesture that she'd called love.

They had been dating for a year when Salvador said he had to return to Mexico for a few months. He told her about the *Candelaria* fiesta the village held every year when its fathers and sons returned from the States. There would be a carnival with bumper cars and a roller coaster, paid for with the money the men wired home. There would be a carousel with small replicas of Volkswagen Beetles like the ones the cabbies drove in the cities, each car with a different shade of muted pastel. His little sisters loved to ride it. "My mother needs to see me," he said, holding Patricia's hand. "She worries."

"Of course," Patricia said. She felt sick. "Don't go," she whispered. She was in college and couldn't leave.

"Don't worry *mi vida*." He kissed her forehead. "When I come back, we'll get married."

She didn't know about that. She was only twenty. Too young to get married, in this country. While he was gone, her friend Vickie from the flower shop tried to distract her by taking her out to a new club, Rock Island, where they danced to music that Vickie liked—Bauhaus, The Cure, The Sisters of Mercy—and Vickie flirted with men. On the dance floor, a man with died black hair rested a presumptive hand on the small of Patricia's back. Patricia jerked away from him and went to sit by herself at a dark table, sipping a Coke until Vickie agreed to go home. "I know," Patricia said as Vickie drove, "I'm no fun. But I can't help it."

She spent their three months apart crying too often and sleeping too little and when he came back she accepted his ring, with its tiny shopping mall diamond. He had a five-inch gash on his arm that had been stitched and partly healed, an angry pink line that he said he'd gotten from an accident with the tractor on the ranch. Now she wondered if he'd been lying even then.

Patricia wiped a soap bubble off her wedding ring with a clean dishtowel. She'd never stopped wearing it, not even in the worst times, when he no longer brought her glasses of water, when he stayed away too long. Lupe fished another trophy out of the water. Patricia and Lupe worked side by side until they had rinsed and dried all of them, and then Patricia arranged them on the kitchen table. They were made of nothing but cheap plastic and fake stone, but they shone like new boys, cleansed of trouble, erased of whatever they had seen in the room Salvador died in.

Ray arrived home from school and opened the refrigerator, but then noticed the trophies glinting on the table. He let the refrigerator door swing closed. He faced down the trophies as he would an opposing batter.

"They're all there," Patricia said. "One for every season."

"You've won a lot of prizes," Lupe said.

"Do you want me to help you carry them to your room?" Patricia offered.

"Nah," he said, shaking his head, shoving his hands in his pockets so she wouldn't try to hand him a trophy.

"Baby, what's the matter?" She reached out to him, extending a hand to feel his forehead.

He skirted her touch, drifting back toward the threshold of the kitchen. "I don't want them anymore."

"What? Your grandma went to a lot of trouble to get these, Ray. You need to thank her."

"I'll win more," he said, throwing her a look, serious and firm. "Those ones are jinxed."

Patricia pulled out a chair and sat, propping her elbows on the kitchen table and holding her face in her hands. Of course he didn't want them. They'd been in the room where Salvador died. There were as good as haunted.

"I'm sorry," Patricia said, turning to Lupe. "I guess he changed his mind." She looked at the trophies again, lined up on the table, the tiny lips of the golden boys that topped each one sealed by the mold that had formed them, their eyes stuck forever open. They were worthless, mute witnesses that you could shake and shake and still they would never tell what they knew.

"It's okay," Lupe said, resting her hands on Patricia's shoulders. "I'll find a box and we'll store them somewhere in case he wants them later."

"Can I have one?" Mia said.

She had been skulking around in the corner, not speaking up. These days, Mia frequently turned up in rooms Patricia thought were empty.

"Go ahead," Patricia said, "Ray doesn't want them."

Mia reached out for the tallest one, then paused, and settled on one with a shiny purple base. She cradled it in her arms, stroking the batting helmet of the boy on the trophy with her index finger.

Patricia followed Mia to her room. Mia had been bunking with Patricia so Lupe could sleep in Mia's room, but she liked to visit her toys after school. Mia reserved one shelf solely for El Johnway and the wooden plaque Salvador had made her with *El Johnway* burned into it. She moved El Johnway and his name plaque to the left and set Ray's old trophy on the right, spacing them for balance.

Patricia patted the bed next to her and Mia sat down. She held Mia and stroked her braids, letting them slide through her fingers. Her hair was thick and shiny and Patricia loved to fuss over it, though Mia would often run away now when she saw her coming with a ribbon and a brush.

"What did you learn at school today?" Patricia asked.

"I don't remember."

Patricia kissed Mia on the part in her hair. "Do you want to talk to someone, a feelings doctor?" Patricia asked, using the term Mia's teacher had offered.

Mia hid her face in Patricia's lap. Her untied shoelaces bore a repeating pattern, *love* ♥ *love*.

When Mia's teacher had called Patricia to set up a meeting earlier that week, Patricia asked her to repeat herself to make sure she'd heard right. "This is Mia's teacher, not Ray's?" she'd asked. Patricia only met Mia's teachers during conferences at the beginning of the year, when they would croon about her, displaying her neat, perfect papers. The way the teachers gushed and cooed over Mia made Patricia wonder just how derelict the other kids were.

"Mia's schoolwork is as excellent as it's ever been," Miss Burson, Mia's third grade teacher had reported. "I'm just a little concerned about the way she's been socializing this year." The teacher suggested Mia visit the school counselor who came two times a month to meet with students. Patricia took the counselor's card, but wondered whether talking to her on the two or three occasions she'd be at the school before it let out for the summer would do Mia any good.

She considered forcing Mia to sign up for some activity that would make her spend more time outdoors, with other kids, away from her books and the notebooks she piled in the corner of Patricia's room. But maybe the teacher was right, and Patricia should find the kids some counseling. Her health insurance wouldn't cover that, and there was no money to spare for it. She could ask the committee to help, but then she'd be begging.

She felt her daughter's warm cheek on her lap and whispered, "For you I'd beg, baby girl. Just say the word."

Mia closed her eyes and hummed a lullaby that Salvador used to sing. Patricia whispered the first verse, holding Mia's hand, "*Qué linda manito que tengo yo, qué linda y blanquita que Dios me dio.*"

"Patricia," Lupe said from the doorway.

"Do you need the room, Grandma?" Mia asked.

"No sweetie, I just need to talk to your mom."

In the kitchen, Lupe told Patricia that their lawyer had called. "Our signs didn't do much good," she said. "The D.A. decided to file charges only against the cop who falsified the warrant. And he's charging him with felony perjury, not manslaughter. He said the other cops were justified when they shot Salvador."

"What does that mean?" Patricia demanded. "Does that mean it's over, that all the cops will get off?"

"No," Lupe said, firm. "We're calling a meeting tonight."

"Give me that phone list," Patricia said, taking the paper from her mother. "I'll do it myself." She wanted to act, even though she hesitated before dialing the first number like a schoolgirl calling a crush.

Lupe and Patricia were arranging chairs for the meeting when Ray wandered out, dressed in his uniform. "I need you to take me to my game now, Mom," he said. "We have to be there in fifteen minutes."

"I forgot," Patricia said, setting down the chair she was lugging.

"You can't leave now," Lupe said. "People will begin arriving any minute."

"Come on, Mom," Ray wheedled. "I can't miss a game. Nobody misses a game."

Both of them looked at Patricia, their eyes challenging, ready to fight her if she chose to oppose them, waiting for her to speak.

Patricia thought a moment. Normally she'd be happy to ditch one of Lupe's meetings for a baseball game, but she was incensed about the D.A.'s decision. "Let me give Coach Pete a call," she said. "He lives nearby. Maybe he can pick you up."

"No!" Ray shouted.

"I'm sorry. We've got an emergency here. I'd never miss your game otherwise, you know that."

He followed her to the phone, so close he stepped on the back of her shoe. "Come on Mom, just take me yourself."

Pete sounded like he would have been happy to make a pit stop by Mars, if that were necessary, to bring his star pitcher to the game. "It's all arranged," she said, hanging up. "He's on his way and he'll be by to get you in a couple of minutes."

Ray stared at her. "No one else gets a ride with the coach," he said. "Everybody else just gets a ride with their dad. And do you know who sits in the stands, cheering for them? Their dads. Now I don't even have you." He jerked up his equipment bag and opened the door. "At least Miguel is going to be there," he said before letting it slam behind him.

Patricia stood rooted in place, desperate to go to him, make things better, take him to the ballfield herself. She wondered if it was true about Miguel or if he'd just said it to worry her. Miguel didn't seem like the baseball-watching type. Maybe she should go to the game to make sure Ray didn't go home with the wrong person. Pete's GTO roared up outside and she walked over to watch from the screen door. The car radio blared AC/DC's "You Shook Me All Night Long" through open windows, but when Ray approached, Pete changed the channel to Ray's favorite hip-hop station. He had a power, that boy, leaving suckers on their knees in his wake. As Patricia watched the muscle car drive out of sight, she sang Salvador's lullaby. "*Qué lindos ojitos que tengo yo, qué lindos y negritos que Dios me dio.*"

"You did right," Lupe said. "There are some things more important than baseball."

"Not for Ray there aren't."

163

Mia shot out of her room and ran to the front door. "Where did Ray go?"

"To his game. His coach took him," Patricia said. "It's all right."

"But I wanted to go. I always watch him play." She held El Johnway, ready for the game.

"Just this once, I'm going to send you over to Nino's house instead. The people will be coming for the meeting soon."

"I'm not leaving," Mia said.

"It'd be boring for you. Wouldn't you rather play with Nino?"

"You can't make me go. I want to hear what you talk about."

"It'll just make you sad, baby."

Mia gave Patricia a firm look. "I'm already sad."

"It's fine, Patricia," Lupe said. "It might be helpful for her to hear what we're doing for her father. She can even take notes. You like to take notes, don't you, Mia?"

She ran to fetch her notebook.

The house filled with perfume and cologne as the committee members arrived, piling their coats on Patricia's bed, the heat of their bodies raising the temperature of the room. Patricia took coats, fetched coffee, and pecked Tío on the cheek. Tío Tiger and Lupe sat at the front, facing everyone, and Patricia dragged her chair up to sit beside them.

"Are you sure you can handle it this time?" Lupe asked.

"Absolutely," Patricia said, hoping that was true. Mia sat cross-legged at her feet, and Patricia rested a hand on her shoulder. She was the mom, she told herself, she had to set an example.

Tío stood to begin. "It looks like we've got a new little committee member up here tonight. That's good, because she reminds us what we're all here for. This child's father was murdered by Denver cops, and as we saw today, they're not going to punish their own. That leaves it to us."

164

"What are we going to do about it?" Mia demanded.

"That's a good question," Tío said. "Any ideas?"

If Mia could speak up, Patricia could too. Patricia stood. "My mom tells me we're filing a lawsuit against the city, and there's a subcommittee trying to get the FBI to investigate the shooting as a civil rights violation. The mayor has refused to meet with us so far, and the police department hasn't made any move to change its policies because of this. I don't think we've been vocal enough." She glanced over at Lupe, who gave her an encouraging nod. "We need to get more people involved so that the city can't ignore us," she continued. "Maybe with a rally at the capitol." Patricia felt her face grow hot, and sunk down in her seat.

"That's a great idea," Tío said.

"When should we have it?" Cop Aware Greg asked.

Patricia thought about how to put their cause before the most people. "The scheduling would be pretty tight," she said, "but there would be no better day for this than Cinco de Mayo." Denver held the largest Cinco de Mayo celebration in the country, attracting over a hundred thousand people to Civic Center Park near the capitol building. "This year people need to come away with more than a stomach full of green chile."

Everyone agreed, and Tío began to give assignments, but Patricia didn't listen as Mia looked up at her. She held Mia's cheek and sang softly, *"Qué linda boquita que tengo yo, qué linda y rojita que Dios me dio."*

CHAPTER 13

Ed

April 24

Ed looked out at the landscape as he walked toward Ruby Hill field for the Z's first game. Denver began life a few miles north of Ruby Hill as a collection of shacks that white prospectors threw up in an old Arapaho campground in the South Platte valley, outlawing the adobe favored by the Mexican gold panners who'd settled the area first. Ruby Hill Park sat along a cut bank of the Platte, separated from the water by a stretch of train tracks. The Arapaho once climbed the bluff for a view of the valley that spread out below, but now the hill served for a sight of the complex of baseball fields, and beyond that the city's skyscrapers. Santillano's family was out there somewhere in the city that had begun to feel too small. Ed might stand in line behind them at the gas station, he might pull up next to them at a red light, he might roll past their front yard on a patrol and not even know it.

Ed nodded hello to Pendergrass, Kitagawa, and Badgett. Chase Reed, the young assistant coach, stood chatting with the dads, his dusty cleated foot resting on the lowest bench. Word was he'd played second base for a California junior college before dropping out. A satin tarp attached to the back of the dugout snapped in the wind, gleaming in the Z's colors, a navy background with ZENITH HOMES spelled out in the sober gray of a banker's tie. The Z's expensive uniforms bore substantial double-layer appliquéd wording, plain and nameless in a way that reminded Ed of the Yankees.

"Look," Chase said, nodding toward a spot beyond the bleachers.

A bantam of a man with a thick black beard stood in the shadow of a sapling. He wore mirrored sunglasses and tight red polyester shorts that marked him unmistakably as a coach or a lunatic.

Boyd emerged from the dugout and approached the bleachers while the boys ran laps in the outfield. The dads sat up straight like they were about to be graced with a visit from a dignitary. Boyd drew his customary pre-game stogie from the back pocket of his navy coach shorts and clenched it in his mouth in a way that emphasized his bulldog resemblance. He nodded to Chase, who produced a Zippo from his pocket and lit Boyd's cigar.

"Look who showed up," Chase said.

"Pete." Boyd said, unsurprised.

"Isn't that the Pirates' coach?" Dr. Kitagawa asked. "Does he think we can't see him?"

"He wants us to see him," Chase said. "He's just trying to rattle us." Chase spit out a spray of barbecue-flavored sunflower shells, and the mess landed inches from Ed's feet. He reminded Ed of any number of good-looking punks he'd arrested over the years. They didn't smirk as much after a night in lockup.

"Let him scout us," Boyd said, the pungent cloud of cigar smoke thickening around him. "We've got no secret weapons."

"Who are the Pirates?" Ed asked, and everybody looked at him like he'd just asked who John Elway was.

"That's right," Darryl Pendergrass said, "You're new to the league. Where did you have your boys playing last year?"

"I coached them on a PAL team," Ed confessed, embarrassed to admit his sons came from a less competitive league, and that he had coached at that diminished level.

"It's a good thing Boyd scouts PAL games," Pendergrass said. "We're going to need Jesse's bat and E.J.'s speed."

Ed nodded, thinking of the first time he met Boyd, a year earlier, after a game in which E.J. had stolen home and Jesse had hit a monstrous dinger that dented someone's car in the lot beyond the field. Boyd had approached Ed after the kids dispersed and handed him a business card. "Ralph Boyd," it read, "Coach."

"The Pirates are enemy numero uno," Chase said, making a gun with his hand and aiming it at Pete. "Their coach runs a pizza joint on Pecos. They win half the championships, we win the other half."

"That statistic is historic," Boyd said, stubbing out his cigar on the side of a metal trash barrel. "The Pirates haven't won districts for three seasons. Their team batting average wasn't even .275 last year."

Ed pictured Boyd up all night working out the stats for every team in the league, a cigar in his mouth, his back bent as he typed numbers into a spreadsheet glowing on the computer in the dark.

"Yeah," Chase said, "but I heard Pete's found himself a pitcher this year. The Pirates scrimmaged Holly Inn and no one could touch the kid."

"Where's he from?" Boyd asked.

"The north side. His name's Maestas. No one's ever heard of him, and this kid turns up throwing heat like he's sixteen."

"Maybe he *is* sixteen," Hank Badgett said. "Did Pete turn this kid's birth certificate in to the league? He probably knows someone who would falsify birth records."

"In exchange for what?" Ed asked. "Free pizza?"

"I think the kid's legit," Chase said. "I saw him throw at the Pirates' first scrimmage." He shook his head and whistled. "Too bad we only scout south Denver."

"We play the Pirates two weeks from Tuesday," Boyd said. "We'll have to throw them fastballs for days, if Maestas is really as fast as you say."

"He's got a slider, change-up, and curve." Chase said. "I've heard he throws eighty."

"A twelve-year-old?" Boyd said as he scratched a pattern in the dirt with the toe of his shoe. "That's uncommon."

"That's what I hear."

"How do you know all this, anyway?" Boyd asked. "You still seeing that girl with a brother on Pete's team?"

Chase shrugged. "Now and then. When she's got something to say that I need to know."

Boyd returned to the field. "All right, men," he boomed to the boys. "Line up for warm-up."

Ed missed that, calling out his "men." He didn't get the same rush, rallying the Purple Unicorns. In the bleachers, moms marked their territories with stadium blankets and their children sprinted off with each other the second they were turned loose. Ed checked his watch. Claire should have been at the field by now. She wouldn't punish him by missing their boys' first game, would she?

Ed tried to explain to her that his staying out all night was an accident. His only defiance was in seeing the protesters' signs. He kept calling her at work to talk to her alone, but she was always busy, and put the phone down once so that he heard her laughing with the orthodontist. The orthodontist made so much money, he worked only four days a week. He'd talked of cutting that to three, which would reduce Claire's hours and paycheck. Ed never doubted Claire before, but since his job was in jeopardy he'd started to wonder if Claire would replace him if he got fired.

He scanned the park for Claire, seeing only women he didn't know, hauling their belongings from the parking lot. The ump called "Play ball!" and Ed turned around to face the field. He felt jittery. What was he nervous about? He wasn't coaching. "Come on Z's!" he hollered as they took the field, a little too loudly, judging from the way the parents around him reared back. Ah, screw them. Ed let out a piercing whoop.

"There you go!" Pendergrass said, pounding him on the back with a meaty hand. "Ed's got his game face on."

Jesse, behind his catcher's mask, took up the cheer, firing up his team. "All right Z's," he barked out in an artificial baritone that he didn't fully own yet. "Play's at one. Let's go one-two-three now." Jesse settled into his crouch and started up his patter to his pitcher, Matt Kitagawa. "Come on now Kid, *rockanfire* now Kid, *whaddoyousay* now huh?"

Kitagawa jammed the opposing team's batter into hitting a dink grounder, and Tyrell Pendergrass fielded the ball and threw the batter out at first. A hand grabbed Ed's shoulder. Ed's fingers moved instinctively toward his holster as he turned to see Claire behind him. Her auburn hair caught the sunlight. She looked good in her work clothes, a crisp blue shirt and a pencil skirt.

"Come with me," she said.

"The game just started," Ed said. "Can't it wait?" He tried to think of a way to delay her revealing whatever decision she'd reached after three days of avoiding him.

"Come on," she said, and began walking away from the crowd, the way she did when the kids were being stubborn. She didn't beg, she just gave her order and expected it to be followed.

"Okay, this is far enough," Ed said when they reached the top of the hill. A few paces away, Polly rolled with other little girls, giggling, bits of grass in her hair. How awful it would be not to live in the same house with his children. "Go ahead."

Claire stood looking at him, a serious expression on her face. Then she smiled, actually smiled, a sight Ed hadn't seen for weeks. He felt like he was driving over a fresh-paved road, all the potholes smoothed over, the asphalt clean. Ed smiled too.

"What are we smiling about?" he asked.

"The D.A. decided not to press charges against you."

"That's it then? I can go back to work?"

"You can start back tomorrow. There's still a procedural review, but the chief's secretary said officers are almost never sanctioned once they've been cleared by the D.A."

"So nothing is going to come of the mistake with the warrant?"

"The D.A. is prosecuting Springer, but that has nothing to do with you."

Ed pulled Claire to him and kissed her.

"So you're happy?" she asked.

"Hey, of course," he said, but happy wasn't what he would call it. His thoughts were a confusing jumble of elation, dread, relief and fear. Something didn't feel right about the whole thing ending so easily. Ed remembered Springer complaining that a place he'd liked to hike, Eldorado Canyon, was suddenly "overrun with Mexicans. They've got their huge families stuffed into their trucks so they only have to pay one entrance fee, and they take over all the picnic areas by the river, leaving their dirty diapers and trash around. All they do is reproduce, get fat, and strain the social system." Maybe Springer had picked Santillano's house because there were so many Mexicans living in it, and figured there would be something inside to justify their entrance. If so, he'd get what he deserved. As for Ed, the law wouldn't punish him, but maybe something else would.

The next morning Ed studied himself in the bathroom mirror and flexed his muscles to see if he could detect any signs of them. A bicep seemed to move somewhere underneath a layer of flesh, as if it were afraid to show itself. He poked at his white belly. It didn't resist.

Claire sat on the edge of the bed in her bathrobe.

"Why are you up already?" Ed asked.

"I wanted to see you off." She rubbed her face against his freshly shaved cheek, her skin soft against his. She inhaled the scent of his shaving cream.

Claire had laundered his uniform even though it had already been cleaned weeks before. She watched him as he put it on, but the audience embarrassed Ed. They weren't newlyweds anymore; they had agreements. He never referred to or touched the slight, below-the-belt pouch that having three children gave Claire, and she never mentioned the latent bald spot that—if his dad's example was a guide—would one day claim Ed's hair. Their marriage was built on these conscious omissions—the moment you mentioned them, the kindness of averted eyes ceased and the whole thing could collapse.

He turned his back to her as he put on his uniform. The waist pinched, and the fabric of his shirt pulled a little between the two bottom buttons. He always ragged on Mitch about the importance of conditioning, and now here Ed was, fat and out of shape. Every time Mitch bought an extra burrito from the ladies outside Coors Field, Ed would remind him that no responsible cop should grow winded when he chased a suspect. If he grew too weak he might violate the first rule of police work: to go home alive at the end of your shift.

He poked at his stomach and Claire came up behind him. "Oh, stop fussing," she said, "you look great."

"Mitch is going to give me so much shit."

"Well, just give him some back." Her whole attitude toward him had softened, like she only loved him when she could send him off to work.

Ed kissed his children goodbye while they slept. He didn't always do this, but his existence felt tentative since he'd killed Santillano, and every kiss he planted on his family sent a prayer shivering through his brain that it wouldn't be the last one. Jesse already looked like a teenager asleep, a little greasy, sunk in slumber, his forearm draped over his eyes and a pillow on top of that forming a head cave to block the morning light. Wiry E.J. slept on his side, curled in a defensive posture, clutching a pillow to his stomach. Polly slept flat on her back like a drunken lord, arms thrown wide, mouth hanging open.

Mitch was waiting for Ed in the parking lot when he arrived at the precinct. "Welcome back, buddy!" he said, then noticed Ed's proto-paunch, easily visible in the uniform Ed hadn't worn for weeks. "Hey, Edward," Mitch said, patting Ed's stomach where the buttons of his uniform strained, "looks like this could be the beginning of a beautiful friendship. You, me, it, and the burrito lady."

Ed shrugged off Mitch's hand. "Cut it out."

"Someone hasn't had his coffee yet. But that's okay, because I've got presents for you." He opened the door of their patrol car, and handed Ed a steaming coffee mug. "New titanium coffee mug in an attractive Kelly green shade," Mitch said, "filled with

7-Eleven sludge, the way you like it. And a pine tree air freshener," he said, flicking a cardboard tree hanging from the rearview mirror, "to keep you from griping about my smelly feet."

"Thanks," Ed said. "But isn't it against the rules to hang that thing from the mirror?"

"Since when have you cared about rules?"

In the briefing room, the watch commander announced, "If everyone hasn't already noticed, O'Fallon is back with us today." Officers all around Ed clapped and whistled. Ed stared at his hands folded in his lap. Their cheers made his unease grow. He'd still killed a man whose house he never should have entered. The D.A. couldn't wave a wand and make the consequences of that stop. Ed had trouble paying attention as the commander listed the incidents that were carrying over from the previous shift.

"We're just going to ride the radio today," Mitch said as they walked to their car. "No Code 3's. We'll ease you back in until you're good as new."

Ed's uniform constricted his stomach when he sat in the passenger seat. They listened to the radio for a while. The dispatcher ran through a number of situations of the kind that Ed used to jump on—high-risk car stops, shots fired, a possible child abduction.

"A child abduction?" Ed said, leaning forward. "Come on, we've got to get in on that."

"Let somebody else be the cowboy for once. It's probably just a dad bringing the kids back from visitation five minutes late."

"What if it's not?"

Mitch looked at him squarely. "In case you missed it, it's in the same neighborhood where you shot Santillano."

Ed fell back. He thought of the neighbors who had stared at him as he walked out of Santillano's house. "Okay," he said. "Noise complaints and grandmas."

The dispatcher began, "We've got a report that an elderly female at 1545 Wabash Street has been unresponsive to the phone and doorbell."

Mitch leaned in. "Bingo!" he said when the report was through. "We've got an old lady, certainly weakened, possibly missing, possibly dead. Not likely to give us too much trouble."

"Some of the worst trouble comes from the dead," Ed said, thinking of the time a few years earlier when he'd entered a hot, reeking trailer in the middle of July on a missing person call. Just in time to witness a decomposing body explode from the build up of its internal gasses.

Ed followed Mitch toward the apartment complex and willed the woman to be alive, in part because it would spare him stacks of paperwork, but mostly because he wasn't ready for another dead body yet.

Inside the building an obese, balding man with a droopy moustache wearing a faded Hawaiian shirt as big as a tent rushed toward Ed. "Thank God you're here!" the man shouted. "My mother won't answer the door, and I've misplaced the key. Oh, I'm so stupid, stupid!" He hit his face with a fist.

"Easy there, friend," Ed said, reaching out to stop his hand. *Friend?* How did he used to handle it, convey authority and spread calm?

Mitch shot Ed a glance and picked it up from there. "We're going to find her, don't you worry."

"Mom!" The man howled at the door, pounding it. "Open the door and let me know you're okay."

"Why don't you just stand back a bit and let us take over," Ed said, finding his footing. "What's your mother's name?"

"Sandra Jenkins."

"Mrs. Jenkins?" Ed called through the door. "Can you hear me? Your son is concerned about you." He turned to the man. "Are you sure she's in there?"

"Her Oldsmobile is parked out front and she didn't show up for her aquacise class today. She never misses it. It helps her back." The man suppressed a sob.

"Hey now," Ed said, looking away. "Nothing's certain yet." Ed decided to give it one more try before he sent Mitch to fetch the tools to break into the place. He brought his hand back to knock and the door opened a crack, as far as the chain would allow.

"Yes, officer?" The woman looked dazed and her thin white hair stuck out crazily as if she'd been asleep. "What do you want?" She sounded crabby.

"Are you all right, ma'am?" Ed had never felt so relieved to see a cranky old woman. "Your son is concerned."

She opened the door and turned to her son. "Sherman, I think I fell. I don't remember." She reached a shaky hand into the pocket of her robe and drew out something that glinted in the light. Ed's gun was out before he could see that it was an inhaler.

"What are you doing?" Sherman screamed, rushing between Ed and his mother.

Mitch shot Ed a glance. "Nothing," Mitch said as Ed holstered his gun. "He's just testing his reflexes."

"You people are sick," Sherman said.

"She could have had a stroke," Mitch said. "I'll radio for an ambulance."

They left the woman enveloped in the arms of her enormous, weeping son.

"Jumpy?" Mitch asked as they walked away.

"A little," Ed said, trying to pretend that his heart wasn't going about forty beats a minute too fast.

While Mitch called the ambulance, Ed leaned against the side of the patrol car, filling out a report, trying to calm himself. A drop of sweat from his forehead smeared the ink on the form. It was a beautiful day, a full blue sky above, and Ed paused to look up at an apple tree in bloom, stirring and sending its sweet scent on the breeze. Ed tried to breathe deep. The ambulance arrived, tearing around the corner, its sirens blaring, and Ed dropped the metal clipboard. He reached down to retrieve it, but then he couldn't see it, he couldn't see anything, he couldn't control his breathing, and the sirens amplified in his head. His hands tingled and his face streamed sweat, his blood pounded in his ears. *What's going on?* he thought. *Am I going to die?* He sunk to the street.

"Ed!" Mitch said, slapping his cheek. "What's the matter? You're white as a ghost."

Ed saw Mitch's face, disembodied, floating in a field of black. "I'm fine," Ed said, though he still gasped for breath. "Just a little light-headed. Just out of shape."

"Are you sure?" Mitch gave him a look that said he didn't believe Ed, but wanted to.

Mitch's body began to come into view now, the tunnel vision expanding to full frame again. Ed concentrated on his breathing, trying to slow it. He shivered in his sweat-soaked shirt as the apple blossom breeze rushed over him. "I'm fine," Ed insisted, "It was nothing."

"Come on," Mitch said, reaching his hand out to help him up. "There's nothing wrong with you that a couple of burritos won't cure," he added, sounding doubtful.

There was plenty wrong with him, Ed thought, none of it curable.

CHAPTER 14

Patricia

May 5

Walking west down 14th Avenue, Patricia heard drums banging and people shouting before she could see the crowd. She held Mia's hand and told Ray to keep close as Lupe led them around the corner onto Lincoln toward the gold-domed capitol building that loomed before them.

Hundreds of people gathered, waving signs and chanting in front of the steps. A half-dozen police cruisers were parked on the grass opposite the capitol. A few yards away from the cops, on the fringes of the crowd, a stout man in a Virgin of Guadalupe t-shirt brandished a dummy on a stick like a piñata—a stuffed police uniform with BAD COP written in messy white paint across the chest. People took turns punching and kicking it and yelled in its face that was childishly drawn in black marker with a checkmark nose. Mia stared and Patricia tugged her deeper into the mass of people, away from the car exhaust fumes and into the dense smell of sweat, patchouli, and competing colognes. On the flagstone steps of the capitol, children beat overturned buckets with wooden spoons and the palms of their hands. Highest up on the stairs stood Cop Aware Greg, yelling through a bullhorn. Patricia realized she shouldn't have brought the kids.

It was Cinco de Mayo, and just down the street people were setting up the annual festival, mariachi trumpeters blowing warm-up notes, vendors arranging rows of *pan dulce, folklórico* dancers practicing twirls in their bright, flaring dresses. Two years earlier, Patricia and Salvador had wandered with the kids through the carnival, sharing cotton candy, Salvador's favorite treat, but a frustration to Patricia, the spun sugar disappearing the moment she bit into it.

Mia stuck close to Patricia and Lupe but Ray pushed ahead, taking in the scene. Patricia and Lupe had been up late planning the rally with Tío for days, and the kids begged to come. "Of course they should be there," Tío insisted, and Patricia felt wary, wondering if the committee meant to display them. Lupe convinced her the kids should see all the people who were supporting their father. Now Patricia doubted it had been a good idea. They climbed the capitol steps, rising above the press of bodies, and Patricia read the signs in the crowd: "SWAT: Swift With A Trigger." "Officer Why Did You Kill My Daddy?" "No Knock, No Justice." "Arrest The Swine." "*¡Justicia para Santillano!*"

Patricia wondered what aspect of Salvador's story had drawn all these strangers here, regular people, in jeans and t-shirts, some shouting along with the chants, others just watching. A few guys with wind-roughened faces might have been homeless people displaced by the holiday from their usual campground in Civic Center Park. A couple who looked like they'd been protesting since Vietnam took turns with the "Arrest The Swine" sign, the man with a gray ponytail extending down his back, the woman in a flowing calico shirt, crystals dangling from her ears. An assortment of college and high school kids milled around, some wearing sandals and shorts, others with dyed hair, dressed in boots and heavy black clothing despite the heat. A group of Indians in embroidered AIM jackets gathered near the front like big-shouldered bouncers. Two men unfurled a *La Raza* banner. Patricia waved at the few people she recognized—committee members, a couple of nurses from Denver Health, Mrs. Sanchez from the post office, and Nino and his grandma, who held a sign that read "Listen to the taxpayers!"

Tío Tiger stood above the crowd at a dais, looking fierce enough to make everyone forget that he portrayed Santa Claus at the rec center every Christmas. Lupe led them up the stairs to stand at his side behind the white banner that read "Justice for Santillano!" in crimson lettering.

Salvador had cared nothing for politics and would have been perplexed to see all these people gathered in his name. As Patricia prepared to speak to everyone who had taken up his cause, she wished she knew what really happened the day he died. Maybe Salvador didn't shoot a gun, and that's why there was no gunshot residue, but he could have still had one. If Salvador did have a gun, he had been prepared to use it. Either he was afraid of the rough, drug-ridden neighborhood he chose to live in when Patricia barred the door to him, or he was so heartsick he had been thinking of shooting himself. Maybe he hadn't had the nerve and when the cops broke in his door, he saw his opportunity, raised his gun and closed his eyes. "Salvador," she whispered, looking out at the crowd, *"lo siento."*

The first Cinco de Mayo after they were married, they were living in a one-bedroom apartment on 12th and Emerson with ancient radiators that hissed and filled the place with the smell of burnt lint. The paint was so thick with fresh coats applied between decades of renters that the windows were stiff to open, and the bathroom door wouldn't stay shut unless you leaned against it and turned the lock.

Salvador was leaving for Mexico again the next week. He'd been gone for a month the previous fall, and made it clear to Patricia that he considered it too short a trip. He decided to quit his latest job and asked her to come with him, but summer school was starting.

"You're always in school," he said. "Just come with me."

"I've got to finish my studies before the loans run out."

She didn't understand why his parents still summoned him home now that he had a wife, and he wasn't explaining it well enough. It had something to do with the crops, the alfalfa and corn they were switching to because the prices had dropped for the drought-tolerant crops they'd grown before. "I've got to help with the irrigation ditches," Salvador said. The night before, they'd fought until the landlord called to report a neighbor's

179

complaint. It shamed Patricia to become the sort of woman who'd receive such a reprimand. They split up to sulk, Patricia studying at the kitchen table while Salvador watched the Spanish channel, some show with too much laughing, a booming host, silly women speaking in helium voices.

The next day they tried to keep their distance from each other in the 500-square-foot apartment. Neither of them was in the mood to attend the Cinco de Mayo street party downtown with its mariachi bands and nacho stands, but Salvador said it was a nice day to go to the park, his way of trying to make up without apologizing.

He used to say that in Spanish apologies meant more, and Patricia thought she understood why. *Lo siento* meant "I feel it," I am by your side feeling it. "I'm sorry" sounded like it came from a remove. But he didn't apologize because he wouldn't admit that she was right and stay home. Instead he invited her to enjoy that one day with him, which was all he could ever seem to promise of himself.

The people who lived in the cramped apartment buildings all around Cheesman Park spilled out into the field, bringing their dogs, children, sweethearts, portable stereos, and blankets. Under stands of pine trees, homeless people and drunks camped out, passing bottles of rotgut. Convertibles drove loops around the perimeter of the park, their radios blasting songs with skittering electronic beats, providing a continuous, mutating soundtrack from one car to the next. The sky above the field filled with buzzing remote-controlled planes, tennis balls tossed for dogs to fetch, kites swooping and rising.

Salvador lay on the grass with his hands under his neck. Patricia rested her head on his stomach and dozed. The sky was becoming overcast when Patricia opened her eyes at the sound of singing. When it grew louder, she looked up to see where the song was coming from. A wedding party was proceeding through the park, the bride and groom at the front, the attendants following behind them, singing in a language Patricia didn't recognize, the tones bright and ringing.

They reminded Patricia of the Ethiopian neighbors at Salvador's old apartment, their bodies tall and lean with bones light enough to permit flight, the long necks of royalty. They were immigrants, tough and vulnerable at the same time. The ladies in the wedding party wore dresses of intricate lace in shades of ivory and cream.

"Why don't more people walk around singing like that?" she asked Salvador.

"In my pueblo, they do. You should come see."

The bride and the groom were the only ones who did not sing. The groom beamed as he walked, holding his bride's hand, but the bride didn't smile, her velvet eyes cast down.

Salvador lifted himself up on his elbows. "We should follow them maybe," he said. "I want to hear how the song ends."

The sun slid from Patricia's back. Salvador watched the wedding party disappear, rapt. She felt that if he left for Mexico again, something would be lost between them.

She wanted to make this moment with Salvador by her side last, but fat raindrops started to smack against her skin. Salvador grabbed her hand and they ran the six blocks back to their apartment. They were barely through the door when they started kissing, pressed against each other in their wet clothes, Patricia trying to make him stay, he trying to reassure her in the only native language they shared.

When she found out she was pregnant, Salvador was at his family's *ranchito*, unreachable by phone. That was the worst part of the previous trips he'd taken to Mexico, how he was utterly gone throughout them, as unavailable to her as if he were dead. He always came home expecting things to carry on as they had before. She sat alone in the too-quiet apartment, studying her textbooks, wiping away tears when they came without acknowledging them, treating them as nothing more than clinical symptoms of her condition. She hadn't told her mother that he'd gone to Mexico again. She was glad Lupe was in Arizona so she couldn't just pop in and see how things were, her married, pregnant daughter periodically abandoned for months at a time.

181

"That's what happens when you marry a Mexican," Lupe would have said.

Salvador had driven their truck to Mexico, so Patricia had to ride her bike to summer classes. It became difficult for her to pedal up hills, and she'd arrive at school sweating and short of breath, dizzy and nauseous. She would head straight for the vending machine to buy a ginger ale, then sit in the air conditioning on the cold linoleum floor and sip it with her eyes closed. Some days she missed part of class because she felt that if she moved, everything inside her would come churning up. One day she puked in the bushes before she made it inside, and she bummed a ride home with a classmate because she didn't have the strength to bike. From then on she took the bus.

Salvador called her a few times during the trip from the town nearest his family's *ranchito* on a pay phone that obscured his voice with crackling static, his accent newly thickened. Who was this man she'd married? He sounded like a stranger. He said that he'd be back a few weeks later than planned so he could stay through the harvest. She told him nothing. He stayed away for three months and she went through the worst of it alone, crying, vomiting, sleeping for ten hours a night, consuming little but saltine crackers and ginger tea.

She wondered if he had another wife or girlfriend in Mexico. She imagined a Friday night dance at the plaza, a band playing *norteño* music, a pretty girl in Salvador's arms. She was never going to let him leave her again. She wouldn't share him with another country the way the provincial Mexican girls did, shrugging as their husbands headed for *El Norte* again, saying *he needs to make a living*. She wanted him to act like the American that he now was since he'd been granted citizenship two years earlier in the 1986 amnesty.

The day Salvador returned, he came in the door and saw her standing in the apartment with her arms crossed over her chest, saying nothing, the lights off, the dying rays of the afternoon sun permitting him to take in her outline. He approached her, recognizing the signs he must have seen a hundred times in

182

his mother and aunts and sisters and cousins, then sank to his knees and rested his head on her belly, kissed it and whispered, *"Mi hijo."*

"No," she said. *"Mi hijo."*

After she told her parents, they offered to cover the down payment on a house and Patricia accepted.

"We don't need their money," Salvador insisted.

"I've already taken it."

"If you would just be patient, we could buy a house on our own."

"This baby isn't going to wait."

Salvador cut meat, he bused tables, he cooked pancakes, he cleaned toilets in an office building at night, he sweated through dusty days on a road crew, hopping from one job to the next whenever he was offered a quarter more an hour.

While they'd been dating, Patricia researched the Immigration Reform and Control Act of 1986, which gave priority citizenship to farm workers who had been living in America continuously since 1982 or earlier. Salvador had been working in the city, but heard of a place on Federal where he could buy a letter saying he'd picked lettuce. Patricia didn't like him using the fake letter, but thought after he had his citizenship he could go to school, get a better job, make something of himself. He was married to her now, and he didn't have to live out the scrappy immigrant existence forever. She could carry him beyond that.

When she nagged him about starting to look into earning a G.E.D.—usually on some nights he was so tired he didn't acknowledge her questions and needed to down two beers before he became recognizably human—Salvador would shake his head and say, "The days for school have passed."

"You're only twenty-five," she'd say. "You talk like you're halfway to death."

Later she began to understand that to be twenty-five in America was to enjoy a carefree life entirely unrecognizable to a person of that age in rural Mexico: the slim-hipped sisters of Salvador's photographs transformed into worn-down mothers the shape of thick, melted candles before their twenty-fifth birthdays. Here Patricia was, twenty-two and pregnant already, taking her place in the line of those women she'd never even met. And Salvador was no longer the boy he had described to her—the smart farm kid who'd read every book he could find, exhausting the bindings on the Lassie novels his father had brought him one year from a flea market in the capital. "Padre Cristóbal said he could get me a scholarship to go to school in Juarez," Salvador had explained, "but then the bishop transferred him to another town when I was twelve and nothing more was ever said about it."

At sixteen, Salvador left the *ranchito* as almost all the men of the pueblo did, heading north with an uncle who worked as a coyote. He'd followed a friend to Colorado, staying with the friend's cousins in La Junta for a few months before growing tired of sleeping on a blanket on the linoleum floor next to the metal bowl of kibble they left out for the matted Chow dog. He'd wrangled a ride north on I-25 to Denver.

When Patricia was eight months pregnant, they settled in the small brick house a few blocks off Federal Boulevard. She began to try to fix up a nursery, culling what she could from thrift stores, thinking while she shopped that her first baby should have new clothes to wear, a clean crib to lay his head in. She felt she was sliding backward, able to provide less for her child than her parents had for her. She'd graduate in a few weeks, but she wouldn't be able to start working for several months. She began to keep a ledger of all of their earnings and bills, quizzing Salvador about his wages and his hours until she caught his lies with her math, and he finally admitted he'd been wiring part of his paycheck home to his family every month without telling her. He didn't even go to a bank to do it—he went to a hairdresser on Federal who had a wiring service to make extra money on the side, charging an unreasonable commission. Salvador always stood in line at King Soopers with his paycheck on the last Friday of the month and bought money orders to pay his bills, but Patricia insisted they open a bank account.

"Consuelo is robbing you," Patricia said. "I don't care if she's Chuy's cousin. Why haven't you gone to a bank?"

Though he was a citizen, he still had the illegal's fear of such places. "The banks will rob me, too. Might as well keep the money in the neighborhood."

Patricia sat at the kitchen table, jabbing numbers into the calculator. "This has got to stop. Can't you get one of your brothers to send more? One of them that doesn't have a family of his own?" Both of his brothers were working in fields in California.

"I am the oldest," he said, removing the calculator from her hands. "I have to take care of my parents. In Mexico, we don't throw our parents away the way you do here."

Patricia stood. "My parents are doing well because they worked hard and they saved and invested so they wouldn't need to look for handouts in their old age. My parents had enough to give us the house that we're living in."

"My parents worked hard, too. They work hard still. This is not about who works harder, and what I give them is not a handout."

"You can't keep squandering the money that should be used for our baby. In the U.S., we look out for our kids."

He clenched his fists. "I have always supported my family. You knew that from the start. That is why I came to *El Norte* to begin with." He punched the wall next to Patricia's head and she flinched, wondering if he'd meant to miss.

"We are your family now," she said, touching her stomach, "me and this baby."

He rubbed his hand and examined it. Maybe he'd have to skip work.

She knew she should stop but she couldn't. "Do you have a wife back there that you're taking care of?"

His clenched jaw made a tendon in his neck twitch. "I left when I was just a boy."

"You didn't answer."

"Of course I don't. The money is for my parents. Why can't you understand that?"

Something in his expression made her wonder if she'd asked the wrong question. Not a wife, maybe, but a girlfriend.

He stopped wiring money home until after Ray was born, but when Patricia started working at Denver Health, Salvador resumed sending part of his paycheck to Mexico. She was too tired to confront him about it, and didn't have the time to keep track of his wages. They staggered their shifts so that one of them would always be home with Ray. While Ray grew into a toddler, there were weeks when they barely saw each other awake. Then she got pregnant again, the one time she didn't take precautions. She'd sat on the toilet and wept with despair when the little plastic wand delivered its impassive result, but Salvador stuck his head in the bathroom and grinned. "A girl," he predicted, kneeling at her feet and singing to her stomach, *Qué linda manito que tengo yo, qué linda y blanquita que Dios me dio.* He was a natural father, full of songs and stories and novel ways to amuse babies. Who was responsible for his death? Was it really the cops that shot him? If there was one thing that could have driven Salvador to suicide, it was what Patricia had done, separating him from his kids.

The shouts of the crowd grew louder, the drumbeats more insistent. The people chanted "Justice! Justice!" and passed the policeman dummy forward, like a crowd surfer at a concert. Tío squeezed Patricia's shoulder, then turned back to the crowd. "The verdict is in," he shouted, feedback whistling through the mic. "Big surprise, right?" Everyone whistled and booed. "The city has let the cops that participated in the murder of Salvador Santillano go free. The goons that entered his home while he slept and pumped him full of bullets are out walking the streets today—your streets—with loaded guns. In fact, the only pig that will even be charged for this crime is the one that signed the no-knock warrant that condemned Salvador to death. If that idiot had managed to get the address right, do you know what the warrant was for? Do you know why eight thugs were granted

186

permission by the city to enter a house with no notice and their guns cocked? An alleged twenty-five-dollar drug buy at the house next door. Who alleged it? A crackhead the DPD calls an informant. Twenty-five dollars, ladies and gentlemen, twenty-five dollars is what this city thinks a life is worth. And guess what they charged the sergeant with?"

Someone in the crowd shouted "Murder!"

"They charged him with perjury. Perjury! How is it that when one citizen shoots another, it's murder, but when a cop shoots a citizen, it's a clerical error? Do you know what the maximum, *the maximum* sentence for perjury is? Six years. On the slim chance that they convict him, he'll be out in six years and have his whole life ahead of him. What about Salvador Santillano and his family? What do they have ahead of them?"

The crowd shouted. Mia flinched and Patricia pulled her closer. What was Patricia thinking, bringing Mia here? This was a child who got tears in her eyes listening to the dramatic reenactment of Jesus's condemnation at Palm Sunday Mass. A man ripped the policeman dummy down from the stick and kicked it in the head until the stuffing emerged.

"The city says they're not ignoring this crime," Tío continued. "Just this week, the mayor formed a panel to study noknock raids. But guess who's on it?"

"Pigs!" someone shouted. A group of people began to chant, *"DPD, DPD, killers, liars, thugs, and thieves! DPD, DPD, killers, liars, thugs, and thieves!"*

"That's right, on the mayor's panel is a bunch of cops and government officials. Not one ordinary citizen from the neighborhoods where no-knocks occur. You know what else? The D.A. has nothing but kind things to say about Salvador Santillano. The D.A. called him a 'gatekeeper' for the drugs being run next door."

Ray took a stone out of his pocket and flung it at the statue of a soldier on the Civil War Memorial behind them. She hadn't told the kids about any of this. What was the use of repeating

187

these hurtful lies to them? Mia looked up at her and Patricia shook her head. "It's not true," she said.

Tío was lit with the fire he must have burned with during all those Chicano rights rallies of his youth. When he and her father had bullshitted over dinner about their radical activities in the '60s and '70s, they sounded harmless—organizing statewide boycotts of grapes, lettuce, flowers, Taco Bell, and Coors beer. And those old photos and newspaper clippings of them with bellbottoms and ridiculous sideburns that she'd laughed at. Now she understood why they called the old man Tiger.

After the boos died down, Tío continued, "A gatekeeper. Anyone that knew Salvador will tell you that he never had anything to do with drugs in his life. The man worked two, three jobs at a time to support his family. When would he have had the time to get up to the mischief they are alleging? They are trying to smear his name. And we have reason to believe that the officers planted the gun that they say Salvador fired at them."

Ray looked to Patricia. "Is that true?"

Patricia put her hand on his cheek and tried to answer his question. "Think of your father, think of what sort of person you know him to have been, and that will tell you the truth."

A few people in the crowd began to shout Patricia's name, and then it became a chant. Her face grew hot. How was she supposed to go in front of them and play the grieving widow? Did she have any right to feel as sad as she did after all that had happened between them? She hadn't been the perfect wife, and he hadn't been the perfect husband. He wasn't a martyr. Just a man who shouldn't have died yet. She kept going over the last fight in her head, trying to replay it so that the outcome would be different.

Less than a year earlier, Salvador's brother had called from Mexico to say their father broke his leg. Salvador hadn't been back home for several years, since they had all gone together

188

during the kids' summer vacation. The family welcomed them with a pig roast, and Patricia enjoyed herself even though she couldn't understand half of what people were saying. Mia had begged to ride an old plow horse, and an uncle indulged her with endless rides. Ray had brought baseballs and gloves as gifts for his cousins and they'd played ball in the fields until sundown every night.

When Salvador told Patricia the news about his father's injury, she told him they could send extra money that month to help.

"My mother needs me," he said. "I need to go home to the ranch. Maybe for a few months."

"I thought we'd planned to go together in the summer when the kids are out of school."

"They need me now."

Patricia sat up in bed. "Who will watch Ray and Mia when I have to work at night?"

"Maybe the neighbor will do it."

"We live in a city, Salvador. This isn't your village where you can turn kids out on the street and expect them to be looked after by some kindly *abuelita*."

"They have a grandmother here," he said. "Why doesn't she come up and take care of them like she should?"

"She lives nine hundred miles away. She has her own life."

Salvador lifted his hand. "That woman—"

"Don't call her *that woman*. She bought this house for us."

He rose from the bed and walked to the window.

"Isn't the money you send every month enough?" Patricia asked. "Because God knows we can't spare it."

"They need an extra man."

"We need you, Salvador. You can take a trip for a week or two, but several months is just too much. The kids hate it when you leave while they're in school. Can't you wait until summer when we can all go together?"

"No," he said, throwing her a challenging look.

Patricia stared back at him. "If you leave this time," she said, "don't come back."

"You're cold-hearted," he said. "You've never understood what family means."

Patricia got up and stuck her finger in his face. "I work my ass off every week to pay our mortgage and keep us fed. I pay the bills, I clean the house, I cook for you." She reached for a photo of the four of them that she kept in a frame on her bedside table, she and Salvador sitting side by side on the front porch, Mia just a toddler on Salvador's lap, Ray, a long-legged kindergartner, spilling out of Patricia's arms. "This is what family means," she said, holding it up to him. "The four of us against the world."

"Patricia," he said, making her name sound light and beautiful as only he could, "That is not the whole picture."

"I mean it," she said. "You choose. If I come home from work tomorrow and you aren't here, don't ever try to come back. I'm too tired to miss you when you're gone and I can't do this anymore. I'd rather be on my own than have half a husband who is half a father to his children." What a thing to say. And she'd said it. She climbed back into bed and snapped off the light so he couldn't say anything else to her. She felt his fingers trail down her back, touching her vertebrae where his kisses used to make her shiver, and she shrugged them off. Was that the last time he touched her?

The next day when she came home from work, she found a single scarlet gladiola in a glass vase on the kitchen table. No note, but she remembered. He'd first carried gladiolas into the flower shop on the day they'd met almost fifteen years earlier, she standing in the parking lot near his van and watching him as he walked into the store, letting her gaze slip from the back of his bronze neck to his tight cowboy jeans.

He would stay away for however long it suited him, calling rarely, then come home and open his arms. But she could change the locks, give him a scare, take the kids to visit their grandparents in Arizona on the day he'd tell her he'd be home,

190

make him see that she'd stand firm. She'd melted for him too many times.

"They're calling for you, Mama," Mia said, tugging her hand. Tío Tiger beckoned Patricia to come up and speak. Patricia squeezed Mia's hand and then walked up next to Tío.

Tío led her to the microphone stand. Patricia looked out at the crowd, still in the frenzy that Tío had incited, and felt dizzy. She couldn't make out individual faces anymore, only a seething mass, bodies pressed close. Her trembling hands drew the note cards that contained her speech out of her pocket, but all the words on them were false. She'd written a rather academic speech about the virtues that the seven major points on the police badge were meant to stand for: honesty, integrity, temperance, fortitude, faith, hope, and charity. She'd sweated over the speech for two weeks, but she'd written it to sound pretty, to make herself seem smart, not to tell the truth. The note cards fluttered to the ground at her feet. Mia started to gather them up, and looked up at her with her hands full of cards, trying to hand them to her. Patricia shook her head.

If she were Billie Holiday, she would wear a white gardenia behind her ear and sing of her pain so that all who heard would feel it. If she were Sonia Sanchez, she would raise a fist and shout her anger into a poem so that all who read would know it. If she were Jackie Kennedy, she would cast down her eyes and let her loss transfigure inside into a kind of grace others could see. But she was only herself.

Patricia took a breath and decided to stare at the microphone so she wouldn't lose her nerve with the crowd. "My name is Patricia Maestas de Santillano," she began. "It is my husband that they killed, Salvador." Her voice wavered, and she took another deep breath to steady it. "I don't usually speak in front of crowds," she said, "but I'm here for my children. They are hurting, and I want them to see that we are not alone." She glanced at Ray and Mia, who looked back at her expectantly. "I want them to see that we never were alone, even when there were only four of us. There were all of you out there, leading your own lives in this city, ready to help us when we needed you."

"Salvador was a good father," she said. "He wasn't a saint. But you shouldn't have to be a saint to be safe from police brutality." She told herself not to lock her knees so she wouldn't pass out. Tío handed her a bottle of water and she took a sip.

"Those of you who know me wouldn't describe me as the most hopeful of people." She glanced at Lupe, faltering a bit. "But I have to have hope now. I hope that we can force a change. There must be changes we can make, laws we can pass so that nothing like this ever happens again. Mr. Mayor, if you're out there listening, I want you to know that I've lost my husband already, but I still have a son and daughter, and they are very angry right now. And we all know that being young and angry will get you into trouble. I just want them to be safe in this city where they grew up. I want this not to happen to anyone else, ever again. Mr. Mayor, you let the cops who killed my husband go free, but you still have a chance to make this right."

She said "thank you" into the mike before stepping away. The crowd cheered, traffic rushed by on Colfax and Broadway, a helicopter beat across the sky. She looked out at all the people and the phalanx of television cameras aimed at her. Her hand slipped from the side of the podium. A few months earlier she had been a wife, mother, and nurse, and now she didn't recognize her life.

That night the celebratory Cinco de Mayo cruising began up and down Federal Boulevard. It would continue the whole weekend, the street jammed with trucks flying Mexican flags from their tailgates, blasting thumping music you could feel in your chest, happy onlookers standing in the parking lots of fast food joints that lined the street, filming passing cars with camcorders. The city would throw a weekend-long party in Civic

Center Park across from the capitol building where Patricia had spoken. There would be Mexican *folklórico* dancers and young men displaying their shiny low-rider cars and even bicycles, lavishly outfitted with velvet, leather, and precious metals. The sweet burnt smell of green chiles roasting in a metal cage over a flame. Carnival food, games, music: the harmless display of culture the city approved of. Denver celebrated as if there were no sadness in the world, no death, as if the words Patricia had spoken went unnoticed. But on Monday when the phone rang and Patricia answered it, a woman said she was calling from the mayor's office. He wanted to meet with her.

CHAPTER 15

Ed
May 15–16

The Z's took the field at Ruby Hill, warming up to play the Pirates, the only other undefeated team in the league. The grass was finally green, the weather balmy, the red-winged blackbirds dive-bombing dogs near their nests, Denver making a little show of spring just before summer hit. The boys threw too hard, bobbling the ball in the pre-game session of situations, Jesse's voice cracking as he called out to the team. Badgett sat in front of Ed and Claire in the bleachers, holding a copy of that day's *Denver Post*. Ed willed him to stick to the sports page, but Badgett had the local section open to an article about Ed.

"It's a shame, this article," Badgett said when he finished reading, turning around to look at Ed and thwacking his leg with the paper.

Ed shrugged. "They just want to sell papers."

Claire threw Badgett a tense little smile, warning him off the subject.

Ed had practically memorized the article, reading it over and over that morning until Claire had snatched it out of his hands. COP DESCRIBED AS "LOOSE CANNON," the headline read. The article wasn't breaking news, just the latest addition to a story that had been gaining momentum since the protestors staged a Cinco de Mayo rally and scheduled a meeting with the mayor. It was buried in the paper, but leave it to Badgett to dig it out. The subtitle ran through Ed's head in a continuous loop: COP WHO SHOT SANTILLANO "YELLED A LOT," "SEEMED ANGRY," SAY PAL TEAM PARENTS.

"I wonder where Chase is," Claire said, too obvious in her attempt to change the subject. She shielded her eyes and searched the field for him. "He usually does the infield warm-up."

Badgett leaned back between them. "If any reporter comes around asking about you," he said, "I won't say anything. You've got my word on that."

"Appreciate it," Ed said.

Ed had been waiting for the reporter to go ahead and print his damn article instead of skulking around all the time. He was almost relieved that it had finally come out. The best Kyle Schmidt of the *Denver Post* could do for quotes was digging up disgruntled parents from his PAL coaching days, the mothers and fathers of children who Ed used to rotate in and out of right field to fulfill the Police Athletic League's minimum play requirement because of their lack of any apparent athletic skill, coordination, ability to concentrate, or interest in baseball.

Parents whose children were coached by Officer Ed O'Fallon say that he frequently lost his temper with players for the Eagles, a baseball team for nine- and ten-year-olds in the Police Athletic League. The article made it sound like all the parents were ragging on him, when it was really just one or two. *O'Fallon stepped down from coaching the team last year. According to team parent Randy Rickenbaugh, prior to O'Fallon's departure, a group of parents had spoken to PAL officials to request a less volatile coach. "We wanted a coach who was more interested in good sportsmanship than winning," Rickenbaugh said.*

"That guy who said all that stuff about you," Badgett said, "his kid must have been pretty lousy, huh?"

"Fat and asthmatic," Ed confirmed. Ed had once chewed out Rickenbaugh's kid after he was late to the plate for an at-bat because he'd been playing with his handheld computer game in the dugout.

Claire glared at Ed and told Hank, "We really don't want to talk about it."

The reporter didn't get much out of his scouting trip to the Unicorns game. *O'Fallon is currently coaching a tee-ball team for six-year-olds on which his daughter plays. Several parents of children on the team declined comment, but one mother, Paige Littlefield—Blondie's mom—said, "He's a fine coach, and I don't know why everyone is giving him such a hard time."*

195

Claire sent Blondie's mom flowers, which embarrassed Ed. It would have been better just to let the whole thing drop.

Pendergrass settled in one bleacher up from Ed, the stands groaning under his weight. "So we finally get to see Mr. Maestas pitch today," he said.

"Should be interesting," Ed said.

"Maestas," Claire whispered to Ed. "Doesn't that name sound familiar?"

"You can't walk down the street without bumping into a Maestas in this town," Ed whispered back. "Apparently this one's some kind of messiah on the mound."

Ralph Boyd approached the bleachers and everyone quieted.

"Say Ed," Boyd said, "Chase got into a fender bender. Would you mind coaching first base for me until he gets here?"

"No, I wouldn't mind," Ed said, jumping up. As he followed Boyd to the dugout, Ed glanced back and saw Pendergrass, Kitagawa, and Badgett watching with longing. Ed felt a swell of pride that he was the chosen dad.

Boyd said he'd be calling all the plays, but he went over the signs with Ed behind the dugout so he could follow them: the third touch after the hat brim indicator was the one that counted. Boyd handed him a Z's t-shirt and ball cap, which Ed put on before jogging out to the coach's box off of first base. He glanced into the dugout and caught Jesse's eye. Jesse smiled at him, nodded. Ed nodded back. Here he was, finally back where he was supposed to be, coaching his boys again. The blue sky stretched overhead, birds warbled in the trees, and Ed stood on the ball field, scuffing his shoes in the base-path dirt.

Ed wondered why Boyd had picked him instead of one of the other dads—Boyd knew that he'd coached E.J. and Jesse before, but maybe there was more to it. Maybe he'd seen the article that morning and felt sorry for him for being demoted to girls' tee-ball.

Ed stood in the coaching box on the Pirates' side of the diamond. They hadn't taken the field yet. Apparently they went in for drama. The Pirates' coach lugged a boom box out to the front of the dugout, crouched near it and gave a quick nod to the boys behind him. He pressed play and as "Eye of the Tiger" began blasting, the boys burst out of the dugout and sprinted to their positions, the loud, discrete guitar chords at the beginning of the song like a revving car. The Pirates wore bright red uniforms even though as the home team they should have worn a lighter color. They winged balls around, putting spin moves into their catches and throws. Maestas had yet to appear, remaining in the bullpen off the first base side. The boys in the Z's dugout busted up at the display, singing along with the music until Boyd silenced them.

Most of the players on the Pirates were Hispanic, and Ed glanced at their parents who sat in the stands just a few yards away from him. He'd worn dark glasses and he settled his baseball cap lower on his forehead. This team was from the north side, and there was a chance that there might be some anti-cop agitators among the parents. The newspapers had been focusing on the race angle lately, running where-are-they-now pieces on minorities shot by the Denver cops in recent years. He didn't want anyone to recognize him from the couple of times the paper and the news stations had run his twelve-year-old police academy graduation file photo. For once, he was glad he'd gotten a little fat.

Finally, Maestas trotted in from the bullpen, stripping off his red satin warm-up jacket and leaving it at the threshold of the dugout. What was he, a matador?

"¡Ándale! ¡Ándale! ¡Arriba! ¡Arriba!" one of the boys in the Z's dugout called out in his best Speedy Gonzales, cracking up the rest of the kids.

Maestas jerked his chin at the boom box and the coach took his cue and silenced it. Maybe Maestas had some kind of Zen pitching thing going on—he couldn't handle the distraction of the noise and he couldn't approach the field until the final moment so that his concentration would be total. Or maybe he just didn't like Pete's music. Ed was ready to see the kid pitch already.

As he warmed up, Maestas' delivery was smooth, windup rhythmic, leg kick high, but his pitches didn't seem unusually fast. He looked like a regular kid. Then the ump told him he had three pitches left and he started to throw heaters, pitches that whistled into the catcher's mitt with a snap. You'd need a real right fielder for this kid, someone who could sprint well enough to snag foul pop-ups—you couldn't use it as a filler position because if any right-handed batter managed to make contact they'd likely be behind it and send the ball off down the first base line. Ed had to watch out.

Finally the ump called, "Play ball!" and E.J. gave Ed a smile as he trotted up to the plate.

Boyd had moved E.J. up from batting eighth to leading off because he was speedy and a fearless bunter. But in order to bunt he'd have to square around, giving Maestas his whole face and chest to aim at with those wicked fastballs. Ed's throat felt thick as he watched to see if Pete would motion the infielders in—if he'd scouted enough Z's games, he'd know that E.J. was a bunter and that would ruin the surprise that was essential to pulling off a lead-off bunt. But the Pirates' coach called no plays as he paced back and forth, clapping his hands, shouting encouragement to his team. Pete's constant movement struck Ed as aggressive and unhinged, like the men in a video about cock fighting rings he'd seen during training one year.

The first pitch smoked past E.J., who was following Boyd's orders not to swing at the first pitch. Ed didn't know if he agreed with Boyd's call on that one—sure, you'd get a good look at the pitch first, but then you wouldn't want to see another.

"That kid's not twelve," Ed heard Hank Badgett call from the stands. "He probably has a twelve-year-old kid."

E.J.'s back leg shook, so Ed could tell that he was going for the bunt with the next pitch. It was much easier for the batter to square around before the pitch, but that would give the play away. Another fastball zoomed by, but came in high, out of the strike zone and E.J. held off, didn't even gesture toward a bunt.

The ump called it a ball. "Good boy," Ed said under his breath. "Good eye."

The next pitch was a slider, and E.J. squared around to bunt and stabbed at his approximation of where the ball would cross, but it evaded his bat. Now he'd given up his move and he was behind 1-2. "Come on, E.J.," Ed boomed, "keep your head in there."

The Pirates' first baseman, a big, lethargic-looking kid with heavy-lidded eyes, turned toward Ed with the expression of a half-interested cow, chewing his gum like cud.

"Don't mind me," Ed said, "In case you haven't heard, I like to yell."

"Are you trying to psych out my first baseman?" Pete roared. "Don't pay any attention to him, Gill."

"Oh, lay off, Coach," Ed said. "I'm just getting into the game."

"Come on, Maestas," the first baseman called, pounding his fist into his mitt.

Claire was right, Ed thought, the name did sound familiar, as he turned to see the ball caroming toward his face, but not in time to move or throw up a forearm before it struck him in the cheekbone under his left eye. Ed fell to the ground. E.J. must have fouled the ball off while he'd been yakking. Lots of people stood over him, E.J.'s face the first one Ed picked out, staring down at him, his eyes big and worried. "I'm sorry, Dad! I didn't mean to!"

"Of course you didn't," Ed mumbled. "I should have been watching. Get back there and finish your at-bat. You hang tough now, you hear?" He felt like the Gipper, spouting athletic advice flat on his back.

"Come on, Yogi Berra," Claire said, emerging from the crowd that had gathered around him. She helped Ed to his feet. "Emergency room."

"What?" Ed said. "I'm fine." Then his cheek throbbed and he touched his index finger to it. It came back bloody. A red drop fell on the new gray Z's coach shirt Boyd had just given him, the stain spreading. The wound began to gush, bathing that part of

Ed's face with the feeling of warm, thick liquid. "Aw, Christ," Ed said. Claire handed him a towel and he pressed it to his face.

Claire tugged Ed forward. "I can see fine," he said, pulling away. He followed her as she walked off the field and headed out toward the parking lot, employing what Ed thought of as her E.R. mission stride—she'd taken the boys often enough to know how to do it: move quickly but don't panic. Polly knew the routine, too, jogging close behind her mother's heels.

Halfway to the car, Ed hung back. "Can't I just ice it until the game is over?"

"Sure," she said. "I'll just get you an ice bag and you'll hold it to your face until it's covered with blood and gore and the mess spreads all over the bleachers and children scream in terror. Sounds like a brilliant plan, O'Fallon."

"But it's such a big game," Ed wheedled. "And I had a chance to coach the team through it and I blew it, I just blew it."

"You sound like a little boy. There are worse things than missing a baseball game." She continued walking to the car.

Polly tugged on Ed's hand and held out a limp clover flower, warm from her palm. "Sorry you're hurt," she said. Ed accepted it, inhaling its sweet crushed scent. As they passed a crab apple tree on the way to the parking lot, a red-winged blackbird on a branch eyed Ed and chirred, asserting his dominance over this stretch of sky. "Fine," Ed told the bird, "I'm going." To the last place he wanted to be: a waiting room.

That night Ed found E.J. huddled up in his bed, his wiry body scrunched tight, weeping softly into his pillow.

"What's the matter, kiddo?" Ed spread a firm hand on E.J.'s overheated back.

E.J. shook his head, tried to catch his breath.

"Are you upset about the game?"

E.J. nodded, then hid his head under a pillow.

Jesse had greater strength and natural ability, but Ed admired E.J.'s fire. When he'd been coaching baseball, he liked to see a kid cry after losing a game. That proved it meant something to him. The loss had lodged somewhere near his heart, and he'd bring that feeling with him to practice and to the next game, a feeling that would make him work harder to improve.

Ed gently tugged the pillow away from E.J., his love for his son rising into his throat again.

E.J. wiped at his tears with the back of his hand and tried to breathe deep. He looked up at Ed. "If only I'd gotten down that first bunt. That's what started the whole game off wrong. Now I'm probably going to go back to batting eighth."

"Yeah, if only, son," Ed said. "If only Bill Buckner hadn't flubbed that grounder, if only Shoeless Joe hadn't thrown those games." If only I hadn't had to shoot Santillano, Ed thought. "There's a whole other world built of nothing but if onlys, and it's a pretty nice place for the guys who ended up losing, but it's a rotten deal for the guys on the other end of it."

E.J. sat up, rubbing his eyes. "So are you saying that I shouldn't be sad because we lost, that I should be happy for the Pirates?"

"No," Ed said, "That's crap. You play to win and you care about winning. I know how it is. You don't like to see the other guys grinning when it's through. It's like a fist to the gut, those grins. I'm just saying that—I'm just saying," Ed paused. "I don't know what I'm saying, E.J. Just don't ever be afraid to let something like this hurt you. It shows that you care."

E.J. squinted up at him, looking confused.

Ed needed to bring this fatherly pep talk around, leave the kid with some comfort so he could sleep. "Look," Ed said, "you've seen Maestas now, you've seen his stuff, and when you play him again next month you won't be surprised by it. A coach like Boyd? He's an expert. After getting a close-up look like that, he'll know just how to coach you so that the next time you face the Pirates, you'll come out with a win."

E.J. nodded. "Will he let you coach first base again, next time?"

Ed laughed. "I don't know, we'll see."

"I hope he'll let you coach first base again because I want a do-over." E.J. settled back into his pillow. "I demand a do-over," he murmured.

Ed leaned over and tucked the comforter around his son's small body, smoothed his sandy hair and kissed him on the forehead. "Yeah," he said, "and get a do-over for me too, while you're at it."

"Phew," Mitch whistled the next day at work when he saw Ed's face. "That don't look good."

"I wanted my eye to match my uniform." Ed's right eye had swollen half shut, the skin around his socket black as the peel of a forgotten banana, his split cheek swollen and stitched with six neat blue stitches along the bone.

"Maybe we'll just sort of cruise around today and have you stick your face out of the window at thugs," Mitch said. "That'll scare them straight."

"I had a rough night. My kids lost their ballgame."

"No kidding? The hotshot team went down?"

"Yeah, they lost 3 to 1 to a team with an ace pitcher."

Mitch drove since Ed's head was pounding and his swollen flesh was moving in on his left eye's peripheral vision. The dispatcher's voice on the radio sounded distant, muffled.

"Can you see out of that eye?" Mitch asked.

"I'll let you know as soon as I figure out which one of you is talking," Ed said.

"Ha ha."

"I didn't want to take a sick day after all that leave."

Ed hadn't had another panic attack since his first day back three weeks earlier, and Mitch seemed to have forgotten it. Ed's heart started to race whenever he so much as thought about it, so he just tried to breathe and put it out of his mind. He hadn't mentioned it to Claire, figuring if it was a one-time thing there wasn't any cause to worry her. They were driving past Colfax and Emerson when a report of a domestic came in over the radio, a mom and a kid trapped inside an apartment, the dad tearing the place apart. The building was on 16th and Pennsylvania, a few blocks away.

When they arrived, a woman stood on the porch. A mass of frizzy, yellowish hair surrounded her face, and she wore a purple exercise outfit, too much rouge on her rice paper cheeks. "They're at it again," she said in a deep, wrecked voice. She stubbed out a cigarette in a tin can full of sand. "It sounds worse this time than before, though."

"Are you Roberta?" Ed asked, "The lady who called this report in?"

"That's right. I'm the property manager here. I've been trying to get the landlord to evict these people for months."

"So you say it's a husband and wife," Mitch said, "and they've got a juvenile in there with them?"

"Their son, Pablo. He's five." She turned to unlock the front door to the apartment building. "I don't know why we bother to lock up the place when there's worse elements already on the inside."

"We need to wait for backup," Mitch whispered to Ed.

"We should call for it, but we shouldn't wait. There's a kid in there."

Mitch went back to the patrol car to radio for backup.

Roberta eyed Ed's shiner. "Are you sure you're up for this?"

Ed took a deep breath. "What's the layout of the apartment?"

"It's a one-bedroom, a living room at the entranceway, a bathroom on the left of the hallway, bedroom on the right, kitchen in back."

Ed nodded, trying to visualize it, to prepare. He took in the surroundings—a small apartment complex with maybe twelve units, tops, arranged on two floors around a long hallway. They heard a crash.

"I take it they're upstairs?" Mitch asked, returning.

"That's right. Apartment 11 up the stairs, on the left."

Ed mounted the stairs, Mitch followed behind him, and Roberta climbed up too.

"Actually, Ma'am," Mitch said, "It would be safer if you'd stay outside and let us handle this. We don't know what kind of weaponry he might have up there."

"But what about the door?" she said. "I don't want you busting it up. It took forever to get a carpenter in here to fix it last time."

Mitch looked at Ed and Ed held up his hand to signal that he should just let her be. Ed pounded on the door. "Police!" he called. The man raged, the woman made low pleading sounds, the kid wailed.

"Open up, it's the police!" Mitch yelled.

There was no response. They looked back at Roberta, who was holding up a crowded chain and carefully examining keys until she found the one she wanted. She stepped between Ed and Mitch and unlocked the door.

"Thanks, Ma'am," Ed said. "Now would you please head downstairs and wait outside so you can stop any other residents who happen to come home?"

She took a few steps back until she was leaning against the opposite wall, then she crossed her arms and stared at them.

Great, Ed thought. "Let's move in," he said. He hadn't been in on a situation this hot since the Santillano shooting. He felt like he was amped on three shots of espresso.

Mitch walked into the living room and Ed followed. An old, scratchy-looking pea green sofa took up most of the space, a child's blanket and a stuffed bear wadded up on one side. The boy must sleep on the couch. Laundry was spilled all over, a Guadalupe votive smashed on the floor, the blinds on the windows dangling from one side. The apartment bore a complicated scent, the dense smell of a home where heavily spiced meals were cooked daily.

The yelling was coming from the kitchen. The hallway between the living room and the kitchen was too narrow. Mitch and Ed wouldn't be able to get a good view of what was going on until they were almost on top of the guy. There was no place to take a defensive position.

"Police!" Ed yelled, hoping the guy would show himself and they wouldn't have to trap themselves in the hallway. The man paused his Spanish tirade—all Ed could make out was *puta* this and *pinche* that—then started it up again. Mitch nodded his head toward the bathroom on the left side. They walked down the hall, then took cover in the tiny bathroom, where they had a clear view of the kitchen, Ed crouching low, Mitch standing above him. The man had the woman pinned in the far corner of the kitchen with a heavy table. He was a large man, six foot easy, built solid as a fireplug, and he paced in front of the table, holding a butcher knife down at his side. The woman held her son's head close to her chest and rocked him, her arm ready to shield his face.

Mitch looked down at Ed and they drew their guns. Mitch moved out of the bathroom, aiming his weapon. There wasn't much space to maneuver, maybe four feet between Mitch and the man, not a safe distance. "Drop the knife!" Mitch ordered. "Drop it."

The man turned around, his eyes wild, blinking at them as if he'd just then realized that they were in the apartment. The whites of his eyes looked bigger than they should have. He was on something. The mother whispered to her son a low refrain, like a prayer, and the boy stopped crying. Now he was shaking as he squeezed an arm around his mother's waist.

The man's chest rose and fell as he stared at Mitch. The man turned back toward his wife, extending the knife forward as if to strike.

"Hey!" Mitch screamed, moving closer—too close, Ed thought.

The guy whirled around, slashing at Mitch with the knife, slamming into Mitch's hand with his elbow. Mitch's gun clattered to the floor. "Shit," Mitch said. Ed burst out of the bathroom, trying to locate the gun—in training he'd learned that cops were frequently killed by their own guns once they'd lost them. Ed couldn't see it and turned back toward Mitch. The man jumped on top of Mitch, wrestling him to the ground, holding the knife above him, ready to plunge it down. Mitch was on his back, grappling with the man's hands. "Shoot him!" he screamed.

Not in front of the kid, Ed thought. He aimed at the guy's head. He couldn't see well out of his left eye. What if he shot Mitch instead?

"Just shoot him!" Mitch yelled, his hands trembling from the effort of keeping the knife from descending.

Ed began to squeeze the trigger, heard the first click that told him if he applied any more pressure, the bullet would launch, and another death would be his responsibility. Instead, he rammed the guy from the side, and knocked him off Mitch. The knife fell to the floor and Ed kicked it away. He beat the man in the head with the butt of his revolver and then hauled him away from Mitch, smacking him across the face with the gun until a trickle of blood snaked out of his ear and he stopped moving. He jerked the man's limp arms around his back and cuffed him, pulling him up by the hair when he slumped over. Ed didn't want him dying from choking on his own blood when he was cuffed and unconscious. He gave him one last kick in the side and the man crumpled. His face swelled, eyes turning to slits.

Ed looked up. The woman's horrified expression told him that she wouldn't be sending him a thank you note for saving her. "Papa!" the kid screamed. "Papa!" He attempted to clamber away from the mother, his hand halfway to reaching his father's ankle before the mother had the sense to grab him by the leg and pull him back.

Ed was afraid to look at Mitch, but then he turned and met his eyes. Mitch was still on the floor, having risen only to his elbows, his face gone fish-belly white, beaded with perspiration.

"Are you all right?" Ed asked.

Mitch looked at him and opened his mouth as if to speak, but then said nothing.

The backup arrived, and the first officers to the scene carried the man out to their patrol car just as he was coming to, his eyes groggy in his bloodied face. Another Mexican beaten by

Ed O'Fallon for the papers to report. They'd love it. Someone gave the mother a blanket. What the hell good does that do, Ed thought, a blanket. People asked Ed if the suspect had done that to his eye, and he just shook his head. Ed passed Roberta on the way out.

"What, did you kill him?" she asked. "Who's going to pay the rent this month?"

"You're welcome," Ed said.

Mitch wasn't hurt, but Ed offered to drive back to the station. They drove in silence, Ed trying to work up something to say.

"You hesitated," Mitch said finally.

"I'm sorry," Ed said.

"Yeah? I'm sorry, too." The color of Mitch's face was still off, the skin under his eyes puffy. "You've got to be sure you can shoot. I'd never hesitate if it was you. I *know* that."

"Look, he's not dead, you're not dead."

Mitch slumped down in his seat. "Close enough."

They spent the afternoon filling out forms, then the district commander told them to go home. Ed meant to go home, but his head was pounding and he didn't feel like telling Claire that he'd almost gotten Mitch killed, and he watched the sign for his exit off the highway come and go. For some reason he just kept on driving, heading west toward the mountains until they loomed up around him, still, red, and massive in their silence.

CHAPTER 16

Patricia

May 16

"Try this on," Lupe insisted, standing in the entryway inside the front door, holding out a garment bag from Foley's to Patricia.

Patricia set down her purse and keys and then took her time unlacing and removing her shoes. "What is it?"

"Something for you to wear to see the mayor. I couldn't find anything suitable in your closet."

Beneath the plastic bag was a navy blue suit made of thick, nubbly material. The dark buttons shone. Patricia held it up to her chest.

"Lovely," Lupe said. "You'll need to put your hair up and find some shoes to match."

Patricia felt the fabric between her thumb and index finger. "This is too nice. Don't I want the mayor to pity me?"

"You should look dignified. You're not a beggar. You have business with the city."

"I have business with the city," Patricia repeated, trying to feel braver.

Patricia felt she knew the mayor after seeing him on TV for so many years, a strapping man with a moustache and toothy grin, a black version of Teddy Roosevelt, ferried across the city in a dark Lincoln Town Car. Last fall the mayor assembled all the city's snowplows and mag-chloride spreaders in the parking lot of Mile High Stadium. Indomitable in his elegant black great-coat, he opened his arms wide to indicate the bounty of trucks and plows that flanked him, and pronounced: "We are prepared!" The image appeared in the papers and on every news channel.

Patricia had been fond of him, and was sorry to see him setting himself up for a cosmic kick in the ass. The next week an ice storm that gave way to a blizzard hit the city. Power lines snapped. Roofs collapsed. People did not go to work. Their children ran rampant in impassable streets. The blizzard was too powerful, even with all the city's equipment lined up against it. The mayor wasn't infallible, Patricia reminded herself.

"This came for you," Lupe said, handing her a letter.

The thin pink envelope rested in Patricia's palm like an unexploded grenade. It was mailed from San Roberto de Jesús, the town in Chihuahua where Salvador's family lived. A woman's name she didn't recognize, Graciela, was on the return address. She must be the woman in Salvador's photos. Why would she write to Patricia?

"What is it?" Lupe asked, stepping closer.

"I'll open it later." She didn't want to read it in front of Lupe. She needed to be alone with whatever it said.

Patricia put the letter on her dresser and stared at it as she undressed. She pulled on the skirt of the suit, which hugged her hips. Then she put on the top, struggling to work the buttons through the tight buttonholes. She hadn't worn anything that formfitting in years. She'd lost some weight, which Lupe must have noticed. Pulling off her ponytail holder, she smoothed her hair into a French twist, fastening it with bobby pins. In the mirror, she looked like a businesswoman. What if she had been? What if she'd broken up with Salvador when she was nineteen, studied finance in college? She'd be married to a professional, living in a different neighborhood. No one would have ever read her name in the newspaper except in a society column about Hispanic business leaders.

Dressed this way, Patricia felt like a different person, someone who could handle whatever was in the pink envelope. When she unfolded the letter, an American twenty-dollar bill fell out. Was this woman sending her charity? The letter was written in Spanish in a neat script. She saw Salvador's name a few times, and recognized several words, but couldn't make out the sense of it. She needed help from someone who knew the language better. She tucked the money and the letter inside the top drawer of her dresser.

She sat for a moment on the edge of her bed, breathing, then walked out into the living room and held out her arms to display the suit. "Perfect," Lupe said, "proper."

Patricia thought of showing Lupe the letter, but she didn't know Spanish much better than Patricia did. She tried to think of who she could trust for the translation. Tío?

Tío and the family's lawyer, John Archuleta, were coming over that evening to discuss their strategy for meeting with the mayor. Mia helped Lupe cook a big meal, pecan chicken with wild rice and green beans, and the sound of Lupe whacking the chicken breasts flat filled the house. Patricia hadn't taken off her suit. It made her feel more confident, better able to strategize. She was running the vacuum cleaner over the living room carpet when Ray walked in the front door, back from baseball practice. Pete picked him up and dropped him off from every practice now. Patricia attended all the games, but with the almost daily practices, it was just too much driving. She was grateful for baseball, grateful for Pete and the competitive league. Patricia had only seen Miguel at one game, and he'd left halfway through with a girl wearing a skimpy top that read "Princess" in pink rhinestones. She hoped baseball was too slow-paced for Miguel, and that he'd avoid the rest and forget about Ray by fall.

Ray threw his bat bag down on the entryway floor. Patricia turned off the vacuum.

"What are you wearing?" Ray asked, circling her with his arms crossed. "Are you going on a date?"

Patricia laughed, but Ray didn't smile. "Your grandma bought me this suit so I could have something nice to wear for my meeting with the mayor."

"You think you can impress him? He's the mayor. He's probably got like thirty meetings tomorrow and he won't even know your name and he'll pretend to agree to whatever you say just so you'll shut up," Ray said. "You think this is like some big date."

"I'm just trying to look presentable so that I feel more confident when I speak to him."

"Confident in what? He's not going to listen to you anyway," Ray said, turning and walking toward his room.

"Get back here and move your baseball bag," Patricia snapped. "We have company coming." He was as strong as she was now, so she didn't know what she'd do if he didn't obey.

He paused and turned deliberately, sauntered back and heaved up his bag. He met Patricia's eyes with a cold glance before he walked away, which was almost worse than if he'd ignored her order. He could diminish her with a single look, just like Salvador had the last few years during the fights about money. She felt ridiculous in the suit and fancy hairdo now, like she was wearing a costume. She yanked out the bobby pins as she walked to her room to take off the suit.

Patricia wasn't sure if Ray would come to dinner after Tío and the lawyer arrived, but he did, bolting his food with barely a glance at anyone.

"You still undefeated, Ray?" Tío asked, braving an attempt at conversation with him.

Ray nodded. "We're 6 and 0."

"Ray's a real fireball pitcher," Tío explained to Archuleta. "Just like I was in my day."

"You threw eighty?" Ray said. "I doubt it."

"Raymond," Lupe cautioned.

"What? I'm just saying."

"Son," Tío said, "for every decade of your retirement you get to add ten miles per hour to the fastball of your youth. So yes, I threw eighty."

After he finished eating, Ray pushed himself away from the table, leaving his plate there for the women to take care of. He threw a challenging look at Patricia before he walked away. That little chauvinistic act infuriated her. The sink was on his way out of the kitchen anyway. It took Patricia two years after they were married to train Salvador to clear his plate, and she'd made Ray carry his plate to the sink since he was three. But no one else seemed to notice and Patricia didn't want to overreact. Mia took Ray's plate along with hers to the sink, and then came back to clear the rest. Patricia guessed Mia was angling to be allowed to stay for the meeting.

"Mia, you have wonderful manners," Archuleta said. He reminded Patricia of a Botero sculpture, an overstuffed, mustached man like the statue outside the performing arts center downtown. Patricia wondered what her life would be like if she'd allowed Lupe to set her up with him when they were teenagers. This was her alternate reality: a Botero with a law degree and a weakness for flan.

"Thank you," Mia said. She resumed her seat next to Patricia, propped her cheek on her hand and waited for them to speak.

"We're just going to be talking about boring grownup stuff," Archuleta said.

"I'm on the committee," Mia said, lifting her chin.

Archuleta looked to Patricia. "It's all right," she said. "It makes her feel better to know what's going on." Mia sank back in her chair with a satisfied glance at Patricia.

"So, the meeting with the mayor," Tío began, "what exactly do we want to focus on?"

"I want the city to admit it did wrong," Patricia said. "And fire the police chief. He allowed this to happen. It was his policies, his men."

"What about no-knock raids?" Lupe said. "I think we should press for their elimination."

"And we want to form a citizen's review committee for the investigation of all police brutality," Tío said. "A panel with the authority to discipline officers."

"What about the officers the D.A. let off?" Patricia asked. "Is there anything we can do about them?"

"Not in the criminal system," Archuleta said. "The D.A.'s decision is final. But we can put together a civil suit if you decide to go the trial route. You would probably have to agree to forgo a civil suit if you opt for a settlement."

"The mayor should say sorry," Mia said.

"That's right," Patricia said. "He should."

"I appreciate all of your ideas," Archuleta said, "But I think the most important goal we can accomplish with this meeting is to propose a financial settlement from the city. We'll name a figure, they'll come back with another one, and hopefully we can avoid a trial."

"But we want a trial," Lupe said, leaning forward and spreading her palms flat on the table. "We could bring attention to this injustice and clear Salvador's name."

"You could also end up with no money at all," Archuleta said. "A trial could drag on for years, and even if you win, you might not get any money out of it in time to send the kids to college. I'll make the case that the city's negligence resulted in Salvador's death. They'll say that Salvador pulled a gun on the officers and they had to shoot."

"But can we prove they planted the gun?" Patricia asked.

"I've gained access to the ballistics tests and the gun is untraceable. There's nothing conclusive. I'll certainly try to introduce doubt, but it ultimately comes down to what the jury believes. And, like I said, you could end up with no money at all. I think we should propose a settlement. If the city doesn't come back with a reasonable offer, we can take it to arbitration or to trial. What number were you thinking, Patricia?"

"Number?" she said. He was asking her to put a monetary value on Salvador's life. Mia looked up at her, waiting for her to speak. "I have no idea."

Archuleta nodded and opened a manila folder. "I've researched some other cases where the city paid settlements. There was a case a few years back when a police officer sexually assaulted a couple of women, and the city settled with them for $650,000. In '96, a cop sped through a red light, striking and killing a

213

man, and they settled with the family for $3.5 million. There are a number of cases like this, none of them exactly parallel to your situation, but I think we should go in there asking for $5.5 million."

"Okay," Patricia said. The number was unfathomable to her. "Whatever you think is best. But I don't know if I'll be comfortable demanding that from the mayor."

"I'm willing to bet he'll bring it up. With all the publicity this case has been getting, he'll probably want to end it. He'll make an offer and then I can negotiate from there."

Mia tugged on Patricia's sleeve. "What am I going to wear to see the mayor?"

"Sorry, baby," Patricia said, "you can't go. I'm the only one going."

"But I'm on the committee," Mia said.

"I know you are, but the mayor might not understand. He might not think that he can talk about Salvador in front of you."

"But he's my dad," Mia said.

"You can come with us to the mayor's office, and then your grandma will sit with you outside while I go in and speak with the mayor. You'll be right there the whole time."

"I'm attending this meeting too," Lupe said.

"He invited me," Patricia said.

"I'm sure the invitation implied that other family members could come."

"I appreciate all the work you've done on the committee," Patricia said, "but I'm going to talk to the mayor myself. If we can't work things out, then the lawyers and the committee and everyone can go at it."

"Do you really think you can do it by yourself?" Lupe asked. "There's so much to remember. You'll have to keep your emotions in check."

Tío put his hand on Lupe's forearm. "Patricia did such a good job with her speech the other day," he said. "It's why she was invited to meet the mayor in the first place. I don't know how this can be any harder than speaking in front of a crowd."

Archuleta nodded. "I think the fewer people we send in there, the less hostile it will seem. We want to accomplish as much as we can, and this might be the best way."

"Fine." Lupe pushed her chair away from the table and then walked into the kitchen to start washing the dishes, something Patricia had never seen her do before with company present.

"Thank you," Patricia whispered to Tío.

After Archuleta left and the kids went to their rooms, Patricia asked Tío to wait. She fetched the letter from her dresser and hesitated, thinking maybe she could translate it with the Spanish-English dictionary, then Tío wouldn't need to be involved. But Tío was doing so much for Salvador, maybe he deserved to know what their marriage was really like. She held the letter out to Tío and asked him to read it. "I'm afraid of what it might say," she said.

"Why?" Tío asked, taking it from her like it was fragile.

"I think Salvador was having an affair." Saying it out loud made it seem true.

Tío squeezed her hand. "Let's just read it first." He replaced his regular glasses with his reading glasses, looked the letter over, and then began to translate:

Dear Patricia,

I feel like I know you. Salvador used to talk about you so often, telling me how beautiful and smart you are, how Mia is just like you.

When I heard about Salvador's death, it pounded me into little pieces. What a cruel loss of a dear man, husband, father, and friend.

As you know, Salvador has helped me and Carmelita greatly since the death of my husband Esteban thirteen years ago. Whenever I could not feed her, Salvador helped me. He always brought us pretty clothes when he visited. You have been so gracious to allow his visits and help. Now we are both in the same position, widows, and I wish you did not have to know the misery that

215

I've known. I feel like that terrible accident that took Esteban has claimed his best friend now too.

I am lighting candles for you at the church. I am saying prayers to Guadalupe for Mia and Ray. Here is a little money to help. I know it's not much, but you have given me so much over the years. Please know that I mourn with you.

With great admiration,
Graciela

Patricia and Tío looked at each other without speaking for a moment. "This doesn't sound like an affair," he said finally.

"Then why didn't he tell me about her? What was this accident?" She thought of the jagged scar he'd come back from Mexico with so many years earlier, the skin on his arm still pink and tender.

"She's left a phone number."

Patricia looked at it. "That's the phone everyone in the pueblo uses, at the general store. The village is pretty remote, so they can't get cell phone signals."

"Do you want me to call, see if I can speak to her?"

Patricia thought a moment. "Yes. Please. Ask her how I can send the money back."

Tío shook his head. "Don't refuse her generosity." He picked up the phone in the kitchen and dialed the number, explained the situation to the shopkeeper. "He says Graciela lives far away, and comes to town about once a month. He says if you call back on Saturday, he'll be able to tell you when she's coming next."

"Saturday? Well, okay." Tío wrote down the number and said he'd call again that weekend. She supposed she could wait a few more days to find out who her husband had really been. Maybe the man she'd kicked out of the house, sending him off to his death, had been innocent after all.

Patricia's heels clicked against the stone floors in the chilly hall of the city and county building. She walked ahead, Lupe and

Mia behind her, both of them silent, still mad at her for meeting with the mayor alone.

Patricia asked the security guard where the mayor's office was, and he directed her around the corner. Patricia stood in front of the desk, her heels sinking into the plush rug. When the secretary looked up, Patricia said, "I have a meeting with the mayor."

"Are you Patricia?" The secretary flashed her a friendly smile.

"Mrs. Santillano." Patricia held her mouth in a line. At least her old tendency to avoid smiling unless she truly meant it, the habitual *La Llorona* face, would help her appear strong in this situation. Too many women spent their lives unleashing smiles they couldn't control, bestowing them on everyone, even their rivals.

"I'll go and see if he's ready," the secretary said, her demeanor suddenly formal.

Lupe and Mia sat on the stiff couch across the room, but Patricia remained standing. The secretary came back out of the office and nodded at her. Patricia followed her into the mayor's office, and the secretary closed the substantial door behind her.

The mayor filled his chair, filled the room, his huge hands resting on the top of his mahogany desk. "Welcome," he said, rising and mauling her hand with a bone-crushing shake. A small chair stood directly in front of his desk. When she sat in it, the mayor loomed above her. She felt like a child at the principal's office. The mayor tried to conceal his weight in an expensive tailored suit. His starched white collar pinched the skin of his neck. A spray of small dark moles dotted his café-au-lait cheeks. His desk was empty except for a blotter, a phone, and a set of fancy pens aligned in a holder. Either he didn't mess with paperwork or he didn't want to appear as though he had to.

"Mrs. Santillano, I first want to apologize on behalf of the city," he said in a deep, grave voice. "I can't imagine the grief that you're going through."

Patricia nodded once in a way she hoped looked strong, non-committal. She had to step up to his intimidation game. This whole meeting might become like one between two animals, all posturing, gesture, and implied superiority.

"I know you probably have a number of concerns you'd like to address," he said, "but first I want to say that I truly hope we can resolve this matter to your satisfaction in the near future. I've asked the city council to approve a settlement that I hope you'll agree is fair."

"What could be fair?" Patricia asked. She thought of Salvador, who may have been true to her after all. "I need you to answer one question. Why did this happen?"

He looked down at her. "I want to assure you that we are launching an investigation into what went wrong."

"Even though the police botched the warrant, Salvador still might have had a chance if it hadn't been a no-knock raid. He was sleeping after working a night shift, and they burst into his house, burst into his room. Of course he was disoriented. With his mind in that state, he might not have known how to react, what to do to save his life."

The mayor stared at her.

"And don't tell me that he shouldn't have pulled a gun, because I don't believe that gun was his. The police say it was, the city says it was, but I don't trust them, because I never knew him to have owned a gun," Patricia rushed on, blurting out her words in a stream. "He didn't know until his door burst open that it was the police breaking into his home. I want you to stop all no-knock raids. They give a person no chance at all."

"Well, like I said, Mrs. Santillano, we have a committee investigating this matter."

They stared at each other. The mayor's silence propelled Patricia on. "The chief of police has no right to keep his job. This happened on his watch. Whether the chief was directly involved with the warrant or not, he is ultimately responsible for the actions of his men."

"We're reviewing the performance of several key players, I can assure you," the mayor said.

"I also want you to establish a citizen's review board that has the power to punish the police. They're clearly incapable of disciplining their own people."

"I'll take that under advisement." He sat with his elbows on his desk, his fingertips together, looking, just as Ray had predicted, as if he were waiting for her to shut up.

Patricia set her jaw. "All you seem to be doing about the murder of my husband is forming different committees to discuss things. Are you ever going to actually do anything? Make some changes? Why did you call me in here?"

"Mrs. Santillano," he said, his voice annoyed. "I invited you to my office so that I could formally apologize on behalf of the city. I invited you here so that I could express my wish that we can resolve this matter civilly in a way that satisfies you and your supporters."

Patricia sat back in her chair. So he was afraid of her, afraid she could command all the Latinos in the city to riot.

"And also," he continued, "I wanted to give you this." He opened a desk drawer and took out an envelope.

"What is it?" Patricia asked, accepting it.

"This is the settlement that the city council has approved. I believe it's a generous one. I hope you'll take it home, think it over, and then we can get our lawyers together."

Patricia flipped the envelope over, finding it sealed. He clearly wanted her to read the letter after she'd left his office. She stuck her finger in the flap and tore it open. She shook out the letter and skimmed it until she found the number: $150,000. More than she'd ever had at one time, but a damn low price for killing her husband. Why was it so low? Because he was an immigrant? Because the cops said he had a gun? "Listen," she said, "the minute I leave, I'm going to find as many reporters as I can and tell them exactly what I requested of you. If you don't make some of the changes I've asked for and make them soon, well—" she paused, pretending to be who he thought she was, "you can just imagine what will happen."

He was up for reelection soon, and he couldn't afford to have thirty-five percent of the population outraged—the Republicans would beat him for certain if he did. Let him think that she could snap her fingers and have thousands of protestors marching in the streets. Let him think that everyone with a Spanish surname would vote as she commanded. "That's all I have to say," she said, and then stood before he could take the initiative to dismiss her.

"It's been a pleasure, Mrs. Santillano," the mayor said as she walked out the door.

Patricia's knees shook, her stomach felt queasy. She thought she might faint, but she had to get out of there, complete her masquerade of strength. Patricia nodded at the secretary, who gave a little wave, and led Lupe and Mia out into the corridor.

Three days later when the mayor announced the termination of the chief of police's contract, reporters gathered in front of Patricia's door. She went out to them herself this time. When they watched the local news later that evening, Mia sat three inches from the television, flipping from one station to the other to catch parts of the story on all of the networks. Patricia watched herself on the screen, crowded by all the microphones around her that she'd barely perceived. "This is a small victory," TV Patricia said, "but the Justice for Santillano committee is not going to give up until all of our demands are met, and the people of Denver are safe from the police." Her voice sounded strange to her, more nasal than it should be.

"That blue shirt suits you," Lupe said. "Your father will get a kick out of hearing that you were on the news with Anne Trujillo." Patricia's father had a longstanding crush on the anchorwoman.

Mia looked back and forth from her mother on the couch to her mother on the TV. "You look taller there," she said.

"Come on, that's enough," Patricia said. She stood and turned off the TV. She wished she could take a break from death and politics and legal action. "My favorite show should be coming on the radio any minute."

On Saturday nights, Patricia listened to the R&B Jukebox on KUVO, Denver's public jazz station. The DJ played old R&B from the forties through the early sixties, when it was raw and good for dancing. Most of the songs covered the same subjects, love that led to ruin or women who looked good in tight skirts. The way they sang about it, love was clover, leaving a sweet taste in your mouth that would last forever. But in these songs love always ended, or was going to. This show was the only overlap between her taste in music and Salvador's, and in the early days they used to listen to the show together, holding hands or dancing.

The first song came on and Patricia pulled Mia up off the couch. They swayed to the music, Mia's feet on hers. Patricia concentrated on the words, trying to let the singer convince her that what he was saying was true. Bobby Blue Bland was singing in a sweet falsetto about taking love while you found it, tugging every syllable back before he let it go. She loved the exquisite torture of these old songs, how all of them related somehow to her, to everyone, she guessed, drawing up a memory that hurt like hell.

Lupe brought out a tray from the kitchen with a bottle of red wine and a couple of glasses, and grape juice in a champagne flute for Mia. So this was a celebration.

Ray came out of his room. "What's going on?" he asked. "Can't you turn down this stupid music?"

"Mom fired the police chief," Mia said. "So we're having juice."

Ray sat on the couch and accepted a grape juice flute from his sister. His hands revealed a natural grace, holding the glass like he was born for caviar and champagne. "The mayor fired him, not Mom," he said. "The mayor didn't do anything but help himself."

Patricia drank the wine too fast, and then filled her glass again. Now Otis Redding was talking to Patricia through the song "Open the Door," saying he'd been wrong, and now he wanted to get back with his baby. The wine made everything feel like a personal message. Otis sounded so reasonable, worthy of forgiveness from whatever woman he'd wronged, though Patricia knew he had probably been a dog. But then Otis began to ask her to let him in, over and over, each iteration causing Patricia a unique pang. Why hadn't she let Salvador come back when he asked to? After he came home from Mexico the last time and she'd locked him out, Salvador tried to change her mind a couple of times, waiting for her on the steps in front of the door until she came home from work. *Please,* he said, *let's work this out,* and took her hand for as long as she'd let him hold it. One time he fell to his knees and blocked her path, a man begging, fit for a song. *Let me come home,* Salvador had said. *I've been away too long. I miss you and the kids.* And she'd told him, *If you come home, you'll just leave again,* thinking, let him ask me one more time, let him stew a few weeks longer, and then when he comes back, he'll really stay. Whatever their differences were, it was no good for the kids to grow up without a father. But he hadn't asked again. Why hadn't she just put her arms around him and welcomed him back inside?

Otis Redding asked his baby to look into his eyes, pleading, knowing that if the girl would just meet his electric gaze once, she'd be a goner for good.

Patricia listened to this show every Saturday, and as she listened she always went over the identical memories until a groove must have been worn in her brain, a path between these songs and those hurts. She yelled at the DJ, "Rolando, play something happy for me!"

When the song ended, the DJ played some Ray Charles, a mischievous song from his early years, "I Got a Woman," and Patricia reached out and pulled Ray off the couch.

"Dance with me," she said.

"You're drunk," Ray muttered.

"Yeah? And you're a jerk." She grabbed his hands and began to lead. "This is a little two-step," she said, "your grandfather

taught me it when I was your age. Watch my feet." She demonstrated the simple dance, right foot behind the left, back to
the center, left foot behind the right, back to the center, repeat,
putting a little shimmy into every move. Ray's big puppy hands
sweated as he concentrated. She wondered how many more Saturday nights she'd spend with him, until he started begging off
to go see a girl. He was as tall as she was now.

"You're a natural dancer," she said, watching Ray pick up the
step with almost no effort.

"So was Dad," Ray said, looking straight at her.

"That's the truth." Salvador had loved to take her dancing,
led her with the lightest, firmest touch, two strong fingers on
her waist telling her to spin until her skirt flared.

CHAPTER 17

Ed

May 16

Ed drove past his exit for home and continued west on I-70. As his car climbed out of the Denver Basin up to the range that crested at Vail Pass, then plunged down into the Eagle Basin, his agitation from beating the man eased. Basin, range, basin. The rise and the fall of the land was calming and rhythmic, and a plan began to form: he'd head to Moab. Soon Ed was out on the high plateau of west central Colorado, the rocks transitioning from cool purples, blues, and grays to ruddier hues, until they were the color of mud mixed with milk and blood. The pines and firs gave way to scrubby desert brush, the flat, bare land laid out like a platter for the big blue sky.

He should call Claire. But she'd order him to head home, and he wasn't going to do that until he found McGill. He would still have been at work if that domestic hadn't gone to hell. She wouldn't expect him yet.

The terrain grew rockier, the mountains rising up on either side of the road as he drove. He should take the kids camping after baseball season. He'd teach them the names of the rocks. His father believed it was a sign of respect to know the proper names of natural things, and Ed would teach his kids to say gypsum, sage, and lark bunting instead of rock, plant, and bird. He tried to remember what his dad had taught him of geology. "That's Pierre Shale, that's Dakota Sandstone," he could hear his father saying, pointing out variations in color and texture. "The I-70 road cut is one of the most beautiful exposures of this rock in the world." It was good to be out of Denver, heading toward the open sky, away from the claustrophobic trailers and musty rented rooms where his job took him, away from those cheap baseball trophies flecked with blood.

When he crossed the Utah border it was almost 6:00, the time to call home if he'd be late. He pulled into a gas station. He dawdled in the store, picking up a Utah roadside geology book. His dad used to have a whole set of these, and said he would have studied geology if he'd been able to go to college. When Ed had told his dad his college major, he'd repeated it back. "Criminal justice?" he'd asked, taking the half-finished cigarette from his lips and mashing it into the ashtray, then saying nothing more. Even though his dad had been dead for five years, Ed still wanted to please him. The rocks that bored Ed as a kid now comforted him. They were here long before Ed's brief life had begun, and they would be here after everyone who remembered him had died. He dug into his pocket for some quarters and approached the pay phone.

Claire answered and he told her that he was going to be back late. "Like tomorrow."

She didn't respond for a moment. "Where are you calling from?"

"A gas station in Utah."

"Nice of you to check in," she said.

"I should have called earlier." Ed waited for her to ask what he was doing in Utah. Her silence made him nervous. "I had a bit of an incident at work today."

"I know. Mitch's wife called to ask how you were." Claire paused. "I told her I had no idea."

"Sorry," Ed said, embarrassed that now Mitch and Mavis knew he hadn't called Claire. He wondered if Mavis had mentioned Ed's earlier panic attack to Claire, and she thought her unstable husband was at large in Utah. "I screwed up," Ed said. "I should have shot the guy that was attacking Mitch."

"No, you shouldn't have. Another body? Another leave?"

"Well, I didn't shoot him, okay? I found a different way." His scraped knuckles throbbed as he thought back to the beating he'd given the man. "I was lucky that Mitch didn't get hurt."

"Agreed."

She wasn't asking him to explain himself, but Ed blundered on. "I'm going to Moab to visit McGill."

"I figured you'd contact him one of these days. Of course, I thought you'd just phone him."

"You mean you're not mad?" Ed fiddled with the coin return on the phone, waiting for her to speak.

"I want some time apart."

"What do you mean? We're married—we're not supposed to be apart."

"You're the one that left, Ed."

"I didn't *leave*. I'm just on a short trip."

"Is that what your grandpa told your grandmother?"

Ed squeezed the receiver of the phone as if to choke it. "That's not fair." Ed's grandfather had abandoned his grandmother, leaving her with Ed's father and uncle. Ed once told Claire he wondered if whatever was inside his grandfather that had caused him to leave was in him too. He shouldn't have mentioned his worry. She could use it against him now—and did.

"It doesn't matter that you're not here," Claire said. "You seem gone even when you're home."

Would Claire try to take the children from him? He wasn't going to let that happen. "Claire, we can work this out. I'll be home tomorrow and I'll do better. I just panicked, that's all."

"I'll let you know when you can see me." She hung up.

Ed could barely keep his mind on driving as he headed into Moab. The rock formations in the dim light made the town look like an outpost on Mars. He pulled into the Red Rock Motel, whose placard read, "Rooms $40."

The room was dingy and smelled of smoke. The huge lighted sign of the truck stop next door shone in the window. He fell, exhausted, onto the bed, expending all his remaining energy yanking off his shoes and collapsing on the mattress. He wished he were in Denver, out to dinner at the Blue Bonnet with his family, eating one of their burritos stuffed with tender, marinated beef. There was nothing lonelier than a solitary night in a grimy hotel. His wayward grandfather probably spent a lot of time in places like this.

When Ed's parents had married, somehow his dad's missing father had heard of the occasion, and left them a leather pouch filled with gold coins on the gift table at their reception. Ed's father had told him this story many times: how he'd picked up the coin purse, felt the weight of it in his hand and recognized the crabbed handwriting on the attached note as belonging to the man he hadn't seen since he was nine years old. Ed's parents left the reception with the coin pouch. They headed out driving on a country road under the stars, stopping when they were far out into the expanse of the eastern plains, where Ed's father hurled the bag of coins as far as he could into a field of winter wheat.

Ed fell asleep, thinking of his grandfather, a man he'd never met. He woke at midnight, his stomach pinching him with hunger. He walked to the vending machines to buy potato chips and a Snickers. He hoped the room's honor bar would have something stiff to drink, but this was Utah: it contained nothing stronger than a decaf Mountain Dew. If he couldn't fix things with Claire, this would be how he'd eat every night, alone in his grim lodgings along Colorado Boulevard, a mangy street where divorced cops took nondescript apartments next to ethnic restaurants, muffler repair shops, and Shotgun Willie's, the largest strip club in Denver. The food stuck in his throat, sending up a wave of acid he could taste in the back of his mouth.

The noise and light of big rigs rumbling into the gas station next door shook him awake all night. He slept fitfully, his mind drifting in half-dreams about Claire. They hadn't had sex since before he'd killed Santillano, over two months now, the longest drought since the birth of each kid. The truth was Ed hadn't really wanted to. Even when he was home, Claire felt farther than one state away.

Ed stepped out of his motel room and into the parking lot the next morning and breathed deeply. Morning in Moab was a bright and beautiful thing, the enormous clear blue sky setting off the stunning red sandstones all around, the black desert varnish on the cliffs glimmering in the sunlight. Everywhere he looked he saw buttes, towers, and arches, fantastical formations carved when the softer layers of the rock had eroded. It was the kind of sweet morning that fooled suckers into braving the day.

Ed planned to find McGill and then rush home and mend things with Claire, but first he needed breakfast. He drove down the main drag past several coffee shops that had sprouted in recent years, selling their fussy little breakfasts of scones and croissants to skinny tourists on $3,000-dollar bicycles. He pulled into a diner, the first place he saw that looked like it believed in grease.

He tucked into a spread of scrambled eggs, bacon, toast, and hash browns, working from left to right, clearing his plate. His wife was probably going to take up with the orthodontist, he'd scarred his kids by leaving without an explanation, and he'd all but gotten his partner killed, but he ate heartily, trying to erase the aftertaste of last night's sad dinner. For the moment, it was a relief to be so far from all the messes he'd made. He asked the waitress if she knew McGill.

"Rod McGill? Sure I know him," she said. "He runs Sunnycide Rafting Adventures just down the road."

"Down Main Street?"

"You see any other street? If he's got a rafting trip to lead, he'd be gone at dawn. You might not catch him until the afternoon."

Ed paid his bill and drove down the road. He saw the sign for Sunnycide Rafting Adventures on his right, a smiling sun beaming down on a river running through a red rock canyon.

He pulled into the dirt lot and stepped out of his Cherokee. A man out front was inspecting rafting equipment, checking items off on a clipboard as he moved past yellow inflatable paddle rafts, oars, water jugs, and orange life vests. He wore a faded blue bandana around his head, his hair tied back in a ponytail, his skin blasted red as the surrounding rocks from the elements.

228

He looked up as Ed approached. "Can I help you?"

"Maybe you could explain your sign to me," Ed said. "It's spelled Sunny C-I-D-E—that means 'killer.'"

"Exactly," the man said, squinting at Ed with his clear blue eyes. "Sunny because nature is prettier than hell around here, Cide because nature will kill you the second you let your guard down. This landscape specializes in the elimination of idiots."

"Are you McGill?" Ed asked.

"Guilty." He crossed his arms over his chest and leaned against a trailer full of rafts. "And what should I call you, officer?"

"Ed. How'd you know I was a cop?"

"Well, your hair is cut like a cop's, you stand like a cop, you watch my hands like a cop—frankly, you reek cop, Ed." McGill let out a piercing whistle and pointed up at the sky. "Sharp-shinned hawk."

"Yeah," Ed said, shielding his eyes with his hands and looking up. He saw a dark silhouette that could have been a pigeon for all he knew. "That's a beaut."

"The earliest rafting trip I could work you into leaves tomorrow morning."

"I'm not here for rafting. I want to talk to you."

"What about?"

Ed scuffed his shoes in the red dirt. "I work for the DPD, like you did. I've been having trouble at work since I shot a man, and my wife thinks I should see a shrink, but I'd rather talk to someone who knows what it's like."

McGill held up his palms. "Hold up, amigo. It's barely 7:30. I need a pot of coffee."

McGill led Ed into a cramped trailer office. On the walls hung faded photos of McGill in various remote locations—he stood alone in the pictures, his nose perpetually sunburned. He didn't seem to have photos that dated from his days on the force. Dozens of Indian dream-catchers hung all around, like the trailer was infested with beaded fur cobwebs. Stacks of yellowing paper and triplicate pink and yellow release forms for the rafting business were scattered everywhere.

"I've been off seven years now," McGill said, clearing room for two steaming tin mugs on his crowded desk. "Are the guys on the force talking me up as some kind of guru?"

"Not exactly," Ed said. Guru was not the word people used. *Nutcase* had come up a lot. "My partner just mentioned you had a rafting outfit in Moab. I wondered how you made the transition out of police work." Maybe Ed could do something outdoors, too.

"I'd love to chat," he said, "but I have to supply some mountain bikers at noon, and I'd better head out if I want to make it. Are you up for a hike?" McGill rummaged around the office, throwing canteens, hats, and food from a small refrigerator into a sun-faded backpack. He must have been in his mid-forties, but apart from his weathered skin he looked much younger, with snapping eyes and a light step. According to Mitch, McGill had been frazzled when he left the force. Ed snuck a look at his own reflection in the glass covering a framed map. He looked older, fatter, and tired. When he was a rookie, he'd sworn he'd never look like the veterans did.

"Sure," Ed said, "I haven't been here since I was a teenager." He'd hiked around Arches with his dad, ticking off each of the delicate rock bridges on his father's checklist, studying ancient petroglyphs and admiring hulking rocks shaped like elephants.

"Canyonlands is a ten-mile hike. How are your shoes?"

Ed looked at his sneakers. He'd intended to jog in them when he bought them a few months earlier, but so far he'd only worn them to baseball games. "I think they'll do."

The parking lot at the visitor's center near the trailhead was packed. Old folks wearing wide-brimmed hats milled around. Ed walked past a motor home with an Illinois license plate that read RETIRED. Busloads of German tourists poured out, and a Mormon family with six kids walked past, the dad with a red beard, the girls wearing bonnets, braids, and dresses, one of them in velvet despite the heat.

"Come on," McGill said, "there won't be any traffic where we're going." He gave Ed a pack to carry and led the way to the Murphy Trail.

The hike began in a ruddy-sand desert area, sparsely covered with juniper, piñon pine, yucca, Mormon tea, and tough grasses. Little lizards darted everywhere. "My dad and I used to have a competition to see who could spot the most lizards," Ed said.

"I'd win that contest," McGill said.

"Wager?"

"A bottle of Maker's Mark."

"Okay. I might have to drive back to Colorado to get it for you, though."

"You're talking like you plan to lose. You do need my help, Ed."

They came to a tall cliff, so sheer it didn't seem possible to descend it without rappelling equipment. "Are you sure about this?" he asked.

"Do you want to win the bet or don't you?"

The trail was carefully marked and arranged with switchbacks so it wasn't too steep in any section, but it took them an hour to pick their way down the mile-and-a-half long path to the bottom of the cliff. Concentrating on where to put his feet helped Ed keep his mind off Claire. To the east rose the La Sal Mountains, a pretty little purple-blue range with snow-capped peaks. A valley cut by the Green River spread out before them, surrounded by red cliffs, mesas, buttes, and spires. The landscape felt open, empty, and clean, free of vegetation, displaying its geology like it had nothing to hide.

"So what's on your mind?" McGill asked as they walked.

"I've been having trouble ever since I killed that man," Ed said, "and I wanted to hear your story, see how you handled it."

"You've got stones in your passway, hellhounds on your trail. That sort of thing." He nodded toward a darting lizard. "That makes seven for me."

Ed had already forgotten about the lizards. "Talking about it is hard," Ed confessed.

"Let me see if I can guess. Bad dreams, night sweats, trouble with the woman, legal issues, hesitations at work, flashbacks, the whole nine?"

"That about covers it."

"Did your woman do that to you?"

"What?" Ed asked, then touched the flesh under his eye, its color now faded to jaundiced yellow with a fringe of eggplant. "No, it's not like that. This was a baseball accident."

"An accident, Ed," McGill asked, "or did you put your head in the way of that ball because you couldn't stand the pain of living?" A chipped-tooth grin broke across McGill's face.

"I'm glad this amuses you."

McGill took a swig from his canteen. "I remember the psychological evaluation they put me through before they gave me a badge. That lipless woman with a checklist on her lap asking, 'Have you ever had sexual thoughts about children? Sexual thoughts about cats?'"

The nostrils of Ed's evaluator had flared periodically when he answered a question, and he'd always wondered what that meant. Back then he thought he was strong, that he'd never go crazy. "How did you end up here?"

"Short version: I couldn't shoot people anymore."

"We've got time for the long version."

"You come out here uninvited, asking me to drag that up again," McGill said, kicking a rock in his path. "Shit." They were walking past what looked like a junkyard for rocks, red sandstone shards piled haphazardly where they'd fallen from the pancake-layered rock wall above. "The department started up a gang unit in 1986," McGill said. "I had only a couple of years under my belt and I was still gung ho—working graves, jumping on hot calls—so I volunteered. I wanted to be right in the middle of the good stuff. In the '70s and early '80s, Denver just had groups of teenagers that would jack radios out of cars and break into stores. But they weren't running drugs and they weren't killing people."

"The good old days," Ed said, struggling to breathe. McGill set a punishing pace down the winding trail. Ed hung back and hoped McGill would slow his stride. "So what changed?"

McGill charged ahead, so Ed sped up again. "In L.A.," McGill continued, "two mothers whose sons were running in street gangs decided to move their families to Denver to get their boys away from trouble. But the boys themselves were the trouble. The two kids met up in Denver and started their own gang, the Rollin' 30's Crips."

Ed nodded. It was a black gang that had been pretty well eliminated in Denver during the late-'90s, as the ringleaders were arrested, and those who couldn't be tied to murders were put away for racketeering. Now the Hispanic and Asian gangs that the police had neglected for a few years were surging. Ed spotted a green lizard that was three times the size of the little ones they'd been counting. He moved toward the rock ledge where it was perched. "Does this one count for more points?"

"Rattlesnake," McGill said.

"What?" Ed froze. "Where?" He heard a rattle, like someone shaking a fistful of bones.

"It's a few inches from your feet."

"I don't see it. Which way do I go?"

"Run," McGill said, calm as a reptile. "Straight ahead."

Ed heard snaky sounds, another rattle, and a hiss as he leapt off the rock. He jogged a good ways off.

"You all right, amigo?" McGill asked, catching up. "You almost stepped on that snake. It was camouflaged, but still, you've got to keep a lookout."

Ed's face burned. "I'm fine." Sweat trickled down the side of his face. So much for his fantasies of moving to Utah and being outdoorsy.

"I'll give you two points for that lizard. Level of difficulty."

"Thanks."

McGill looked Ed over and shook his head. "You remind me of myself my first year here, when I didn't know to check the clouds before I went out exploring slot canyons."

"I think you were younger than me when you started over."

"You're not that old."

"I feel it."

They started walking again. "So what happened to you with the gangs?" Ed asked.

"The two California bangers organized one of those neighborhood groups of teenagers," McGill said. "They held meetings, drew up hit lists, and watched gangster movies as instructional videos. They studied the police's habits, identified unmarked cars and undercover officers. They even sent members on pilgrimages to L.A., and Crips from there would travel to Denver to run gangbanging seminars, basically. They brought back semi-automatic weapons. Soon there was a pipeline running crack cocaine from L.A. to Denver, the Bloods started up a faction, and then all hell broke loose."

The ten-foot sides of the gully tapered off and the view opened up again. "I started patrolling the neighborhoods in northeast Denver where the gangs were based," McGill said, "studying the graffiti, learning the hand signals, the code words that changed every week."

The next mile rose sharply uphill on a wheel-rutted road to a hogback. Ed puffed along next to McGill, who wasn't even winded and kept talking. "I'd been on the gang unit for a little over three years when I answered a call to break up a fight at Cole Middle School. It was one of the schools that the Crips and Bloods recruited young kids from, so I went there a lot. Usually the middle schools weren't as violent as the high schools, so I'd often go without backup. On this particular day, the principal said an eighth grader—a suspected Crip—had beat the hell out of a female teacher in the middle of class. A bunch of teachers hauled him off her, and locked him in an empty classroom—but he was still worked up and they were afraid."

"So when I get there," McGill continued, "I open the door to the classroom they'd locked him in, and he's gone. The window's open, so I go around to the outside and see a movement in some bushes in the schoolyard. I order him to come out. I take a few steps toward the bushes. Nothing: no movement, no response. All of a sudden he comes roaring out of the bushes, pointing a gun at me. Before I can think, I shoot him in the chest." McGill stopped walking. "He was thirteen years old."

"I remember looking at his sneakers as he lay on the pavement, white K-SWISS jobs with fat blue laces, Crip sneakers. On my rounds, I always checked the kids' footwear, like that was the cut-and-dried indicator of whether they were good or evil. But they were still just sneakers."

McGill soaked his bandana with water from his canteen. "The kid must have had the gun on him the whole time he was assaulting the teacher. I'll never get over that—he could have shot the teacher, but he didn't. So would he have shot me? Maybe he just wanted to earn his street cred by threatening an officer, go to juvie for a couple years, get some tats. The paramedics tried to save him, but he'd lost too much blood. I expected community outrage—I mean, I'd killed a black child—but apart from the usual protests from his family, there wasn't much. We were coming off the bloodiest summer for Denver ever. People were sick of gangs, sick of drive-bys, and they took me at my word. I wanted them to hate me."

"From personal experience, being hated isn't worth the aggravation." Ed weighed McGill's story against his own, thinking of the rallies and signs and media attacking him. At least he hadn't shot a kid. He couldn't bear that, killing a kid. "Did you leave the force right away?"

"I stuck it out for a year, but my head wasn't in it anymore. I fought with my wife constantly. She finally divorced me. I knew I could never shoot another person, and once you decide that, you're a danger to the other cops."

"How did you recover?"

He looked at Ed sharply. "When you kill a man, his life and yours are intertwined until you die. He'll be the first guy waiting for you when you cross. But I've seen cops that can pick up and go on. They carry their ghosts all the way into retirement. At that point, a heart attack finishes most of them."

Ed had killed Santillano at close range; his face would always be in Ed's mind. He'd never asked his father if he remembered the faces of the men he'd killed in war. Ed finally had something in common with his dad. "I've never been anything but a cop," Ed said. "I've got a wife and three kids." The burden of this felt as heavy as one of the rock elephants in Arches. He had no real choice about how to live the rest of his life. They needed his pension, his insurance.

McGill started walking again. "Some cops are able to keep going. But if you don't decide to stick with it, I can always use some seasonal help at Sunnycide." He glanced back at Ed. "I'd have to send you out with a snakebite kit, though."

"Thanks. I'll keep that in mind." It sounded relaxing, floating down the Colorado River with McGill for the rest of his days. Would Claire be up for moving out here, to Mormon country? Sticking Polly in a bonnet?

"Here are our guys," McGill said as two string-bean men in spandex pedaled up the slickrock toward them. McGill arranged some food and drinks on a blanket. The men went for the energy bars and protein shakes, leaving the turkey sandwiches. They had the faces of retirees and the bodies of twenty-year-olds.

"You going to eat that sandwich?" Ed asked.

The cyclists shook their heads. "Go ahead," one of them said. "It'd weigh too heavy on me."

Ed ripped off the cellophane and tore into the sandwich. A truck rumbled up out of the empty land behind them and pulled in next to them. A man climbed out and waved at McGill. "You seen our cyclists?" he asked. "A short guy and an Amazon woman?"

"Not yet," McGill said.

"You mean we could have driven here?" Ed asked.

McGill smiled. "It looked like you could use the exercise."

Ed sank down on the ground.

McGill put a hand on his shoulder. "I'm having a barbecue tonight. You're welcome to come."

Ed's throat was scorched and his feet were sore. He would have liked to hang out here and do nothing for a few days. But Claire was back home, trying to get rid of him, the hours he

236

was gone piling up against him. He missed her and the kids. He didn't want to be single, he didn't want to live alone. He could not do what his grandfather had done, say *forget you* and hit the road. "I can't this time," Ed said.

McGill handed him a dog-eared Sunnycide business card with a smiling sun in the corner. "Here's where to send the booze," he said. "Call if you're interested in my offer."

Ed caught a ride with the truck back to Moab. A six-mile hike was enough for one day.

When Ed pulled into his home in Denver, it was almost 8:00, Polly's bedtime. From now on, he'd do a better job. He'd convince Claire to give him another chance. He'd gone over his speech to her as he drove, imagining her replies, working out comebacks. He pictured Claire in the bathroom, blowing Polly's hair dry after a bath. But the house was dark. He came in from the garage and called out to his family, but no one answered. His legs began to shake from the exertion of the hike followed by the long drive. A wave of intense loneliness broke inside him. He picked up the phone and dialed Claire's cell. It sent him to voice mail. "Claire, I'm home," he told the phone, "call me."

CHAPTER 18

Patricia
June 8

Patricia was near the intersection of Federal and Speer, driving toward Ray's baseball game at Ruby Hill, when Mia shouted from the backseat. "Wait! I forgot El Johnway."

"Oh, Mia," Lupe said, turning to look at her, "it's just a toy."

Before games, Ray rubbed El Johnway's football-clutching hand over his bat for luck. Mia pointed El Johnway at her brother when he was pitching, as if the action figure emitted game-influencing rays. The longer Ray's undefeated streak lasted, the more superstitious the kids became. But kids were naturally superstitious. Patricia had started knocking on wood when she was nine after two of her grandparents died in the same year. She feared the bad times that lurked around the corner, so she knocked on wood, hoping the gesture would keep calamity at bay. It hadn't saved Salvador, but the habit remained ingrained. Maybe she could borrow El Johnway for luck tonight—Tío had arranged a phone call with Graciela after the game.

"If we turn around now, we'll be late," Patricia said.

"But Ray will lose if we don't get him," Mia said.

"Isn't El Johnway powerful enough to work his magic from home?"

"Patricia," Lupe said, "don't encourage her superstition."

It was worse than Lupe knew. Ray dressed for games in a particular order: sliding shorts first, then socks, then pitching sleeves. Then he'd eat a snack, always one banana and two sticks of beef jerky. "Pitchers need potassium and protein," he explained seriously, like a retired ballplayer on a commercial advertising a pain reliever. While he sat at the kitchen counter chewing his banana, he positioned a one-inch photo of Roberto Clemente under his sock next to his skin. Finally, Ray would go back to his room to button up his jersey, pull up his stirrups, and finish with his pants. He always put his baseball cap on with the brim at a slight angle, then swiveled it forward to lock. After that, he wouldn't sit down again until he was in the car on the way to the game, afraid to leave his luck lying somewhere in the house.

"El Johnway isn't superstition," Mia said. "It'll be your fault if Ray loses."

"Mia, don't talk to me that way." Patricia didn't want Mia to go through life as she had, fearing she could cause bad things to happen if she lapsed in her rituals. So she continued driving toward the field, hoping this would prove to Mia that Ray was in charge of his power.

Gloria Sandoval intercepted Patricia on her way to the bleachers, catching her arm with her warm, manicured hand. Lupe and Mia walked ahead and settled into their seats in the stands.

"I saw you on TV the other day," Gloria said, her eyes wide and solemn, exaggerated with heavy makeup. "I'm so sorry to hear about your husband."

"Thank you," Patricia said. The curved edges of Gloria's nails depressed her flesh faintly. She wanted to escape this conversation, but felt like a rabbit in a raptor's talons.

"It's amazing that Ray is pitching so well this season," Gloria said, then dropped her voice to a whisper, "after what he's been through."

Patricia could smell Gloria's grooming products—the candy apple scent of the hairspray she applied like a coat of lacquer, the violent mint of her breath spray. "Well, he loves baseball," Patricia said.

"When I first heard about the shooting in March, I had no idea that Salvador was your husband. I didn't make the connection." She leaned forward, like they were friends, sharing a secret. "Why doesn't Ray use his father's last name?"

239

Patricia wanted to tell Gloria to mind her own business, but that might lead to a scene and an aftermath of bad feelings that would last the rest of the season. "Ray wants to keep baseball separate from what happened to his dad," Patricia said. "He doesn't want people talking about it or feeling sorry for him. So we signed him up under my maiden name."

"The poor thing." Gloria shook her head. "I talked with Coach Pete, and we're going to dedicate this Pirates season to the memory of your husband."

People were always acting as though the loss of a life could be redeemed through a triumph in some game, Patricia thought. Like the football announcers on TV talking about a patch players wore to commemorate a fallen teammate, injecting a false note of sorrow into their voices before resuming their jocular banter. Was Gloria attempting some publicity stunt? "That's kind of you," Patricia said, "but Ray doesn't want to be reminded of his dad's death while he's playing. Please don't mention this to anyone."

"We're planning to embroider Salvador's name in the corner of the team banner we hang on the dugout," Gloria continued as if she hadn't heard. "In gold thread. And we're purchasing a commemorative cross."

"A cross?" Patricia pictured a cross large enough for a crucifixion looming behind the mound, Ray pitching in its shadow.

"Yes, a three-foot white cross with Salvador's photo in the center that we can display at each game. They sell them at the Dollar Store on Wadsworth. You do have a picture, don't you?"

Did she have a picture? Was that a test to find out if she loved her husband so little that she would have destroyed all the images of him during their separation? "Ray doesn't want a cross," Patricia said. "Baseball should be fun for the boys."

"It's the least we can do to help you through this. And it would be so motivational. Every time the boys saw the cross, they would be inspired to try harder." She seemed earnest, as though she really believed what she was saying.

"Gloria, I said *no*." Patricia removed Gloria's hand from her arm. Ray played to forget. When Ray was intent on pitching, his self-consciousness dissolved. "Please tell Pete not to mention this to anyone for Ray's sake. Ray went out of his way so that no one on the team would find out. Everyone at his school knows, and that's hard enough for him. People treat him differently. Baseball was safe for him."

"But I called Coach Pete last night, and we've already dedicated the season to Salvador. Coach Pete made the announcement in the team meeting before they took the field today," Gloria said with a pleading look.

"I never gave you permission," Patricia said, and then walked away, searching the field for Ray. He eased into his warm-up as he always did, his movements slow and deliberate, snapping his arm down and across his body, sending the ball speeding toward the catcher. She considered driving back to fetch El Johnway, but then Pete called the boys in to begin.

Patricia sat next to Mia and listened to the dads in the stands discuss the situation. The Pirates were playing the Z's for the second time that season. If they won, they'd automatically become the Denver champions for the league and qualify for the state tournament in Ft. Collins in July. If they lost, they might have to play the Z's again in a league championship. As the game started, Ray untied his cleats, pulled the laces taut, and retied them snugly. He stepped into the on-deck circle and closed his eyes as he took his first cuts with a weighted bat.

"I hate the Z's," Joey Santiago's dad said. He worked construction and his biceps bulged as he crossed his arms over his chest.

"What? That Speedy Gonzales crap they were saying last game?" Gloria's husband replied. He was smaller than his wife and he rarely spoke in her presence. But she wasn't in the stands yet, probably off badgering someone else. "We shut them up."

"Didn't you see? Their right fielder was flinging those little hot tamale candies at our boys during warm up."

"We should just throw something back at them."

"Like what? Crackers?"

241

The men laughed and the first Pirate grounded out. That brought up Ray. Ray entered the batting box and tapped the lower outside corner of the plate three times with the end of his bat, holding his right hand up to signal the pitcher to wait. Then he took three slow half-swings and sank into his stance, maintaining an almost imperceptible yet constant motion as he waited for the pitch.

Mia squirmed next to Patricia, moving her hands in and out of her pockets, drumming a beat with her fingers on the bench, as if she didn't know what to do with them when they were not holding El Johnway. Patricia thought of the dog-eared Guadalupe prayer card Salvador kept in his wallet, how he used to kiss it before he headed off to work with a road crew. She'd have to dig through the box of Salvador's belongings from the morgue to find it.

Ray swung at the first pitch and sent a pop-up looping straight into the right fielder's glove.

"See," Mia said, her face sour.

"He doesn't get a hit every time he's up," Patricia said. "Nobody does. You can't blame that on me."

The afternoon sun struck the Pirates' stands. "I'm thirsty," Mia complained. "Didn't you bring anything to drink?"

"I'll get you some water," Patricia offered.

"I want a pop," Mia said.

"You're fidgety enough as it is," Patricia said.

"Say please," Lupe said.

Patricia walked to the snack bar. The teams in the league traded off working the little booth during games to raise money for uniforms and travel, and today was the Z's parents' turn to staff it.

A woman with reddish-brown hair wearing a Z's t-shirt stood behind the counter and Patricia asked her for a bottle of water, handing her a dollar.

The woman stared at Patricia. "Does your son play on the Pirates?" she finally stammered. Her pale, freckled skin flushed.

"Yes," Patricia said. "He's the pitcher."

"Maestas, right?"

"That's right." This woman obviously recognized her from the news. Patricia was tired of being Denver's most famous widow.

The woman nodded, kept nodding like she was nervous. "I'm Claire. I've got two boys on the Z's. Catcher and outfielder, but sometimes my younger one just pinch runs," she blurted out.

"It must be nice to have them both on the same team," Patricia said. "Less driving. Could I have that water, please? My son's about to start pitching."

"Sure, sure." Claire turned to fish out a bottle from a tub of icy water, her hand shaking as she handed it to Patricia.

"Thanks," Patricia said, and turned to leave without waiting for her change. How many years of this kind of reaction would they face if the case went to a trial, the cameras recording them as they headed into the court building each day?

Something was wrong with Ray, Patricia could tell from the first pitch he threw. He normally straddled the mound like he owned it as he bent forward to receive the call from the catcher, the whole sequence from the first movement of his hand to when the ball struck the leather of the catcher's glove completely fluid. Today Ray scrunched his shoulder blades up until they were even with his neck, and his motion was choppy. He walked the bases full and Pete and the catcher trotted out to the mound for a conference.

"Just breathe, baby," Patricia whispered. "Let your muscles go."

"What's happening?" Mia asked. "He doesn't look right." She shot Patricia a glare. "I told you we should have gone back."

"Mia," Lupe said, holding up a warning finger. "It's all right. The game has just begun." She hugged Mia. "I had no idea you were such a fan. When the Broncos lost the Super Bowl in 1987, your mother sobbed in front of the little TV in the basement. She couldn't stay upstairs to watch the game with the rest of us because we were making fun of the Broncos. She didn't get her win for ten years. But some days it's not your day."

"It's not my year," Mia said, leaning her head against Lupe's shoulder.

By the time Ray got himself out of the inning, the Z's had scored three runs. Ray loosened up in the second, and only gave up one more run for the rest of the game, for as long as he lasted into the fifth inning. But nobody on the Pirates could hit the ball that day, and by the end they had lost five to three.

Ray was one of the last to leave the field after the post-game talk with Coach Pete. Patricia, Lupe, and Mia stood watching him from the parking lot as he walked toward them, his head hanging, his bag dragging against the dirt, his cockiness drained. Mia ran out to him and picked up his bag. He didn't try to stop her from taking it as he would have on any other day. When they reached the car Patricia opened the door for her son.

"I'm sorry, baby." Patricia left off the platitude, *you'll win the next one*. In this moment, the next one didn't matter. Even Lupe knew not to tell him that it was just a game.

"Mom wouldn't let me go back to get El Johnway," Mia reported.

He looked up at Patricia through his long eyelashes. They drove in silence, the radio off, until they were a few blocks from home.

"Mom?" Ray said.

"Yes?"

"I wish you hadn't gone on TV." He sounded tired.

"I'm sorry they all found out like that. I didn't want them to. And I had no idea they'd make such stupid plans."

Ray didn't speak for a moment, then said, "Why does everyone act like what happened to us belongs to them?"

When Ray didn't come out for dinner, Patricia brought him a plate as she had in the first days after Salvador's death. "Aren't you hungry?" she asked, peeking around the door.

He shook his head. He held a framed photograph that normally stood on his dresser. In the photo, Salvador wore a cheap

244

adjustable Pittsburgh Pirates ball cap, the team of his favorite player, Roberto Clemente, and he held Ray, a fat baby, on his lap. Baby Ray was laughing.

Patricia put the plate of food down on Ray's desk and gently took the picture from his hands. "You were such a cute little fatty. And look at you now." She squeezed his shoulder with her free hand. "All muscles."

"Why do babies laugh so much?"

"Babies can laugh at all sorts of things. You liked it when Dad tossed you in the air, when he blew a raspberry on your stomach, when he made a funny face."

"How come I don't get baby jokes anymore? Instead, things get less funny, and you forget why they were funny before."

Patricia stroked his hair. "It's hard to laugh these days."

"Did Dad play baseball?"

"When he was a boy. He didn't have much time for it when I knew him. He had so many jobs."

"No time for baseball," Ray echoed.

"That's why you've got to play now. Enjoy yourself. I don't give a rat's ass if you win."

"I wouldn't take a rat's ass if you gave me one," Ray said with half a smile. But only Patricia laughed.

At 8:00, Tío dialed the number of the general store in Salvador's pueblo on the kitchen phone and Patricia picked up the extension. She wanted to hear Graciela's voice, even if she couldn't understand everything she said. She wasn't sure what she was hoping for. Perhaps some sense of certainty about Salvador, a man she knew less about the more she learned.

"*Bueno*," Graciela said, her voice soft and high-pitched, nervous.

They greeted her back. "I want to know about the accident first," Patricia said. Tío translated, and Graciela began to tell a story. Salvador and her husband had been childhood friends. Salvador left for the U.S. as a teenager, and Esteban had married

Graciela. A few years later, he moved to California to make enough money to buy some land. Esteban had been back in Mexico for a year when Salvador came for a return visit.

"This would have been soon after we married," Patricia said to Tío, "when I was pregnant with Ray. Salvador didn't know until he came back."

"Salvador and Esteban were celebrating seeing each other for the first time in ten years," Tío translated. "They drank in town, then went out riding the new tractor Esteban had just bought for the farm with the money he had made in the States."

Graciela began to cry. She struggled on with her story, Tío translating slowly so she could catch her breath.

"The tractor hit a dip in the road and overturned," Tío said. "Salvador was thrown clear, but the tractor crushed Esteban's chest. Men came running from the pueblo, but by the time they could move the tractor, he was dead. Graciela was eight months pregnant with Carmelita, her only child," Tío translated.

"Eight months pregnant," Patricia said. "So the girl in the picture is not Salvador's daughter." Patricia felt desolate, like a tumbleweed was blowing around inside where her heart should be.

Graciela continued, and Tío translated. "She didn't have any money. Esteban had spent it all on new equipment, thinking they'd make more once the crops were in. Salvador gave her all of what he had and said he'd send more."

"*Patricia es una buena mujer*," Graciela remembered Salvador saying. "She will understand."

"*Gracias*," Patricia said. A good woman. She didn't feel like one. But why didn't he just tell her about the tractor accident instead of hiding his reason for sending money all those years? It would be insulting to ask if there had been anything between Graciela and Salvador. She knew the answer anyway now: Salvador was guilty only in that he didn't tell her everything.

Graciela told Patricia she was praying for her, lighting candles at the church, and then they said goodbye. Patricia pictured the candles, white and flickering, throwing yellow light against an adobe wall. Tío sat in silence, looking down.

"I killed him," Patricia said.

"The cops killed him, *hija*," Tío said, putting his hand on hers.

"It's good that I know," Patricia said. She thanked him for his help and led him to the front door. As she closed the door behind him, the blender whirred in the kitchen.

Lupe stood at the kitchen counter. A bowl of chunked pineapple, a carton of orange juice, a bag of coconut, and some limes were on the countertop. Lupe poured spiced rum into the blender. She must have found Patricia's stash in the high cabinet behind the refrigerator. Patricia hadn't touched it since the day after Salvador left for Mexico that last time. Lupe cranked the knob to blend it, then poured two tall glasses full and handed one to Patricia. It tasted tropical, and Patricia pictured herself as one of those carefree women in commercials for beach resorts. The drink cooled her tongue and left a moustache of froth above her lip. "This is good," she said.

"It looked like you could use a drink," Lupe said.

The alcohol hit Patricia in the knees first, sending a wave of relaxation up her spine. The blessing of low tolerance. "Let's sit on the porch."

They stretched out on the patio furniture, enjoying the slight breeze that stirred the mild June air. Crickets sang in the neighboring backyards and the traffic on Federal was muted by distance. From some open window wafted the scent of familiar shampoo. An airplane passed overhead, a great dark whoosh in the night.

"He didn't have an affair with her," Patricia said.

"He was a decent man."

"If I hadn't kicked him out, if I hadn't been so mad about him always sending money to Mexico, leaving us to go help with farm chores."

"You were incompatible," Lupe said. "That happens to a lot of people, and they don't die because of it. Now you're going to have to decide whether you want your case to go to trial soon."

"I know." Patricia sipped her drink.

247

"The whole committee wants a trial. They would support you all the way through it."

"Even if it takes years?"

"Of course."

"But what about Dad? Are you going to stay here all that time?"

"I miss him. We've been apart three months now. I'm probably going to leave soon. But I'll be back for the trial."

Patricia imagined what Mia would be like when she was grown. Patricia hoped to be as much help to Mia as Lupe had been to her. But Mia's life would turn out better, and she wouldn't need Patricia as much. "I'll miss you," Patricia said.

"*Hija*," Lupe said, "I miss you every day."

Patricia leaned over and kissed her mother's cheek. Was having a daughter grown and living far away like it was with a dead loved one, how you thought of a million things you wanted to tell them throughout the day? With Salvador, she'd never be able to say these things. But with Mia and Ray, Patricia would save these thoughts and try to remember all of them when they talked on the phone. Patricia's house would empty of children, and she'd be left alone. She shivered from the thought, the breeze, and the frozen drink. "What if there isn't a trial?" Patricia asked.

Lupe sat up. "Are you really thinking of settling?"

"I'm considering it." Patricia didn't want to disappoint her mother again, but she had to make her own decision.

Lupe sank back. "Then you don't need my help. You'll keep working, the kids will go back to school in the fall, and that will be the end of it."

Patricia refilled their glasses from the pitcher. She settled into the plastic chaise lounge, feeling decadent—stretched out, drinking a tropical cocktail. Tonight, she didn't want to choose. She just wanted to be here, next to her mother, listening to the sounds of the streets.

CHAPTER 19

Ed

June 9

Ed pressed the bell at Claire's aunt's house in south Denver and stood on the porch holding a bouquet of mauve lilies wrapped in cellophane like he was here to pick his wife up for the prom. Claire had agreed to go to Grimaldi's as a family for the Unicorns' championship banquet. E.J. opened the door. "I can't wait to get out of here," he said, and brushed past Ed, dragging a bulging backpack out to the car.

"Come back, E.J.," Ed called to him. "We'll leave in a minute." E.J. plopped on the sidewalk by the car, leaned his cheek against a fist and flung pebbles into the gutter. Ed wanted to comfort E.J., to tell him everything would be all right, but first he had to win over Claire. So he stepped into the house, his feet sinking into the pink carpet that Claire's aunt had installed the year before she moved to the nursing home. It matched the floral prints in gold frames on the walls and the frosty pastels of the upholstered furniture. There were no toys or video games and only a single, tiny TV without cable. The kids must have been bored out of their minds, pestering Claire, which worked in Ed's favor. His flowers were the same color as the rug, and he wished he had bought a different kind.

Polly ran out and hugged Ed. "Did you bring the trophies?" she asked, a finger in her mouth. She'd bitten her nails ragged, but her hair was combed, tamed with barrettes.

"Sure," Ed said, patting her curls, careful not to mess Claire's styling efforts. He kissed her brown neck, glad to feel her little body humming next to his. "Have you been enjoying Aunt Ruth's

249

pool?" There was a public pool a few blocks away, and Polly's skin had a new tan.

Polly shrugged. "I want to go home." She was quiet, but it was more than just her voice, like the volume of her entire personality was muted.

"Tonight. You'll be back in your own bed." He hoped Claire wouldn't change her mind. She could stay here forever and no one would know until Aunt Ruth, suffering from about three flavors of dementia at Trail Ridge Assisted Living, finally died and her children came back from California to claim their inheritance. It was Claire who checked up on the house, Claire who visited her aunt every week and baked her pecan tassies at Christmas. She'd more than earned a free, clandestine vacation in Aunt Ruth's house. But it wasn't doing the kids any good.

Jesse came out, lugging a couple of bags, trying to pretend this was normal. "Here sport," Ed said, handing him the keys. Ed never called Jesse 'sport'—he was as nervous as the kids. "Why don't you take your sister and load up the car?" If their stuff was packed, Claire might not change her mind. Jesse threw an arm over Polly's shoulders and hustled her outside, whispering something to her. Ed wondered about their secrets, about how they were taking this.

"Claire?" Ed called.

"Coming." She walked out from the back room looking beautiful in a lavender linen dress, pinning her hair up. "Can you zip me?" she asked, presenting her strong freckled back to him.

She was trying to make him suffer, Ed thought as he tugged the zipper past places he hadn't touched for weeks. She smelled like rain on a summer afternoon.

"I brought you these," Ed said, giving her the flowers.

"Thanks." Claire sank her nose into the blossoms, avoiding his eyes. "But what am I supposed to do with them while we're at the banquet?"

"So you're really coming home?" Ed said, wanting to hold her but not sure if he was allowed. "Let them wilt. I'll buy you some new ones."

Grimaldi's was one of the only sit-down restaurants on Hampden Avenue, the main drag in Ed's neck of Denver, a wide, ugly street marred by perpetual construction, flanked by strip malls and gas stations. Grimaldi's served watery marinara, undistinguished pizza, lasagna whose layers of sauce, cheese, and meat were applied in inconsistent and unappetizing proportions. But the owner employed everyone's kids when they turned sixteen. So teenagers came to the restaurant to flirt with their latest crush, parents came to patronize their child's place of business, and every sports team held its banquet there. The owner, a tan middle-aged man with thick silver hair and bleached teeth, drove a gleaming Mercedes, conspicuous in a parking lot full of minivans and Subaru wagons.

The O'Fallons walked into the banquet room fifteen minutes early to set up. Ed gave the kids a handful of quarters and they ran off to the vending machines out front. He took a deep breath as he looked out at the room, the tables set with paper placemats, napkins, and old white plates covered with silvery marks from years of forks scraping across them.

"Are you nervous?" Claire asked.

"Always." He was no public speaker, and the parents expected him to say a few words about each kid as he called them up to receive their trophies. The parents would lean forward when their child's turn arrived, staring at Ed attentively. If he didn't appease everyone, they might turn on him and tattle to the reporter, saying that in addition to shooting a man, Ed was a lousy coach and worthless human being. "Let me practice my b.s. a minute," Ed said. "Moe's got a lot of heart. Blondie's play was greatly improved."

"Larry is really a team player," Claire offered.

251

"But what am I going to say about Muscles? That girl's a mess."

"Muscles is always smiling and upbeat. There you go." Claire began to unpack the trophies from a cardboard box.

"I miss you, Claire," Ed said. "I wish we could talk."

"We will," she said, something stern in her voice as she looked at him. "But now we've got a banquet to run."

The first week Claire hadn't returned Ed's calls. The loneliness at home was almost audible, like a waterfall rushing overhead, so he took on extra work, providing security at bars and Rockies games. It was no time to think about changing jobs. He had gone as far as driving out to Aunt Ruth's street and parking a few blocks away. But if he approached Claire, she might feel stalked, so he just watched as she and the kids trooped home from the pool, his chest constricting with a sob that wouldn't break as he drove home. He couldn't stand being a spectator to his children's lives. The second week she'd called him every couple of days, and they'd started to make some agreements. There would be counseling, and new rules Ed had to heed, like not bugging Claire at work. But he hadn't talked to her in person since before he'd left for Utah. He'd seen her at the games, but she'd volunteered to work the snack stand and Ed couldn't say anything important to her from across the counter in the booth.

The kids and their parents began to arrive, and Ed greeted them. Polly hung behind him, like she didn't want to let him out of her sight. "Hey, Moe!" Ed said, slapping the leftfielder's hand. As the season wore on, Ed figured out that the parents found it endearing when he called the kids by their nicknames. No one seemed to suspect that he simply couldn't tell one Emma or Madison from another, whereas Lefty and Muscles—those were clearly different girls.

Ed pretended to pay attention to whoever was in front of him, but watched Claire as she worked the room, asking parents about children and pets, keeping the names straight. Ed felt a flare of pride in her as he often did on such occasions of bad speeches and worse food. Whenever he messed things up, she smoothed it over, or at least she had until he'd shot Santillano.

Blondie made her entrance, wearing a purple cheerleader outfit with a white number one on the front. "We're number one!" she shouted, pumping a pompom in the air. The girls rushed over to her, joining in the cheer.

The Unicorns had placed first in their league, averting the inevitable season-end struggle with various parents over whether the kids would receive trophies or not. Ed always thought the practice of awarding kids just for showing up taught them nothing. A few years back, when the PAL team Ed coached placed fourth in its league, Ed refused to order trophies, and Claire diligently constructed felt pennants in the team colors because she knew there would be a revolt if Ed gave the kids nothing at the banquet. Most of the kids were glad to have the pennants, but one complained, demanding his trophy.

"You didn't earn a trophy this year," Ed had told him. "Trophies are for the winning team. Not everybody gets them." The kid ran straight to his mom, and she must have borne Ed a grudge all these years because she told the *Denver Post* reporter, "Ed didn't seem concerned for the feelings of the children." Since when has it been a coach's job to care about feelings? A coach was meant to shape a kid into something better, and sometimes that hurt.

Polly didn't join the general rush toward Blondie, but she finally left Ed to speak to her friends, and some of her old spirit returned. She looked sturdy and confident, like a girl who had been raised with the security of her mom and dad and brothers surrounding her—not like a couple of the kids with divorced parents who were on the team, either so shy they could barely speak or so loud and theatrical you wanted to lock them in a closet. He wanted Polly to stay how she was. He wanted to hold his family together, to make it right with Claire. He'd forget about rafting in Moab and be a better cop, a better husband.

"Good evening," Ed began when everyone had returned from the buffet, their plates filled with steaming food, the smell of it triggering Ed's gag reflex. "We're going to start with the trophy presentation. The first one goes to Moe, a real team player who's always smiling. Moe, you really improved this season."

When they arrived home, the kids ran inside, eager to visit their rooms for the first time in three weeks, and Ed hung back with Claire in the car.

"So," he said, drumming his fingers on the wheel.

"So."

"How do we start?"

"By getting out of the car, I guess."

He took her hand and kissed it, tried to read the faint smile on her face. They left the car and as they entered the kitchen, the phone began to ring.

"Damn, that's Mitch," Ed said, "I told him I would come over after the banquet." At the time he didn't think he'd have any plans. "Let me just tell him I can't make it."

"Just go."

"I don't want to go, Claire."

"Please," she said. "I need a chance to settle back in with the kids. And you owe Mitch, too."

"Not as much as I owe you. I want to be here tonight." The phone stopped ringing.

"Go Ed." Claire filled a vase with water. "I need to do some laundry and be alone." She turned her back to him and stuck the limp lilies in the vase.

Ed hesitated, wondering if this was some kind of test, but Claire was done talking to him. "I'll be home soon," he said.

Ed brought a six-pack of Coors over to Mitch's house. He felt nervous as he waited for him to answer the door, preparing to court once again, this time to smooth things over with Mitch.

Ed didn't know where to begin with Claire half the time, but Mitch seemed pleased to welcome beer and male company into his house full of women. The day after Ed returned from Utah to an empty home, he'd apologized to Mitch, who was taking the week off to recover from the knife fight. Mitch had stopped him in the middle of his feeble speech, saying, "I'm glad you didn't kill him, Ed. I'm gladder that he didn't kill me, but I'm glad you didn't kill him. Then I'd have to deal with the homicide investigation, the internal review, the trial, and on and on." Mitch had even covered for him on the day he took off for Utah, feeding some excuse for Ed's absence to the district commander. Despite this, for the past few weeks, Mitch had been hesitant at work, convincing Ed to lay off hot calls, domestics, and in-progress situations. Mitch claimed it was because he was trying to get over his nerves, but Ed suspected that he'd lost faith in his ability to cover him.

Mitch accepted the beer from Ed, then snorted as he checked out Ed's purple t-shirt with the word "Unicorns" spelled out in glittery rainbow colors, a little unicorn sticking its horn up to form the "i." "Nice," Mitch said.

At the banquet, it had been Ed's gift for coaching, and he'd put it on immediately for the girls. "You like it?" Ed asked.

"I'm surprised that shirt comes in size Man. You'd better step inside before anyone sees you."

His daughter Shelley and an androgynous friend sat in the front room, dressed in black, strumming guitars. Mimi had some giggling teenage friends over, hanging out in the living room.

Mitch turned on the lights to the basement with an angry flick. Only dads could flip on lights in a way that expressed their moods. "I built this rec room for these girls," Mitch complained, as he had for years. "I spent all of my weekends for months working on it, and do you think they use it?"

"It looks like they prefer being upstairs."

"Yeah, so the old man is banished down here."

"At least they're home."

The walls of the rec room were a lurid shade of red. A thick white shag rug covered the floor. On one end stood a pool table upholstered in felt the color of pumpkin pie, and on the other sat a large TV, ringed by orange beanbags. Mitch's deluxe Scrabble board sat, neglected, on a folding table in one corner. The rec room looked like the fantasy retreat of a '70s adolescent. When Mitch finally accepted that this was to be his lair, he set up a bar near the pool table and put up a Corvette poster.

"How long do you have to wear that shirt?" Mitch asked.

"Come on. I remember that "Number One Dad" shirt Mimi gave you for Father's Day, with the cartoon tiger dad and all his kids, and the baby tiger was sitting in his diaper in a puddle of piss. You wore that for years."

"Father's Day?" Mitch said. "Does that exist anymore? It hasn't been observed in this house since 1995."

Ed pulled his t-shirt away from his chest and looked down to inspect it. "I mean, this is who I am now, Mitch. I'm a goddamn Unicorn. Covered with glitter and crap."

"I thought you liked coaching those little girls."

"I do. But it doesn't make me miss coaching the boys any less. And once you're a Unicorn, you can't be a Raider or an Outlaw or a Viking anymore because you're a goddamn Unicorn."

"Maybe you could convince the girls to switch the team name to The Valkyries next year. You know, sort of work your way back up."

"Once a Unicorn, always a Unicorn." If there was anything Ed could handle without screwing up, it was being a purple unicorn.

Ed and Mitch settled down into the beanbags with the six-pack between them.

Ed took a sip of his beer. "What did you tell the district commander on that day I was in Utah? He's been looking at me kind of funny."

"I told him you took the day off for personal reasons," Mitch said.

"Nice. That doesn't make it sound like I'm going nuts. Couldn't you have said I was laid out with the flu? Or something manly—like lockjaw?"

"Or strychnine poisoning. Hey, he's fighting through it, but he's a little stiff."

"Don't be giving Claire any ideas. She came back with the kids tonight."

"Then why are you here?"

"She sent me."

"Are you sure it wasn't a test to see if you'd go?"

"I'm not sure of anything."

They sat drinking without talking for a while, staring at the blank TV screen. Mitch finished his can and reached for another. "Must be a game on, huh?" Ed asked, feeling nervous, craving the distraction of sports.

"Sure," Mitch said, handing him the remote.

Ed flipped through the channels, past cooking shows and news programs until he came to a college baseball game between Arizona State and Oregon State.

"Go Beavers," Ed said.

"So what was McGill like?" Mitch asked. "Nuts?"

Ed shook his head. "He was where he needed to be."

"When I first went on, he was the guy all the rookies looked up to. He was fearless."

"Not anymore," Ed said. "But at least he knows it."

"Can I ask you a question?" Mitch kept his eyes on the game that neither of them cared about.

"Sure." Sometimes talking with Mitch these days felt like talking with a woman, working on a relationship.

"Do you think you can still pull the trigger if you need to? Because if you can't, you need to think it over, for your own safety." He rubbed his shoulder, still sore from the fight.

"Sure," Ed said. "That situation was unique—I mean the guy's kid was right there, and I knew I could get him off you without shooting." He didn't know, actually. It had been a guess.

"All situations are unique." Mitch took a sip of his beer.

"I just went with my instincts."

"That's what I'm afraid of."

Ed stood. He was doing the best he could and he was tired of this. "Believe me or don't. But I'd rather let my wife badger me instead of you."

Mitch stood, an apologetic look on his face. "I didn't want you to blow the guy away in front of his kid. I just thought you could have acted quicker."

"I was thinking the situation through. But I can shoot when I need to. I really can." Ed wondered if he was trying to convince Mitch or himself of this.

"Okay," Mitch said. "Stay for one more beer?"

Ed clinked his can against Mitch's and they sank down in the beanbags in front of the TV, done talking. One more beer and Ed could return to Claire.

When Ed arrived home, he found Claire alone in the kitchen. Sometimes she sat there at the counter once all the dishes had been cleaned and put away, the table wiped down, the trash emptied, to admire the order of it before the kids tore it apart again.

"Did you have a good time at Mitch's?" she asked.

"Yeah," he said. "I think he's finally coming around. He doesn't have too many other friends."

Claire glanced downstairs, where the kids were absorbed in a video game, its repetitive music loud and vaguely Japanese. "Sit with me a minute?"

"Sure," Ed said. Great. Another confrontation about his weaknesses.

Claire sipped her coffee. "I've been debating telling you about something since yesterday."

"Go ahead," Ed said. "I can take it." He wondered if he actually could take whatever it was. He thought of Claire driving off with the orthodontist in his yellow Porsche convertible, her auburn hair blowing wild in the wind. That he couldn't take.

"When I was working the snack bar at the game yesterday, I saw that woman—the wife of Santillano." Claire's face was ashen and weary.

"Are you sure?" The lights in the kitchen felt too bright.

"I am never going to forget that woman's face."

"Was she there to watch the game?"

"Ed," she said, reaching out to touch his arm, "her son plays for the Pirates."

"He does? But none of them is named Santillano."

"The pitcher. That's their son."

"Ray Maestas? He's the best player on that team. The best pitcher in the league. The best twelve-year-old pitcher I've ever seen."

"The man you killed was his father." She set her coffee cup on the counter. "I don't know what to think about it. I feel sorry for that woman though, and that boy."

Ed sank down on the stool next to Claire's. He thought of the baseball trophies in Santillano's room, toppled and flecked with blood. They were Ray's. "Santillano must have taught Ray to throw like that."

"Why does it matter how well he plays?" Claire asked. "What are we going to do?"

Somehow it did matter to Ed. "In all of Denver, our kids have to end up in the same league."

"Denver isn't that big. I still run into people I went to high school with at the grocery store. If your kid is a good baseball player, he plays in this league."

"Did she recognize you?"

"How could she? I've never been in the paper or on TV. It's you that she might recognize."

"From that old police academy picture the papers ran a few times?"

Claire appraised him, moving her eyes from his face to his gut, and shook her head as if to agree that he didn't look much like his former young, slim self. "Maybe not, but she'd probably recognize your name. The media has focused on Springer and the warrant, not so much on you, but still. If that happened to me, I'd remember the names." Claire picked up a wet dishrag and rubbed at a spot of tomato sauce on the counter. "What are we going to tell the kids?"

For about the thousandth time, a brief fantasy of driving out to Springer's house, ringing the doorbell, and swinging a baseball bat at his head flashed through Ed's mind. "I don't think the boys should know." He looked at the three kids, cheering as E.J. blasted somebody on the video game. He felt like grabbing them and carrying them far away. "It would be too much for them."

Claire thought a moment. "I guess I agree. I don't see the point of the boys finding out about this if they don't have to."

Ed stood and paced around the kitchen. "They're going to have to play the Pirates one more time for the district championships, probably." He leaned against the kitchen sink. "If she hasn't made a connection with our sons' last name yet over the course of two games, she's probably not going to. She must not keep score or pay attention to the names of the opponents. If we can get through that last game without her finding out, that would be the best. I can stay far away from the Pirates' stands."

"Maybe it will work," Claire said, without conviction. "Can I get you anything? Some coffee?"

"No, thank you," Ed said. They were being too polite with each other, as formal as strangers.

Ed walked down the hall and looked out the front window that faced west. When he was upset as a child, his mother would take him outside and she would hold him and point at the peaks, naming them until he calmed, *there's Bear Peak, there's Green Mountain, there's Long's.* But it was too dark to see the mountains and there were too many buildings blocking them now, anyway.

Through watching Maestas pitch, Ed felt he knew more about Santillano now than he'd ever wanted to. Santillano must have loved baseball. In his mind, Ed returned to the musty, dim room where Santillano's body bled out next to Ray's trophies. Santillano had taught his son to play the game just as Ed had taught his own. Given the statistics of police work, Ed's kids should have been the ones growing up without a father, not the kids of a man who'd worked at a soda bottling plant. If one change had been made in the events of that March day, one tiny change—if Springer had written the right address on the warrant, if Santillano had gone out to the store, if Ed had turned down the SWAT assignment just that once—then they would still be strangers to each other, two Denver fathers on opposite sides of a ball field, rooting for their sons.

Chapter 20

Patricia
June 21–22

Patricia led her kids through the front door of Pete's Pizza for the 6:00 team meeting. The restaurant had no air conditioning and the heat hit Patricia in the face. Pete propped the front and back doors open, letting in the traffic noise from Pecos, but little breeze. The grizzled fleet of ceiling fans, mired in dust, stirred the dry air.

The boys sat at a long banquet table in the center of the restaurant and their parents filled the booths along the perimeter. Gloria Sandoval raised the team banner on the front wall. "Dedicated to Salvador Santillano" was embroidered along the bottom in gold script letters. So Gloria had done it anyway. Patricia wanted to tell her off, but it was more important to protect Mia, who was intent on showing El Johnway the restaurant and hadn't noticed her father's name. Patricia steered Mia to a booth facing away from the banner.

Two boys at the far end of the banquet table bent plastic straws into triangular footballs. The shortstop flicked the football across the table toward the goal posts the catcher formed with his hands, and it struck the catcher in the face, cracking the boys up. Ray sat down next to them, leaving an empty seat between. The catcher flicked the football and it landed under the table. Ray picked it up and handed it to the catcher, but they didn't resume their game. From Ray's wistful expression, Patricia sensed that he wanted to play, but he didn't ask and they didn't offer. She could no longer rush over and encourage them to play together like she did when Ray was three, a stranger in the sandbox.

Kids only knew to avoid the wounded, the rule they'd learned on playgrounds. They couldn't laugh or joke around someone who had been through something like that. It was as though Mia and Ray among all the children in the restaurant bore a faint, somber glow that everyone could sense. If Patricia chose arbitration instead of a trial, people would stop talking about what happened to them sooner and maybe the other kids would forget.

Patricia's thighs stuck to the vinyl seats in the booth. Periodically the fans blew an unpleasant waft from the dumpster in the alley. Mia positioned El Johnway on the table to face Pete, as though he were a member of the team, awaiting instruction. After Ray lost, Mia started carrying El Johnway around everywhere in a white lace purse, like a talisman.

Pete's waitresses—good-looking high school girls wearing short shorts, each of them swinging long, straight hair—brought out pizzas, one for every two guys on the team, and a large one for each family in the booths. There was an uneven number of boys and when they reached the end where Ray sat, one of the waitresses plopped down a whole pepperoni pizza in front of him.

Ray looked at his non-communal pizza, the grease glistening on the slick of its cheese, tugged one slice away from the rest and slid it onto his plate. While the other boys stuffed their slices into their mouths, point first, Ray picked up his silverware and cut neat little squares, eating them with a fork, a peculiarity he'd copied from Salvador, who hadn't been raised on pizza.

Pete stood at the head of the table and watched them chew. "Eat up, men," he said. He circled the table, resting a hand on a boy's shoulder now and then, his attitude both paternal and militaristic, like a king at a feast before sending his knights into battle. When Pete completed his circuit, he stopped and faced the crowd. "Parents," he said, the chatter in the booths dying out during his pause, "I've enjoyed coaching your sons this season. I've enjoyed it so much that I don't want it to end next week at the city championship. They're the best group of guys I've ever coached. But since we dropped that game to the Z's, they haven't been living up to their potential."

The catcher's father shot his son a knowing look. He had struck out a lot during the past few games, as had many of the boys. The catcher's shoulders sank. Fathers had the sort of power over their sons that Mia attributed to El Johnway, able to sap or bolster with a glance. After games, Ray used to always watch Salvador's face for the truth about how he'd done.

"We're lucky we've been playing weak opponents," Pete continued, "or else we wouldn't have qualified for the city championship. Baseball is a game of streaks and slumps. The worst thing that can happen is to be hot all season and then go into a slump just before tournament time. But I'm not going to call what we've been in a slump."

Pete rocked back and forth on his heels. "The Z's used to laugh at us. They're not laughing now. We've got their number. Speedy Gonzales could kick their asses." The boys laughed. "They've gone to state four years in a row. Now we have a chance to end that streak and start one of our own. And I don't know about you, but I'm not ready for this season to end."

The boys pounded the table with the butts of their forks and knives. Mia joined in.

Pete held out his hands to quiet them. "We've dedicated this season to the memory of Ray's dad," he said. "But Ray can't do it all by himself." Ray studied his hands in his lap. "You need to wake up those bats, men." Patricia hated the way the coach set Ray apart in his speech. The kid was already an island. She could understand now why he'd clung to Miguel. A friend was a friend.

"From now on I want each of you practicing like you mean it. We've got about two weeks before the big game. Moms, make sure they get enough sleep, and feed them right—tell them to lay off soda, chips, and women." This drew a laugh.

"Dads," Pete continued, "extra practice never killed a kid. Why not take them out into the backyard for some soft toss so they can work on their bat speed? Throw an old blanket over a clothesline and have them hit into that. I'll also be sending around a clipboard for everyone to sign up for some batting cage time."

The parents nodded along with what Pete said. If he'd told them to pour whiskey down their sons' throats every night at 8:00, they'd be into it. Mia was nodding, too. Patricia could feel the energy in the room, everyone inwardly balling up the disappointments of their lives into a single hope, to win this one game. Patricia wanted this win, too, even if it was just a game. She didn't want to think about how badly Ray would feel if he lost, or what street corner he might head toward when she couldn't watch him and baseball didn't occupy his time.

"And now our team mother would like to say a few words," Pete said.

Gloria Sandoval made her way up front. Patricia imagined sticking a leg out to trip her. "I want to talk about a new fundraiser," Gloria began. "I've arranged for all the parents and players to work next Thursday night at the Bingo Emporium in Arvada so we can earn money for tournament travel expenses. We'll be selling pickles and helping the bingo caller. Every family is expected to have at least two representatives there."

The heat, the noise of the fans whirring, and Gloria droning on made Patricia dizzy. The pizza suddenly smelled vile. A dark-haired man wearing ostrich-skin boots and a plaid shirt tucked into tight jeans entered the restaurant and for a split second, something about his build made Patricia think it was Salvador. Patricia stood, and the man turned and showed his face: he was no one she knew. "Mia, I've got to get some air," she whispered. "I'll be back in a minute." She walked out in the middle of Gloria's speech, brushing against the stupid banner on the wall as she passed behind Gloria, everybody looking as she left.

At home, Lupe stood by the kitchen counter, collating some papers for the next committee meeting. Mia snooped around the papers, and Ray took out the orange juice from the refrigerator and chugged it directly from the carton.

"Hey!" Patricia said. "Use a glass."

"I'm going to finish it anyway," Ray said, wiping off an orange moustache. "The vitamins are good for my pitching arm."

"Why don't you give Nino a call," Patricia suggested.

"What for?"

"I don't know, so you can hang."

He threw the rest of the juice down his throat, and then bank-shot the carton into the trash. "We're going to win," Ray said. "I know it."

"So the meeting must have gone well?" Lupe asked.

"It was nothing, really," Patricia said.

"It wasn't nothing," Ray protested.

"Sorry," Patricia said. "Pete wanted to get the guys pumped for the city championship, and it looks like it worked. He told us ladies to make sure we feed our sons right."

"They put Daddy's name on a banner," Mia added.

"What?" Lupe said. "Gloria did that?"

Patricia nodded. "At least there wasn't any cross."

"Are we going to work at bingo like she said?" Mia asked. "There has to be two people from each family."

"I'm not spending my free time working at a smoky bingo hall in Arvada just because Gloria Sandoval told me to," Patricia said.

"But it's for tournament travel money," Ray said.

"I'll make sure you get to your tournament," Patricia said. "If the team is that hard up, I'll just write a check."

"Won't Gloria get mad?" Mia asked.

"I'll tell her I sent Salvador's ghost to work bingo. The dead are convenient that way—you can use them for whatever cause you want and they have no say."

"Have you seen Daddy's ghost?" Mia asked. She glanced at a photo of Salvador that they kept on the refrigerator.

"No, baby," Patricia said, softening her tone. "I'm sorry I said that. I'm just tired of people using him. It seems like half the newspaper is about him some days. And none of these people who are so interested in him now paid him any attention while he was alive." She pulled Mia close, stroking her hair. Maybe now was as good a time as any. "I wanted to talk to you kids about something," she said.

Mia tensed in Patricia's arms.

"We're going to have to decide pretty soon whether to take your father's case to trial or go to arbitration," Patricia said.

"What's arbitration?" Ray asked, sitting on one of the kitchen stools.

"It's a process where our lawyer and the city's lawyer will work out how much settlement money to give us."

"I've heard of that," Ray said. "It's like when a free agent baseball player wants a lot of money, and his team says no, and he and his agent go to a judge to figure out what his salary will be."

"Something like that," Patricia said. "If we choose arbitration, the whole thing could be over soon. If we choose a trial, there's a chance we could get more money, but there's also a chance that we'll get nothing. A trial will take a long time—years maybe, before it happens. There will be lots of stories about it in the newspapers and on TV, people talking about us in public, TV cameras outside our house, and who knows what else."

"Don't you think we should discuss this with the committee tomorrow?" Lupe asked. She banged a stapler down on a pile of papers. "It's a big decision to place in the hands of kids."

"I just wanted to hear what they think," Patricia said.

"Well, you know how I feel," Lupe said. "A trial is the only way we'll have a public hearing on this, and clear Salvador's name once and for all. We've got the ACLU on our side, and Tío's going to announce the findings of our independent investigator tomorrow. The whole city has rallied around us, and it would be a shame to waste that support."

"Salvador was an honorable man," Patricia said. "We already know that. What we don't have is college money for the kids."

"Let's have a trial," Ray said, firm.

"If we have a trial," Patricia said, facing him, "they'll say all kinds of stuff about your dad. They'll call him a drug dealer, they'll bring up how he lived in the U.S. illegally for a while. Who knows, they might be able to search through his files and find out he faked a letter saying he'd picked lettuce so he could get citizenship."

"He faked a letter?" Lupe asked, alarmed.

"During the amnesty in the '80s. Everyone was doing it, because they'd only accept farm workers."

"What does that have to do with the cops shooting him?" Ray asked.

"It could affect what the jury thinks of him," Patricia said. "With a trial, it's all up to a jury—their judgment, their prejudices."

"Dad would want a trial," Ray said.

"No, he wouldn't," Mia said. "He would want us to go to college."

Patricia tried to decide what Salvador would have wanted. His name cleared? He never cared anything about that. *Take the sure thing*, that's what he would have said. Tomorrow was another country that no one could predict. "I think Mia's right," Patricia said.

Ray pushed himself away from the counter and jumped down from the stool. "Why did you ask us, anyway? You're just going to do whatever you want to, like always."

"That's not true," Patricia said. But she did want arbitration. She wanted to end all the publicity, all the committees, all the meetings, all the fighting, and figure out what their lives would be now, without Salvador.

The Justice for Santillano committee had grown too large for Patricia's home, so they gathered in the sweltering community room of Our Lady of Perpetual Sorrow. The seats filled with Lupe's old friends, Patricia's neighbors, other families who had been wronged by police, people of every color and age. The Cop Aware crew, a bunch of college kids, and Latinos who were big in La Raza sat in the crowd, the same people who'd been there at the rally, the same people who'd been there all along. Patricia, Lupe, Mia, and Ray sat up front next to Tío. It was the first meeting Ray had attended, and he studied the crowd as he would an opposing batter. Patricia shifted uncomfortably in her seat.

Tío held up a stack of papers. "The results of our independent investigation are in," he said. "Lupe made copies for everyone, but I'm just going to highlight a few details. Based on what our investigator found, I believe that if we go to court on this, we could make a good case that the cops planted the gun."

Patricia knew what he was going to say—she'd read the report as soon as the investigator delivered it. But she still looked forward to hearing the results spoken aloud. If they didn't have a trial, at least they would have this public airing of the facts. Tío had invited several reporters. Patricia picked them out in the crowd, aiming their tape recorders and scribbling notes.

"Police reports that we've gotten released indicate the cops found no fingerprints on the gun they say Salvador fired. The D.A. told the press that doesn't mean anything—he said, 'it's not a particularly good surface for fingerprints.'"

"Neither was my ass when the cops beat the shit out of me," a man in the far corner shouted. Ray and Mia stared at him. The crowd began to chatter.

"Let's watch the language," Tío said, the noise dying down. "I'd like to continue." He put on his reading glasses and held the papers out in front of him. "Several of the cops couldn't say for certain that they saw Salvador fire a gun. The main shooter said, 'I thought he was going to fire, and then I fired at him.' Ballistic reports couldn't match the two recovered slugs with what they say is Salvador's gun. The gun that they claim is Salvador's was manufactured in 1963, and it was missing a crucial piece that keeps the cylinder from falling out. The cops say that Salvador pointed a gun at them and fired, but they can't even prove that he was holding this gun, that this gun matched the bullets they recovered, or that this gun they say they found in the room was even functioning. Our independent investigator has concluded that the cops never saw Salvador with a gun—that they fired at him through the bedroom door that he was hiding behind. The cops deny this, of course. In a trial, it'd be our and our investigator's word against the cops, but as you can see, I think we've got a good case. Any questions?"

Nino's grandma raised her hand. "Does that mean the cops could go to jail?"

Tío shook his head. "The D.A. already declined to press charges. The best we could do against them would be a civil suit."

Cop Aware Greg shot his hand into the air. "When would the trial start?" he asked. "We can plan some demonstrations to lead up to it."

"Well," Tío said, "we're not sure about that yet. The family is still considering their options."

"What's to consider?" Greg asked. "It's another clear case of the cops' blatant disregard for human rights."

"Amen," a woman in the crowd called out.

Greg had never been a victim of police violence himself. Being an activist was some sort of hobby to him. Patricia wasn't going to let Cop Aware Greg and a bunch of strangers run her life. She'd made up her mind. "I have something to say," Patricia said, raising her voice above the noise. She walked to the podium and stood next to Tío. "Thank you for all the support you've given my family these past few months. I'm glad we got this chance to see that my husband is innocent of whatever the cops have accused him of to cover their mistake on the warrant." She paused, holding the sides of the podium to steady herself. "But we've decided not to take the case to trial."

"We?" Ray whispered, shaking his head.

"Are you sure?" Tío said, loud enough that the mike picked it up.

Lupe put her hand on Patricia's arm. "You don't have to decide this now," she said.

Greg stood up. "But this case could help so many people," he said. "Think of all the publicity it will generate. It'll bring to light the abuses of cops in this community, and set the standard for other cases around the country. This room is full of families who have been harmed by cops, but who didn't have as strong a case as you do. You could speak for all of us."

Before Patricia could respond, another man stood up. He had skin the color of tea leaves and thick white hair. "I just wanted to say that we haven't seen anything this explosive since the old days of the Chicano movement, when we were organizing lettuce boycotts and storming Denver Public School board meetings. If this comes through, it could really shake things up. It could make this city safer and better for everyone. A policeman would have to think twice before he harmed one of us again."

"Well, what does Patricia want?" Tío asked. Everyone turned to look at her. Patricia took in their faces, their eyebrows lifted, waiting for her to speak. Overheated men and women who rung up groceries, cleaned offices, poured asphalt, or answered phones all day and then spent free evenings helping her. There was a heaviness to their faces, bags under their eyes with a discernible heft, skin sagging like it was too tired to cleave to bone.

Patricia shook her head. "I'm sorry," she said. "I've got to do what's best for my kids. I'm grateful for everything you've done. I'm as angry as any of you. But I'm thinking about my kids."

"You're not thinking about me," Ray muttered.

Patricia glanced at him and then faced forward again, less confident than ever. "I don't want their dad's death discussed in public for years. And I want them to go to college. I don't want to gamble that on what a jury may decide. Can you understand?"

Some people in the crowd nodded, and a couple of old ladies murmured *bless you* and *of course we can*. A few of the more militant members of the committee stared at her stone-faced and whispered to each other.

"Patricia, I've got to ask you to reconsider," Greg said, standing again. "Isn't it more important for you to set an example for your kids by fighting? Shouldn't they see you defending their father's name? Think of how many other husbands and sons will be endangered if you do nothing."

"You've overstepped," Tío said. "Let somebody else have the floor."

"No, it's okay," Patricia said. "I understand. You've all worked hard because you believe what the cops did to Salvador wasn't right. And you're scared that it could happen to your families. But I'm in a different position than you—my husband is already dead. You made a difference. The mayor fired the police chief. The legislature is in the process of changing the rules for no-knock raids. They're at least considering our suggestion about a police oversight committee. I'm sorry I can't help you get the public fight that you want, but if any of you ever has a reason to go after the city, I'll be right behind you."

Patricia sunk down in her chair and hardly heard the rest of what was said at the meeting, overcome by the full weight of her decision. She felt like half the people in Denver were looking to her with upturned faces, holding their breath. She just wanted them to turn their backs to her, the way they had before.

After the meeting, Patricia didn't know if her family would follow her to the car. They were all mad at her, except Mia. Ray wouldn't look at her as she unlocked the door. She was not his friend, she reminded herself as she had since he was a defiant toddler, she was his mom. She drove, her passengers silent, until she was about to make the turn for home. "Don't go home yet," Ray said from the backseat.

She looked at him in the rearview mirror, slumped with his cheek against the window. She tried to make out whether there were tears in his eyes. When Lupe made no comment, Patricia said, "All right."

She took Federal south to Speer, and drove over the bridge that led to downtown. A few years earlier, the area had been a wasteland of railroad tracks and abandoned warehouses. Now the bridge led to the new basketball arena, the nostalgic baseball stadium, and lofts going up everywhere. Near the highway, the roller coaster and swooping rides of Elitch Gardens amusement park—which had relocated from deep in Hispanic Denver—were silhouetted against the mountains.

The city was in bloom, its colors red and green, the colors of the mountain rock and of the streams that cut through it. New buildings sprung up, derelict neighborhoods snapping into respectability around them, and old warehouses became expensive homes. Salvador and other men like him had built all this, cooked in the restaurants, toiled on the construction sites, and cleaned everything up while the rest of Denver slept. Rents rose, hopes soared, the landscape changed. Patricia watched in the rearview mirror as Ray rolled his window down and stuck his hand out, catching the breeze on his palm. Patricia wanted the bad times behind them. She wanted something new to begin.

CHAPTER 21

Ed

July 7

E d sat next to Claire in the second-to-last row of the bleachers at the city championship game, hiding behind sunglasses and a hat. Normally he would have joined the other dads in the front row, but he couldn't risk that. Santillano's wife might glance across the field to the front row of the Z's bleachers and recognize his face. For once Ed was glad for the Z's Yankee-like practice of not putting names on the back of their uniforms. Polly ran off to play and Claire began to whisper directions to Ed. "Pull your cap lower. And don't yell. Just sit and be quiet."

"Okay," Ed said, but the word came out like a pout. Ed didn't know how he was going to remain silent and still during the most important game of the season. But it was better than staying home like Claire had suggested.

"I hate this," Claire whispered. "I wish I could talk to her, but they could still sue. If they see us, if we provoke them—"

"We could lose everything," Ed finished. He'd be relieved when they were past the announcement of the lineup, a special touch reserved for the championship game that he hoped by some chance Santillano's wife wouldn't pay attention to.

Thunderheads built in the distance. During Ed's rookie summer as a cop, he pulled people over during the almost daily afternoon storms, leaving him with a soggy uniform for the rest of his shift. After a couple of evenings sitting in damp pants, Ed noticed the veterans laughing at him and learned most cops wouldn't bother to pull someone over during the brief storms unless they spotted a car heading the wrong way down a highway on-ramp.

But this summer, Colorado was in a drought, and the thunderheads were bound to disperse into high, wispy clouds. It seemed the whole state was cinder. Denver had a foreign, dead white haze from the fires in the mountains that made the sky feel close and puny. Still, Coach Boyd shielded his eyes with his hand and studied the clouds as he would an opponent.

"Of all the days it could pick to rain," Ed said, watching the clouds darken. "I think it's really going to this time."

"I hope not," Claire said. "The last thing we need is a do-over."

The boys ran in from their warm-up and Ed braced for the announcer to call the lineup. The head ump conferred with the coaches and elected to skip the announcements and the national anthem because of the threatening sky. Ed sank back with the relief of a batter granted a fluke walk by an ace.

Maestas struck out the first batter in the top of the first, but then he got behind on Badgett, walking him. Jesse came up to bat next. Ed looked from his son to Santillano's. Jesse opened his stance slightly. Maestas leaned in for the call from the catcher. Ed clenched his teeth and felt Claire tense beside him, her thigh moving away from his. Jesse and Santillano's boy were just playing a game, unburdened by what Ed and Claire knew. It was knowledge only a god should bear, the weight of the hidden connections between everyone.

"Nervous?" Hank Badgett turned and asked, startling Ed.

Ed coughed out a fake laugh in response, the only sound he could get out of his throat.

"Ease up, Ed," Pendergrass said. "Jesse's a pro."

Maestas threw a knee-high fastball that cut in toward Jesse, and Claire flinched. Jesse took it for a called first strike. The catcher threw the ball back to Maestas, and the process began again, Jesse taking a few soft practice cuts, bouncing a little in his stance to keep loose while Maestas leaned in for the call, wound up, and delivered. The fastball came in letter high, and Jesse tore into it, connecting with the ball on the sweet spot of his aluminum bat. Ed ripped off his cap and whooped as the ball sailed over the fence. Then he felt Claire's glare and shut up. Jesse ran the bases at a dead sprint, too shocked by his success to gear down into a glory trot. As he rounded third and headed for home, he finally seemed to realize what he'd done, and threw his arms in the air.

All the dads pounded Ed on the back, while the mothers reached in from every side and patted Claire, congratulating her. The parents stood up and clapped Jesse home, but Ed followed Claire's lead and rose only half-way, remaining hunched. The Z's emptied out of the dugout and lined up at the plate, holding their hands out for high fives and low fives, Jesse smiling, red-cheeked, as he slapped their palms. Tyrell held his arms open and Jesse leapt into them, though he outweighed the shortstop by at least thirty pounds.

Past the raised arms of jubilant parents in the Z's stands and the boys bouncing around Jesse, Ray Maestas stood talking to his catcher, his face shadowed by his cap. He rested his hands on his hips, ball in his left hand, glove on his right, one knee bent. He nodded as the catcher talked to him. The catcher couldn't have anything that useful to say. Maestas knew what he was doing, knew what he'd done. He'd let a fastball get away from him, a mistake he didn't often make. But when Ed watched him out there, a subdued pitcher, his head bent in conference with the catcher amid all the celebration, Maestas became just a boy again, with skinny arms. A boy without a father.

Ed looked across through the chain-link fence to see if he could find Maestas' mother. It was hard to pick her out. A lot of the women were about the right age. One woman had risen from her seat and gazed forward, intent on the pitching mound, silent and solemn, like she wanted to send the boy a telepathic hug. "Is that her?" he whispered to Claire.

She nodded. "Don't stare."

"Come on, Claire, smile!" Rosa Pendergrass said, squeezing Claire's shoulder muscles. "Your boy just hit a home run in the big game."

Claire produced an unconvincing grin for Rosa.

276

"Yeah, Claire," Badgett's wife said, "Live it up a little," a hint of reproach in her voice like she was mad that Jesse was hitting better than her son.

After the catcher trotted back to home plate, Maestas looked down at the mound in front of him and took such a deep breath his shoulders rose with it. He performed some sort of ritual with his hands, bringing them together as he inhaled and pulling them apart as he blew out. He took three breaths this way, and then he assumed his stance on the mound. Tyrell Pendergrass came to bat, and Maestas smoked three fastballs by him before he had a chance to think. Maestas struck the next batter out on four pitches and deserted the field as soon as "strike three" left the ump's mouth. Going into the bottom of the first, the score stood 2-0, Z's.

Kitagawa looked sharp warming up, snapping his glove down to catch Jesse's tosses, his motions crisp as he threw. Jesse also mustered some extra pop, firing the ball to second and throwing out a base runner who got on with a bloop single to start the inning. Kitagawa retired the side with no runs scored.

In the second inning, the clouds rolled in until the field was canopied in gray. It grew so dark that Ed removed his sunglasses. Claire checked him with a look, and he put them back on. The wind picked up and the rain came, fat drops falling intermittently. It hadn't rained since April, and the parents turned their hands up to feel it pattering on their palms. The ump called the coaches over to confer. Hank Badgett, sitting in the front row, turned around and announced, "The ump said they're going to try to keep playing until at least five innings so the game is official. He'll call it if there's lightning."

Ed willed the rain to hold off for a few more innings. If the ump had to call the game before they finished five, they might have to play the rest another day. He couldn't take another game like this, his leg jiggling until Claire pressed her palm firmly on his thigh. She took the plastic ponchos from her bag. Ed pulled one over his head, even though the rain was still light and none of the other parents opened umbrellas yet.

"I'll go give Polly her raincoat," he told Claire, glad for the excuse to move. He found her playing with the other girls, and helped her wriggle into her coat before heading out to join the dads where they paced near the first base fence. Shrouded in rain gear, he felt free to roam. The rain picked up, tamping down the dust on the base paths and darkening the dirt.

They played on as it rained. Water puddles formed in depressions in the grass. The pitchers focused despite the weather, each dispatching the opposition, three up, three down. Kitagawa worked around the batters, but Maestas threw so fast that it didn't matter where he placed his pitches.

In the bottom of the fourth, the lead Pirate batter hit a double off of Kitagawa, water spraying from the impact when bat and ball connected. Then a wild pitch evaded Jesse and the runner stole third. Jesse beat himself in the chest pad with a fist, angry he hadn't stopped the ball, but he recovered well, holding the runner to only one base. The next batter hit a single, driving the runner in. Jesse went out to talk to his pitcher, and after that Kitagawa settled down. The Pirates grounded into a double play, and then Kid struck the last Pirate out. The score stood 2-to-1, Z's.

The rain picked up in the top of the fifth. The fans hid under umbrellas and raincoats, and Ed couldn't make out Santillano's wife anymore. Maestas danced around the strike zone, the ball skimming above the black border of the plate, his stuff turning nastier each inning. Claire collected Polly from where she was playing behind the bleachers and led her under the awning of the building at the center of the complex.

In the bottom of the fifth, E.J. snagged a dink pop-up in right field to end the inning. The ump threw up his arms, calling the game. The Z's thundered out of the dugout and a half-dozen of them sprinted to the outfield, where they slid belly down through the soaked grass, sending up waves around them. Lightning crackled through the sky and the coaches whistled the team in. The Pirates fled before the customary hand slaps. Boyd sent his team to their parents' cars without a post-game debriefing, and the league officials skipped the trophy presentation, instead handing over a cardboard box of trophies to each coach.

Ed found his sons, rain-soaked and radiant, skipping through the field like kindergarteners. They ran together to the car. Ed tried to share the boys' joy. The Z's win was perfectly legitimate according to the rules, but something about it made Ed uneasy. It felt unfair, and Santillano's son deserved a clean shot at the championship. It was a lame ending to the season, like a soccer match decided through penalty kicks. As he climbed in the Cherokee with his boys, who were reliving Jesse's home run, Ed thought of Maestas, who had no father to comfort him over his loss, no one he could give his second-place trophy to.

The next day the Pendergrasses hosted a victory celebration at their house in a Zenith Homes community in the suburbs south of Denver. At the gate, Ed spoke to the security guard in the booth, who wore mirrored sunglasses and a uniform, playing cop, glancing at a surveillance camera monitor before replying to Ed.

"How many in the car?" the guard asked.

"Five," Ed said, and the guard lifted the gate arm. Were the people who lived in these million-dollar homes worried that a roving band of Mongols was going to attack? "Good work," Ed couldn't resist adding before he drove through.

The immense houses loomed, crowded together so that each spanned nearly its entire plot of land. The streets all had the same name—Trail Ridge Lane, Trail Ridge Circle, Trail Ridge Way. Ed finally happened on the right street.

Ed parked and walked with his family to the front door, where he assumed a habitual position, off to the side, holding Polly behind him out of gun range, before he reached to ring the bell. "Ed," Claire whispered. "Stand in front of the door like a regular person." Ed did as she said, drawing the leg on his shooting side forward to align it with the other one, and then he stood looking like anybody else, pretending this felt natural to him.

Rosa Pendergrass answered the door. "Ed and Claire! Come in!" Rosa was a tiny woman in coral Capri pants, and Tyrell took after her in size. Ed had sensed a little regret in Darnell that his boy was better at baseball than football, but if he'd wanted his son to play his sport, he should have married a beefier woman.

"Thanks for inviting us," Claire said.

"Of course!" Rosa said. "It wouldn't be a party without our home-run hitter."

As Jesse's parents, Ed and Claire enjoyed special status among the Z's fans, and all the parents of the best players rushed up to greet them, while the parents of boys with worse batting averages huddled around the onion dip. Over the course of the season, the parents had formed a sort of tribe, sharing newspapers and boxes of doughnuts, rooting for each other's sons, razzing the umps about bad calls.

As they crossed the living room, Claire paused before a print that hung on the wall. A Mexican peasant dressed in white carried a load of blooming flowers on his stooped back. "Nice," Ed said. He never knew what Claire wanted him to say when she pointed out art to him. In college, she'd majored in art history for a couple of semesters before succumbing to her parents' advice and switching to accounting, so she saw more in paintings than Ed did. "Diego Rivera was a socialist," Claire said. "But his paintings also happen to match a lot of sofas."

"Do you not want to be here?" Ed whispered.

"I'm happy to be here. I was just making an observation."

"Maybe we should take the kids to the art museum after baseball is over," he offered.

"You'd be bored stiff, like the last three times we went," Claire said.

"Give me a chance, huh?" But Claire was already halfway across the room, heading for the catered spread in the kitchen, a Tex-Mex-themed buffet of miniaturized food.

The children piled their plates with two-inch tacos, enchiladas the size of index fingers, and guacamole heaped into dainty corn chip boats. The boys demolished their food and ran off to play video games and bludgeon each other with pillows. Some of the boys asked Darnell for permission to swim in the pool.

The parents poured out of the house to watch their children clowning in the pool: chicken fights, belly flops, the bigger boys tossing the smaller ones as far as they could heave them. Rosa Pendergrass handed out drinks, and all of a sudden, everyone was drunk. Darryl kept blending strawberry margaritas, draining several bottles of tequila. The margaritas were potent enough to cause the men to lose their fascination with the beer tap next to the kitchen faucet that dispensed a microbrew. Everyone walked around holding big round glasses of pink slush with paper umbrellas, ceasing to notice their sons in the pool.

Although he was holding back compared to some of the parents, Ed had a buzz going, and the Pendergrass backyard began to look like the grounds of a tropical resort, a crystal blue swimming pool with a springboard, little solar-powered Japanese lanterns casting a glow on the lush lawn as the sun faded, a bit of fancy landscaping at the far end of the yard with a rocky terraced garden, a small waterfall burbling through it. A high wooden fence surrounded the yard, so they couldn't see anything beyond it and they could have been anywhere. Ed sank down in a chaise lounge by the poolside and watched the boys launch off the springboard and strike split-second Egyptian poses before plunging into the water.

Ed and his friends disdained the cops that worked in these neighborhoods, ranking them only a notch above shopping mall security men. These cops must do nothing but respond to calls about yowling cats and kids skateboarding on private property. But maybe it would be nice for a change to serve as the friendly neighborhood cop in a place like this, just the guy you'd wave over for help if you were stuck with a flat or locked out of your car. No need for a gang unit; instead the police here could hold car washes to raise money for schools. Cops in this neighborhood could afford to be kind.

But Ed knew he couldn't transfer here. He needed to be where he felt useful, where he'd always felt useful, until he killed

Santillano. When he used to work graves, he felt protective toward the people of the city as he drove through Denver at dawn. He'd picture everyone asleep in warm beds, unaware that their alarms would soon ring. As the night sky gave way to morning colors and the lights flicked on in the houses along the highway, he'd think of the people in them stretching, scratching, groping their way toward coffee machines. He'd felt that he was watching over them, if only because he was alert during the defenseless hours of their slumber. And then he'd gone and killed someone whose house he had no business entering.

He gazed out at the Pendergrass sanctuary. Was it some failing in him that he hadn't provided his family with such a place to live? Maybe Claire wanted more.

Claire's laughter cut through the noise of the party. She stood on the patio amid a group of parents, the melon-colored paper lanterns that hung from the eaves casting a warm glow on her pale skin. The breeze swayed her cotton sundress around her legs and her cheeks grew pink from the margaritas. Ed wanted to kiss her like he used to before all this had happened, before he'd killed Santillano, before he'd become a cop, before they'd had children, before they'd had anything at stake between them.

They'd met when Ed had just entered the police academy, and Claire was a senior in college, working as a waitress at a Mexican restaurant. The place was subterranean, with stucco walls. Little red candles flickered on every table, and a bar stood at one end, looking out on a dance floor that nobody used.

The cops-in-training came after classes let out because of the women who hung out at the bar, long-legged in tight jeans, their hair falling in curtains down their backs. Ed's classmates hit on them, the easy marks, and sometimes managed to take one home. Ed occasionally flirted with them, but he had his eye on the waitress with the auburn hair.

Claire's uniform was simple, a black t-shirt and jeans with an apron to stow her notepad in. Her messy hair curled every which way, and her eyes were green. Her skin was freckled and back then she wore too much eye makeup, the heavy black liner underneath the lid making her look smutty and tough.

"You're working too hard," Ed said to her one day, after watching her for months. "Why don't you rest for a minute?" He was sitting with a group of men from the academy. They'd goaded him into speaking to her, and watched their interaction with shit-eating grins on their faces.

"Good one," she said. She nodded her head at the dance floor. "Why don't you dance? Keep me entertained, then I won't need a rest."

"Where's the music?" Ed asked, his belly full of too many Dos Equis.

"There's never been music." She turned away and wiped a table.

Ed took down the guitar that hung on the wall next to a poncho and a *rista* of chiles. He strummed it, working the five chords he knew, and Claire turned to look. In his croaky voice, he sang "La Cucaracha" and "Guantanamera" and "Cielito Lindo," and every hackneyed Mexican folk song Colorado third-graders were trained to belt out during school assemblies. Claire hurried around, but he caught her looking back at him several times because he never took his eyes from her during his serenade. The ladies at the bar howled and came over to clap along, a lanky blonde trailing her hand down Ed's back as he played.

At the end of the night, Claire pressed a slip of paper with her phone number on it into Ed's hand, saying, "No more singing." He started coming to see her when she got off work. When he first kissed her, she tasted of salt, limes, and tequila. This is the story that Ed thought of first when he told his kids, "Your mom and I used to be fun."

Ed, damp from the pool spray, rose from the chaise lounge on slightly unsteady legs and crossed the yard to Claire. She shivered when the breeze blew across her bare shoulders and he reached out to wrap his arm around her. She flinched.

"Sorry," he said, taking a step back.

"It's okay." Her eyes were bright from the margaritas. She dropped her voice to a whisper. "Is it over now?"

For a moment, Ed had forgotten about Santillano. "I hope so."

"No criminal charges, no lawsuit, no confrontation with his family."

Ed took her hand. "Do you think I have a chance with you?"

She pulled him close and kissed him. "I hope so."

Standing there next to her, the length of her body pressed against his, breathing in her perfume, it was possible to forget that at the end of the evening they would have to collect their kids, who were running around the yard and cannonballing into the pool in the glow of the tiki torches. But he couldn't forget that Ray was out there somewhere in the city, a boy who'd lost his father and the baseball championship in the space of a few months.

CHAPTER 22

Patricia
July 7–13

When the other team's catcher, a solid oak of a boy, hit a home run off Ray in the first inning of the championship game, a canyon opened in Patricia's chest as she watched the ball fly, gone. The centerfielder took off running, but he didn't even bother to reach for the ball. The Z's fans burst into cheers. The Pirates' parents sat, hunched and grim. Mia scolded El Johnway for not preventing the hit. Patricia stood, a gesture of support for Ray, but he didn't look over.

Ray recovered from the home run, pitching well in the rain for four innings, but then when he was rushing out to the mound for the top of the sixth, the ump shouted, "That's the game. I'm calling it." Ray stopped short as though he'd been yanked back on a tether. He kicked at a puddle. Pete whipped off his cap, water flying from his hair as he hollered. But the ump crossed his arms and turned his head. Ray remained on the field after all the other boys ran for shelter, bent over with his hands on his thighs, letting the rain hit his back. Thunder rumbled in the distance. It took a while for Patricia to understand that it was really over, that the championship was going to end this way.

The parents gathered their belongings and ran for cover. They hurried to their cars, heaving lawn chairs and coolers. "Can you take Mia?" Patricia asked Lupe as the rain intensified. "I'll wait for Ray." Lupe and Mia fled as pea-sized hailstones plinked against the metal bleachers.

Patricia stood under the awning at the center of the complex while she waited for Ray to appear. The Pirates, burdened with heavy bat bags, ran to the parking lot and sorted themselves into their parents' cars. So much for the boys of summer. In a few weeks, the kids would return to school, and Ray would see Miguel. Patricia would do everything she could to keep Ray from trouble, but she couldn't watch him all the time.

The field was deserted, so Patricia went to look for Ray. Tiny ice pellets beat her and her hair dripped. Had Ray left with Pete? She tried the bathrooms, calling into the men's and getting no response. A brief vision of Ray lying in some gutter, covered with hail, flashed through her head. But then she finally saw him, sitting in the dugout alone.

She ran into the dugout, where Ray huddled in a corner, hugging his glove close to keep the leather dry. The hail rattled the plastic dugout roof.

Ray turned and looked at her. He seemed like a little boy again, small and soaked. He had the same dazed expression as when he was a toddler needing a nap. "How come weathermen always say hail is always pea-sized, then marble-sized, then golf-ball-sized, then baseball-sized?" he asked. "They never say grape-sized or peanut-sized or tennis-ball-sized."

Patricia shook her head. "I'm sorry about the game."

Ray looked out at the empty field. His eyes seemed too bright.

Patricia resisted the urge to feel his forehead for fever. "Don't you think we'd better go home now? Get warmed up?"

Ray shrugged. "Are you all right? Did the hail hit you?"

"I'm okay." She rapped her skull with a knuckle. "It's hard. I should have figured you had enough sense to find shelter."

"Yeah, you should've."

"But, you know." Patricia shivered. "A mother worries." She looked at Ray, thinking, they're just legs and arms and neck at that age, with no cushion from the weather. They could both pretend his cheeks were wet only from the rain. The drumming on the dugout roof gradually faded to a patter, and then to a gentle beat.

"We'd better head to the car before your sister and grandma worry." She stood, but Ray didn't move. "I'm sorry, Ray," she said, taking his hand. "I know how much this meant to you. It wasn't your fault. You got your team here, and they couldn't score any runs in the end."

"I want to stay right here," Ray said. "I don't want to go through the rest."

"The rest of what?"

"The end of summer. Back to school. My birthday. The World Series, Halloween, Christmas. All of it without Dad."

"You can't stay here, baby." She took a deep breath so she wouldn't cry. He was right. There were times when it seemed like the only safe thing to do was to stop moving forward. But that was never an option. "Come on now. The rain's stopped." She tugged his hand to pull him close. He felt warm next to her chilly skin.

Water dripped from the dugout roof as they walked out. A mocha puddle formed a moat around the mound. In the distance, a short, squat man wearing navy rain gear hurried in from the parking lot.

"That's the other team's coach," Ray said. "Pete hates him."

Patricia and Ray moved aside on the sidewalk to let him pass, but he came right up to them.

He was an odd-looking man, with a doorknob nose and dark little eyes. "Maestas, you pitched a great game," he said.

"Not great enough." Ray shook his head.

"I'm glad I caught you before you left," Boyd continued. "There's a rule that says we're allowed to pick up two players from our league to take with us to post-season play. The only one that stands out is you. Would you join us? We could sure use your arm and your bat."

Ray looked at Patricia, and she was touched that he deferred this decision to her, after their disagreement on arbitration. She wanted to tell him to go for it. If baseball lasted the whole year, her Miguel problem would be solved. Instead she said, "It's up to you. You choose."

He thought for a moment, weighing loyalties. Water rushed through the streets around them. "My team let me down," he said. "They should have gotten some runs."

"You shouldn't have to throw a perfect game to come up with a win," Boyd said, nodding, eager to sign an ace. "The Z's will back you up."

Ray looked at Boyd, then down at his shoes. "Yeah," he said. "I'll throw for you."

Boyd produced a sealed plastic bag from his pocket, took a folded form from it and shook it out. "This is a release. Fill it out and have your mother sign it."

They used Boyd's clipboard and pen to complete the form. Patricia's hair dripped on the ink as she signed, making her name run. Pete wouldn't want Ray to take on this mercenary role with the opposition, but after all, it was allowed in the rules of the league. It was an honor to be chosen, and Patricia wouldn't let anyone take that from Ray.

Boyd extended his hand to Ray. Ray shook it, and now he looked grown up to Patricia, a free agent already.

When Boyd walked off, Patricia put her arm around Ray's shoulders. He sighed. "What's the matter?" Patricia said. "You should be proud. You earned the right to go to state."

"I know," he said. "I just wish I'd done it with my own team."

On the day of arbitration, Patricia gave her name to the man at the front desk in the courthouse downtown, and he showed her and Lupe to a windowless, gray-walled room. Archuleta was already sitting at the table, which was empty except for a stack of paper cups and a plastic pitcher brimming with tepid water. The city's lawyers were in another room, and the arbitrator would go between them until they reached an agreement.

The arbitration attorney arrived, a tall, elegant woman with a skunk stripe in her black hair, and all at once the talks began. The arbitrator presented the city's case to them, saying that the beginning offer was $175,000. Patricia blew the breath out of her mouth slowly when she heard the first number. So that's what a man was going for, in Denver, these days. It was higher than the first offer the mayor had made, but it was still a pittance compared to the $5.5 million her lawyer sought. Archuleta had told her they'd come in low at first. It was hard to think of the money as real—it was like pink and yellow board game currency in her head. Any price seemed cruel, even if the first offer was a sum that Salvador would have considered riches. He would have bought a new truck for them and a tractor for his father, taken them all to Elitch's to ride the roller coasters.

The arbitrator said, "The city's counsel wants me to remind you that Mr. Santillano fired at the cops, and it is their belief that the jury wouldn't award you anything."

"Depends on the jury," Archuleta said. He had taken off his jacket and rolled up his sleeves. "I think you will find that the people of Denver will be sympathetic to our case. Sergeant Springer claims that he made a clerical error, a judge signs a warrant for a no-knock with a wrong address, and the cops kill an innocent person. Furthermore, Springer has a history of racist behavior toward Latinos."

"There's no proof that Salvador fired at them," Patricia said, her voice sounding shrill to her ears. "They can't even prove that he had a gun. They're just trying to do anything they can to make themselves appear less guilty." She clenched her fist, her palms sweaty. "And you know what really gets me? After they killed Salvador, they tested him for drugs, hoping they'd find some so he'd be nothing more than a Mexican drug addict. What right did they have to touch him?" She reached for the pitcher and tried to fill a glass, but she shook so much that the water spilled on the table. Maybe she should have had a trial after all, like Ray and Lupe had wanted.

"It's all right, Patricia." Archuleta pushed a box of tissues toward her. "This isn't a trial. You don't need to answer anyone's questions or complaints. You just tell me if they come back with a number that sounds like it would work for you."

The arbitrator chanced a flicker of a smile at Patricia. "We could always discuss this separately and have your lawyer confer with you," she offered.

"No," Patricia said, "I can take it." Arbitration was supposed to be more civilized, freeing them of the accusations of the courtroom. But now that she was shut in this room with a woman offering fake sympathy, she didn't want to let the city dispatch with Salvador's death so efficiently. "You were right," she whispered to Lupe.

"You're doing fine," Lupe said. "It'll be over soon."

Patricia thought of the back of Salvador's neck, how good it was to kiss, how he had this subtle scent that drew her to him. It was faint and familiar and comfortable, like sheets that had been on the bed for a week, a hat he'd worn to work, a t-shirt he'd slept in. She could still create his voice in her head when she thought of things he used to say, *nada nada limonada*, but feared the sound would become uncertain to her. She didn't want to forget his smell, or his voice, or how her cheek felt, pressed against the middle of his back. She worried that a decade from now, she would lose the ability to conjure his face from memory, and begin to take the pictures in the photo albums into her mind, her image of him generated from without instead of within.

As the arbitrator came and went, offering a figure and then retreating to the other room to consult with the city's lawyers, Patricia practiced remembering. The way she used to close her eyes when she felt alone and afraid and couldn't sleep as a child, and try to remember her dead grandparents' house. She ran up the concrete front steps and turned the small metal knob to open the screen door. She walked across the carpeted kitchen, running her hand over the glass-fronted armoire where they displayed their good dishes and the cheap porcelain sculptures their grandchildren gave them for Christmas. She walked up the creaky wooden stairs to her mother's former bedroom, with the rag rug at the foot of the bed. She smoothed her hair with the yellow-bristled hairbrush on the doily in front of the mirror on the vanity, next to the bowl of dried rose petals, then ran her hands over the lamb-soft white chenille bedspread. She stared at the picture of Mary on the wall, her eyes betraying centuries of pain, her chest superimposed with the flaming sacred heart, and the other picture that hung beside it, of praying alabaster hands, entwined with a rosary, pictures a child could see in the moonlit dark and be comforted. If she could keep a house in her head, an entire house, she could keep Salvador there, too. She just had to practice.

The lawyers went back and forth, suggesting figures, making counter-offers. She shook her head when Archuleta told her the numbers. At the end of the day the offer was $750,000, and that was final, take it or they'd go to court, Archuleta said. Patricia thought of Mia and Ray, the faces she didn't have to practice to know. If they went to a trial, there might be no money for them. She looked at Lupe, questioning, and her mother nodded, "Do what you think is right." There would be no trial, no lawsuits. She would give up some imaginary future money so that her family could have security now. "All right," Patricia said. "We'll settle for that."

That evening, Lupe began packing to leave, pulling her red suitcase out from under Mia's bed. "I've stayed away from your father too long," she said to Patricia as she stacked the neat squares of her folded shirts into her red suitcase. "He may have turned savage." He called every night, and when Patricia spoke to him, it sounded like he was enjoying himself, golfing nonstop.

Patricia wondered if Lupe was mad at her for settling with the city. But she couldn't read her reaction. It was the same as when she'd decided to marry Salvador. Lupe argued her point until she saw that she couldn't win, then never brought it up again.

Mia sat on the bed next to the open suitcase, swinging her legs as Lupe packed. Ray paced, picking up objects from the dresser and examining them. Patricia meant to leave her mother to pack in peace, but she kept wandering back with some excuse, bringing Lupe's clean laundry or plastic bags for her to stow her lotions and soaps in. It seemed like all the light and life of the house was in Lupe's room and it drew them in.

"This little room is crowded today!" Lupe said. "Thank you for lending it to me, Mia."

"You can keep it, Grandma," Mia said.

"It's time, dear." She cupped Mia's cheek with a palm. "I came to help you. Your mom is doing well now. She can see you through."

Patricia steadied herself with a hand on the dresser. With Lupe leaving, she felt doubtful of every decision she'd ever made.

Ray opened and closed a small jewelry box. "When can we visit you, Grandma?" he asked.

Lupe hugged Ray. He was taller than her now by an inch. "I hope you'll come out to visit us in Arizona. Maybe for Christmas break? You can stay for three weeks if you want. Grandpa will teach you how to drive his golf cart."

"If this team I'm playing with wins state," Ray said, "we'll go to the regionals in Las Cruces. We could all meet there."

Lupe looked surprised at the invitation. "Sure. Southern New Mexico isn't too far from where we live. If you make it to the regionals, your grandpa and I will see you there."

"I'll get us to regionals," Ray said with an efficient nod like he belonged on his new, businesslike team, away from the flash and disorder of Pete and the Pirates.

Patricia sank on the bed next to Mia. Lupe was so graceful, her back straight, her hands nimble as she folded her clothes. Patricia studied her mother's hands, and then reached across the bed and grabbed Ray's hand. "So that's where you got them from," Patricia said, inspecting the long, tapered fingers of his pitching hand that were a perfect match for Lupe's. Lupe had supplied all her family's grace.

The next morning Patricia helped her mother load her suitcases into the trunk of her butter yellow Cadillac. "Thank you, Mama," she said. "I'm sorry I settled. I'm not a brave fighter like you."

Lupe shook her head. "You did the right thing. I see that now. You did what a mother should do." Her voice broke and she couldn't get any further.

Lupe reached out and pulled Patricia into an embrace, rocking her gently as Patricia rested her head on her shoulder. Her mother's touch felt as bolstering to Patricia as it had when she was in labor. Salvador had dutifully attended the childbirth preparation classes before Ray was born, and agreed to be in the delivery room with Patricia, though he doubted this American custom. But when she was in the middle of active labor, he had no idea what to do. Patricia wanted someone to wipe the sweat out of her eyes, give her a sip of water, but she was too weak to speak. Salvador's touches were tentative, and brought her no comfort. Then Lupe had shown up, charging into the room, finding Patricia hunched over, shaking uncontrollably, too dehydrated for an epidural. When the next contraction came Lupe wrapped her arms around Patricia fiercely, holding her with all her strength, as if preparing to bear the brunt of a wave that was about to crash.

Patricia held on until Lupe eased free. "You're safe now," Lupe said. "With that money—if you're careful with it—you can take care of the kids, send them to college."

"I'll be careful."

After Mia kissed Lupe goodbye, she hung around Patricia's waist like she was a toddler. Lupe waved and then stepped into the car. Patricia turned her head. She couldn't watch her mother drive away. When they headed back into the house, Mia began to cry. Ray retreated to the backyard. Patricia could hear him winging tennis balls against the side of the house, something he hadn't done since Lupe had told him not to.

The afternoon after Lupe left, Patricia drove Ray out to south Denver so that he could practice pitching with his new team's catcher. With the long drive across town, the whole thing would take several hours, so she left Mia with Nino and his grandma.

"Isn't one catcher the same as another?" she asked Ray as they drove.

"No," he said. "You need a catcher that knows how to frame your pitches so that the ump will call a strike. A catcher who will call the right pitches for the right batter. Someone who can handle your curve balls."

"That's what I need," Patricia said, missing Lupe already. "Someone who can handle my curve balls."

The field was forty minutes away from home, so Patricia decided she'd stay at the practice. The diamond was empty except for Boyd. He talked to Ray, too softly for Patricia to hear. Compared to Pete, he seemed subdued, calm. Patricia sat in the bleachers reading the newspaper. The catcher who'd hit the home run off Ray walked up to the field, followed by his dad. She wondered about the catcher's life. Was his room brimming with gadgets, his own TV and computer, and would he attend one of the huge suburban schools that won high school baseball championships every year? She hoped she wouldn't have to make small talk with the dad. She glanced at him and he met her eyes and stopped walking. He was tall, a little chunky around the middle, and there was something unsettling about how he carried himself, with arrogant authority. He turned away and leaned against the fence, his back to her. He gradually edged away, never turning his face toward her again, until he was seated in the bleachers on the opposite side of the field. Was this some kind of racial snobbery? But there were black and Asian kids on the Z's. The dad seemed familiar—maybe from the earlier games. She'd met so many new people in the past few months, it was hard to say how she knew him. She tried to concentrate on her newspaper, but instead she watched the man through her sunglasses, trying to place him.

After practice, she and Ray climbed back into the car to head home. "So how was the catcher?" Patricia asked.

"He's proper," Ray said. "Shows a good target, stops what I throw. He's got a good arm so I won't have to worry about base runners stealing on me. I can just throw. I think we can get to regionals."

"Good," she said, and although her instincts told her not to, she asked what the catcher's name was.

"Jesse O'Fallon," Ray said.

When they got home, Patricia kept glancing at the computer in the living room. If she used it in front of the kids, Mia would come up and look over her shoulder, ask her what she was doing. Patricia let the kids stay up an hour past their bedtimes so they wouldn't be suspicious, and then said she was going to bed and made the kids turn off the TV and go to their rooms.

An hour later, when it was quiet, she crept out and turned on the computer, leaving the lights off. It didn't take her long to find out who the man was: Ed O'Fallon, a Denver cop. She could only find one picture of him, an old one. He must have gained thirty pounds since then. And then all the articles came up. She hadn't recognized him at first because most of the articles only mentioned Sergeant Springer, the man who botched the warrant. Springer was still on unpaid leave, and various committees and judges were in the process of deciding whether he'd lose his job over the mistake and have to serve jail time. She found an older article from the week of Salvador's death, listing O'Fallon as one of the three shooters. A door creaked down the hall and she jumped. She tried to shut the computer down, but the cursor wouldn't respond to the mouse. "What are you doing, Mom?" Mia asked as Patricia finally closed the browser.

She settled Mia back into bed, and went to sit in the kitchen. Her first instinct was to call Lupe. She got as far as picking up the phone before she decided that she'd depended on her mom enough already. She was a single mother now, and she needed to figure out how to handle her own curve balls.

Patricia didn't want to think about cops anymore now that the arbitration was finished, but here she was, drawn in again. The way O'Fallon edged away from her today infuriated her—he knew who she was. The coward. He'd probably learned they signed a settlement, so now they couldn't sue him. She didn't want to know this man's face. She didn't want to know he had a son, or anything else about him. And she had to keep Ray from finding out who O'Fallon was. What were her options? Forbid Ray to play with the Z's? She might as well buy him a six-pack and drive him over to Miguel's house to hang out with the gangsters and pit bulls. Or she could let him play in the tournament, and pretend she didn't know. She would have to sit there in the stands and watch, with a smile on her face, while her son played catch with the son of the man who'd killed her husband.

CHAPTER 23

Ed

July 13–21

J esse sat shotgun, fiddling with the laces of his catcher's mitt, as Ed drove back from pitching practice. "Boyd didn't mention Ray Maestas would be there," Ed said, trying to sound nonchalant even though his jaw was tight from clenching it throughout the practice.

Jesse shrugged. "How am I supposed to know what pitches to call against the batters at the state tournament?" he asked, a panicked tone in his voice. "Guys I've never seen before?"

The houses flew past as Ed drove. When he'd seen Ray up close, Santillano's dying face had come back to him, and now that was all he could see as he looked out his windshield. Answer Jesse's question, Ed thought. "If San—" Ed began, "I mean if Maestas is pitching, you probably don't need to worry about that too much." Ed glanced at his speedometer and eased his foot off the gas.

"You might as well speed," Jesse said. "You'd never get a ticket anyway."

"I have to obey the law like everyone else," Ed said.

But Jesse was already back on baseball. "Maestas is good, but I've still got to call his pitches. A catcher's best weapon is information, like you always said."

Ed nodded. A year ago, he would have delivered a rambling coach lecture at this point. *Note where the batter is in the lineup, estimate his height and weight, check his stance—is it open or closed? Is he up in the box or back?—and judge what pitch will probably fool him.* But he wasn't a coach anymore. And he had other things to think about. "I'm sure you'll figure it out," he said.

Jesse looked at Ed, as if waiting for something more. Then he took a deep breath, blowing it out slowly, an old man of twelve. "The pressure is getting to me."

A baseball rolled around in the backseat, and Ed waited for it to shoot under his seat and wedge against the gas pedal, sending them flying through somebody's front yard. At least if that happened, he could delay telling Claire that Ray was now an official member of the Z's.

"We're on the back patio," Claire called. Ed steadied himself as he passed through the house. "Steak and corn on the cob," she said, displaying a platter of New York strips. Claire had been cooking his favorite meals lately, and Ed had been offering back rubs, buying flowers, both of them making gestures they hoped would get them back together somehow. The kids, at least, were relieved at such outward displays of harmony. But the truce was tenuous and it might end once Ed told her about Ray.

"Mommy says we can make s'mores after dinner," Polly said. A watermelon slice the size of her head spanned her plate. She took a bite out of the middle, chewed, and spit the seeds out into the grass, her sticky cheeks glistening. Santillano had a daughter, too.

"Everything looks great." Ed settled into a patio chair.

"How was practice?" Claire plopped down a slab of meat on Ed's plate, its juices oozing.

Ed's mouth felt dry.

"Good," Jesse answered, as Claire loaded his plate.

"Well, that's informative." Claire began to pour the iced tea. "Did Kitagawa pitch well?"

"Boyd had a new pitcher for me to work with," Jesse said, sawing through his meat.

"Oh?" Claire started to fill Ed's glass. He touched her hand in warning.

"Yeah, we picked up Ray Maestas, that awesome pitcher from the Pirates."

The tea splashed over Ed's glass as Claire poured it. "Here, let me," he said, taking the pitcher from her hands. He sopped up the spill with a handful of paper napkins, glad he didn't have to break it to her.

"We're going to be sweet," E.J. said, drumming a beat on the table with his fingertips.

"We're going to be swee-eet," Polly mimicked, kicking her legs back and forth.

"What do you mean you picked him up?" Claire asked, straining to keep her tone light as she yanked the sodden napkins out of Ed's hand and shot him an exasperated glance.

"Teams are allowed to pick up a couple of ringers from their leagues before the state tournament," Ed explained, glancing at her quickly.

She turned to him, her face stern. "Did you know about this?"

"I just found out today." He threw up a tense smile like a white flag. "The rules are different in this league." It was the most competitive league in the state, and the pick-up rule was meant to reward the all-stars with an extension of the season.

"It's good Maestas gets another chance," E.J. said. "He's better than the team he was playing for."

Claire balled up the napkins. "I don't understand why Boyd would want to mess with the team's dynamics after you've already won the district championship."

"Don't worry, Mom." Jesse patted her arm. "Kitagawa will still get to throw. It'll be all right with him."

"Who knew Mom was such a fan of Kid?" E.J. said, pinching his sister underneath the table.

Claire and Ed lay flat on their backs, neither of them sleeping in their hot room. The battery of fans Ed had positioned in the windows to combat the heat droned on.

"You told me it was over," Claire said, her voice flat. "You said after Santillano's family signed the settlement, everything would be okay."

"I had nothing to do with this," Ed said, thinking about how after the party at the Pendergrasses' house, he and Claire had sex for the first time since the shooting. Now they lay with twelve inches of bed between them. "We'll just have to try to avoid her."

"Won't that seem strange for us to be distant when her son is playing on our team?"

"She's got more complicated things to worry about than a couple of parents on the team snubbing her." Of all the years he'd been a cop, he'd rarely encountered people repeatedly, except for court dates. The family of the man he'd killed was dogging him, making the city feel too small.

"She's bound to hear our names." Claire rolled over onto her side. "I bet the state tournament has announcers for every game."

"Maybe she won't assume we're the same people."

"Did she see you at practice?"

Ed considered telling her he'd accidentally all but walked up to Santillano's wife and introduced himself. "No," he said. "I sat far away from her." He'd lied more often in the past few months than he ever had before. It was beginning to feel natural. "The season will end," he continued, "and if she had figured out who we were by now, she wouldn't have let Ray play on the team."

Claire sat up and hugged her knees to her chest. "If she finds out, she'll take her son off the team."

"That's right."

"We could take our boys off the team."

"I can't tell them they can't go to state because I killed the pitcher's dad. I want to keep them out of this. They shouldn't have to carry this."

"But we do," Claire said. "I wish I could tell her how sorry I am for her loss. Help her in some way. You didn't make the mistake on the warrant. This happened to us, too."

"She'd never see it that way." He wished he'd scrutinized the warrant himself before the raid. Maybe he would have realized the mistake, stopped everything before it had a chance to go wrong and end up with Ray's dad lying dead in that stuffy house.

"When I saw her working in the snack stand a few weeks ago," Claire said, "she wasn't how I pictured his wife."

"I didn't picture her at all," Ed said. But he knew what she meant. If Santillano's wife had been an illegal immigrant like those who crowded the hospitals and jails, looking out at the world with that filter of incomprehension and insularity—would he have felt less guilty?

Ed drove his family north to Fort Collins' main youth base-ball complex on the Friday the tournament began. He glanced at Jesse in the rearview mirror, worried about all the time he and Ray would spend together this weekend. He hoped they wouldn't get to talking about anything but baseball. Polly demanded a window seat so she could watch for the isolated taxidermy shop along the side of the highway with a stuffed giraffe mounted on its roof. Claire stared out the window. Ed blasted Springsteen and threw the sun roof open the way he would have before any of this happened. The kids were quiet, always responding to tension between him and Claire by turning down their volume. They passed a neglected-looking farm with a weathered barn bearing the faded words GENETIC ENGINEERING on its side, as if DNA could be spliced in an old feeding trough once used to slop hogs. Jesse broke the silence by socking his brother in the arm and saying, "That's where you were made, E.J."

The fields at the main complex had tawny base paths lined with pristine chalk, and green, smooth outfields stretching to the fences. The boys spotted Coach Boyd and the Z's gathering under a tree, and zoomed off to meet them. Ray wasn't among them. Claire rubbed Polly with sunblock, and then let her join some other girls making dandelion chains in the grass between the fields.

"What's the plan?" Claire asked when they were alone. They brought several lawn chairs so they could sit as far away from Santillano's wife as possible.

"I'm just going to stay away from the field until the game starts," Ed said.

"I'll wait to set up our chairs until I see where she sits." Claire shook her head. "I feel ridiculous. Sneaking around like a criminal."

Ed's left eyelid twitched behind his dark glasses as he walked to the tournament's command center that stood on a rise overlooking the four fields spread out around it, fat pie wedges divided by fence and concrete paths. On one side stood the concession stand. A Hispanic man worked in it, drowning a paper basket of nachos with molten plasticky cheese, jalapeño rounds bobbing in goo. The man glanced at him and Ed looked away. How many people in the state would recognize his face?

Ed walked by the booth where coaches submitted their team rosters, game outcomes, and documentation. A woman in an official tournament t-shirt chatted with the umpires. Behind her on the counter sat a pile of first aid kits under a defibrillator mounted on the wall. Boyd approached on his thick, short legs, his skin tanned from the season into a glove-leather brown.

"Turning in the roster?" Ed asked.

"I'm submitting a copy of Ray's birth certificate. There's always some team mom accusing you of cheating."

"Is he young enough to play on the Z's next year?" Ed asked, his eyelid spasming again.

Boyd nodded. "If I can get him away from Pete. I don't want him ending up like Cisco."

If Ray played for the Z's next year, Ed would have to move his boys back down to PAL. They'd hate that. "Who's Cisco?"

"A promising pitcher that Pete made throw too much, too hard. He messed with his delivery until the kid was a burnt-out head case." Boyd shook his head. "I've seen too many kids ruined by coaches hopping up their sore arms with Flex-It and Red Hot so they could keep throwing."

"That's a shame," Ed said. "Their arms will be worth more later."

302

"Hell," Boyd continued, "last time I was in Las Cruces for the regionals, there was this Oklahoma coach doling out horse liniment to his pitchers, blazing them up just to win a few games."

If things had been different, Ed would have warned Patricia, telling her not to let Pete use Ray too much, and he would have shown Ray how to take care of his arm after an outing. When Ed was coaching, he'd split a couple of old tires in half and cut them down the middle so the pitchers could fill them with ice and attach the U-shaped rubber to their arms immediately after they came off the mound, cooling their muscles.

"Nothing worse than a washed-up fourteen-year-old," Ed said, thinking of the dozens of them that he'd come across in his work. Before he'd become a cop, he hadn't known it was possible to screw up your life so permanently when you were that young, but now he saw it all the time. Unless baseball came through for Ray, Ed figured he was ruined. Losing a father at that age, in that way, was bound to affect him. He could see Ray, rangy and dangerous at sixteen, scaling a chain-link fence while sirens blared, a blade in his back pocket.

Boyd's turn came up at the registration window, and Ed continued circling the command center until he found the wall where the tournament brackets were posted. He joined a herd of men staring at it and took off his sunglasses so he could read better. The women had already purchased programs to read their sons' names and found a copy of the tournament schedule on page one. But men liked to gather around tournament brackets, which appealed to them on a primal level, pitting weak against strong.

Ed looked up from the brackets as Santillano's wife walked around the corner, leading her girl from the bathroom. Ed turned away, but Santillano's wife tugged her daughter around to the other side so that she was between Ed and the girl as they passed behind him. Ed's eyelid twitched double-time like a broken turn signal and he put his glasses back on. Had she figured everything out?

"I don't see any team names," one man wearing a Yuma Bears t-shirt said. "Where are the teams?"

"Now you see," began a squat man with a round gut who had been standing there for hours and had memorized the thing, "today they'll play the round robin games for seeding, then on Saturday they'll enter the brackets according to their records from those games, and from then on it'll be double elimination. What pool is your son in?"

"Apache."

"No, that's his division. The pools are named for colors."

"Oh, blue, I think."

"Tough draw," he said. "The Denver Z's are in that pool, and they picked up a ringer. Took him from Pete's Pirates."

"I saw that kid throw once," another dad said. "I hope we don't face him."

Ed drifted away from the crowd, not wanting to hear any more.

When the first game was set to begin, Ed scanned the stands but didn't see Santillano's wife. Then he spotted her in a lawn chair set up in the shade of a tree a good way back from the bleachers. Her girl sat beside her, turning the pages of a book, a sweet expression on her face. She was close to Polly's age.

Ed helped Claire set up their lawn chairs on the opposite side of the bleachers from the Santillanos. Claire hoisted a big beach umbrella, saying, "This will keep off the sun." Ed considered telling her about how Santillano's wife had avoided him. But he didn't need to make this weekend feel any longer than it already would.

Santillano's girl walked in front of the bleachers, holding an action figure in her hand. "What have you got there?" Pendergrass called out.

She held up a John Elway toy.

"Don't stare," Claire whispered to Ed.

"Not that guy again," Pendergrass said, smiling. "Come see me tomorrow. I'll give you a real doll."

She looked up at the huge man. "Are you a Bronco?"

"Sugar, I'm the best Bronco."

The boys sped out of the dugout as the announcer called their names and lined up along the base paths, each kid slapping the hands of the boys in line before him. The announcer hammed it up a bit, booming, "Number 7, Jesseee Ohhh Fallon." Ed studied the faces of his boys, eager and amped for the game, E.J. rising up and down on his tiptoes. He wished he could feel like his sons did, with one desire—to win the game—consuming all their attention. There wasn't a thought in their minds apart from baseball. Ed had to keep it that way. The announcer called "Ray My-ESSS-Tas!" Ray trotted out and pounded the fists of his new teammates, then assumed his spot on the line, putting his cap over his heart for the anthem.

The first team they faced was Moe's Auto Body Diablos from Greeley. Boyd started Kitagawa pitching—he'd need all the arms he could get to survive the tournament's grueling three-game-a-day schedule. Jesse stood behind the plate at the top of the first, checked that the fielders were in place and that Kid was ready to throw. "Play's at one," Jesse yelled, as if to try out his voice. He settled into his crouch and the game began.

The day began to fly by, at-bats and innings accumulating into games, runs that led to wins, bunts and stolen bases and squeeze plays, bubblegum and sunflower seeds, sweat and sunblock, dirt and dust and lukewarm water tasting of plastic bottle. The heat of the day ceded to the peace of the evening, when the lights blazed on above the fields. That first evening, Ray pitched a one-hitter under the lights. Ed wasn't the only one riveted on Ray as he worked on the illuminated mound like a star in a spotlight.

On the second morning of the tournament, Ed watched from a distance as Darryl Pendergrass, dressed in a massive pastel polo shirt and khaki shorts, walked up to Santillano's girl. Her hair hung in two long, shiny braids. He bent down and handed her a Pendergrass action figure. He must have stockpiled them before they were discontinued. The little girl beamed up at Darryl as she held the toy, and her mother came up and shook his hand.

Ed felt like his eyelid twitch might take over his whole body. Here was the girl he'd deprived of a father, the woman he'd made a widow, chatting with an ex-Bronco bearing gifts, a man Ed was beginning to consider a friend.

The tournament made use of most of the baseball fields tucked all over Fort Collins. The parents consulted the maps printed in the program and drove their children to this field and that, crisscrossing the town over the course of the day. The mothers took turns buying bagels and doughnuts to share for breakfast, but Santillano's wife never had any. She sat in a folding chair with her daughter, away from the others, though occasionally one of the mothers or fathers would wander out to talk to her, to compliment her on her son's pitching, Ed guessed.

The Z's beat Ulockit Storage from Grand Junction, and Roybal Concrete from Pueblo. They entered tournament play as a top seed, and so were matched against some of the more pitiful teams early Saturday, ACE Plumbing & Heating from Westminster and VIP Roofing from Durango, who lost as they were statistically expected to.

Too much time in the sun addled Ed's head. He was sunburned, his skin covered with a paste of sunblock and dirt, and he ceased to have a sense of himself as a distinct human being. He stopped watching Santillano's wife and daughter, and let the rhythm of the games lull him.

As the boys kept winning, Claire relaxed, too, and didn't call Ed back when he went to pace the fence and holler, dispensing instructions, advice, and praise along with the rest of the fathers. Ed jumped up and down and waved his arms when a batter from the Z's rounded third, and he grabbed his head theatrically when runners from his team were felled by a double play.

"I wish I could be out there, playing ball," Darryl Pendergrass told Ed. If his knees had even one original, functioning ligament left between them, Ed could tell, he would have tackled someone just to feel it again.

"Me too," Ed said.

"Playing behind a pitcher like Ray has got to be fun." Darryl sighed. "It makes me nervous, just watching them play, waiting. I'd rather be in there myself, taking care of things."

"I know," Ed said. "Maybe that's why I'm a cop."

"That's where you're wrong," Darryl snorted. "You're a cop because you're nuts. I'm talking about playing ball here. You ever been shot at?"

"Twice. But my vest stopped the bullets."

Darryl took a handkerchief out of his pocket and dabbed at his face. "I've been stung silly, laid out, had the wind knocked out of me, my ligaments shredded, tendons snapped, cartilage dislodged, and bones broken, but I've never been shot. My left kneecap is floating somewhere in my thigh, and a dead man's parts are holding my right knee together, but there are no bullets in me." Pendergrass shook his head. "I could give you a job at one of my stores if you ever get tired of dealing with that mess."

Ed shook his head. "Thanks, but this is what I do, you know?" He had two offers now. Working as a river guide, or hawking TVs in an electronics shop. Claire wouldn't have to be married to a cop then, but neither job would pay enough for a grown man to support three kids.

The Z's made it all the way to the championship game on Sunday, where they would play the Lamar Cougars. Lamar, a small town on the eastern plains, always put together a good ball team despite its small population. Maestas and Kitagawa had each only pitched one game on Saturday, so Ed wondered which of them Boyd would start.

"The only time I've ever heard of half these towns is during emergency storm warnings," Claire said as Ed settled into his lawn chair next to her.

"Look at that," Ed said, nodding toward the visitors' stands. Some of the teams the Z's defeated had begun to stick around for their next game and fill the stands, rooting against them.

"I guess we're the bad guys," Claire said.

"So what else is new?"

307

"I never used to be the bad guy, before I met you."

Ed glanced at her to see if she was joking, but she didn't smile.

Boyd started Kid out of loyalty, but he looked ragged on the mound. He'd thrown most of three games in two days. Ray had thrown two. In the first inning the boys from Lamar took batting practice off Kid, socking his pitches beyond the outfielders or in front of them, through the gaps. Jesse scuttled after balls like an injured crab, the youth gone out of him. This was the seventh game he'd caught in three days and he was bruised and sore. Every time he crouched, the scab on his knee opened up and spots of blood showed on his uniform. He smelled of Ben Gay. Ed was proud of how tough Jesse was, but wished Boyd would sub someone else in.

The Z's had gone and blown the game in the first inning, letting the Cougars score a half-dozen runs, and Jesse would have to shepherd them through this one respectably.

Boyd put Matt Badgett in to finish the inning, and then for the first time that season, he yelled at the Z's in the dugout. Boyd had spent hours scouting these boys from every league in the city and more hours cajoling their parents into joining up, and more hours refining their skills. He knew all the fields around Denver, could choose among the sons of half a million people, and he had culled the talented few. He didn't have to settle for a fat kid in right. All of the Z's could field and all of them could hit. "Wake up!" he yelled, "Remember yourselves!"

While he listened to Boyd's pep talk, Ed scanned the crowd and saw a familiar man standing between the two teams' bleachers, putting away a hot dog. "That's the reporter from the *Post*," Ed whispered to Claire.

"Does he know?" Claire stiffened in her seat.

Ed knew better than to hope that the paper had demoted the reporter to covering the little league baseball beat. "If he does, everybody's going to."

Tyrell Pendergrass began the inning with a leadoff single. Then E.J. came up and stepped out of the path of a wild pitch.

He watched it pass by as Tyrell rounded second and stole third. E.J.'s patience, so little demonstrated when he wasn't playing ball, gained him a walk. And then came Jesse, who did what he had always done, who did the thing he'd spent his whole boyhood training for: he and E.J. smuggling a blanket to the backyard and clipping it to the clothesline and throwing soft toss to each other, hitting the ball into the blanket all afternoon; he and E.J. playing home-run derby with a Wiffle ball and a plastic bat as the light faded late on summer evenings. Jesse smacked the ball clean, clear out to pasture, and Tyrell came home, then E.J., as Jesse gained third, sliding into the base in a billow of dust. It continued, this onslaught, until the score was tied and the Lamar coach indicated to the ump that he would substitute another player for the pitcher.

After the new pitcher had warmed up, Matt Badgett came to the plate and teed off on the first pitch, sending a liner screaming straight toward the third baseman. It hit the fielder dead in the chest with a thwack and he fell to the ground.

A man who must have been the third baseman's father jumped up from the bleachers and ran onto the field, the gate rattling behind him. He dropped to his knees next to his son. In a strained voice, the man shouted, "He's not breathing!" The parents rose from their seats but the outfielders stayed deep, ready for the next batter. A half-dozen parents took out their cell phones and started to dial for an ambulance.

"Is there a doctor?" a woman screamed, "Is anyone a doctor?"

Ed sprinted past the banging gate and saw the boy stretched out on the dirt, his coach and parents bent over him. They looked older than most parents, well into their fifties. The woman was heavyset with gray hair curling around her face, her husband lanky and washed out, his watery blue eyes panicked under his John Deere cap. The boy was as small as E.J., a spray of brown freckles across his nose. Santillano's wife came running in from the other side of the field and reached them before Ed did, saying, "I'm a nurse."

She kneeled in the dirt next to the boy, putting a competent hand on the boy's forehead, tilting his chin back. She leaned in close to check for respiration. Ed wanted to help, but didn't speak. She pinched the boy's freckled nose and gave him her breath. She pressed two fingers to his neck. "No pulse." She turned to Ed, who crouched beside her. She didn't seem surprised to see him. "I can handle the CPR for a while," she said. "Go see if they have a defibrillator."

Ed sprinted up to the command center in the middle of the complex, everyone clearing out of his way as he rushed past. He vaulted over the counter, grabbed the device, and ran back.

Santillano's wife held her hand on the boy's breastbone and she compressed his chest rapidly, her elbow locked, her pony-tail swinging as she rocked with each press, intent on saving the boy.

"Oh please, oh please," the mother repeated over and over. The dad kneeled beside her in the dirt, twisting his cap in his hands.

Ed threw the defibrillator case down on the ground. He took out the scissors and Santillano's wife stopped compressing so he could cut open the boy's jersey. He'd never defibrillated a child before. He turned on the device and flipped its voltage from adult to child, and then applied the pads to the boy's chest. His small body shuddered as the initial shock worked through him. The ambulance wailed into the grass next to the field, and finally the boy came to with a gasp. He tried to sit up, his eyes unfocused. "No, wait," Santillano's wife told him, holding him down with a firm hand, stroking his hair with her thumb.

The paramedics jogged over and asked questions while they examined the boy. "Line drive straight to the chest," Ed explained. He squatted there in the dirt, his eyelid twitching from being so close to Santillano's wife, until the paramedics loaded the boy onto a stretcher and carried him to the ambulance. As they took him away, his mother held his hand, trotting to keep up with the paramedics' pace. Ed glanced at Santillano's wife, who sat across from him, her butt in the dirt. She held her face in her hands, unable to rise. He didn't know why he cared what she thought, but he did: he wanted her to know he was more than just a killer. She gave Ed a long, dead stare that could have seared the ground around him.

A frisson ran through him as the breeze blew over his sweaty neck. She clearly knew, and yet she was letting her son play with Jesse and E.J. anyway. He wondered when she'd figured it out. He'd underestimated her. Ed dusted the red dirt off his legs. They had obliterated the chalked third base line with their efforts, stirred the white into the dust so that it now was the blood and milk color of southern Utah. Ed slowly walked across the field, opened the creaky fence door and eased it closed, silence all around him.

The boys stood in their dugouts, motionless. Finally the ump gestured for the coaches to meet him at the plate. After they spoke for a while, Boyd approached the Z's stands. "He gave us a few options," Boyd said. "We can either keep playing the game, take a break for a couple of hours and then resume, or try to meet up somewhere mid-week and finish the thing. The regionals are next weekend, so they need to get this championship resolved. I let the Cougars' coach decide."

The Lamar coach was over with his boys, asking them what they wanted. Finally, he approached the ump again.

Ed sank down in the lawn chair next to Claire, who held Polly in her lap. She handed him a bottle of water, and Ed twisted off the cap and sucked down the whole thing.

"Will he be okay?" Claire asked, barely above a whisper.

"Is that boy alive?" Polly asked.

"He came back," Ed said. "He'll make it." He threw up a prayer to whoever was listening to the voices in his head, a thank you for the defibrillator. He was impressed that Santillano's wife had thought of it. The survival rate from CPR alone was only ten percent, and with the defibrillator, it shot up to eighty percent. Ed thought of telling Claire that Santillano's wife had recognized him, but Polly was right there in her lap, squeezing Claire's hand and staring out at the empty third base, where the boy had fallen. Polly shivered, despite the heat. Claire took a curl from the nape of Polly's neck between her thumb and fore-finger and stretched it straight, her hands always playing with the children's hair when she was worried.

"You saved the boy, Daddy," Polly said.

"Ray's mom saved the boy," Ed said.

"That's right," Claire said with a grave glance at Ed, "she's a nurse."

"How do you know?" Polly asked.

"Just something I heard." She leaned in to kiss Polly on the cheek and the girl turned her head, squirming away from affec-tion. Then Ed saw the reporter talking to the Lamar parents, taking notes. The whole story could come out at any moment.

The Lamar boys walked out onto the field and then tossed the ball around to each other. They looked nothing like they did before the start of the game, when they'd led with their chests. Now their shoulders drooped and they seemed smaller.

"I guess they're finishing the game," Claire said.

Boyd volunteered to declare Badgett out from the line drive, so that left a runner on third, and only one out needed for the Cougars to end the inning. The pitcher was rattled, and he sent a couple of balls sailing out of the catcher's grasp, allowing the Z's runner to steal home, an apologetic look on his face as he crossed. The Cougar pitcher walked the next two batters and then got the third to ground out.

Boyd put Ray in to start the next inning. He was the only kid who didn't look like he was sleepwalking. His acute focus on his target, Jesse's glove, reminded Ed of the gaze of a bird of prey, a creature that had no use for doubt. He was a twelve-year-old boy, but to everyone watching him he threw like Tom Seaver and Nolan Ryan and Roger Clemens combined. The pitches whistled through the air, smacked the glove and produced an echo. The ump called strike after strike in a calm tone. The parents hardly cheered, the silence broken only occasionally with the half-hearted "Go Billy!" of a mother rooting for her own son. With

Maestas in the Z's lineup, the Cougars were goners before they'd eaten their Wheaties that morning.

Maestas didn't give up a single hit. The final innings melted away and the game ended with the Z's on top by three. They'd won the championship, but the boys refrained from their customary post-win taunt, "Who dey say dey'd beat dem Z's? Who dey? Who dey?" They simply sat in the dugout until the announcer called them to collect their enormous trophies, three feet tall. Maestas measured the weight of the trophy in his arms, opening and closing his fingers around the base. The Cougar's coach presented him with the game ball, and an official brought over the tournament MVP trophy, a golden glove for him to rest the ball in and a state tournament t-shirt. The loot filled Maestas' arms so he could barely carry it all. Santillano's boy was the only one on the field smiling.

Polly ran over to her brothers and tugged at the trophies in their arms.

"She knows," Ed whispered in Claire's ear.

Claire looked like an air raid survivor, not totally convinced that she wasn't dead. "So we're going to New Mexico," she said, "land of enchantment."

CHAPTER 24

Patricia
July 23–30

A few days after the state tournament, Patricia dreamed about the fallen boy. The colors in the dream were supersaturated, the sky too blue, the dirt too red, the skin of the child pale against the dust. He didn't respond to CPR and rescue breathing, and when she looked up from his still chest to his face, she saw Ray's sharp chin and cheekbones. She turned to the man she could sense beside her, the man who had killed her husband. He stood there, doing nothing but casting a shadow while he let her son die.

Patricia rubbed her eyes and looked at the clock: 6 AM. Ray wouldn't notice if she cracked open his door to check on him as she had when he was a baby, staring into his dark room until she could see his chest rise. With her hand on the doorknob, she listened to Ray talking. "Well, Tim," Ray said in a deepened voice, "I'm here with the Cy Young award winner. How did you win so many games, Ray?"

"I just take it one inning at a time," Ray replied to himself.

Patricia knocked. "Yeah?" Ray said, and she walked in. He looked sheepish, standing barefoot in Broncos pajamas he'd outgrown, next to his trophy shelf, a cowlick in the front of his hair.

"Why are you up so early?" Patricia put her arms around him, feeling his sleep-warmed body.

He stooped to rest his head on her shoulder. "I want to go for a run before it gets too hot."

"Since when have you run?"

"A good pitcher needs stamina." Ray pulled away and attacked an imaginary foe with a three-punch combination. "I bet those Texas pitchers jog before breakfast every morning."

Patricia picked up the MVP trophy, and ran her index finger over the raised laces of the game ball. "I kept your old trophies," she said, "They're in the basement if you want them." When she passed them on her way to the laundry room, she got the same feeling she did when walking by a mannequin at a store, a creepy shiver from something being not quite right.

"These are better," Ray said. "They're for the state championship."

The first-place trophy stood tall and gaudy on the shelf, glinting with gold-colored plastic, shiny blue chrome, and imitation marble.

Patricia hadn't made up her mind yet about the regionals in New Mexico. As they drove home from the state tournament in Fort Collins, the kids had chatted about the incident. "That was cool how you and Jesse's dad saved that kid," Ray said. "How did he know what to do? Is he an EMT or something?"

Patricia had tightened her grip on the steering wheel. "I don't know," she said. "I think he just took a class."

Patricia tried to think of how to talk Ray out of New Mexico as he dropped to the floor and pumped out a set of push-ups. They ran into Miguel the night before when picking up some takeout from El Pollo Loco. Miguel was hanging out in the parking lot under the streetlight with some other guys in oversized t-shirts, clowning and chucking their chicken bones into the gutter, warming up for a night Patricia assumed would include gang-infested parties, the kind that frequently ended with a gunshot victim wheeled into the emergency room. As Patricia approached, one of the kids ditched an empty beer bottle behind a bush. Miguel slapped Ray's hand and although it pained her, Patricia left them to chat while she and Mia bought the food.

When Patricia returned, Miguel said to Ray, "You should come with us, man." Ray shook his head. "I can't," he said, "I've got early practice tomorrow." Ray followed Mia and Patricia back to the car before she'd even asked. She didn't want baseball season to end, yet the only way it could continue was for Ray to play on O'Fallon's team.

"I've got to get ready for work," she told Ray. "Do you need anything before I go?"

"Did you get the weekend off for the tournament?" he huffed between push-ups.

"I haven't asked yet."

"What?" He flipped over to face her. "We've got to go, Mom."

As soon as they'd come back from Fort Collins, she'd scribbled a pro and con list about taking Ray to the regional tournament in Las Cruces. She'd have to add a few more items to the pro side: Ray bouncing out of bed at dawn, letting her hug him, operating in a different time zone than Miguel. "There will be scouts there," he told her, switching to sit-ups. "Big League scouts."

"Really? They find players this young?"

"Half the Dominicans in the majors were recruited in elementary school."

That didn't seem possible, but Ray knew a lot more about this stuff than she did. Mia had begun packing her bag the moment they returned from Fort Collins, thrilled she would be staying at a hotel with a swimming pool. And Patricia would get to see her parents again, the only people she could talk to about everything. In a few weeks, school would start, and Ray would be thrown in with Miguel, but New Mexico would delay their reunion.

Then there was the con: the cop. She'd underlined this word three times on her list. Ray would be playing with his sons, and Patricia would have to bear it without telling anyone. She didn't know how to hide what she knew. After they had defibrillated the kid, she'd shot O'Fallon the ugliest look she could, trying to match the dead stare of a lady her cousins said was a *bruja* who gave people the evil eye. O'Fallon should pull his own sons off the team.

"Don't worry," Patricia said, touching Ray's cheek to see if he'd still let her. "I'm sure they'll give me the weekend off."

He continued his sit-ups, arms crossed over his chest. "Just ask today."

"Okay, baby," she said. For him, maybe she could endure the tournament. She could sit on the bleachers next to O'Fallon and his wife, clapping along while John Fogerty's "Centerfield" boomed over the loudspeakers, and pretend they were all on the same team.

Before Patricia left for work, the phone rang. It was Ralph Boyd, the Z's coach. "I've been getting some calls from scouts about Ray," he said, sounding uncomfortable, the sort of coach who didn't know how to interact with all the parents that came with the kids.

"I thought Ray was exaggerating."

"There are always scouts at regionals. He just doesn't know they're coming to watch him. I had one inquiry from the director of Suncrest Sports Academy."

"What's that?"

"A private school near Tucson."

"That's where my parents live."

"They've been known to give scholarships to promising pitchers, and several of their athletes have gone on to play baseball in college. Anyway, I don't want to waste Ray on our first game against Navajo Nation. I'll have him throw the second, against Dallas, so the scouts can get a good look."

Patricia tried to sort through everything in her head as she escorted the kids to Nino's. Two games. Maybe she could endure two games to give Ray this chance. Salvador would want her to. "A baseball school, can you believe it?" Patricia told Salvador out loud as she drove to work. It was like something out of the old immigrant's dream of America, gold-paved streets, land for the taking, a school where you studied baseball. She stopped and bought a road map of New Mexico, unfolded it on the dashboard and traced the route with her finger. To get to Las Cruces from Denver, you took I-25 south and just kept on taking it.

They left for Las Cruces the Thursday morning before the tournament began. In Pueblo, the last major town before they hit the southern Colorado border, Patricia pulled into a gas station. While she waited for Ray and Mia to return from the bathroom, Patricia picked up a copy of the *Denver Post* by the checkout counter and skimmed the headlines. In the lower right corner she read, SONS OF COP, SLAIN MAN TO TEAM UP FOR REGIONAL YOUTH BASE-BALL TOURNAMENT, by Kyle Schmidt, a reporter who'd been leaving messages she hadn't returned. She felt like someone had taken a bat to her sternum and she tried to breathe in enough air to keep from crumpling inward. She'd half hoped the whole situa-tion was a paranoid trick her mind had played on her, but here it was in print.

Everyone was going to think she was insane to allow her son to play on that team. She pictured the people on the committee reading the article at their breakfast tables, saying *I knew she was nuts*. Coach Pete would choke on his coffee. She dug in her purse and checked her cell phone, which she kept turned off in the car since she'd cleaned up the victims of too many dis-traction-induced accidents at work. Two messages from Tío and three from Lupe. They would tell her to turn around and head back home. But now more than ever, she wanted to move Ray to a new school in a different state. She shook her head. Her belief in that baseball school was as bad as an immigrant's fantasy of an America full of ease.

"What are you reading, Mom?" Mia asked, coming up behind her and setting a Coke on the counter.

Patricia placed the paper face down next to the Coke. "The usual," she said, "bad news." The Z's parents had probably all read the article. Knowing competitive baseball parents, they were calculating whether this would hurt the Z's chances. But surely O'Fallon wouldn't show his face at the tournament now that everyone knew what he had done.

As Patricia buckled herself into the driver's seat, she glanced at the newspaper on her lap. She couldn't read it in front of the kids, so she wedged it on the side of her seat. Now what? Tell the kids they were turning around? Or continue on toward the El Dorado of the baseball school? She looked at Ray, stretched out in the backseat, practicing his pitching grips on a baseball. "Let me have a swig of that," she said to Mia in the passenger seat, reaching for the Coke. She downed some of the cold, syrupy liquid to fortify herself as she pulled onto the road again, dreading talking to Lupe.

They approached the New Mexico border and the landscape changed from high plains broken with rugged mountains to dry, hilly terrain, pink earth dotted with scrubby brush and piñon pine. Some of the small towns near the border looked as though they had been standing for centuries. The paint on the signs of the businesses had faded to faint shadows of their original colors. There was still something charming about these places with their small boxlike houses and abundance of rust. Almost exactly at the New Mexico border, the housing materials changed from weathered wood and dusty brick to adobe, the color of the earth. She thought of the cantina in Salvador's village, the boards of the shack thirsting for a fresh coat of whitewash, the 1960s Coca-Cola sign sun-blasted to a salmon color. They were driving over the same road Salvador had taken on visits to Mexico through the years. How could she ever explain this to him?

They stopped for dinner at a McDonald's in Albuquerque. Patricia tucked the newspaper under her arm, gave the kids some money and told them to order what they wanted while she went to the bathroom. She locked herself in the handicap stall and read the article.

The sons of Edward O'Fallon and Salvador Santillano, two men on opposite sides of a recent officer-involved

319

shooting, will play on the same team representing Colorado at the Amateur Baseball Congress regional tournament in Las Cruces, N.M. this weekend.

The dramatic finish to last weekend's Colorado State championship took a surreal turn when O'Fallon and Patricia Maestas, the widow of Santillano, came together to save the life of a young participant in the tournament.

Sam Hilliard, 11, of Lamar, was playing third base for the Lamar Cougars when a ball batted by a member of the Denver Z's struck him in the chest. His parents and coaches found him unresponsive and called for help.

Maestas, 34, a Registered Nurse at Denver Health Medical Center, and O'Fallon, 37, a Denver police officer, rushed to the boy's aid, and revived him with a defibrillator and CPR until paramedics arrived. Hilliard was released from Memorial Hospital Monday, and doctors expect him to make a full recovery.

But Maestas and O'Fallon share more in common than emergency medical response training: O'Fallon was among the officers who shot and killed Salvador Santillano in a March 11 drug raid authorized by an immediate entry warrant with a mistaken address. After months of community protests, Maestas recently settled her wrongful death case against the city for $750,000.

O'Fallon's sons, Jesse, 12, and E.J., 11, have played with the Denver Z's, who went on to defeat Lamar for the state championship title, for the entire season. Maestas' son, Ray Maestas Santillano, 12, joined the team for tournament play, according to Hank Badgett, a father of another team member.

The Denver Z's will play in the Regional ABC tournament this weekend in Las Cruces, N.M.

As much as she wanted to delay the conversation, Patricia had to call Lupe before the kids worried about her absence.

Lupe answered on the first ring. "Where are you?"

"In a bathroom in Albuquerque."

"You're going to the tournament?"

"I just now read the article. We're halfway to Las Cruces and the kids don't know."

"Someone will tell them. It had better come from you."

"Maybe Ray doesn't have to find out. How could that cop come to the tournament now?"

"Did you know his sons were on the team?"

"Not when we signed up. But I figured it out."

"Skip the tournament and come stay with us in Arizona. He can't play baseball with that man's sons."

The lemon scent of bathroom cleaner suddenly overwhelmed Patricia and she steadied herself with the cold metal rail next to the toilet. "Ray thinks this is going to be his big break. That some scout from the major leagues is going to see him. The coach told me a recruiter from a baseball school will be there."

"That's a fantasy."

"He needs his fantasies."

Sneakers squeaked against the bathroom floor. "Mom?" Mia's voice came from behind the door. Patricia hung up the phone.

"We're done eating," Mia said, studying Patricia with concern. "Aren't you going to get something?"

"I'm not hungry," Patricia said, faking a smile. "Let's go."

Patricia led the way to the car. Her hands shook and she dropped her keys to the pavement as she tried to open the door. She bent to pick them up and saw that she'd trailed some toilet paper out on the bottom of her shoe.

"She was talking to someone while she was in the bathroom," Mia reported.

"Who?" Ray asked, only half-interested.

"Just Grandma." Patricia adjusted the rearview mirror. "We don't have to go to this tournament. We could visit Grandma and Grandpa's house instead."

"Are you crazy?" Ray said, snapping a baseball into his glove. "We'll see them at the tournament."

Now, she willed herself, tell them the rest. She couldn't keep driving her son to play a game with the sons of that killer. "There's something I need to tell you."

"Is it about Coach Boyd?" Ray asked, eager. "I saw his number on the caller I.D. Did he tell you about the scouts?"

Patricia let out her breath. "He mentioned them," she said, and pulled back onto the highway, heading south. It was O'Fallon who should stay away.

As darkness fell outside of Albuquerque, she could just make out the silhouettes of distant mesas, reminding her of a tale her dad had told her when she was about Mia's age. She turned down the radio. "How about a ghost story?" she asked.

"Sure," Mia said from the passenger seat. Ray gave a non-committal grunt.

"Once, hundreds of years ago," Patricia began, "there was a Pueblo tribe who lived on a mesa with sheer sides. They built their city on the top, where they were safe from enemies, wild animals, and flash floods in the arroyos. The men would go down the secret path from the mesa top every day to hunt. Only the tribe that lived on the mesa knew how to find the steep, hidden path up to the top, and when all the men hiked down to hunt one day, another tribe ambushed them. They tortured the mesa dwellers to tell them how to find the path, but they wouldn't say. Their wives and children and grandparents were up there, waiting for food. The marauders killed the hunting party and the people on top of the mesa starved to death. Years later, some people wanted to open it up as a national park, but when the officials toured the mesa, they heard the ghostly moaning and weeping of the dead women and children echoing from the dwellings. They left and never came back."

For a moment they heard nothing but the wheels over the road. The story had spooked Patricia so thoroughly that she remembered it all these years later, and now she could identify with the people in it. Here she was, wife of a dead man, waiting with her children in suspended animation, hoping for a sign of what she should do.

"But why didn't the women go down and get some food?" Mia asked. She hugged her knees to her chest and wrapped a jacket around her legs. Patricia had blasted the air conditioner to keep herself awake. "They must have seen where the path was when the men went down every day."

"Maybe I'm not remembering it right—maybe the marauders waited at the bottom so long that the women starved."

"But the marauders must have gone to get food," Ray said. Patricia had insisted he wear his seat belt, but he'd managed to twist around and spread out his long legs in the back. "So those ladies became ghosts out of laziness. They shouldn't let you turn ghost unless you've been wronged."

"But their husbands and fathers were all murdered," Patricia countered. "That's wronged enough."

"Well, then the men should be ghosts. The women could have gotten off their asses."

Patricia glanced at Ray in the rearview mirror as he settled his arms behind his head. His hands were as big as a man's, his wrists delicate as a boy's. "What about *La Llorona*?" Patricia asked. "Her husband left her, she drowned her children, then started haunting the riverbanks and snatching children. It's not only the wronged that become ghosts. She's the one who did wrong." Patricia didn't believe in ghosts, and here she was, arguing for their existence.

"The way I heard it, the kids drowned by themselves in a flood," Ray said, "And that made *La Llorona* so crazy that she goes around trying to replace them, and she drowns living kids to take them with her."

"I've heard she's more like a zombie than a ghost," Mia said. "This girl at school, Brenda? Her auntie saw *La Llorona* once and said she isn't see-through. She wears a white dress and tempts men with her beauty. But if you try to kiss her, her face turns zombie ugly and she kills you dead."

Patricia had been collecting *La Llorona* stories ever since her cousins gave her that nickname, but she hadn't heard that one before. The car returned to silence, and Patricia felt small

323

on the open road with little but the black, starry sky and desert sand surrounding them.

"Maybe dad will come back as a ghost," Mia said softly.

"No," Ray said, leaning his head between the front seats, "he wouldn't do that."

"Why not?"

"He wasn't like that, all dramatic." Ray slumped back again.

Patricia turned up the radio, to bless what Ray had said, letting Otis Redding howl them through the dark desert night.

Las Cruces Brisas looked more like a motel than a hotel, with three floors of rooms arranged in a U-shape around an outdoor courtyard with a pool in the center. Even at 10:00, as they walked across the parking lot, the day's leftover heat rose off the asphalt. "Can I go swimming?" Mia begged. Patricia pointed to the sign that said the pool closed at 9 PM. She scanned the doors and wondered whether the cop and his family were behind one of them. It reminded her of that story, "The Lady, or the Tiger?"— except there were only tigers. Maybe she should confront him, ask him what had happened that day. Did Salvador have a gun or didn't he? He'd probably repeat what the police reports said: Salvador had fired at them first. Patricia's cell phone rang. It was Lupe, calling to see if they'd arrived. They'd arranged for rooms next to each other.

A moment later, Lupe knocked and Patricia opened the door to see her mother dressed in linen pants and a crisp shirt, her lipstick fresh. Patricia tucked a strand of her lank hair behind her ear.

"I want to show Grandpa Ray this new grip Coach Boyd taught me," Ray said, gathering up a glove and ball. He walked on his toes, light and lithe, his calf muscles bunched, as he headed out the door.

Mia stayed, flipping through the channels on the TV, playing with the air conditioner, and inspecting the little wrapped soaps in the bathroom before her energy faded and she crawled into bed.

Patricia and Lupe sat down at the particleboard table by the window. "That's the longest stretch I've ever driven by myself." Patricia yawned. Salvador, who had the stamina of a long-haul trucker, used to do most of the driving on road trips. Patricia was still buzzed on the caffeine she'd been downing, and didn't think she'd be able to fall asleep. Famished from skipping dinner, she ate one of the tamales Lupe brought from Old Mesilla, relishing the burnt smoke taste of the chipotles and the smooth bland corn paste.

"Have you told the children?" Lupe asked, while Mia was in the bathroom.

"I tried."

"What are you planning to do?"

Patricia chewed her tamale. "I'm going to let Ray play two games, so the baseball school director will see him pitch."

Lupe gave her a puzzled look. "What are you talking about?"

Mia stirred, turning over to her side. Lupe and Patricia sat in silence until they heard Mia's gentle snores resume.

The long day began at 7:30 AM with breakfast in the hotel's café, the temperature mounting in its daily climb toward the triple digits. Ray packed away a bowl of oatmeal and a hardboiled egg, looking up every time people entered the restaurant and favoring his teammates with a quick, macho lift of the chin. Nobody from the cop's family was there. This was the first time they'd gone out for breakfast in over a year.

"Why did you get oatmeal?" Mia asked.

"It's good for endurance," Ray said.

Mia ordered a pile of sugar for breakfast—Belgian waffles covered in whipped cream and strawberry syrup. Patricia stirred her cornflakes around in her milk as she watched for O'Fallon.

"Coach is leaving," Ray said, rising. "I've got to go."

"Wait," Patricia said, following him.

"I'll be late." Ray said over his shoulder as he walked with three other boys to the coach's van outside, while Coach Boyd gathered up some clipboards from his breakfast table.

"Coach," she said, rushing up to him.

He looked at her. The lineup was on the top of his clipboard, but Patricia couldn't scan the names before he turned it upside down.

"I didn't tell Ray yet," Patricia said, ashamed to admit this to someone she barely knew.

"We're here to play baseball," Boyd said in a hushed voice. "I'm sure everyone realizes that. Twelve-year-olds don't read the paper."

"I'll let him pitch that game against Dallas," she said. "After that, I don't know."

"Fair enough," Boyd said.

Patricia tried to feel reassured as she retreated to pay her bill.

The games were held a few miles down the road from the hotel at a complex of baseball fields near a flat stretch of desert. Somehow the groundskeeper had coaxed outfield lawns into growing, with only a few scorched patches. Outside the park, meager bushes and spiky growths, yucca and yellow-flowered cactus, clung to the red dirt. Beyond the park, the fringe of the Organ Mountains jutted into the blue sky. Compared to the Rockies, it was a tiny range, with naked knobby peaks that reminded Patricia of animal teeth.

Patricia led Mia over to the bleachers at the field where Ray would play, and sat at the far end of them with her parents. A canopy of netting, with ragged bits of camouflage cloth woven through, hung above the bleachers, casting mottled shadows on everyone's skin. No one from O'Fallon's family was there. A few of the other parents glanced up when Patricia approached and said hello, then turned away. She didn't blame them. What was she doing here, letting her son play baseball after everything that had happened? The groundskeepers hosed down and raked the field to prevent dust from rising, then a man chalked precise lines over the infield, trundling a metal device along in front of him.

"You told him?" Lupe asked.

"I tried. I decided to tell him after he pitches today." Patricia looked away so she wouldn't have to see her mother's disapproval.

"*Hija*," her father whispered, a frown flickering at the corners of his mouth.

Mia hopped down from the bleachers, El Johnway in one hand, the Pendergrass doll in the other, and walked by Darryl Pendergrass, who sat in the front row. "Hey, Mia," he said, patting the seat next to him. She showed him her action figures. She'd made the Pendergrass doll a little blue coat out of construction paper and tape. Pendergrass praised the outfit, and glanced back at Patricia. "You have wonderful children," he said. "You are going to be just fine."

"Thank you," Patricia said.

Mia sat next to Pendergrass and Patricia thought of the times Salvador came home exhausted, covered in drywall, but still submitted to Mia's teddy bear tea parties.

The first game was against the Navajo Nation team that drew its players from the nearby reservation. Mothers whispered about how they hadn't actually qualified for the regionals, but were allowed to play in the tournament because they were the host team in Las Cruces. Their bodies were skinny instead of sleek, the bigger ones doughy instead of muscular. They reminded Patricia of Ray's old Catholic Youth team, in those days that seemed so far away now. They wouldn't be here now if she'd left him in that league.

The Navajos achieved each out with great difficulty. They had a handful of competent players, but somebody always screwed up a throw or bobbled a ball. As the Z's batted around, it was painful to watch the Navajos field. Neither of O'Fallon's sons was in the starting lineup. She couldn't make out which of the boys sat in the shadowed dugout.

In the second inning, Coach Boyd put Ray in at third base, a position he'd never played before. The boys all swapped positions and laughed as they headed out to start the new inning. Some right-handed boys tried hitting lefty. Surely the other team knew they were being mocked, but they were giving it a go anyway. The Z's should play their game as usual and get it over with. In the third inning Coach Boyd sent O'Fallon's sons in to play outfield, and Patricia felt nauseous, her mouth flooding with saliva. She searched for the cop but didn't see him.

During the middle of the third, O'Fallon's wife, who Patricia recognized from the Fort Collins tournament, walked up and sat in the bottom row of the bleachers. She didn't turn around like the other mothers did, laughing and chatting their way through the blowout. Her daughter kept coming up to her, asking for a bottle of water, then a stick of gum. The girl was curly-haired and dimpled. Maybe Patricia would grab her as they left, raise her as her own, leaving O'Fallon to wander the streets, calling her name, making useless pleas on TV for her return. The coward still hadn't shown his face, sending his family alone. But when Patricia looked at her parents, it was she who felt like the coward.

Back at the hotel during the break between the first two games, Mia changed into her swimsuit and ran out to the pool, Patricia dragging herself behind. The coach kept the team together at the field between games, separating them from their parents, perhaps to avoid any incidents the newspaper article would cause. Patricia wondered if Ray knew anything. Coach Boyd could try to prevent him from finding out, but one of the boys could ask a simple question that would stagger Ray. She'd tell him right after he pitched. She would.

Patricia sat on a chair at the poolside, wearing dark sunglasses. Mia dove and swam underwater, her kicking legs disappearing beneath the blue surface. Dozens of other kids splashed in the pool, happy to be free from their older brothers' endless baseball games.

The door in the chain-link fence surrounding the pool banged, and Patricia opened her eyes. O'Fallon's girl walked into the pool area, her mother a few paces behind her. The woman stood in the far corner, leaning against the fence while her daughter jumped into the pool. Patricia stared at her but O'Fallon's wife kept her eyes on her daughter. This was the one experience Mia had wanted all summer, and the O'Fallons were determined to ruin this, too.

The cop's wife sat on the opposite side of the pool. She was pale and freckled, her nose peeling with sunburn. She scratched at a mosquito bite on her arm and fanned herself with a program from the tournament, looking altogether unadapted to the desert. O'Fallon's wife kept glancing up at Patricia until finally she stood and walked up to her. Patricia didn't acknowledge her for a moment, staring at Mia as she dove and kicked. "Yes?" she said finally, looking up to see tears in her eyes. This woman had nothing to cry about.

"I am so sorry," O'Fallon's wife began, her voice hoarse. "I know that probably doesn't mean anything, but I think about your family all the time."

"If you're so sorry," Patricia said, "then why didn't your husband admit what he did was wrong? Why didn't the police tell the truth about the gun? Why did you bring your boys to this tournament when you knew Ray was going to be here? Why can't you go away and let my daughter swim in this pool?"

"I understand you're mad," she said.

"Did he tell you they planted the gun? Or does he lie to his family too?"

"They didn't plant the gun. I asked him myself."

"But you suspected him of it. Why else would you have asked?"

"That's not true." She straightened her spine.

"You still have your whole family, your husband still has his job. You can go back to pretending that nothing happened."

"It's not that simple." There was an edge to her voice now.

"It isn't? Tell me your problems. I'd really like to hear them."

"There is more than one way to lose a husband."

"Your husband is alive," Patricia said.

The cop's wife looked off at the kids in the pool for a moment. Her girl was in line for the diving board, and Mia was on the opposite side of the pool, playing Marco Polo with a couple of other kids. "I don't know why I thought that I could say something to make you feel better."

"You didn't," Patricia said, "You thought that saying something to me would make *you* feel better."

O'Fallon's wife turned and walked back toward her seat.

Patricia's face felt hot, her anger fading as suddenly as it had flared. It wasn't this woman's fault what her husband had done. Maybe Patricia would forgive her someday. But Salvador had been dead for just four months—what did she expect? The smell of chlorine stung Patricia's nose and she felt woozy in the heat. She needed to tell Ray, right now, before he pitched. He could not play on the same team with the sons of that man, not for one inning more. The baseball school could wait.

Patricia called her parents in their hotel room, and a few minutes later they arrived at the pool, dressed in their Arizona gear, white linen shirts and wide-brimmed hats. They made a perfect pair, retired, marriage strong. Patricia didn't want to think about the lonely years ahead of her, the unoccupied pillow on the bed.

"Can you watch Mia?" Patricia asked. She rose from her seat, her knees weak.

"Of course," Lupe said.

"She's wanted to go swimming this whole summer and we haven't had a chance until today. That's all she wanted. And they won't let her."

"Are you all right?" Lupe asked.

Patricia took her car keys from her pocket. "I'm going to the field to talk to Ray."

At the baseball complex, Patricia shielded her eyes with her hand, trying to distinguish between the boys. She pushed past people streaming around her, and scanned the stands for her son. A group of Z's were watching Houston play Albuquerque, but Ray wasn't with them. She asked Coach Boyd if he'd seen Ray, and he pointed beyond the field. In the distance, past the outfield fences of the farthest fields, a single tree stood in the desert landscape, with a shape that might have been a person next to it. As she drew closer she saw Ray's back resting against the tree trunk, his knees drawn to his chest and his face buried in his arms. He looked up as she approached.

"What are you doing out here, all alone?" she asked.

"Visualizing," Ray said. "I take the mound in twenty minutes."

"Aren't you too hot? Do you have enough water?"

Ray held up a water bottle. "I'm hydrated."

"I'm sorry I brought you all this way," Patricia began, faltering. She hadn't felt this bad since she told him Salvador was dead.

"Why?"

"I can't let you pitch. Not on this team. Those boys—the catcher and his brother. They're the sons of the cop that killed your dad."

"How?" he demanded. He looked off, shaking his head. "Last weekend, Jesse mentioned his dad was a cop. I almost wanted to quit the team. But he didn't say what cop he was." Ray's mouth twitched around the edges. "You let me play all this time with the kids of that killer." His voice grew louder. "This is who you want me to play with? At least Miguel is one of us."

Patricia kneeled in front of him and took him into her arms, knocking his ball cap off. "I'm sorry," she said. "I'm so sorry."

"I miss Dad," he said, his voice breaking.

She held him tighter, his sharp shoulder blades poking up under his uniform. "I know," she whispered. She looked up at the vast blue sky, the dry New Mexico air parching her throat.

"What do I do?" he asked. "How am I supposed to get out of this?"

"We'll leave right now. We can go home."

"But I'm supposed to pitch." A note of the little boy he once was crept back into his voice, his eyes frantic.

"You don't need to pitch. You don't owe these people anything."

"No," he said. "I'm tired of you deciding everything. You always choose wrong." He shrugged out of her arms and stood up.

He started to walk away, then turned and kicked a spray of sand at Patricia like she was an ump who'd made a bad call. His figure grew smaller in the distance, a wavy heat mirage in the dust at his feet.

The announcer was calling out the starting lineup by the time Patricia had picked herself up and walked to the field. She couldn't catch her breath, as though the air had thinned.

"Pitcher, number 27, Ray Maestas," the announcer boomed.

Ray ran out of the dugout, but instead of lining up along the first base line with the others, he marched up to the backstop and yelled at the announcer, cupping his hands around his mouth, "My name's Santillano!"

"What?" The announcer asked, a burst of feedback screeching through the loudspeaker.

He took off his hat and stared up at the announcer's booth, his gaze fierce. "My name is Ray Santillano."

"Scratch that," the announcer said, after a pause. "Pitcher says his name is Santillano."

Ray slammed his cap back on his head and took his place on the first baseline as his teammates turned and looked at him. Ray faced straight ahead, his chin lifted, his cap over his heart as the national anthem played. O'Fallon's sons, one on either end of the line, froze. The small one didn't remove his cap until Whitney

Houston belted "the bombs bursting in air." The catcher, his gear already on, searched the crowd. Mia sat in the shade of a tree, playing with her dolls. Patricia didn't see the cop anywhere. She sat next to her parents in the bleachers. "I told him," she told her parents. "He chose to pitch this game."

"He's brave," Lupe said.

"You wouldn't guess that he's my son," Patricia said.

The Texans came up to bat first, and when Ray let a fastball rip, someone in the Dallas stands shouted "Who—eeee!"

"Come on Stingray!" Pendergrass shouted. "Now that's a nickname," he added.

Patricia remembered the baseball school scout and scanned the men in the stands to see if she could pick him out. A Dallas fan rang a cowbell every time Ray began his windup. "What's with the cowbell?" Patricia asked, mad that they would try to break Ray's focus.

"All the Texas teams have them," Rosa Pendergrass said. "They pass them down from one team mom to the next, all decorated with ribbons and puffy paint."

Ray struck the first kid out. Patricia watched in a daze, wanting it over, wanting to run out to Ray and win him back, explain her side of things. As the next batter entered the box, O'Fallon arrived, his arm slung defensively around his wife's shoulders. He steered her toward the stands.

"I can't believe he showed up for this," Lupe said.

He was a big, hale man, enjoying himself, enjoying his life. He would have seemed unremarkable, another middle-aged man in a world full of them, but now he was grotesque. Ray stood alone on the pitching mound, probably still seething at Patricia as he wiped the sweat from his forehead with a sleeve. O'Fallon had done this to them, torn her son from her, turned her daughter sad.

Ray retired the side, but his edge didn't last for long. The other team's pitcher threw almost as fast. Z after Z struck out, cowbells ringing their return to the dugout. The Texans began to figure out Ray, first fouling off, and finally, by the third inning, getting around on him. They were relentless, each player in the lineup as good as the next, so that Ray had no easier time getting the ninth batter out than he did the third. The worse Ray pitched, the louder the cowbells rang. Ray took exaggerated breaths between pitches, trying to regain the concentration Patricia had broken when she told him who his teammates were.

As the noise crested, Ray started winging wild pitches every which way, the ball bouncing in the dirt. O'Fallon's son, the catcher, had to stop them with his body to prevent runs from scoring, and his thighs must have been tattooed with the ball's laces. The catcher didn't trot to the mound to give a pep talk to Ray, he just squatted there behind the plate and accepted the beating.

"This is terrible," Patricia said.

"It's worse because he's here," Lupe said, nodding toward O'Fallon. "I don't like him watching Ray."

"I'll talk to him," Patricia's dad said.

"Why?" Patricia reached toward her dad to stop him, but her fingers slid off his sleeve as he picked his way down the bleachers.

He sat beside O'Fallon. "Tell me something, Officer," her dad said in an elevated voice, hushing everyone's chatter. "You knew that the son of the man you killed was pitching here today, and you still came. Don't you have any respect?"

"My sons are playing, too."

"But you're alive. They don't need you here. They'll see you tomorrow."

O'Fallon and Ray Sr. looked at each other.

"Fine," O'Fallon said finally. "I can leave."

O'Fallon walked off toward the parking lot. The cop's wife remained, her shoulders hunched. The other parents on the Z's kept their distance from her, the ringing of the cowbell now the only sound on the field besides that of ball hitting glove.

Patricia stared at Ray and between pitches, he glanced at her, his eyes as dull as stagnant water. He stopped assaulting the

334

catcher, and settled in to work, but the other team was already ahead, and the Z's ended up losing, 5-3.

"Maybe Ray could live with you guys for the rest of the summer," Patricia told Lupe as the parents filed out of the bleachers. "Something tells me he won't want to put up with me for a while." The city of Denver felt too small.

"Of course," her father said, squeezing her shoulder. "I'll teach him to golf. Mellow him out a bit."

"I want to go to Arizona, too," Mia said, joining them.

"And leave me alone?" Patricia couldn't drive herself back to an empty house in Colorado. Maybe they would all pack up for Arizona. O'Fallon had killed Salvador, he'd ruined Ray's baseball, and now he was banishing them from their home. If he wasn't one of the four horsemen, she didn't know who was.

Patricia waited at the gate by the dugout for Ray, but the field emptied, and he still didn't appear. She checked the dugout to see if he was hiding there, but it was empty except for crushed Gatorade cups littering the concrete floor. She asked the mothers who hadn't left yet if they'd seen Ray. Rosa Pendergrass said she thought she saw him getting into Boyd's van.

Patricia thanked Rosa, and then wondered why Ray would want to arrive at the hotel before she did. She left Mia with her grandparents and raced to the parking lot, thrown into the internal free-fall she'd felt all the times Ray had nearly dashed in front of cars, all the moments she couldn't find him in a crowded public place, all the days she'd heard a terrible crash and raced to find out what damage it had inflicted. Was Ray planning to find O'Fallon?

At the hotel, Patricia ran in from the parking lot to the front desk. "Can you tell me what room Ed O'Fallon is in?" she asked the docile, heavy woman at the desk.

"Just a sec," she said, chewing her gum and typing at her computer. "Are you a relative?"

"Please," Patricia said.

The woman looked at her. "213," she said, finally.

Patricia ran up the concrete steps to the second floor. Finally she came to room 213. She knocked on the door, which was slightly ajar. No one answered, but she heard the low voice of a man, and then Ray. She pushed the door open. Ray stood at the foot of one of the beds, pointing a gun at O'Fallon, who stood across from him in front of the window, his hands raised. Her son, like her husband, was now in a place he wouldn't have been if she'd protected him better.

CHAPTER 25

Ed

July 30

As he left the baseball field in the middle of the fourth inning, Ed tried not to think about what came next. The sun was blinding. Even through dark glasses, all he could see was light glinting off metal fences and cars. Claire was wrecked from the way Santillano's wife had lit into her at the pool, and Ed hated that he'd put Claire in that position. He still wanted to apologize about the mistake on the warrant to the Santillanos. He'd have done it on his knees if that would have helped.

He sweated as he walked, salt stinging his eyes. The car was an oven, and the air conditioner wouldn't respond fast enough.

In the chilled air of his hotel room, Ed shivered in his sweat-soaked t-shirt as he flipped through the sports channels on TV. Eventually he decided to take a shower. Ed removed his gun belt, thinking about how Santillano's wife had told Claire he'd planted the gun.

He took the gun from the belt, feeling its weight, and pointed it in front of him, closing his eyes. He flicked off the safety, and tried to recall the moment he shot Santillano, what he'd seen in that dim room, but the memory came back to him shrouded in cobwebs. Every time he replayed it, he saw Santillano standing near his unmade bed, that hole in his t-shirt, his right hand empty, his left hand hidden. Ed yelled at him to show his hands, to drop the gun, and then he heard that pop, and the mirror shattering behind him. But after everything, the mirror was intact. All the reports said that Santillano had fired first. "He didn't fire," Ed said aloud as he opened his eyes. And the gun that Ed saw Santillano holding might not have existed. He'd lost enough faith in his perceptual abilities to allow that. You go in there thinking *gun,* you see a gun. Ed set his weapon on the bed and went into the bathroom.

He turned off the water from his shower, and then heard a knock at the door. Probably Claire and Polly, home from the game. He pulled on his pants and left the bathroom. Peeking through the peephole, he saw Ray in the hallway, wearing a dust-covered Z's uniform, arms crossed over his chest. Ray knocked again.

Ed owed this boy whatever he wanted—an explanation, a fistfight. He took a deep breath, and then opened the door. "Hello, Ray," he said. "You want to talk to me?"

The boy nodded, a deep shadow from his baseball cap obscuring his face.

Ed's tongue tasted gummy. What could he possibly say to the kid? Did he want to know about how his dad died? "Come in," Ed said, opening the door. "I just need to put on my shirt."

Ed went to the bathroom to find his shirt. The boy was silent. Then he remembered: the gun. The one day he was careless with it.

Ray was standing, his back to Ed as he came out of the bathroom. Ed glanced at the bed—his gun belt rested where he'd left it. "Ray?" Ed asked cautiously, stepping toward him.

Ray turned, the gun in his left hand. "Call me Santillano," he said.

Ed swallowed, raising his hands. "Sure," Ed said. The placid sounds of a golf commentator on TV droned on behind them. Maybe Ray wouldn't know how to use it. But who knew what these north side kids knew. Maybe he'd been playing with guns since he was in kindergarten. "You don't want to do this," Ed said.

Ray tightened his grip. He wiped the sweat off his forehead with his right forearm, knocking his cap to the floor. Someone banged on the door. *Please don't let it be Polly*, Ed prayed to

338

his mother's God. If it was Polly, he'd have to try to disarm Ray before he wheeled around on her. The knock came again. "Do you want me to answer that?" Ed asked. On TV, the golf crowd clapped politely.

"Shut up." Ray gestured with the gun as he must have seen criminals do in movies.

Ed studied the room. Two beds, Ed at the foot of one, Ray near the other, the TV to Ed's right between him and Ray, the door beyond the boy. He tried to get some sort of plan together, but nothing was coming to him.

The knock came again. The television grew louder as a Mercedes commercial came on. Ed wanted to find a way to wind Ray down, to make this stop before any more lives were ruined. If anyone but his children or Claire came through that door, Ed decided, he'd let Ray shoot him. He'd had enough of killing. He'd try dying instead.

The door swung open and Ray's mother stepped in the room. "Ray!" she screamed. "What are you doing?"

Ed hadn't guessed she'd find them, and tried to refigure the math of the situation with her in it.

"You should have told me," Ray said, shifting his weight from side to side, squeezing the handle of the gun, his finger on the trigger.

"Give me the gun," she said, holding out her hand. "I messed up. But they'll put you away forever if you do this."

"Please," she said, reaching her hand out. "Please."

"Think of your future," Ed said, lowering his hands a bit. "My life's half gone already, but yours—don't you see what you can be? But not if you go to prison. Cop killers never get out."

Ray jerked the gun at Ed. "Don't talk to me," he commanded. He squeezed the trigger, the first click telling Ed that if he pushed it farther, the bullet would launch.

"Ray," his mother said. "Put the gun down. Give it to me. Put it down." She started to shake, keeping her hand out, palm open. "Ray. Do this for your father. Put the gun down so that you can live a life, a real life. It's what he came north for—opportunities for you. Don't take that away from him here."

Sweat soaked Ray's short dark hair at the temples and nape. Ed's cop sense told him Ray wouldn't do it, but who knew if his intuition was working right anymore?

Ray's hand trembled. "What's going to happen to me?" he asked, his voice catching.

"I'll take care of you, baby, if you put the gun down."

"Nothing will happen to you," Ed said. "I promise."

"Why should I listen to you?" Ray snapped, the gun rising again.

Ray's mom met Ed's eyes and shook her head once. *Shut up.*

"Don't listen to him," she said. "Listen to me. We'll get back to where you want to be. But it all has to start with you putting down the gun."

Ray's arm shook as he lowered the gun out to his side. Then he dropped it, and the explosion came. Ed crumpled onto the floor.

So this is what it felt like to be shot, Ed thought. All these years of wondering, and here it was. It didn't surprise him, how he didn't feel anything until he looked at the gushing wound in his thigh, and even then it took a moment for the pain to come. He hit the ground, his leg stretched out before him, blood pumping out.

"I didn't mean to," Ray stammered. "I was putting the gun down."

"I saw you," Ed rasped, wincing. He inspected the damage. The skin of his right thigh was torn open, as if a shark had bitten him. He might die if he didn't get the bleeding under control. The bone was probably splintered, ligaments ruptured. But if he could stop the blood, he'd survive.

Ray's mother tugged her boy close and stepped in front of him.

"I'm not going to hurt him," Ed said, retching. He fumbled toward the bed with his hand, and managed to pull off the comforter. He tried to strip off a sheet, but flailed, and couldn't raise himself. He looked up at Patricia. "Can you help me with this?"

She maintained a protective stance in front of Ray, unwilling to step forward.

"I won't hurt him," Ed said. "Send him out if you want. I just need some help."

She whispered in her son's ear. She squeezed Ray's hand once before she let it go, and then he backed away, out of the room, his face gray, his eyes wet. She stripped the sheet off the bed and fixed a tourniquet around Ed's leg. "You need to get to the hospital," she said, inspecting the wound. His blood coated her hands, and she reached for the beige hotel phone, covering the receiver with fingerprints.

Ed held his hand out for the phone. "I will. But you need to be long gone first."

She stared at him.

Ed's breathing was shallow, but he spoke as best he could. "Take Ray and drive back toward the field. If anyone asks, say you hadn't gotten to the hotel yet." He needed the rest of his breath to make the call. He dialed 911 and spoke to the dispatcher. "I shot myself with my gun," he huffed. "I'm losing a lot of blood." He gave her the name of the hotel, and waved at Patricia to leave.

She began to walk away, then stopped. "Tell me," she said. "Did my husband say anything at the end?"

"Sorry," Ed said, covering the phone with his hand. He would have paid better attention to the words Santillano had uttered if he'd known that anybody would have cared about them. "Nothing I could make out. Names." He couldn't speak more. The ambulance wailed into the parking lot. "Go."

"Okay." Her face was desolate, like the downcast, fragile look of the porcelain statue of Mary in the church he'd gone to as a boy. These mothers, how they suffered. His answer hadn't erased her questions. She gave him one more worried glance before she

341

disappeared into the hallway. He hoped she wouldn't spend the rest of her life fearing a lawman's knock at the door.

Just before Ed blacked out, a feeling of lightness washed over him, and he had a vision of freedom, Ed running like he had when he was a boy, over a green baseball field, knees loose and young, no fence in sight.

Four Years Later

Ray's got a lead off of first base, he's crouched over, his arms dangling down, fingers twitching as he watches the pitcher. Ray tries to make him nervous by stepping out a little too far. The Arizona sun heats up the number on the back of his jersey, 21, burning it into his skin.

The pitcher throws a ball past the catcher and Ray takes off, sprints down to second base and looks for third. As he heads back to the bag, he glances at the stands, but there is no one there—this is just another scrimmage at the baseball academy. A few of the parents used to show up every day, but then they got too bored, had to work, or deal with the rest of their lives, so the boys play against each other to empty stands. Ray's mom works day shifts so she usually isn't there.

Ray pictures his father watching him. Not from above like people always say when they get weepy, but from somewhere that's near and yet too far away to reach. Left field, maybe. That's where Ray would look for him back in the church ball days, when his dad was running from one job to the next, but had time to stop off and stand down by the left field fence for a few innings. There's his dad leaning on the fence, alone, and he's happy because he doesn't have to work anymore and he can just stand there and watch baseball in the sunshine.

The pitcher and the catcher confer, and Ray kicks the dirt around second base like a roadrunner keeping house. Ray didn't have enough of his dad. He was at work a lot. Sometimes it made Ray edgy to be around him, like he had to be careful not to waste time. Ray would be all "look at me, look at me, Dad" at the top of his lungs, showing him a new pitching grip, reporting his stats from the latest game, leaving out the stuff about school. His dad didn't much care about that, anyway. After he'd be home for a few weeks they'd settle back into a rhythm, Ray talking in English and his dad talking back in Spanish, both understanding each other just fine.

Weren't fathers supposed to waste time? Shoot hoops, watch a game, goof off, play catch, wrestle on the ground like they used to when Ray was little, all of it a waste of time if you wanted to look at it that way. With Mom it always had to be something educational, like reading a book, playing some word game that wasn't fun but was supposed to be good for your brain, never any decent TV, just PBS if you were lucky. When Ray was home with his dad they could kill a whole afternoon just looking at whatever came across the TV, in either language. Ray never felt guilty about it until Mom came home and said, "That's all you did today?"

Ray is sixteen now, practically grown. The pitcher starts to work again, sending a fastball to the batter, who fouls it down the left field line. Ray can hear his dad out there, that Mariachi-sounding yip he made when a ball blazed by too close. His dad would never know Ray as a man. He would think of him as this goofy kid. If the dead got to think, that is. If Ray had one more day with him, he wouldn't do anything special. Play catch maybe. Or just watch TV, his dad near enough to reach over every once in a while and run his knuckles over Ray's scalp like he used to.

The batter hits an easy grounder to short. The shortstop snags the ball and wings it to first. Ray likes to think that his dad had the last laugh when Ray got to go to baseball school. They came down to Arizona the summer after his dad died, soon after Ray shot O'Fallon. Grandpa met the director of the Suncrest Sports Academy when he was golfing and convinced him to give Ray another tryout. Grandpa Ray was good at that, turning on his charm from the old restaurant days, winning over janitors and presidents. The Dallas game was a fluke, anyone could see that. They offered Ray a scholarship so Mom couldn't say no, even though she said it seemed like too much baseball and not enough school.

Ray was always trying to do his homework in front of her, spreading it all around the living room so that she'd see he was doing school and let him stay at Suncrest. Because really, it was a lot of baseball. Weightlifting, conditioning, scrimmages, batting practice, position work, nutrition class instead of regular science, weekend road trips to play other teams. School was for Mia. She'd end up being a doctor or a philosopher or something. She went to a Catholic prep school and won every award. "Saint Braids," Ray called her, tugging on her long ropes of hair while she studied the evenings away.

Ray decides to mess with the pitcher a little. His lead off second is ridiculous, a bet that he's fast enough to beat the throw back to the bag. Stealing third is a fool's game and they both know it, but Ray dances around off second and tries to make the pitcher think he doesn't. Ray has the mechanical baseball stuff down by now, and is deep into mastering the psychological side.

If everything went okay, if he didn't hurt his arm, Ray would end up with a minor league contract by the time he graduated from high school. That's what Coach was always telling him during their weekly conferences, Coach with his red, meaty face. Coach was always beaded with a light sweat, his foot jiggling when he crossed it over his ACL-surgery scarred knee because he was just so damn excited about Ray's future. Coach would sit for about the first five minutes of the conference, then leap up and pace, talking fast, telling Ray his future. "Can you see it, Sting? You're going all the way." And Ray would say, "I'll try," and think about asking Coach not to shorten his nickname.

Ray's leadoff game works, turns the pitcher skittish. He hurls a wild one to the backstop so that Ray takes third standing.

Making it to the majors is the plan. Ray has no plan B. If Ray's life were a movie, he'd end up making it to the major leagues and he'd pitch in the World Series, and the announcers would dig up the sad story about when he was a kid; and when he won the Series and cried tears of joy, the announcer who said the annoying stuff—because there was always one of them in a television pair—would say he must be thinking of his father and how proud he'd be of him. But life isn't a movie, and Ray doesn't want to think about the million non-movie ways things might turn out.

The pitcher and catcher confer again. Coach should yank him, he's too tired. The kids at baseball school are all right, most of them a little too uptight and redneck for Ray, but Ray never needed many friends. He lost touch with Miguel. The guy is banging with his uncles now. Ray could have been just like him, a cop killer at twelve. Or a cop wounder, in prison until his body was buried under muscles and tattoos, and his mind shriveled up into an angry raisin.

It was decent, what O'Fallon had done, letting Ray go like that when he could have locked him up for almost ever. Still, it didn't make it right, the way Ray's dad died. And it kind of pissed Ray off that the cop got to feel like the noble one, when the way Ray saw it, they weren't close to even.

Right after he shot O'Fallon, Ray would wake up screaming about how he had the chance to kill him and he didn't, sobbing into his mom's nightgown like a baby. "What would your life be like if you'd done that?" his mom said, rocking him. "Nothing you'd want to live in."

After the regional tournament in Las Cruces, they went to Grandma and Grandpa's house in Tucson. They drove back to Denver to pack their stuff into a U-Haul before school at the baseball academy started, and Ray asked his mom if they could visit O'Fallon. He didn't know why he wanted to see him, exactly—maybe just to confirm that he'd done it, he'd shot the cop that killed his dad. Because it all seemed too unreal. His mom tried to talk him out of it, checked to make sure Ray still didn't want to kill him, but then gave in. O'Fallon had been transferred to Denver Health from the hospital in New Mexico a couple of weeks after the shooting. She talked to some nurses and they found O'Fallon in the rehabilitation center, working with a physical therapist, lifting weights with his busted leg under the fluorescent lights of the clinic.

Ray and his mom stood in the corner and watched until the therapist looked up. She started to say something to them, and then realized who they were. She turned to O'Fallon and said, "I'll be in my office when you're done," and walked away. Ray was glad to be leaving Denver. They were too damn famous for no good reason.

"Hello," O'Fallon said, trying to stand. He looked goofy happy to see them, like a golden retriever, and Ray felt sorry for the guy.

"Don't get up," Mom said. "Ray just wanted to see how you're doing before we left."

"You're leaving?"

"Yeah, we're moving," she said, but didn't tell him where.

O'Fallon nodded, accepting that. "It's as you see. I'll be a gimp for a while."

"Sorry," Ray said.

"I'm sorry, too," O'Fallon said, turning his eyes on him, reaching out his hand so that Ray didn't know what to do but shake it. O'Fallon didn't let go of Ray's hand. "It didn't turn out so bad," he said and Ray flinched, wondering what he meant. But then O'Fallon continued, "No damage to the bone or nerves."

As soon as O'Fallon loosened his grip, Ray took his hand back. He'd had ideas of different things to say to the guy, but now that he was here, his mouth was all dry and he couldn't speak.

O'Fallon filled in. "I hope I'll see you pitch again."

"Who knows?" Ray said, finding his voice, thinking, *if I get good enough that everyone can see me play, I guess you can, too.*

Coach orders a new pitcher from the bullpen, and Ray squats down on third to rest his legs. They did weight training at 6 AM and his legs give out by the end of the day. Getting up that early just about killed Ray, but that's the deal with baseball school.

They did stuff like that so that it'd look like they were being all disciplined with you, so your parents would think they were getting their money's worth. There are other sports at the school, too, golf and tennis, but Ray doesn't hang with those kids. He doesn't understand the games they play, one of them with a ball too small, the other one with a ball too soft.

Ray doesn't want to return to Denver unless he's in a big league uniform, playing at Coors Field. That's how he sees it. When he walked away from there, he left for good until he'd return famous for a proper reason. And if he never got famous, well then screw Denver. He does miss the mountains, and driving down the highway some March morning after a heavy evening snowfall, pickup trucks kicking up slush like cowboys trailing dust, the sun breaking out over the whole mess to melt it. Ray likes sun, but snow is good too. So much baseball is played where there isn't ever any snow. He needs seasons to set his clock right. So he hopes he'll be at Coors Field some day, knocking the snowmelt off his cleats at some early spring game.

The pitcher is warm and a new batter comes up, so Ray stands. Ray glances out to left field and wants to shout out to his ghost dad, "What are you doing out there?" That's what it was like, having him gone. When he was alive, Ray could go whole days without thinking about him. But since he died, he's been something Ray has to carry with him all the time. Ray doesn't like how as the years pass, his dad gets farther away. His dad's clothes and haircut will always be the same in photos, even as fashions change. Death traps you in that last bad sweater. His dad will never know any of the songs that Ray likes as a teenager, he'll never meet whatever girl Ray picks, or any kids he'll have. Ray's dad has no place in this decade, the one Ray lives in. But Ray dreams of him all the time, wakes up with a soul ache, like a haunting, half-remembered song playing through his mind.

Ray's tired of being out on base in the sun and Coach hasn't fed him any signs, but Ray thinks what the heck, it's just a scrimmage and he's never stolen home before. The pitcher is a lefty like Ray, the batter a righty, so Ray creeps down the third base line. The second the pitcher raises his arms to begin his windup, Ray takes off at a dead sprint toward home. It's too late to stop as he flies over the dirt, so he's got to throw himself across the chaos of the plate and hope the pitcher and catcher can't make the play. He hooks his leg and slides his body through the dirt in front of the plate. He collides with the catcher, who misses as he tries to tag Ray. And Coach comes charging out of the dugout to yell at him about taking a stupid risk that could have injured him, and Ray thinks, you don't know the first thing about risk.

ACKNOWLEDGMENTS

Julien, I can't thank you enough for your constant support. Maya and Theo, my joys, thanks for putting up with my divided attention over the years I wrote this book. I am grateful for my parents, John and Paulette Shank, who raised me in a house full of books and baseball, my brother Jonathan, who I followed to baseball tournaments every summer of my childhood, and my brother Jordan, who gave El Johnway to the world, and for all my family, Shanks and Hottovys, especially my grandparents, Harry and Rita Shank and John and Agnes Hottovy. Where would I be without such a tight tribe?

Thanks to my agent, Gary Heidt, for his enthusiasm and diligence, and for taking a chance on me. I am grateful to my publishers Judith and Martin Shepard and everyone at The Permanent Press, who made this dream come true.

I couldn't have written this novel without the help of my friends, especially Paula Younger, a brilliant writer, and a tireless, giving editor, and Gesenia Alvarez, a true, uncompromising artist and an insightful reader, both of whom saw me through several drafts of this book. Thanks also to Ashley Simpson-Shires, Greg Glasgow, Kate Jenkins, Doug Kurtz, Cat Altman, Nancy Horowitz, Rachel Horowitz, Lisa Molinaro, Jeni Mullan, Jessica Martinez-Milligan, Erron Ramsey, Shane Oshetski and Vince Darcangelo.

Thank you to the Denver Public Library and the Tattered Cover Book Store, those great nurturers of the imagination. Thanks to all my teachers in the Denver Public Schools, especially Pam Fisher at Cole and Matt Spampinato, Virginia Sheridan, and Steven

Gensits at TJ. I am grateful for the guidance and encouragement of Valerie Sayers and Father John Dunne at Notre Dame. And I am forever indebted to the late, great writer Lucia Berlin, my teacher and friend, a lifelong fan of the Oakland A's who shared with me her love of Chekhov, Tolstoy, and Ricky Henderson.

I appreciate all the people who helped me better understand the lives of police and their families, especially Mike and Becki Swanson, Mike Mosco of the Denver Police Protective Association, who patiently discussed the procedures followed after an officer-involved shooting, and Angie Mullan, who told me what it was like trying to date when your dad is a San Francisco cop. *Deadly Force Encounters: What Cops Need to Know to Mentally and Physically Prepare for and Survive a Gunfight* by Dr. Alexis Artwohl and Loren W. Christensen, *Into the Kill Zone: A Cop's Eye View of Deadly Force* by David Klinger, and *I Love a Cop: What Police Families Need to Know* by Ellen Kirschman were extremely helpful books. Thanks to the many journalists at the *Rocky Mountain News*, the *Denver Post*, *Westword* and elsewhere whose reporting on the shooting of Ismael Mena helped inspire my fiction.

Thanks to Patty Limerick and everyone at the Center of the American West and the Barbara Deming Memorial Fund, who supported me on a prior novel that never quite worked out.

And Denver, I love you.